GRIT City

a **BALEY NOAL** *novel*

Also by

Clandestiny

The Starstruck Duology:
Starstruck
Starstruck: The Trials

Cover by Baley Noal & ElfElm Publishing
Interior and ebook formatting by ElfElm Publishing
www.elfelmpublishing.com | Tacoma, WA

ISBN (paperback, black & white): 979-8-9914667-5-2
ISBN (paperback, color): 979-8-9914667-9-0

10 9 8 7 6 5 4 3 2

First Edition 2025

To my very own Boo, Bayne, who was a born-and-raised Grit City boy. Thank you for helping to inspire all of these loveable four-legged friends in our books. I love you always, buddy

CHAPTER
One

S HAW AND BAZ WAITED FOR THE GATE TO SLIDE OPEN AT HEAD-quarters. It was their first day back to the grind from their short weekend. Baz noticed his partner massage the back of his own neck as he sat in the passenger seat looking more tired than usual.

"You alright over there, fam?" Baz shook his head. "Please tell me you didn't try out your nephew's hoverboard again and end up on your ass."

"Only needed to learn my lesson once on that one," Shaw reassured him with a smile. "I'm straight. Just a kink or something."

"You won't ever catch my big ass on some damn hoverboard." Baz laughed at the thought.

"I've seen your big ass pussy out on a Razor scooter." Shaw chuckled. "So, I can't imagine you on a hoverboard."

Baz flipped him off and turned onto the mainroad to start their patrol route.

Many who knew them throughout Tacoma's Police Department often referred to Shaw and Baz as Chip and Dale—their dumbass spin on a Chippendales reference. And when a refresh was needed in the rotation, they used Ebony and Ivory.

There was no denying that the duo was hands-down the best look-ing in the department. Sure, there were other handsome officers, but not ones partnered together like Shaw and Baz. They had been the cause of countless false reports by local women who simply wanted to shoot their shot after catching a glimpse of the duo. Many times when the department had to select officers for any kind of marketing campaign or when there were community events of a high-profile nature, they would send Baz and Shaw. Baz's uncle happened to be Tacoma's Police Chief, which created even more pressure for his partnership to always be seen in a good light across the public.

Hunter Shaw had celebrated his thirtieth birthday a couple months prior. He stood at precisely six feet and never missed a workout. His light brunette hair was always cut into a perfectly clean cop fade. He chose to style it with pomade almost every morning and sent most women over the edge with his mesmerizing green eyes that popped against his skin tone. He went through phases of facial hair but lately had settled on a smooth face to show off his flawless light olive complexion and strong jawline.

Bastian 'Baz' Haywood, on the other hand, was what a perp the previous week had described as "one huge-ass brotha" while Baz had him on the ground after he'd tried to flee. Baz was a solid 6'6" with darker skin than his bi-racial parents may suggest. He wasn't ripped, but the man had the build of a refrigerator. He maintained a curly top fade that was meticulously barbered like clockwork and had a matching well-groomed beard. His caramel colored eyes and lush lashes had broken countless hearts.

"You do anything exciting this weekend?" Shaw asked as he observed the traffic around them.

Baz shrugged. "Fucking slept for a good fourteen hours after that last damn shift we had." He continued by disclosing details about the date he'd gone on. "I *did* actually end up going out with Tickle-Me Tinsley on Sunday night."

Shaw laughed, he thoroughly enjoyed the luxury of living vicar-iously through his partner when it came to dating. Although Shaw was only a few months younger than Baz, he hadn't quite made his way back into the dating scene. He never deprived himself of the stories Baz entertained him with though, and he would hop in the chats for Baz on occasion because Baz didn't have the respectful finesse that Shaw did.

Tickle-Me Tinsley was actually the name Shaw had come up with for this new gal. Based on looks alone, Tickle-Me Tinsley's profile was similar to the types of girls Baz would always swipe yes on. With a more in-depth review, however, she appeared to be so much more than most of the girls he'd actually met up with. Baz had a rule that any woman he swiped on had to pass the ten second scroll effort to even get that extended look. She had to be under 5'8" and 160 pounds, include at least two full-face photos with no obstructions like sunglasses or a hat, and have at least two full-body pics. If they passed that test, he would only give their profile a true read if she was his definition of 'fuckable' at first glance.

Tickle-Me Tinsley passed the philandering Baz assessment with flying colors because she was a knockout. Her profile name was Tinsley, but she introduced herself in her bio as 'Tins.' Tinsley's first photo showed her full body *and* she didn't have anything obstructing her gorgeous face. Baz especially liked that her hair was slightly different in almost every photo. Her occupation was listed as salon owner on her profile, so the guys assumed her change in hair color was due to that fact. She wasn't outrageous with her color choices by any means. Based on her eyebrows it appeared she was a natural brunette to some degree, her photos showcased blonde, darker brunette, or sometimes auburn highlights. The answers to prompts in her profile, along with pictures and their captions, provided the inspiration for Shaw's nickname. He'd determined she was a sweet, girl-next-door type who wouldn't be all that open for a Netflix and Chill situation as a first date; so he told Baz he would happily settle on a good tickling from the beauty and her manicured nails.

"Oh yeah? Did she provide you with a nice little tickling?" Shaw smirked. His friend wasn't shy when it came to sharing conversations with his current roster picks or date details—when he managed to follow through on those.

"No." Baz shook his head with a smile. "She *is* fucking sweet, I'll give her that. I felt like a damn lost puppy for the first half of that date."

"Really?" Shaw was skeptical because his best friend had never gone for a good girl type. It was difficult for him to believe he'd been a lost puppy like he claimed. "Where'd you guys go?"

"I met her at Indita Mia down on the water."

Shaw quickly sat up straighter in the passenger's seat. "You didn't pick that sweet little thing up?! Damn Baz, didn't realize you were slippin' like that these days."

Baz chuckled and wiped his beard. "I tried. She asked to meet me there because she wasn't comfortable giving out her number or her address quite yet." He shrugged. "For real, I almost canceled on her and then I was like, you know what? She's just out here tryna be safe… And also Big-Tittie Tilly was out of town this weekend, so it wasn't like I had a good back up lined up right away."

"Big-Tittie Tilly doesn't deserve a waterfront date—that girl's just a fucking booty call and you know it." Shaw shook his head remembering not only the woman's profile that looked like an ad for *OnlyFans*, but also how conceited her messages sounded. "She's a bitch, honestly. She *must* be good in bed because her conversation skills suck ass."

"She's left me with *no* complaints multiple times and she doesn't seem to be too worried about commitment or monogamy." Baz smirked. "So, kinda suits me while I'm looking for wifey."

"So, what happened with sweet little Tickle-Me? You said you were a lost puppy?"

Baz let his entire chest deflate when he exhaled. "I was genuinely enjoying the date. She looks exactly like her pictures, so not the filtered mess some of these catfishing bitches be using on their shit—which was a pleasant surprise. She showed up looking like a goddamn angel and she wasn't even showing a lot of her body off. She's funny—her laugh is damn adorable and contagious as fuck. We didn't even have any dead air either through the first set of drinks. I thought things were going really well." Baz shrugged his broad shoulders and held out one of his mammoth-sized hands. "I went to the bathroom shortly after our dinner got set down and then like ten minutes after that she's getting a damn phone call." He rolled his eyes. "She's a great actress on top of all the rest of her wonderful attributes, I'll say that much."

"Did she give you the whole 'my friend has an emergency' excuse?" Shaw listened but watched as two seemingly homeless men pushed an overflowing cart across the main road.

"Better than that." Baz pulled into the parking lot of their favorite coffee shop. "She said her *dog* was having an emergency."

The men got out of the car and walked toward the shop.

"Apparently, her friend who was watching him called and she had to go right then and there. She had the audacity to put down cash on the table, told me she'd message me, apologized, and just straight up left. She didn't even look back."

"Did she message you?" Shaw opened the door for them.

"Fuck if I know. I unmatched with her the second she took off."

"Baz! Bro, what?!" Shaw smacked his partner's shoulder. "You were genuinely enjoying your time and you didn't even want to see if she was going to message you?! How do you know she wasn't telling the truth? She did have a dog in one of her photos, you know." Shaw remembered the bully breed looking dog that they only got a profile view of in one of Tinsley's photos. He was shocked his best friend didn't give this one a better chance. Shaw had thoroughly enjoyed her profile, and the conversation he'd had with her. As was usual for them, Baz had given Shaw his phone for some help when he didn't have the right words to keep the conversation going, and to him this girl seemed to be the type of perfect that was too good to be true.

"Good morning, Bronwyn." Baz winked at his favorite barista who had their drinks ready for them even before they ordered.

"Hey, Baz." She returned his gesture. "Shaw." She nodded. "You guys be safe today."

"We always try." Baz grabbed both coffees and handed one to Shaw.

They were walking back out of the coffee shop when Baz started again. "Look, the timing of the bathroom and her phone call were suspicious enough. But a call about her dog needing help? What—like she has a dog sitter or something when she leaves for a two hour fucking date? And leaving cash is like a slap in the face—some kind of guilty conscience move for bailing on me is kinda how I took it."

"Damn, bro!" Shaw was in a full on belly roar. "I had no idea you were so damn sensitive! Or that your ego is so fucking fragile anyway."

"Fuck off, Shaw." Baz gave him a friendly jab to the bicep. "I don't need to end up catching feelings for some flighty chick who doesn't know what she wants."

"*You* don't know what you want!" Shaw couldn't help but continue laughing at him. "You're out here building a damn football size roster and *still* don't know what you want, bro!"

"*Baz, Shaw, what's your location?*" Dispatch interrupted their conversation as they opened the car doors.

Shaw reached for his radio. "We're near the 3800 block of Cedar Street."

"*We have a reported vandalism and robbery near the 5400 block of South Tacoma Way and the caller is requesting a police response. Suspect just fled the scene.*"

"We're on it," Shaw confirmed. "Send the address."

Shaw took a drink of his coffee before looking at his partner again. "I'm just trying to point out that you've *never* talked so highly about a date that you didn't sleep with. Let's hope that unmatching bullshit doesn't end up haunting you."

"Thanks." Baz rolled his eyes. He wasn't mad at Shaw, he'd already wondered if his reaction was too quick. Unfortunately for him, he'd never know.

CHAPTER
Two

Baz pulled the patrol car up to Grit City Pretty, where there were signs of obvious vandalism in the form of a completely shattered front window. They heard a high pitched, flamboyant shriek as they approached the open door of the salon.

"Oh, thank you, Jesus!" The man waved his hands around and made haste toward the officers. He made a slightly awkward pause upon first glance and gave Baz a quick, sassy snarl before he continued toward them. "We need police assistance—some goddamn crackhead just busted through this place." His hands were flying everywhere and somehow the pitch in his voice got even higher. "In broad daylight while all our lights were on in here?! What the hell is this world we live in coming to?!" The dainty man held his hands to his chest. His skin tone was a sand color and the tips of his short, black hair were bleached. His khakis hugged his legs, showing his toned thighs under the fabric, rolled up to expose his ankles and the wedge style clogs on his feet. The man wasn't afraid to show his body because the white Gucci shirt he wore was tight, revealing a sliver of his midsection.

"Alright, there." Shaw put his hands up a bit to slow the man down. "Is anyone hurt?"

"No, thank God!"

"Are you the owner?" Shaw asked.

The man put his hands on his hips. "No, but I live and work here."

Shaw looked back and forth at the man and Baz as he gave his partner another unfriendly glare. Baz's face was just as confused at the dramatic man's judgemental stares.

"The owner *is* here," he continued along at increasing speeds. "Do you need to speak to her too? I was the one who called but we were both here when this all happened not even ten minutes ago. You'll need to give my girl a minute if you're wanting to talk to her, she's been through it this week." The sassy snarl came back to the man's face and he gave Baz a harsh once over just before rolling his eyes.

"Harv! Wait! Oh shit!" A woman's voice called out from a room in the back of the shop. "Brin, grab Harvey! Keep him out of the glass!"

The man twirled and clapped his hands like wet noodles before waving his arms about. "Harvey!"

A dog made his way toward the familiar face and happily sat right by him while panting in excitement and thumping his nubbed tail on the floor.

Shaw looked at Baz—they knew this dog. But the unphased look on Baz's face meant he was clueless. Looking at the dog now, he would be very recognizable seeing his full face even once. He was on the larger size and resembled a silver cane corso, but almost a mini version given his stature. He also had a split face of sorts; he was an AKC pedigree version of the breed on the right side of his face but the left side looked like someone put the poor dog through a blender. Starting from the top of his head, he was missing chunks of hair in the shape of scratches. While his right ear was cropped, it looked like the left one had been bitten right off his head. As if that wasn't enough for the poor dog, he was also missing his left eye and a couple of his teeth permanently showed due to his small cleft lip. Despite his appearance, the dog seemed to be quite happy as he leaned all of his weight against the animated man.

"I got him, girl!" He held the dog's collar. "The law men are here and need to talk to you too, Boo."

"I caught my damn heel in this stupid grate again. I'll be right there," she called out.

The man, Brin as he was referred to, turned back toward the officers and directed his attention to Shaw. "I told you, my girl's been goin' through it this week. Can you hold him, or go back and help her? I swear, poor thing's probably trying to take her shoe off at this point—that grate is treacherous."

Shaw looked at Baz who was still trying to place the man to figure out why he was getting such an attitude.

"I'm gonna go back and check things out—just to be sure." He had a pretty good idea of who he'd find back there and wanted to give Baz another moment to figure it out.

"Really? Gah, today of all days," the woman mumbled to herself. "I knew I shouldn't have even worn damn heels today." She was crouched in an awkward squat trying to reach for at least one of the zippers of her booties because now both heels were stuck in the most uncomfortable placement.

Shaw walked around the corner and saw Tickle-Me Tinsley with her head upside down as she struggled to squat low enough for her hand to reach the zipper of her bootie to take it off. He was going to have to do his best not to give any indication that he was familiar with her.

"Ma'am, can I help you out there?"

Tinsley's head bounced right up and her face looked a bit flush. "Oh my gosh, this is so embarrassing."

Shaw continued toward her. Baz was right, she did look like her pictures—easily a ten out of ten in his book. Her hair was up in a high ponytail so he couldn't see the full length, but the bottom of it touched just below her shoulder line. The black jeans she wore couldn't have been any tighter—they hugged every one of her voluptuous curves. Shaw never knew himself to be an ass guy, but the glimpse he got of Tinsley's backside had him convinced that's what he was now. The cream colored, long sleeve top she had on was tucked into her jeans and just as tight as the pants, offering the same flattering fit over the attractive curves of her plump chest.

"Here." Shaw got down on a knee next to her. "You can hold my shoulder, I'll work on your boot there."

"I can't wait to tell Brindle we get to add this to my week from

Hell." She shook her head but took him up on the offer of balancing herself on his shoulder. "Thank you though, I do appreciate this. I know better than to walk across this without the rug being here, but Harvey heard new voices and he took off, I tried to chase him—" She felt the zipper slide down on her first shoe. "Oh my gosh, thank you." She lifted her foot out of the bootie and noticed Shaw going for the other one. "Oh, you don't have to do both—I'm so sorry."

"Ma'am." Shaw chuckled. "You don't have to apologize." He tugged the other zipper down and then looked up at her. "We can't let the grate win. You won't have to add it to the week from Hell if we get you outta here without further incident."

Tinsley removed her second foot from her booties and watched as Shaw carefully wiggled each of the high heeled shoes to free them from the clutches of the grate. Tinsley caught eyes with Shaw, her blush returned as he finally stood up next to her. He was the most handsome man she'd ever seen in person—something about a man in uniform only made her heart beat that much faster. And on top of how nice his body looked, she couldn't take her gaze off his electric green eyes or that smoldering smile.

"Tinsley." She reached her hand toward Shaw. "While ma'am is very respectful—and I do appreciate it—it makes me feel ancient." She chuckled.

"Fair enough," Shaw agreed and took her hand in his. "Hunter Shaw"—he quickly shook his head—"Officer Shaw," he corrected himself.

"Well, Officer Shaw, thank you for hopefully helping turn my week around."

"Glad I could be of assistance." He smiled, momentarily mesmerized as he looked into her beautiful brown eyes. Her skin looked like glass, she had perfectly maintained eyebrows, and long lashes. To top it off, Tinsley's smile was something that belonged on a magazine cover. Her profile pictures didn't quite do her the justice she deserved and he was more than appreciative of her figure.

"Boo, are you alive back there?! Harvey's getting antsy and now all the nosey neighbors are starting to gather around the front of the shop!" Brindle called out, presumably more irritated from being left with Baz.

"Sorry—I'm coming." Tinsley slipped her feet back into her booties, zipped them up, and then grabbed the broom she'd gone into the back room for.

"Look, there's your mom—go." Brindle let go of Harvey's collar and shooed him away with his hands swinging in the air. The dog happily did his best to trot toward Tinsley with a slight lean to his head.

"Tins." Brindle rolled his eyes and gestured towards Baz. "This is *Officer Baz*. He and his hot partner—who I didn't get a name for—are here so we can file the report."

Tinsley attempted not to showcase her surprise too much when she made eyes with Baz. She tried clearing her throat but chickened out and instead squatted down to her dog who was now in front of her, wiggling his body and leaning his head into her.

"Oh, hi." She halfheartedly waved in Baz's direction and then looked at Brindle. "This"—she gestured toward her heel-grabbing grate savior—"is Officer Shaw."

"Oooh, Officer Shaw." Brindle sauntered over and took the broom from Tinsley. "You can cuff me anytime, sir." He pumped his eyebrows at Shaw.

"Brindle!" Tinsley's face went scarlet and she swatted at her friend. "I'm so sorry." She shook her head.

Shaw did his best to suppress his laughter and looked up at his partner, who was still trying to find some level of professionalism now that his weekend date—who he cut all ties to with no explanation to her—stood in the same room.

"Why don't we start with the report, huh?" Shaw suggested with a red face, not wanting to look at Brindle at all. "Were you both out here when this happened?"

"Harv and I were rotating laundry in the back and Brindle was upstairs." Tinsley now stood, avoiding all eye contact with Baz who hadn't moved since she walked into the room.

"So, let's take separate statements. Officer Baz will stay out here with you, Brindle, to get your statement. And Tinsley"—he turned to her—"why don't you and I go in the back and get yours? It'll keep Harvey here out of the glass while it's getting cleaned up." He didn't wait for Baz to say anything, he trusted his partner would find his calm and get his job done.

"Sure, let her take the hot one while I'm out here stuck with some Kevin Atwater wannabe." Brindle continued to sweep and make his dislike of Baz very well-known.

"Brindle," Tinsley hissed. It was bad enough to have to be reunited with Baz now, she wasn't interested in dissecting their failed date in front of everyone.

Shaw looked at Baz and at that moment they were convinced Tinsley had fully informed Brindle about their date and had obviously shared pictures for him to have recognized Baz so easily.

Shaw followed both Tinsley and Harvey to the back of the shop and he noticed the dog looked a little off-center with his head tilting toward the right as he walked. Shaw watched Tinsley carefully step over the grate this time and then bend down to pull a rug over the heel trapper.

"Officer Shaw, do you mind if I make a quick phone call before we get started?" Tinsley reached for a landline.

"Not at all." He pulled a small notepad out of his pocket. Shaw couldn't help but listen to her phone call, which sounded like she was leaving a voicemail at a veterinary clinic. Harvey made his way toward Shaw so he squatted down and gave the dog a few scratches.

Tinsley tossed a few more towels in the dryer and set the phone down before she turned back toward Shaw. "I'm really sorry, it's just been a hectic morning." She held her head for the slightest moment. "Do you need a drink or anything? Sorry I didn't offer earlier—how rude. We have water or I can make you a coffee if you need one?" She started to move around the kitchenette to show him the coffee pods they had available.

"Tinsley," Shaw noticed her anxious demeanor and smiled to try and ease her mindset. "Why don't you take a seat? No need to worry about me." He pulled a chair from the small bistro style table that was against the wall.

"Oh, sorry. The report. Right." She sat down and nodded.

Shaw didn't sit. He stood near her and decided to reach out and lay his hand on her shoulder. "Tinsley, are you alright?"

She continued to stare at the table, thinking about how terrible her luck truly seemed to be this week and then finally shook her head. "I'm sorry."

"Tinsley, you've apologized at least a dozen times already this morning." Shaw chuckled. "I need you to just take a couple good breaths with me and then we can talk about what happened this morning. Do you think you can do that?"

"Sor—" Tinsley stopped herself. She took a second then looked up at Shaw. "Yes, I can do that."

Shaw set down his notebook. "Let's start off with an easy question. What kind of coffee do you take?" He walked over to the Keurig.

Tinsley shot out a quick exhale that was more of a chuckle as she rubbed her dog's deformed ear. "Well, unfortunately my kind of coffee is the one that's all over the floor out front."

"Right… Week from Hell." He nodded a few times and then grabbed her a bottled water. "Here, start with this then and tell me about the morning." He twisted the lid off before handing her the bottle and taking a seat himself.

Tinsley took a sip and looked up at him. "Thank you. And I apologize, I really only have two modes and you're being subjected to the spastic setting that runs a hell of a lot faster than I can keep up with so I tend to look and sound like I belong in the looney bin."

Shaw laughed. "You're apologizing again," he gently reminded her. "Why don't we start on a different topic—tell me about your guy here? This is Harvey, right?"

Tinsley leaned down to hug her dog around his neck as he sat next to her. "Yep, this is Handsome Harvey… Two-Face, ya know?"

"I actually wondered if that's where his name came from," he happily admitted with a charmed smile on his face.

"Well, technically his full name is Harvey Handsome-Face Dent-Adams, but I only pull that one out when he's giving me a run for my money… Which is currently every other day."

Shaw let out a short chuckle before he gave Harvey another few rubs to the side of his head. "Can I ask what happened to him? He looks like he may have seen a couple unfriendly days."

Tinsley leaned down and pecked Harvey just above his missing eye.

"I'd been on a waitlist with this super reputable cane corso breeder for like three litters or something crazy, and one day I got a call that I could skip the line if I was willing to take the nearly discarded runt. Poor Harvey here was not only barely half the size of his siblings, but he was also born with his cleft lip. It's definitely not as bad as most with the same condition—it hardly qualifies as a full on cleft lip anyway— but obviously not the standard for the breed to be showing a couple of scraggly teeth. I fell absolutely in love—not even head over heels, just purely in love with him the second I saw him—so, I had to have him."

She shrugged and watched Harvey find his bed to lay down from his exciting morning. "Unfortunately, after about a month into Harvey's life, one of the other older dogs in the house got a hold of him and did the damage to his ear, that scar on his head, and he lost his eye. The breeders let me know they could just put him down, but I insisted I still very much wanted him. He didn't deserve that fate—I knew he was a good guy who just needed the right home. I did take him about two weeks before he should've been away from his mom, but it just wasn't safe there for him anymore. I wanted to take care of him while he was recuperating from that damn traumatic event. He lost his eye, obviously, but also most of his hearing in that ear and then he has structural epilepsy—most likely from that attack. So, he does get seizures from time to time. Most aren't too bad, but he just had his worst episode on Sunday night and I wasn't even home." She took a deep breath, gazing at her dog. "We ended up spending the night and a portion of the next day at the emergency vet. He's still recovering from that one a bit, so that's why he's got the little lean and some wobbles going on today... Week from Hell and all." Her head rolled side to side and she finally took her eyes off her dog to look at Shaw who'd already been staring at her. "But that's also why I needed to just call his vet—my damn purse was stolen during the commotion this morning and his seizure meds were in there... Along with the rest of my life. So, there's going to be that fun task to tackle." Tinsley rolled her eyes. "Honestly, I'll figure all that out but he can't be without his meds—especially now."

"Seems like you've done really well for good ol' Handsome Harv." Shaw smiled down at the dog who did look like he was exhausted if nothing else. He also had every intention of informing his best friend he'd *definitely* been wrong in doubting Tinsley. He'd completely fumbled by cutting ties with her for bailing in the middle of their date.

"Oh, it's been a mutual caretaker thing he and I have. He rides the spastic bouts with me and I play nurse to every ailment imaginable," she disclosed with a soft giggle.

Shaw felt like Tinsley was finally starting to relax from her anxious state—she'd just needed a second with her mind off of what had just happened. While he enjoyed talking to her, he knew a report was needed so he continued his questioning.

"Is Harvey also tasked with security at the shop?"

Tinsley laughed more freely this time. "I mean, he *is* basically deaf in one ear and can only see with the one eye... Not to mention Harv's like the nicest guy you'll ever meet—so he does his best with security. Honestly, with Brindle being his only competition he may have the job by default."

Shaw smirked at the response. "So, is Brindle your only employee?"

"No." She shook her head. "Brindle is the only one who's here full-time with me during the week—we have the same hours. But I have another stylist, and then a few days a week there are two estheticians providing services as well. Technically, they rent space and mainly operate under their own licenses, so I'm not like a *boss* boss for them—if that makes sense? And it just so happens today is the only day of the week where it's just me and Brindle."

"He mentioned he lives here, is there a dwelling above the salon?"

"Yep, it's just a little two bedroom apartment and he lives there alone—well, with a cat that is. But he was upstairs when the guy broke in because I realized the barista forgot the cream cheese for my bagel so he was grabbing some from his place." Tinsley grabbed her forehead. "Well, I actually lost my entire breakfast this morning because the bagel was *also* in my purse."

"You weren't lying when you said you've had the week from Hell." Shaw shook his head at the series of unfortunate events that she seemed to be battling. "Do you remember what all was in your purse, besides Harvey's meds, that would be of value?"

"The purse itself was quite expensive, and of course my wallet was in there which has all my cards—my personal favorite being my license with my home address so whoever took it can now head over there and burgle the place. My phone as well—not to mention my car keys. And then for good measure, I had a pair of diamond earrings I was going to bring into the jeweler during lunch today to have cleaned."

"Shit." Shaw tried to hold his laugh back but couldn't help it. "I'm sorry, Tinsley. I don't mean to laugh at you, but it sounds like you just need a break."

"Now you're the one apologizing for no reason, Officer Shaw."

"The 'Officer' part actually makes me feel ancient." Shaw smirked.

"So, should I just call you Shaw, or would you prefer Hunter?"

Shaw took a liking to her saying his first name but he didn't project that on his face. "Typically at work I go with Officer Shaw. But you're the one that's had the shitty week, I'll let you decide what fits best."

"Since you're at work and all, Officer Shaw it is." She shrugged, grinning.

Brindle interrupted them when he poked his head around the door frame. "Boo, the whooped version of Khloe Kardashian circa 2007 is here for her appointment."

"Brindle"—Tinsley held her forehead in response to the nickname—"you are so mean." She took an elongated breath and then looked up at her best friend. "Did she notice we aren't exactly operational quite yet this morning?"

Brindle put one hand on his hip and whipped his other hand around while he went on a rant. "Who the fuck are we talking about right now? The better question is whether or not she cares and I'm sure you can find the correct conclusion there—even with your damn scatterbrain." Brindle rolled his eyes. "And I'm reconsidering how good of a friend I want to be to you right now. I got the shit end of the deal having to talk to Black Casper out there." He flung his arm toward the front of the salon.

"Brindle!" Tinsley slapped her hand to her forehead this time. "I'm so sorry." She glanced at Shaw before standing up. "I just need to go talk to this client real quick and I promise I'll provide a full statement when I come back."

"Boo, you didn't even give the statement yet?!" Brindle gave her a quick look up and down as she passed him. "Better not be taking *my* man's number back here."

"I swear…" Tinsley's voice trailed off and Shaw directed his smirk and his attention back down to his notepad to avoid looking at Brindle or listening any further to Tinsley.

"We're both single, by the way," Brindle offered to Shaw with a flirtatious touch of his tongue to his top lip before he skipped off to join Tinsley.

"Thank you, Tinsley. I think I've got everything for my report." Shaw gave his notes another quick look after they'd reviewed the events of the morning for the last twenty minutes or so. "I'm sure it's not a settling feeling that your information and keys are out there. Do you have a way to get into your home or car?"

"Not sure what to do about the car right now—my spare set's at home. I'm not super excited that it can now be stolen basically whenever with the other set out there. My brother has my spare house keys though," she confirmed. "I'll need to call him because I'm not actually in the mood for a lecture from my parents on how I need to pay attention, especially while I'm at the salon in such a seedy part of town." She rolled her eyes. "I grew up in a gated community over in Gig Harbor and let's just say my parents weren't exactly happy when I told them I leased this place."

"I remember coming by this spot a couple years ago when it was all boarded up. You've really created a nice and welcoming environment here. And this area, despite your morning, has been getting better with all the businesses taking over."

"Yeah, maybe a little too inviting… But thank you."

Shaw wiped his smile before continuing, "Tinsley, I'd recommend changing your locks at home if you can. I know it's not going to stop the perp from knowing where you live, but it's something."

"Yeah, another task my brother'll be holding over my head when I have to tell him what happened. He's the lesser of the two evils though." She shrugged.

"Younger?"

"Older, by six years," Tinsley informed him. "He tends to get much more credit than I do most days—and he's for sure the golden child. I, personally, will always argue we're roughly the same age if we're just talking about maturity and not actual years."

Her comments elicited a laugh from Shaw, who also reached out and patted Harvey on his head when the cane corso decided to rest his chin on Shaw's lap.

"Would you mind if Baz and I did a drive-by of your house to check things out when we leave here?"

Tinsley considered what he was asking. It would be nice since her brother wouldn't be able to get over there until later, but she wasn't wild about Baz having her address. She had zero intention of welcoming him back into her life after he ghosted her—he literally cut off their only line of communication so she didn't even have an opportunity to fully explain. She'd learned very quickly to not offer second chances when it came to men. Baz wouldn't be an exception to that rule—no matter how good looking he was, how much she'd enjoyed one of their late night chats on the app, or how many laughs they'd shared in the short time they were at dinner.

"I, uh…" She inadvertently glanced toward the doorway to the salon before shaking her head to politely decline. "Please don't trouble yourself even more than you already have this morning. There are probably actual crimes out there requiring your attention over some ditzy girl who lost her keys."

"Tinsley, you didn't lose them—someone *stole* them from you. And that's the kind of stuff we try to prevent or at least correct around here." He wasn't settled about simply leaving it at that. He looked down at the address she'd given him and knew the city had their own small police force. "I'll call over to Fircrest PD when we leave here and see if they'll do a drive-by. Would that be okay?"

"You don't have to do that." Tinsley shook her head but was fully appreciative of the gesture.

"It's no trouble at all," he smiled. "And it'll make me feel a little better about this situation."

She felt almost giddy at his last statement but masked that feeling from projecting on her face. She watched as Shaw reached up toward his trap, wincing slightly, and she noticed purple-shaded markings on the back of his arm.

"Oh gosh." She stood up and got closer to him. "Is that a bruise?"

Shaw was surprised at the concern in her voice, but even more so when she moved in and placed her hand on him.

"I don't mean to pry, but that looks uncomfortable. Do you want something for it?"

Shaw laughed. "I appreciate that, I'll tough it out though—I don't do painkillers."

"Not a painkiller, tough guy." She smirked before turning around to walk to a drawer at the kitchenette. "I always have this ointment on hand." She gestured toward Harvey who'd made himself comfortable at Shaw's feet. "That guy has zero spatial awareness and has bruised me on countless occasions. This arnica stuff is all natural and helps with inflammation and healing time—full disclosure, it has *some* pain reduction tendencies. I wouldn't want you to be fooled into feeling better." Tinsley smiled. "Just put it on your bruises twice a day and they'll be gone in half the time." She held the clear container out to him.

"I'm not supposed to be accepting gifts out on the job," Shaw replied as his hand grazed Tinsley's.

"I won't tell if you don't," she offered. "Unless of course that line's going to be taken as some kind of bribe that I'll be arrested for—that would really just put the dang cherry on top of this amazing week I'm having."

Shaw tucked the ointment in his pocket and laughed. "No, I didn't see or hear anything at all. And thank you for that—I might have to start bathing in the stuff if it works."

"I can imagine your job can be pretty physically demanding." Tinsley watched him and started to appreciate his physique even more. His forearms had several veins popping and it looked like actual grapefruits or some kind of melons had been placed under his skin to double as his biceps. Her appreciation was cut short when Brindle popped his head back there again.

"Tins, Boo, the neighbors are dropping by with some plywood and you know my pretty ass isn't helping to lift *any* of that shit."

"Oh my gosh, how sweet of them." She popped right up. "Is it the Kims? I'll help them."

"You don't have to do that." Shaw followed her back into the salon. "I'm happy to help out."

"Thank you." She turned to Shaw and lowered her voice so Brindle wouldn't hear. "Heaven forbid Brindle ruin *his* manicure." She playfully rolled her eyes.

Shaw had thought she was sweet chatting with her on Baz's dating app before physically meeting her, but after spending time with her in person, he was completely captivated.

When they got back out to the salon they heard an older Korean couple arguing in their native tongue while Baz was holding an entire sheet of plywood in the window.

"Sir—" Baz tried even though he was facing the plywood and not the couple. "Sir, hand me the drill and we'll get this hung… Ma'am…" He continued with no luck as the couple got louder. "Sir—" Baz repeated.

"*Annyeonghaseyo.*" Tinsley quickly made her way toward the couple.

"Oh, Yang Tinsley!" The woman greeted her with arms open wide. "We brought this wood." She pointed toward Baz who was still holding the sheet, waiting. "We gonna cover the hole for now. Du-Ho will call his brother—get glass in no time," she assured Tinsley.

Tinsley did a small bow but also hugged the woman. "Thank you."

"Shaw, you wanna grab the drill?" Baz didn't want to stand around and hold the board all day.

"I'll grab the other sheet and Mr…?" He looked at the man and then to Tinsley for an answer or assistance in communicating with the man who held the drill. "Perhaps he can drill these in place while we hold them?"

"Du-Ho. My name is Du-Ho," the man said in a gruff voice. "Hold the wood, I will drill." He flicked his wrists at Shaw to fit the board into the window next to Baz's sheet.

"Take your time, Mr. Kim." Brindle stood back with his phone out to record the scene. He received a swat from Tinsley when she looked over and Brindle had zoomed all the way in to only have Shaw's backside in the frame of the video.

"What?" Brindle sassily shook his shoulder. "Don't act like you have some claim over him because you got to spend time with him in the back."

Tinsley held her face and tried to be discreet with her response. "I literally want to fire you right now, I swear."

"But, Boo, you won't—you'll be begging for a copy of this video later. I'm calling this cinematic masterpiece 'Officer Shawberry Beefcake Hangs Wood.'"

Tinsley swiped the phone from his hands and stuck it in her back jean pocket.

"You bitch! You know I'm not going in there for that, but you better not have fuckin' deleted my recording."

Both Baz and Shaw heard the entire exchange and tried their best to not laugh out loud. Shaw was so red he could feel his entire body heating up. Being deemed Shawberry Beefcake was probably what he deserved after all the nicknames he had given Baz's online girlfriends... Including Tickle-Me Tinsley.

"Well, you're a *fucking* idiot." Shaw couldn't even wait until both of the cruiser doors were shut. "She's a *dime,* as sweet as a goddamn peach, *and* her dog had an actual seizure the other night. She wasn't lying about that emergency." He shook his head at his partner who'd been way too quick to pull the trigger on cutting ties with Tinsley.

"Fam, what the fuck?! What are the chances we get called out and she's there?! I about shit myself. And her little friend—what the fuck? She clearly has an accomplice while scrolling through those dating apps too."

"Can you blame her?" Shaw laughed out loud. "She's probably met a Baz or two in her time. Honestly, the sass and ogling is scarier than a burly big brother type—she's a smart girl to be recruiting that guy to help."

"You're just trying to make that guy seem anything but cringe since he has a crush on you, *Officer Shawberry*."

"Fuck off. You're just jealous he prefers my handsome ass over a Black Casper." Shaw smirked.

"A *what*?!"

"Your boyfriend called you Black Casper—you have no idea how bad I had to fight my urge to laugh out loud at that. He definitely knows you ghosted his friend, you asshole. I'll take Shawberry over Casper any goddamn day of the week."

"How was I supposed to know? I thought she was giving me some damn runaround." Baz shook his head and stopped at the light closest to the salon they'd just left. "Did you happen to get a phone number from her?"

"For the report, yes," Shaw confirmed as he was typing on their laptop to clear the board of this call.

"Don't pull that bullshit now." Baz swatted his buddy's chest. "I need to apologize to her."

"Her phone was in her purse when it was stolen. But also, that entire *two hours* we were at her salon would've been the time instead of acting like you didn't even damn know her." He laughed at Baz. "Besides, you've got Big-Tittie Tilly and the rest of the roster. Give this one a break, she's had a shitty week already."

"Oh, and I had time for that when? You took it upon yourself to be in the back with her while I got stuck with the fucking protective gay chihuahua in her life." Baz took a sip of his now cold coffee.

Shaw smiled at his partner. "I can't believe you didn't have any damn clue that was her dog. I thought I was doing you a favor giving you an extra minute to figure it out when I volunteered to go back there initially."

"Shut the fuck up. You didn't know that was her raggedy-ass Frankenstein dog when he came out there either."

"You are *definitely* an asshole." Shaw rolled his head back, still laughing at his best friend. "And yes, I did. Come on, he was on her profile. Granted not a full face photo—so, I'll give you that. But how many salon owners, in Tacoma, do you think have a dog that looks like that? The wall behind her cash register was in the background of her profile picture too. Not to mention, why do you think the protective gay in her life was mean-mugging you the second we were on scene? And *how the fuck* did you not recognize her voice!? You're the one who claimed to be a lost puppy around her and you didn't realize that was her voice?"

"Shit." Baz shook his head. "I keep telling you you're missing your detective calling. I'm the one with the dating profile and you're sitting here like you memorized the damn thing."

"You'll want to remember she was the topic of discussion when we were on that stakeout a couple weeks ago… *We* basically tag teamed that effort chatting with her all night." Shaw peered at Baz from under his brows. "So, you're goddamn welcome for having set you up to look like you even deserved a date with her in the first place."

Baz flipped him off before responding, "That's right. That *was* Tickle-Me Tinsley we were talking to that night. I'll give it to you, you're a fucking poet, fam. She was eating that shit up." A wide smile took over Baz's face. "So, see—I told you she was sweet. My ass shouldn't have removed our match. Now I can't even contact her without looking like a fucking stalker or a tool. I don't even know what excuse I could possibly spin for her to give me another shot."

"I'm gonna call it and let you know that ship has sailed." Shaw scanned the board for another call they could respond to. "You fucked it up. She deserves a gentleman."

"Oh, and you know this because you're a fuckin' dating expert now and just spent a whole five seconds with her?" Baz laughed as he glanced down at the address on the laptop screen Shaw pointed at for their next destination.

"I'll admit, I'm no dating expert." Shaw held his hands up. "But, I did just spend longer with her than you probably did on your date…" He gave his partner a sly side gaze.

"You're an asshole." Baz shook his head, smiling.

"Takes one to know one, dick."

They sat in silence for a bit until Baz broke it. "She's fine as hell though. Ten outta ten fuckable."

Shaw didn't disagree with his partner that Tinsley was gorgeous. He nodded along but inside was a little offended Baz referred to her as 'fuckable.'

CHAPTER
Three

"Thank you for doing all this." Tinsley sat on her porch steps that evening while her brother removed the lock on her door to install a new one with a keypad. Vance was almost an entire foot taller than Tinsley and had a lean runner's build. She'd always been jealous of her brother's curly hair; he had natural brunette ringlets while she had to manufacture any kind of curl to her healthy hair. Vance had a lot of their father's features—larger ears for his head, hazel eyes, and a deeper olive skin tone compared to Tinsley's.

"Leave it to you to have your entire damn life taken in a matter of minutes." Her brother shook his head, almost laughing at his out-of-luck sister. "You better replace that bag too. You'll never hear the end of it if Dad finds out you had it swiped from the shop."

"Yeah, I'll be adding that to the list of things I need to replace like yesterday." She rolled her eyes. "You're sure you don't mind swapping cars for a couple of days?"

"Tins, like I'm going to expect you to have your car here when the key's out there with Lord knows who. In fact, you should just sleep over at our place tonight. Even with the locks changed, it's not a great idea to just be here with Helen."

"Screw you." She reached over to scratch Harvey between his shoulder blades as she stuck her tongue out at her brother. "You're always so mean to him—he's your only nephew you know." Tinsley had to constantly remind Vance how rude it was to refer to her dog as the Helen Keller of the animal kingdom. Despite having a slight disadvantage when it came to seeing and hearing, Harvey was still very much aware and capable. And Vance's in-laws all had girls, so Harvey truly was his only nephew.

"I'm just saying, you should go in and pack an overnight bag for both of you. Alaurra will be over the moon to have her favorite Auntie Tins stay the night, and *I'll* sleep better knowing some fucking crackhead isn't crawling through your windows while you guys are sleeping."

"Well, doesn't that just paint the most comforting picture."

"I'm serious… Unless you want to tell Mom and Dad what happened and stay with them tonight?"

Tinsley stood up. "I'll go pack a bag."

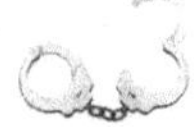

Their twelve hour shift had finally ended and both Baz and Shaw were in the locker room putting on street clothes to presumably go home.

"What do you have goin' on tonight?" Shaw had just pulled on a black cotton shirt.

"Shit, I was gonna go hit the sack, but Big-Tittie Tilly just hit me up." Baz shoved his foot into his sneaker. "So, probably a little detour first."

"Oh, so not working on that apology you were gonna try to spin?"

Baz flipped off his buddy. "It's been a long fuckin' day—not tryna put in that kind of emotional effort."

"You wouldn't have a choice about that if you were wifed up—just so you know." Shaw continued to pick at him.

"Depends on wifey." Baz shrugged. "Plus, gotta live it up while I'm single. Settling down is for another day—no harm in visiting something enjoyable and familiar tonight."

"Do you, bro." Shaw reached his fist out to Baz and once they dabbed, Shaw grabbed his hand. "But don't be a fool, wrap that fuckin' tool—Big-Titties is definitely sleeping with more than just you."

"Thanks, Mom." Baz shook his head and left the locker room.

Shaw decided he'd encouraged his grown friend enough to let him make his own decisions. He took a deep breath after his long day while pulling out his phone. Like usual when he ended a shift, he had no notifications. The silence hadn't bothered him in quite some time, so he shoved his phone in his pocket and headed out. He'd usually go to the gym and then pursue his off-duty activities before going home. Tonight, however, he was going to look for a discarded purse and very likely end up driving by the address he had for Tinsley.

Shaw had searched every dumpster for eight blocks west of Tinsley's salon when he decided to head the other way and start his search eastward. He only had to dig into four bins in that direction before he found some of what he was looking for. Thrown together were a few cards—Tinsley's driver license, memberships to Costco, a local gym, the library, and a punch card to a coffee house.

He spotted a black zipper pouch and picked it up to inspect the contents. He knew it was likely Tinsley's when he saw a roll of disposable dog waste bags and a small container of similar looking ointment to what she'd given him earlier that day. It was also very clear it was a woman's bag when he found chapstick, hair ties and a few bobby pins. The only other thing he saw in the dumpster that could belong to her was a book. It looked to be in good condition and wouldn't be something a thief would be much interested in, so he plucked it out of the trash just in case.

As he got ready to shut the lid a glittering phone case caught his eye—it had the logo to Tinsley's salon. He grabbed it and noticed all she'd get back was her case, there was no phone in sight.

Shaw walked back to his car with a bag of Tinsley's items in his hands and started to really think about what he was doing. Sure, this aligned with his desire to correct wrong-doings, but really—a stolen purse? This was a pretty light crime compared to what he'd previously corrected. It was certainly a far cry from the string of violent carjackings he'd been investigating on his own time. He wasn't sure if he felt some kind of obligation given Tinsley's familiarity with his partner, or if it was something else, but for some reason he couldn't walk away from making this as right as he could for her.

After checking another couple of dumpsters—just to be sure—he made his way toward the address he had for Tinsley. He'd talked to the police department in her city to ensure someone drove by her house earlier that day. Shaw had even given them his personal cell if they needed to follow-up, but he never heard back. He assumed they truly did check on Tinsley's house and all was well. He wasn't one to leave things to chance though, so he made his way across town.

If she was home, he figured she wouldn't recognize him because she had no idea what he drove. He just wanted to check that nothing looked out of place around her house. He slowly passed by Tinsley's initially to circle the block and then parked his black, third generation Ford Raptor across the street and a few houses down from Tinsley's.

His tinted windows offered him further concealment, but also made it harder to see anything in the dark of the night so he rolled his window down halfway. It was eleven o'clock and the neighborhood was quiet.

She lived in a little subdivision-turned-city called Fircrest which was generally a very nice, family-friendly place to live. He remembered her talking about how her parents were so appalled by her working in what they assumed were the bowels of Tacoma—maybe this was her compromise with them to justify living beyond the gates of their Gig Harbor community?

Her house was a smaller Craftsman that had a very well-kept lawn, similar to all the other homes in the neighborhood. The front porch and at least one light inside were on, but truly he didn't know if she was home. The garage that was to the left of her house was shut, and he wasn't curious enough to go creeping around the windows of that structure just to see if her car was in there.

After about twenty minutes of just watching the neighborhood Shaw decided to head home. His shift would start again before he knew it and he needed to let his body recover if he was going to pull two more shifts like the one he had today. Not to mention, he'd have more intense homework for the rest of the week besides just looking for a stolen purse.

"Alright, it's bedtime, sis." Delilah, Vance's wife, walked into the guest room to retrieve her daughter that night.

"Mommy, Auntie Tins brought over *Pickle-Chiffon Pie* and she helped me read it!"

Delilah smiled and shook her head as she leaned against the door frame. "You guys love that book."

"Yeah, because Auntie Tins loves Prince Musslebaum *and* we want to get some puppy snozzles!" she said in an excited voice.

Tinsley chuckled along to Alaurra's commentary. "He could use darker hair, but he's a dreamboat, right, Laura Loo?"

Alaurra giggled and bumped her head into Tinsley.

"Better get to bed." Tinsley hugged her niece. "You did so good reading tonight too, Auntie Tins is proud of you."

"Love you."

"Love you too." Tinsley smiled as her niece rubbed Harvey's head before jumping off the bed.

"Good night, Tins." Delilah waved and shut the guest room door.

Tinsley rolled over to her side and stroked her dog's large and boxy head. She'd usually fall asleep either doom scrolling on her phone or reading her newest book, but both of those items had been stolen from her that day. She was left to simply get lost in her thoughts instead.

She was still stunned by the robbery, but on top of that, her *ghost* of all people had been sent to respond. Tinsley held firm to the belief that things happened for a reason and the universe always put you exactly where you needed to be, but she found it difficult to dissect exactly what the universe wanted from her with today's experience. They were both grown adults and had equal opportunity to have a conversation about what had happened that weekend instead of pretending not to know each other. She couldn't help but wonder if she was the one who needed to apologize. She'd done just that right before she up and left the restaurant, but it was Baz who basically deleted her on the dating app instead of letting her explain. When she'd tried to check in at an ungodly hour that morning from the emergency vet—once Harvey was stabilized—their conversation was completely gone and his profile nowhere to be found.

She knew very well he initiated that because she'd been forced to do the same thing to an unfortunate date a couple months back. A date in which she also had to establish another rule about offering her last name or phone number until at least date number four or some kind of reliable sign that the guy wasn't going to be a creep. Cutting someone off who only had access through the app was much easier… Until it was done toward her.

They had an amazing conversation on the app. He was interested, or at least pretended to be, when she went on and on about her bigger dreams with the salon. And then she did have a genuinely fun time at dinner until she had to leave. She'd even tried to offer some money toward the tab for being so rude, but he still removed their match.

Tinsley finally decided she wasn't the one who needed to apologize. She wasn't going to say sorry or feel guilty for rushing home to her dog who was having a legitimate medical emergency; and he didn't so much as acknowledge even knowing her when he saw her earlier.

It didn't seem like he was all that upset that things weren't going to work out between them. She appreciated that Brindle had also done a perfectly fantastic job showing his disgust of Baz and the entire situation.

As Tinsley decided she could check that off her mental list of things to do, her focus turned toward the new face she met that day, Officer Hunter Shaw—or as Brindle referred to him, Officer Shawberry Beefcake. She couldn't deny that her best friend's nickname was pretty spot on. The guy was an absolute hunk—no question. Tinsley appreciated everything from his seemingly freshly cut hair to the way that uniform complimented his amazingly sculpted body. And his eyes—that green was burned into her memory.

He'd had a calming presence about him as well, which had soothed and helped ground her that morning when she spiraled into another frantic and anxious Tinsley scramble.

She could be overthinking their entire interaction because he was probably trained to be calm under pressure, but there was no reason for him to be so kind to her specifically. She continued getting caught up on the fact that he seemed to know he would be better suited to talk to Tinsley over Baz. Which she wondered about because Brindle had been so rude to Baz—it would've made logical sense to flip flop interviewers.

In addition to his intuition on the awkwardness between Tinsley and Baz, Shaw had been kind toward Harvey and there was a tenderness in his voice when he'd asked what happened to him. It wasn't the normal shocked 'Oh My God' expression when people saw her beloved pup. He'd genuinely seemed like he cared and wanted to know what Harvey had been through.

Whether it was one thing or a combination of all those things working in conjunction with how good looking Officer Shaw was, he was *definitely* taking up space in her thoughts that night.

CHAPTER
Four

"**H**EY BOO, HOW'D YOU SLEEP LAST NIGHT?" BRINDLE HUGGED his best friend when she and Harvey finally walked into the salon that afternoon. "Did you get your ID and a new phone too?"

"Sleep was decent and I got this super dope paper version of my ID to go in my new phone case for the phone I did manage to get this morning." She shook it around. "Restored with all my settings—shout out to the cloud and sales associates who understand technology much more than I do. I just have to wait for my debit and credit cards and get a new purse before my parents find out… Oh, and of course next time I hit up all the dang places I go with memberships, I'll need new cards."

"Sorry, Boo, I know that's a bitch." Brindle went back to his client's hair and quickly teased the style he was working on. "I'll take you up to Louis this week if you want to go replace your bag."

"I appreciate that." Tinsley nodded as she prepared her station for her first client of the day. "Let's pencil that in, and only because I'm not too sure which day they're coming to fix the window."

"For sure." He waved his hands around in his signature sassy swish through the air. He barely let silence take over before he was yapping along again. "So, don't act like we're not going to revisit the topic of

Black Casper and whether or not that sexy Baztard tried to get a hold of you since seeing him yesterday. He may be an asshole, but in-person"—Brindle fanned himself—"*DAMN.*"

Tinsley chuckled. "No, I haven't heard from him." She shook her head. "And honestly, it's more than fine."

"Is it though?" Brindle practically sang out the question with squinted eyes. "I watched that video I took about ten thousand times already and I'm telling you, I will be dialing 9-1-1 for literally any potential crime I see. Like, Boo, if there's a medical emergency and I need mouth-to-mouth *please* don't let the EMTs at me. I'll hang on for the Black Casper and Shawberry Beefcake to show, thank you." He snapped his fingers with his lips puckered.

Tinsley laughed as another one of the stylists headed to her station with a client who had a towel wrapped around her head.

"Hey, Tins!" Farrah waved with her free hand.

"Hey, girl," Tinsley responded and then greeted the familiar client as well. "Hi, Mrs. O'Hara."

"Hi, honey." The older woman smiled.

"So, is Brin still up here wetting his pants over the officers that I'm pissed I missed out on yesterday?" Farrah asked.

"How'd you know?" Tinsley winked at her.

"I've seen that video at least twenty times this morning… on the actual television up there, mind you. Not that I'm complaining."

"Brindle!" Tinsley threw her head back laughing.

"What?" He asked with a high-pitched voice, trying to act innocent.

"Actually, Tins"—Farrah shot her friend a suggestive look—"Brin was telling me you had the pleasure of going out with that fine chocolate man."

Tinsley laughed again as she shook her head, bending down to scratch Harvey's ear. "That's not going anywhere. Didn't Brindle inform you? He acted like he didn't know me yesterday."

Tinsley's head was in her cabinet grabbing a few tools for the client coming in when she noticed Farrah swat Brindle.

"I'm sorry, Tins. I didn't know that."

"It's honestly okay." Tinsley looked at Farrah again when she stood.

"Apparently *I* was the rude one when I left in the middle of our date because Harv was headed for the emergency vet."

"Boo," Brindle chimed in, "you know you're always about signs and shit. Harv's incident happened because you were meant to find out Black Casper has an even *hotter* friend." He bit his bottom lip before smacking his lips at Tinsley.

She immediately turned red and tried to hide her face from him. She knew exactly what he was inferring and didn't want to admit exactly how hot she thought Shaw was.

"On looks alone, I'd happily take mouth-to-mouth from either of those boys in blue." Brindle whipped his hands around. "And it's not just because I think Black Casper is an asshole now, but that Shawberry muthafuckin' Beefcake has it goin' on. I'd let that man have his damn way with me." He rolled his eyes back and bit his lip.

"Shit, based on what I saw, I'd take either of them," Farrah admitted.

"Boo, did Shawberry give you his card at least?" Brindle asked.

"No."

"But he got all *your* info…" He shimmied his shoulders around.

"Yeah, I doubt we'll be seeing that duo again," Tinsley replied. If she was being honest with herself she was actually hoping her path would cross Officer Shaw's again.

CHAPTER
Five

IT WAS SHAW'S TURN TO BE BEHIND THE WHEEL LATER THAT WEEK and he was feeling another nearly sleepless night. He'd just finished yawning for the umpteenth time when Baz swatted him.

"Hey, fam, you good?"

Shaw nodded. "Yeah, I'm straight." He readjusted his position in the driver's seat. "Just a long damn night."

"Me too." Baz stretched. "Didn't leave ol' Big-Tittie Tilly until the early hours of the morning."

"Oh, did she have other company coming over?" Shaw shook his head. He truly didn't like Tilly for his best friend. Baz could do much better.

"Fuck if I know. I needed to be in my own bed though." Baz shrugged and then pointed toward a corner market. "Hey, stop here, I'm gonna need an energy drink today."

Shaw stayed in the car while Baz ran into the store. He simply sat, watching the happenings around him. He thought about telling Baz that he'd found some of Tinsley's things, but he decided it wasn't the time quite yet. He'd figure out what the hell it all meant first and then have a talk with his best friend.

Baz opened the passenger door with not only an energy drink, but a few of his favorite candy selections as well. "We've gotta make it back to HQ in time to chat it up with Unc tonight."

"Everything all good? We in trouble?"

"Nah." Baz chuckled. "Based on the tone of the text I'm guessing it's another assignment for a community outreach thing."

Shaw only nodded. He didn't mind those assignments—it gave him a break from stressing and living in his past. Not to mention, it was always easy overtime.

"Yo, lemme get a quick drink of that water." Baz pointed to Shaw's water bottle.

"Fuck. No." Shaw laughed out loud. "You think I want Big-Tittie Tilly taste all over my shit?"

Baz wiped the smile that was on his face.

"What do you need water for anyway? You can take your chlamydia meds with your damn energy drink."

"Fuck off, it's just my vitamins." Baz threw up his middle finger, grinning.

"That shit's not going to protect you from what Big-Tittie Tilly's likely sharing."

"You really hatin' on her like that?" Baz narrowed his eyes at his partner. "Or are you still mad at me for the whole Tickle-Me Tinsley thing?"

Shaw held his tongue initially, not wanting to admit anything about Tinsley. He still had plenty to sort in his mind before making any of that known to Baz. So, he focused on Tilly instead.

"Bro, I'll keep sayin' it until you hear me—Big-Titties is a ho. You can't possibly believe you're the only one seeing *and* sleeping with her." Shaw turned his head and watched Baz. "If you're just having a good time then do you, but you can do so much better. Don't get caught up in that shit expecting her to be wifey."

Baz chewed a chunk off the sour strip he just freed from its packaging.

"And wear a goddamn condom." Shaw made a left and then accelerated.

"You know what I think?" Baz smirked and waited until Shaw looked at him before he continued. "I think your ass needs to get laid so you aren't so damn wound up all the time." He reached over and grabbed Shaw's shoulder to give him a few good shakes.

Rather than replying vocally, Shaw held up a hand gesture toward his best friend.

"To put your damn mind at ease, I've been wearing a condom, *Mom*."

"I'm glad to hear it… Your ass still isn't getting a drink from my water bottle though."

Baz threw his head back laughing and turned his attention to the laptop so they could start chipping away at the dispatch calls on the board.

Shaw and Baz were spent by the time their shift ended that day. Two of the calls they'd responded to demanded much more—physically—from them than usual. Despite the exhaustion, they made their way toward the Chief's office as promised.

"Hey boys, come have a seat," Chief Haywood greeted the men when they walked into his office.

While the chief held a strong resemblance to his nephew, he was much smaller in size all around. Additionally, Chief Haywood was bald, by choice, and only maintained a goatee.

"Unc," Baz greeted him before taking a seat.

"Chief Haywood," Shaw offered a more proper greeting despite having known him on a personal level, as if he were also a nephew, for over a decade now.

"How are Tacoma's finest doing these days?" The chief leaned back in his chair.

"Can't complain." Baz shrugged.

"I heard the two of you had some excitement today?" The Chief leaned his forearms on his desk in anticipation for their version of the events, off the record.

"Oh, you heard about how I had to be the one to chase *and* catch the coked out version of Usain Bolt today because Baz over here was weighed down by his Sour Patch Kid breakfast?" Shaw laughed.

Baz socked his partner and then flipped him off while the chief laughed.

"Oh, I do miss the days of beatin' the streets with my old partner. Best times in my career were rolling around the city streets," Chief Haywood recalled. "You fellas do a phenomenal job out there and I don't wanna pull my two best guys off patrol, but I have to keep saying it anyway." He shook his head. "There are so many opportunities throughout the department for you two to advance—you aren't limited to working every OT shift imaginable and keeping a simple patrol. You both have *very* bright futures in this department—you just need to let me know when you're ready for that move. We have multiple teams that have *specifically* asked about the two of you, SWAT, HEAT, SARS, detective positions, really anything you fellas may wanna do—you just have to say the word. The world is your oyster," he added with his arms held open wide.

This wasn't the first, or likely the last, time they'd heard this speech. Baz and Shaw had regularly been given this pitch—as if there was a script somewhere for it—from not only the Chief but every other leadership position throughout the department for at least four years. Like every other time, they simply nodded their heads in unison.

"Well, with that said"—Chief Haywood clapped his hands together—"let's talk about the assignment I called you guys up here for."

Baz leaned further back into his seat and reached in his pocket for an opened bag of Skittles.

"Really?" Shaw looked over and laughed.

"Hey, we're done chasing down bad guys for the day—I deserve a sweet treat." Baz popped a few Skittles in his mouth.

"Your big ass didn't chase down shit today," Shaw reminded him but continued to laugh.

Chief Haywood walked around the desk and held his hand out to his nephew before leaning on his desk. Shaw just watched them shaking his head with a smile on his face.

"There's a community event coming up." The chief chewed on a couple of Skittles. "It's developing into something much bigger than what was originally anticipated. We're gonna shut down a large section of the streets and will need to have a fairly solid presence for it. The mayor's involved now and it's not just businesses putting on a little open house—it's expanding into a multi-vendor market, some community services, and an opportunity for our department to do a little outreach." He leaned over for another handful of Skittles. "So, obviously I'd love for the two of you to be very involved in that effort day of."

"Sure." Baz shrugged. "We know the community loves our fine asses." He dumped a few more Skittles into his own hand.

The chief rolled his eyes. "You're your damn father, I swear. But yes, we've caught some bad press lately and the whole damn carjacking scheme we're battling hasn't exactly improved public opinion about the boys in blue. We could use a few good media spots to help. The department will be partnering with Metro Parks to provide a Children's Health and Safety Fair at the event. I also want to get you two into a few of the carnival activities the businesses are hosting." He stared directly at Baz before his next statement. "You know, since the community loves your fine asses and all."

"When's the event?" Shaw asked, not that it actually mattered since his life revolved around his work schedule.

"Almost two weeks from now, it'll be on a Sunday afternoon."

"Where's it at?" Baz asked.

"We're going to have South Tacoma Way from 52nd to 56th blocked off from vehicle traffic to make the street safe for all the tents and patrons. I'd like you fellas roaming the event—and actively participating in some of the carnival games for photo opps."

Hearing the location, Shaw did his best not to look at Baz and knew his partner was fighting the same urge.

"That area's been a focus lately for the Mayor since it's been turning around so quickly. I know you fellas just responded to an incident there this week, but that seems to be a one-off from the neighborhood as of late. Did you guys notice anything concerning about that incident?"

Shaw shook his head and decided to answer for them. "No, it looked pretty standard for any low-budget thief; no other motive or pattern from it." He distinctly did not mention to the chief he'd gone back to the scene and recovered some of the victim's items—some of *Tinsley's* items.

"What types of carnival things are you trying to have us in?" Baz asked and ate the last of the Skittles so he didn't have to keep sharing.

"Not too sure yet. The department publicist will be getting all that information from the event committee and I'll let you guys know where we'll need you."

The men chatted for a few more minutes before Chief Haywood declared he needed to get home before his wife threatened divorce again for another late night at the office.

As they walked down the hall from the chief's office, Shaw started in on his partner.

"Shit, someone better work on that apology before the event."

"Fuck off." Baz gave him a healthy jab. "You don't think I've already contemplated calling in sick for that one?" He chuckled.

"It sounds like a pretty big event, you may not have to see him." Shaw shrugged.

"Him?" Baz's face twisted trying to figure out why Shaw said *him*.

"Your new boyfriend, Brindle."

"You asshole." Baz laughed and grabbed his partner around his neck to put him into a friendly chokehold.

Shaw bent over to have Baz basically hanging on his back. "I'll have to let him know you like to be the dominant one and you prefer a choking style foreplay."

Baz hopped off his back and gave him a firm shove. "You're an asshole."

"You and your boyfriend are the experts on assholes, so you might be right."

"I swear to God…" Baz just shook his head smiling, not wanting to say anything else and allow Shaw another opportunity to take a shot at him.

While Shaw thoroughly enjoyed watching his partner squirm, he was also grateful Baz hadn't said anything else about Tinsley. He knew he'd been spending more time with Tilly lately, so Tinsley was likely drifting off Baz's radar completely. Shaw, however, hadn't *stopped* think-ing about her—since meeting her, her smile popped up in his mind more times than he'd like to admit. The chief's assignment was a very welcome surprise and Shaw couldn't wait to catch a glimpse of Tinsley again.

CHAPTER
Six

After Baz and Shaw parted ways that night Shaw decided to pick up on his own self-appointed investigation. Chief Haywood's short mention of the carjacking ring had Shaw's mind swirling back to all the leads he'd gathered over the last couple of months. The city had been terrorized by an increase in carjackings that had more recently turned violent.

Shaw's need for justice grew as the incidents escalated. At first, there were just a few scattered reports of stolen vehicles, but lately the calls were from victims who'd sustained serious injuries and reported multiple assailants during the attacks.

A week earlier, Shaw had discovered a garage on the eastside of town that appeared to have been some kind of home base for a handful of the stolen vehicles. There were various parts from four of the models that had been associated with carjacking reports over the last month. By the time he'd caught wind of that garage, it looked like they'd already made a quick exit and only left remnants of their make-shift chop shop. There'd been no helpful evidence to pinpoint a suspect by the time he got there either. He'd made his best attempt to plant suspicious enough evidence around the garage to prompt neighbors to phone the police in hopes the task force would be alerted of the potential scene.

Tonight, however, Shaw had another area of the city in mind because of the newest reports that had come in the last couple of days. He wasn't sure he'd find another headquarters for the ring that night, but the recent reports had all been clustered in the south end of the city. His plan was to roll around the area of the last few incidents in hopes of catching the ring in action—or at the very least, find another lead.

Shaw parked his truck near a Starbucks in the Lincoln district to simply observe and run through everything he'd discovered since following this case. He hadn't been parked long when he noticed a beauty school across the street. The building caught his attention for a long moment as a picture of Tinsley flashed in his mind.

Damn—she was gorgeous, he thought. He chuckled at himself for thinking about her like he was, but he couldn't help it. Initially, he'd simply wanted to help his buddy out—who couldn't put a charming sentence together to save his life. Baz always had a 'player' tone to everything he said and was completely lost when it came to actually making a woman like Tinsley swoon. He'd given Shaw full access to his app several times, and some of the things he said to select women was enough to make Shaw embarrassed for him. So it wasn't odd when he'd passed his phone to Shaw one night when they were on a stakeout.

"Fam, this is one of them good girls. She hasn't responded for almost a day, help me out?" Baz had said.

Shaw remembered scrolling through Tinsley's profile to get an idea of what he was working with. He'd ended up shaking his head to scold Baz after he looked at their messages. Tinsley had responded to one of Baz's compliments by politely telling him he'd make a handsome wedding date after seeing him as a groomsman in one of his pictures. His friend had the audacity to tell this sweet woman something along the lines of 'if he decided she was lucky enough, he'd let her see what was *under* his three-piece suit'.

Shaw had to do some creative back pedaling for his suggestive buddy, but once he did he genuinely enjoyed chatting with Tinsley. Baz eventually decided it was his turn to take over. After that, Shaw had assumed that Baz would dig himself into another hole. Either way, Tinsley had made an impression on Shaw that night.

Since they'd responded to Tinsley's salon, Shaw couldn't stop thinking about her. He'd driven by her salon multiple times since their official meeting in hopes that he may just catch a single glimpse of her. Each time he'd done that he laughed at himself. What did he truly expect from that? It had been so long since he'd courted a woman that he felt completely lost. Not to mention, he wasn't even sure he was ready for anything like that. Still, each time since meeting her, the mere thought of Tinsley made him smile—and that had to mean something.

He realized he'd been parked for almost an hour when he decided to finally head home. Shaw was disappointed to have come away empty handed on the carjacking case, but somehow left with a grin on his face as Tinsley's picture-perfect smile flashed through his mind again.

CHAPTER
Seven

"**Y**OU SHOULD GET THIS ONE TOO." BRINDLE HELD UP A SMALL crossbody option while they were shopping at Louis Vuitton one afternoon.

Tinsley smiled but shook her head. "It's super cute, but I'm only replacing the purse and wallet. You know I'm trying to save and this isn't exactly helping out."

"This is another reason you need a man." Brindle put the purse down.

"Brindle." Tinsley shook her head smiling. "That's awful." She looked down as Harvey's heavy head plopped onto her foot when he decided he'd been standing in the store long enough.

The sales associate who was helping Tinsley looked down at the cane corso. "He's been a very polite visitor today," she complimented the friendly dog.

"Thank you, he does his best." Tinsley smiled down at her favorite guy.

"Boo"—Brindle shoved right next to Tinsley—"smell these. Which one should I get? And keep in mind I plan to go out with that fine-ass African man I was chatting with on the way up here."

Tinsley chuckled and leaned in to smell the blue bottle—it was decent. The clear bottle was better.

"Hmm, is there like a mini collection? That way you can change it up for the flavor of the week until you settle on one."

"That's a great idea, I'll be doing that." Brindle decided and walked back to the fragrance area.

Tinsley was taking her card back from the sales associate when Brindle set his items down on the counter. She had to laugh because in addition to his fragrance set, he had also grabbed a belt and a pair of socks. He'd spent the majority of the car ride up to Bravern complaining about how much it was going to cost to put new brakes on his car, yet here he was spending over a thousand dollars on unnecessary items.

"Let me see another picture of this guy you're going out with tonight." Tinsley didn't remember seeing anything overly notable to warrant Brindle getting this fancy.

"I'll show you when we get back in the car." Brindle knew full well Tinsley would have something to say about this guy. Her standards for her bestie were *impossible* and she always managed to have some critical observations about his dates.

They walked out of the store and the door had barely shut when Tinsley started in on Brindle. "Well, looks like *you're* the one who needs a man to be taking you shopping. I *cannot* believe you just spent four hundred dollars on a pair of dang socks. You are hands-down the bougiest person I have ever known. Your date better be taking those off with his teeth this evening to justify that spending."

"Bitch! You're gross!" Brindle threw his head back and laughed. "If a man ever came for my feet!" He whipped his head around in disgust.

"And let me see him. We're not waiting to get in the car so you can come up with another excuse." Tinsley stopped Harvey and held her hand out, waiting for Brindle to get his phone. He took his time, which Tinsley knew was her best friend delaying the inevitable because the guy wasn't going to be worthy of a four hundred dollar pair of socks in her mind.

"Brindle. Lawrence. Graves." Tinsley snatched the phone from his hand the second she had a view of the guy's profile picture. "Have you not been getting enough attention lately or something?! Four hundred dollars on socks for *this* guy?! What the hell is he wearing on his feet? Did he just get out of some Cambodian prison or something?" She gaped at the profile picture which was the man's feet propped up in front of a fireplace with a starlit city skyscape in the background. The plastic-looking basket weave sandals he wore were almost more offensive than having to see his hairy feet as the first picture in his profile. She scrolled, hoping that there would be something redeeming after that.

"He's not the worst you've ever dated, but that first picture is grotesque. I cannot believe you didn't swipe him away at first glance."

"Well"—Brindle snatched his phone back from Tinsley—"we know why your judgemental ass is still single."

"I'd rather be single than have a man show up wearing *those* Jesus jandals thinking he was about to take me anywhere."

"Well, you're not a gay man, so your taste is very different." Brindle looked through his date's profile again. "Honestly, I like the shoes." He shrugged.

"Where are you guys going?"

"Dinner at Dusty's and then who knows? Hopefully his place if this is his balcony." Brindle zoomed in on the foot picture again.

"You think that profile picture is from his *OnlyFans* or something?" she teased.

Brindle gave her a quick little shove. "You can be such a bitch."

"I just don't want my bestie to settle is all." Tinsley reached up to put her arm around Brindle. "You are a priceless little gem and only someone very deserving should be occupying your time."

"I'm not gonna be young forever. Beautiful, yes—but not young. So, I have to ho around now." Brindle stood on his behavior, he was having a good time and that's all that mattered to him.

"As long as you're happy… And safe." Tinsley finally conceded with a friendly shaking of her head.

"You haven't sent along any profiles in a while. You have anyone notable on the chatline you want me to stalk?" Brindle bumped into his best friend's shoulder. He was a master investigator, it didn't matter how private someone tried to make their socials, Brindle was a wizard when it came to finding information.

Tinsley shook her head and stopped, looking down when Harvey wanted to sniff a trash can. "I haven't checked the app in a few days."

"Prince Charming could be sitting in your inbox right now! What are you doing, Boo?!"

Tinsley shrugged. "I just don't really feel like being on there right now."

"Please don't tell me that Baztard has scared you away from online dating. Don't let that asshole have that kind of power."

"I mean, that sucked getting dropped and ghosted. But, no, it's not like that." Tinsley lightly shook her head.

"Then give me your phone. Let's find someone to amuse you this evening." He held out his hand.

Tinsley didn't reach for her phone, she simply declined with her head.

"You're not gonna be young forever either, Boo." Brindle put his hand on his hip. "And unlike my fine ass, your eggs are drying up with each passing day."

Tinsley rolled her eyes. "You'll have to let me know how Hell is, because that's where you're going for being so rude."

Brindle opened his mouth for a sassy reply but Tinsley continued.

"And you know very well I don't want a man just to *amuse* me or simply foot my bill at Louis." She stuck her tongue out at him. "I'm looking for my husband—and I'm not so sure I'll find him on that app."

"*Maybe*," Brindle sang out, "you say that because you've already met him." He pumped his eyebrows at her.

Tinsley didn't respond to her best friend's suggestion, she maintained her focus on Harvey who was thoroughly enjoying all the new smells as they made their way back to Brindle's car. She couldn't help but smirk as a picture of Officer Shaw flashed in her mind.

Before she could linger too long on that mental picture, she looked over at Brindle who was pushing his phone out to her. He had the video of Officer Shaw holding up a piece of plywood.

Tinsley laughed and gave Brindle a gentle shove.

CHAPTER
Eight

DESPITE IT BEING THE ONLY DAY OFF HE'D HAVE FOR A WEEK, SHAW decided it was time to bring Tinsley the belongings of hers that he recovered. He felt like keeping them any longer would be border-line stalker behavior versus his true intentions of wanting to simply return what was stolen from her. In addition, he genuinely wanted to see her again. Based on their talk earlier in the week he knew she worked four-day workweeks. Since they'd caught her on her version of a Monday morning, Saturday was her official Friday. He checked the salon hours and decided to try and catch her right at opening to hopefully avoid taking any time from her clients.

Shaw parked his truck across the street from the salon and grabbed the bag of Tinsley's items. He did a quick shuffle through the cards to make sure everything he found was still there. When he thumbed by the coffee shop punch card, he noticed she was only one purchase away from her free one. The logo of the card was familiar and he knew the stand was less than two blocks from him, so he started his truck to head that way so the next time she used her card she could redeem the free drink.

"Good morning," Shaw greeted the barista when he pulled up to the window. "This may be a little odd, but I was wondering if I could order a drink for someone who I assume is a regular patron here. Are you familiar with the regulars?"

The barista looked at him with suspicious eyes.

"Listen, dude, I don't know your kink or what angle you're trying to take, but we don't do any stalker shit with our customers." She banged one of the stirring spoons around on the counter to flick the moisture off. "Being good looking might help in some situations, but that doesn't mean you'll be getting away with shit around here."

"No…" Shaw shook his head and reached for his badge to show her. "Nothing like that," he tried to assure the protective barista. "I'm a police officer with Tacoma PD and we actually recovered some stolen property for a citizen." He held up the punch card. "Listen, she just looked like she's been down on her luck and I noticed she's one punch away from a free drink so I thought when I drop these off, I can also drop off a coffee. I appreciate you looking out for each other, but it's not like that—strictly business. I can even leave you my card so you know who I am."

"Uh huh…" The barista walked toward the window. "Can I see your badge again, Officer?" She inspected it and then looked at Shaw. "Can you describe the victim of these stolen items? I can't very well tell who it is based on the card."

"Her name is Tinsley. You'll probably remember her dog, Harvey, as well."

"Okay…" The barista finally lightened up a bit. "Yes, I know what she gets. I'm actually surprised I haven't seen her yet this morning. She's probably running late again today. Bless that woman and her ability to show she's human from time to time." She shook her head with a smile on her face as she flipped a couple of handles on the espresso machine.

"What do you mean?" Shaw was intrigued.

"Well, clearly you've seen her!" The barista laughed. "Tins exudes perfection. From her adorable little body to that cute-as-a-damn-button style she rocks, right down to her outrageously aesthetically-pleasing salon that she designed herself. By all accounts she looks perfect from the outside, but you even spend five minutes talking to her and you soon realize she's just as human as the rest of us." She dug into the ice bucket to fill Tinsley's cup.

Shaw could feel a smile forming on his face, but he stopped it before it became obvious and instead nodded. "So, you must've heard about her shop the other day then?"

"Yes!" She shook her head. "Of all the places on the block, I can't believe they'd hit hers. You know what a dick that tattoo artist is a couple doors down? Or try even just walking into that plant shop on the corner—they make you feel like you need to pay to get in or some shit, they're so damn bougie. You get shit service at the bar across the street from her too. Yet somehow, when there's all those amazing candidates for bad karma, it's the Saint of South Tacoma Way who has her front window shattered."

Shaw grabbed his wallet from the center console while thinking about Tinsley's unofficial title—it made him smirk.

"Here's her usual. Can I get you something too? I still need to grab Harvey his treat—that one's always on the house."

"Actually, I'll take an Americano, please. Thank you," Shaw agreed.

"Boo, what the fuck?" Brindle put his hands on his hips. "You know you can't be late like this on a day your mom's coming into the salon."

"I know, I know—but you know I was here late last night so the window could be fixed. I'd be busted for sure if she saw that." Tinsley set her phone down on her workstation and watched as Harvey circled a few times before settling onto his bed nearby. "I didn't even have time for coffee. It's going to be a long damn day."

"You know I'd help, but I'm busy. Send Farrah or Lacey." Brindle continued placing the extensions he was applying for his client.

"I'll be okay." She started pulling all of her tools from her cupboard and was in a squat when the salon door opened.

Brindle let out a quick screech that made Tinsley jump.

"Officer Shawberry!" His hands fluttered about. "We were hoping we'd see your beefcake ass again soon." Brindle took in Shaw's dressed down appearance. He'd fully appreciated him in a uniform, but now he looked like he was ready to hit the gym. Shaw had on a charcoal gray Ariat ball cap and a black quarter zip long sleeve that clung to his pecs in the most flattering way to showcase how strong his chest was. Further down, the entire salon watched and waited in anxious anticipation for precisely the right movement because Shaw wore a pair of gray shorts that were made of sweatshirt material.

"Brindle!" Tinsley hissed and her face burned into a new shade of pink.

Shaw turned red at the greeting in front of a much larger crowd than they'd had a couple of days ago. "Brindle." He tried to wave his hand that was holding a bag and not the drinks. "Nice to see you again."

"Oh trust, Shawberry—the pleasure is *all* mine, sir." Brindle gave him another once over with a suggestive expression on his face.

Farrah and Lacey gawked, their heads poked around the corner of the back room when they'd heard Brindle's screeching. Farrah decided Brindle's little video that he'd been showing everyone from the day they met the officers didn't come close to doing Shaw any justice. Having the uniform off, she could tell he was actually very fit.

"Good morning, Officer Shaw," Tinsley greeted with a smile and watched Harvey grab his now legless monkey stuffie to bring to his new friend.

"Good morning." Shaw made friendly eye contact with Tinsley before noticing Harvey's animated trot toward him. "Harvey's looking good today." He noticed the tilt he had with his head the first time they met was completely gone.

"He's definitely on the road to recovery—finally," Tinsley happily agreed.

"I've actually got something for you, big guy." Shaw looked over at Tinsley. "The barista at the little stand down the street said this is his usual." He held his hand out where he was double fisting both Tinsley and Harvey's drinks. "I have no idea what the other one is, but she also assured me this is what you order."

Brindle let out a high pitch, giddy groan that Tinsley and Shaw tried not to acknowledge.

"This is really nice of you, thank you. I was just complaining to Brindle about not having time for my coffee stop this morning."

"I was lucky to have managed this because that barista initially wasn't trying to give up any information to help me out." Shaw handed over the coffee, smiling.

"Oh, yeah"—Tinsley chuckled while accepting the drinks—"one of her customers had like a crazy stalker guy and he started showing up at the stand when he knew she'd be rolling through. So, Shelly's super protective of all us girls now."

"Nothing wrong with that," Shaw agreed and watched Tinsley hold out Harvey's treat.

The jubilant cane corso dropped his monkey and then carefully took the cream filled, biscuit topped cup back to his bed to dig in.

"Thank you for bringing Harvey's treat too—he would've known if he got cut out of the deal." She fondly watched her dog who was making sure he didn't leave anything in that cup. "Can I give you some cash for this?" Tinsley shook her cup.

"No." Shaw shook his head. "Absolutely not, I just figured it would give you that little break from Hell you've been needing." He chuckled.

Brindle unapologetically stared at the interaction intently while Tinsley blushed.

"Plus, you were only one punch away from your free drink." Shaw held up the small, plastic GNC bag he'd brought.

"What's this?" She smiled and accepted it.

"I know it's not everything, but we did recover a few things that I assume may have been in your purse." Shaw watched her dig through the items.

Brindle rushed to Tinsley's side to peer over her shoulder.

"Where did you... How did you find this?" Tinsley thumbed through her cards.

"It was in a dumpster a couple blocks down. I did my best to sanitize the items, but I'm really not sure how to clean a book... I'm not even sure if that's your book anyway."

Tinsley put everything back in the bag and then looked at him with infinite gratitude. "Honestly, this is so much more than I expected. I really appreciate this, Officer Shaw—thank you." She wasn't sure about hugging him, especially in front of Brindle and the other girls, so she just reached for his forearm and gave him a gentle squeeze with a bright smile on her face and in her eyes.

Shaw didn't generally initiate affectionate touching toward anyone, but Tinsley's touch was warm and welcoming. "You're welcome, I really hope this helps out."

"Oh, I know how you can continue to help out," Brindle offered, completely railroading the moment.

Tinsley immediately held her forehead, sighing. "Brindle…" she complained.

Brindle took the bag and hung it on a hook that was next to Tinsley's workstation.

Tinsley suddenly felt warm from the embarrassment so she slid her long jacket off to hang over the hook where Brindle just put her things. She turned back around to talk to Shaw and watched as he bit his lip, trying to suppress a smile, as he looked away from the mirror behind Tinsley. Then Brindle let out yet another high-pitched sound from deep within his throat.

"Bitch, can't take you any-damn-where!" He marched over with one of his hands in the air and Tinsley felt him grab at something on her backside. "How many damn times have I told you to do a couple full rotations in the mirror before leaving the house?" Brindle held up the black lace thong that had been sticking to the back of her jeans.

Tinsley's bright red face immediately fell into her hands.

Shaw tried and failed miserably to not join the laughter when he heard not only Brindle's client, but the two employees who were still stuck in the doorway listening, cracking up as well.

"I think I'll go find a rock to crawl under now," Tinsley mumbled through her hands, unwilling to look at anyone at the moment.

Shaw gathered enough of his voice to try to lighten her embarrassment. "Tinsley, I didn't even see anything," he fibbed and reached out to gently touch her wrist in hopes she would uncover her beautiful face.

She finally began lifting her head when Brindle doubled down. "Oh you didn't?" He held the thong by the hip strings so it was fully visible. "Well, here it is in all its glory. I can't believe guys go for this shit."

Tinsley scrambled over and snatched them from him. "You are the literal worst."

Everyone was laughing when a voice cut into the room from the front door.

"Good morning! Aren't we all having fun?" The well-put-together, older, brunette woman smiled.

Brindle scurried back over to his client while Tinsley quickly shoved the thong in her back pocket that barely had any room because of how tight her jeans were.

"Hi Mom." Tinsley waved initially and waited for Harvey to say hi to his grandma before she walked over and hugged her.

"Hi, Tins, honey. Sorry I'm late, looks like I'm missing all kinds of fun this morning." Tinsley's mom immediately lasered in on Shaw. "Am I interrupting another appointment?" She walked toward him. "I don't believe we've met before, I know a lot of my daughter's clients. I would *certainly* remember you though."

Tinsley worried because she didn't want her mom to find out about the break in. Brindle held his breath, he didn't even have a good segway to save anyone in this scenario—and that was a rarity.

Shaw held his strong hand out to the woman and offered a warm greeting, "Hi, Mrs. Adams, I'm—" he was immediately interrupted.

"Oh!" She put her hand to her chest. "Sweet Jesus, Mrs. Adams is my mother-in-law." She laughed. "Please, call me Colette." She shot a sly glance at her daughter. "That is, unless I am indeed going to be your mother-in-law?"

"Mom!" Tinsley whined in a tone that was only slightly less sharp than when she was scolding Brindle.

"There's a line!" Brindle informed her. "Shawberry's in high demand around here, Colette."

"Shawberry?" Colette looked at Shaw, who was—once again— trying to suppress his smile.

Shaw held up his hands. "Just Shaw—Officer Shaw."

Tinsley's eyes went wide and she tried not to look too quickly toward Brindle's direction.

"Officer?! Tinsley, what happened? Are you okay, honey?" She held her daughter's hands up and inspected her for any signs of distress or injuries.

Shaw remembered his interview with Tinsley and the implication that her parents were less than thrilled about her being in this neighborhood.

"Mom, I—"

"No need to worry, Colette." Shaw smiled and then gestured toward his outfit. "I'm not on duty today. I was just in the area and figured I'd stop to check in."

Colette looked at her daughter and then back at Shaw.

He continued along, "This area's been really popular the last couple of years with so many successful businesses moving in. My partner and I have this neighborhood in our sector so we like to be sure we've always got a pulse on who belongs and who doesn't, you know?"

A visible sigh of relief left Colette's body. "I'm so impressed to see good police work these days. You have no idea what kind of relief that gives me." She turned to her daughter.

Tinsley shrugged. "Mom, I've tried to tell you, it's not as bad as you and Dad think out here. I'm perfectly safe—the business is fine here."

"Well"—she stole another glance at Shaw—"you didn't mention you had such an attentive police presence around." She leaned in closer to whisper, "and so attractive."

"I didn't want to worry you and Dad," Tinsley assured her while trying to ignore the 'attractive' comment.

"I'm certainly a *lot* less worried now." Colette gave Shaw another once over. "I have to use the restroom before we get started, honey. I'll be right back."

They all made sure Colette was out of earshot before everyone exhaled relief from their lungs.

Farrah finally walked to her workstation and Lacey went into a small room off the side of the cash register to prepare for her first client of the day.

Tinsley turned toward Shaw and her eyes were big but she had a gorgeous smile painted across her face. "Thank you for that, and I'm sorry."

Shaw chuckled. "You're apologizing again, ma'am."

"I'm sor… *Gah!*" She laughed. "That's a difficult one to drop."

Shaw's eyes were still grinning when he responded, "I know you mentioned they worry, I didn't want to put you in a bad spot." He nodded. "Plus, this neighborhood *is* part of our sector, so I didn't actually tell any lies."

"Well, truly, I appreciate it. Actually everything you've done this morning… Officer Shaw, you've got an amazing ability to cast a calmness over things. I need that energy bottled up to carry around with me." She laughed.

Shaw's smoldering smile finally made its way onto his face that morning, despite his attempts to continue hiding it. "I think that's the first time I've had that compliment."

"You've been hanging with the wrong crowd then." Tinsley shook her head.

Brindle immediately perched his hands on her shoulder. "You're welcome to join our crowd *anytime*, Shawberry."

Tinsley, again, held her forehead. "Brindle." She put her hand down when he sauntered back to his station. She watched Shaw laugh under his breath and apologized again.

"I'm going to need to get one of those jars where you have to pay up each time you say 'I'm sorry,'" he joked.

Tinsley's smile completely took over and she just shook her head at Shaw.

"Well," Shaw decided, "I better let you all get back to work." He walked over to Harvey who was happily lying on his bed. Shaw squatted down to scratch his head and it didn't take long for his new four-legged friend to get excited enough to stand up and lick his face. "Good boy." Shaw gave his sides a healthy pat down before he stood up.

"Thank you again. I really appreciate everything, Officer Shaw," Tinsley said, smiling when he looked her way again.

"My pleasure, Tinsley." He grinned. "You all enjoy your day," he offered before he left the salon.

A collective squeal took over the second the door closed and Brindle did a dainty run in his platform shoes to put his arms around his best friend.

"Boo! Are my gorgeous-ass eyes deceiving me or did Shawberry Beefcake just shoot his shot?!"

Tinsley tried to conceal the red in her cheeks but didn't stand a chance with Brindle literally hanging off her and hopping around like a little school girl.

"Brin, he was just being polite. I don't even have a way to get a hold of him… Not to mention, wait until he finds out I went out with his *partner*."

"Oh, get the fuck outta here, Boo." Brindle flicked his wrist around. "Black Casper definitely told him yet he still came by and bought you a coffee. That's some-damn-thing. I don't see a drink for me anywhere." His animated movements whipped his head around Tinsley's workstation. "And don't get me started on him with Harv."

Tinsley shook her head, knowing full well her mom would be coming out of the bathroom any second and very likely heard all the screaming that she'd now have to explain.

Brindle could tell she was trying to find her calm so he walked up behind her and put both of his hands on her shoulders to whisper to her. "You better welcome that shot with open fucking arms when he comes back."

If, Tinsley thought to herself.

"Wow, you all sure have a lot of energy this morning." Colette commented when she headed back toward her daughter's workstation.

"Must be something in the coffee." Brindle winked at Tinsley.

"Where's Officer Shaw?" Colette looked around.

Tinsley answered before Brindle had the opportunity to, "Oh, he was just doing a quick check-in, he had to go."

"Uh huh," Colette stared at her daughter through the workstation mirror while she was getting a cape buttoned around her neck. "And how often have we been getting check-ins from Officer Shaw?"

Brindle, for reasons unknown that Tinsley was grateful for anyhow, held his tongue.

"This was his first morning check-in." Tinsley shrugged. She hoped that would be enough for now and then she quickly suggested they go to the sink to wash her mom's hair.

CHAPTER
Nine

Later that week, Shaw pulled yet another twelve-hour over-time shift but decided to roll right into his self-appointed side job—despite the invitation from Baz and a few of the guys to grab a beer. They had responded to an incident earlier in their shift that had Shaw's blood boiling. He decided to take the night, at least the first part of it, off from any carjacking theories so he could deal with this new issue. The street clothes he left the station in weren't dark enough, so he went home to change first.

Shaw lived in a very simple apartment. After selling his house a couple years earlier he'd reduced his life to just this one-bedroom apart-ment, the gym, and work… both on and off the books. Tonight would be no exception to his off-the-books duties. As he did most nights, he heard the kids who lived above him stomping around. He knew they regularly circled their apartment on some kind of wheeled toy given the sounds sometimes.

He walked into his bedroom and locked his glock securely in the safe he had near the bed. In the closet he checked his secondary safe to be sure it was still locked. On the right side of the closet he had a collec-tion of items that could be used as weapons—he decided to grab a metal baseball bat for his duties this evening. Shaw had collected various bats and golf clubs from garage sales and thrift stores because he never had to use a credit card at any of those places and there was less chance of being recorded during his purchases. Once he was in darker clothes and had selected his weapon of choice he headed out.

Shaw returned home a couple hours later and had to tend to a few cuts. One probably needed stitches, but he wasn't going to bother. He stripped his clothes and threw them in the washing machine before he stalked to the shower. Shaw let the scalding water fall on him to wash away what he'd just done. Like every other night, he wasn't proud of what he was doing, but it helped relieve some of the anger and grief he permanently carried. After a while, he scrubbed his body. He looked down and knew he'd have a couple new bruises by the morning. His deeper cuts continued to bleed and he decided he'd try to glue one of them when he got out of the shower since it truly looked like it needed stitches. Shaw watched the red stain the water below him and spiral down the drain.

He quickly washed his hair before getting out of the shower. Once he gave himself a brief towel dry he dug in a bathroom drawer for the ointment Tinsley had given him. As he opened the jar he started to think about her. She'd actually been on the forefront of his mind since he last saw her at her salon two days prior. He didn't know what to do with the feelings he'd been wrestling with.

She was a gorgeous woman, but on top of that she had an absolutely addictive personality, and that smile… Shaw felt a short flutter in his heart when a picture of that sweet, bright smile of hers consumed his mind. He had only been exposed to a sliver of her and he still craved another opportunity to see Tinsley and learn more. He knew the ball was in his court but he didn't want to be too forward too quickly—and he needed to feel Baz out on the subject. He decided he'd be prioritizing that since they'd likely see her at the upcoming community event.

CHAPTER
Ten

"**H**AVE YOU BEEN HOLDING OUT ON ME, OR WHAT?" SHAW started in on his buddy the next morning just after they finished responding to a call along the southend of their sector.

"Holding out? What do you mean?" Baz asked, confused.

"You haven't been sharing any online dating stories in a few days. You and Big-Titties moving toward a bigger commitment or something?"

Baz laughed out loud. "I certainly have been seeing her more often than not." He shrugged. "I was thinking about actually taking her on a date."

"Are you kidding me?!" Shaw laughed. "Bastian"—he pulled his full first name to make his sincerity known—"I may not know her like you do, but her messages, bro… I don't know about her."

"What?" Baz joined the laughter.

"Hopefully she can carry a better conversation in person because she seems pretty shallow online." He shook his head. "Just let me know when I need to start calling her Tilly instead of Big-Titties, I wouldn't wanna disrespect your girlfriend."

"Hey now, pump the fucking brakes with that shit." Baz put up his hand. "I only said a date—your fucking romantic ass tryna get me all boo'd up too quick."

"You're the one that dropped the comment about looking for 'wifey' not too long ago," Shaw reminded him. "I'm just sayin, if she's not giving that vibe then be careful about catching real feelings."

"I hear you, fam." Baz nodded. "Honestly, I think I just need a break from the online dating thing." He rolled his head around. "I kinda feel like shit about being such a dick to Tickle-Me. I need some separation from the app before I do some dumb shit again."

"Soooo… you're not going to be apologizing to her? You know, before we see her at the community event and all?" Shaw enjoyed teasing his buddy. If he was being honest with himself, he also wanted to see where Baz stood regarding his feelings for Tinsley—if he had any.

"No." Baz shook his head. "You're probably right. I'm sure the ship has sailed." He shrugged. "And even if it hasn't, I'm not looking to end shit with Big-Titties yet."

There was a long pause in the car, Baz picked up on it and called his partner out.

"You got somethin' on your mind?"

Shaw rolled his head around.

"Shit, fam."

"What?" Shaw narrowed his eyes at his best friend.

"Say it already!" He laughed. "Damn. You embarrassed or something?"

Shaw shook him off. "Not embarrassed. Just want to be sure I didn't cross a line or some shit."

"Don't tell me you been fuckin' Big-Titties too." Baz gave him a sideways glance knowing full well his friend had been very celibate for a couple years.

"If I can't even stand her suck-ass conceited conversational skills, do you really think I'd give her a go in bed? She probably calls you Big Daddy or some shit and you know that grosses me out." Shaw rolled his eyes.

Baz laughed out loud at him. "I *knew* you were fuckin' her—that's *exactly* what she calls me!" He rolled his head back and continued laughing, his enthusiasm finally got Shaw going too.

"C'mon." Baz swatted Shaw's chest. "Out wit it already, fam."

"You know I like to close loops on things," Shaw started. "So, I went to the salon the other day because I found some of Tinsley's things from her purse…"

Baz quickly shook his head back and forth. "You *found* some things?"

"Okay!" Shaw threw his head back and his hands up. "I went damn dumpster diving that same night and found a bunch of her cards and stuff a few blocks from the salon. So, I went back the other day and brought them to her."

Baz was quiet for a long moment. He didn't look upset at all, but Shaw didn't know how to read him.

"Honestly," Baz finally spoke, "I think that's a good thing."

"What do you mean, a *good thing*?"

"Fam…" Baz gave Shaw a flat look. "You don't think I noticed a difference in you when we went to that salon? That protective ass Shaw was showin' face," he pointed out. "And the lines you were pulling when we talked to her that night on the chatline? You haven't used that kinda material on any of the other girls you've helped me talk to. That was a full on convo you two were having"

Shaw just gazed out his window as they drove down the street.

"Shaw, fam, I'm gonna be real with you. It's about time you got out of your solo journey. You've been doing this dark and gloomy life for far too long now. No one wants that for you—*Sloane* wouldn't want this for you and you know that."

Shaw's strong arm rested itself on the windowsill of the door, he wasn't interested in following Baz down this path.

"I won't keep digging on that topic, fam. All I'm sayin' is take chances on something that might feel right. You got no hate or worries comin from me if something's *or someone's* drawing you back to that salon."

Baz checked Shaw's expression a few times when he didn't move.

"I'll be giving you so much fucking shit if you're going back for your little gay parade buddy though. Just know that, *Shawberry*."

"Fuck. You." Shaw finally laughed. "You're just goddamn jealous I got the better nickname."

"For real though, do you Shaw. You got no shade coming from me—on everything."

Shaw finally reached his fist up to Baz, but didn't look at him. Baz just met his knuckles and simply continued to drive along in silence.

CHAPTER
Eleven

HARVEY THREW A FIT HAVING TO SIT INSIDE THE SALON WHEN EVERY-one else was out front but Tinsley was going to be occupied and didn't want him to wander. She decided it was best he just stayed inside for now—they were only on the sidewalk right outside the window anyway.

"Boo, didn't you say you picked up pineapple too?" Brindle looked around the table to organize all the cotton candy flavors. Tinsley had signed up for the salon to offer facepainting and cotton candy for the event.

"I did… Maybe I left it inside or in my car though, I'll go look." Tinsley didn't see the carton anywhere in the salon so she grabbed her keys and headed for her car. She decided the alleyway was probably pretty empty so she let Harvey come with her. She stood at the back of her 4Runner digging through a box when Harvey barked.

"Harv!" she called before seeing what caused his friendly bark. To Tinsley's surprise, Baz was in the alley. "Come here, buddy." She reached down for Harvey's collar. "Sorry, I know he should be on a leash out here." She didn't look at Baz, she just stroked her dog's head, praising him for listening.

"It's all good." Baz shook his head as he made his way toward her. "I'm not worried about that."

Tinsley grabbed the pineapple cotton candy mix and shut her tailgate. She wasn't sure what else to say to Baz but listened when he started.

"Hey." His voice was gentle. "I just wanted to apologize for the other night."

Feeling unsure, Tinsley didn't look up at him.

"I genuinely thought you were giving me the runaround or something. I had no idea." He gestured toward Harvey.

Tinsley kneeled down to her dog to offer him a better chin scratch. "I wouldn't lie about him. Well, I don't actually make it a habit of lying anyway."

"I know I fucked up." Baz put up his hands. He wasn't trying to fix things to move forward with her, but he wanted to be sure that if Shaw pursued her, their past wasn't going to cut his best friend off from being given a chance. "I'm not standing here asking for another shot with you—you deserve so much better than how I treated you. I just want to genuinely apologize for being an asshole." He shook his head. "And the other day… I didn't expect to see you again… And I didn't know what to say, but I know I should've apologized at the very least."

Tinsley was taken by surprise. He'd pretended not to even know her the last time they saw each other, so the last thing she ever thought she'd get from Baz was an apology. She wasn't interested in having some kind of grudge against him either though. It was what it was—and they probably wouldn't have to see one another again anyway.

"I really appreciate that." She nodded but maintained her focus on Harvey instead of looking up at Baz who stood only steps away from her.

"Baz, you fucker, where you at?" His radio interrupted them. *"I know you didn't leave me to do this pie thing alone. Get your big ass back over here."* Shaw's light tone projected just enough urgency that made it clear he didn't want to participate in the pie event alone.

Baz smiled and Tinsley tried to hide her own amusement.

He reached for his radio. "Coming, Princess."

Tinsley and Harvey started to walk back toward the salon.

"Bye, Tins."

Tinsley turned around and looked at Baz. "Bye, Baz… Maybe we'll see you guys around today." She waved.

You guys… Baz's thoughts lingered on. His apology had done what it needed. Tinsley wasn't going to completely ignore his presence in the future and whether intentionally or not, she'd just referenced seeing his partner too. He had hope now that if Shaw wanted a shot, the door would be open.

"You dick." Shaw bumped Baz's shoulder when Baz swaggered up to the pie-eating contest. "I thought you were ditching out on this shit." Shaw lowered his voice with all the kids around.

"Nah, fam." Baz shook his head. "Just had to take a leak," he fibbed.

"Slight change in plans." The bakery owner who was coordinating the pie-eating contest hurried to the duo. "I didn't realize we'd have a representative from the paramedics here as well, so really we only need one of you to participate, if that's okay?"

Both Shaw and Baz were ecstatic to find out one of them would get out of this obligation. They turned toward each other knowing full well how they'd settle who'd have to be the representative.

"Roshambo, fam." Baz held out his hand.

"On three," Shaw confirmed and mirrored him.

They shook their fists and flashed their selections.

"Shit." Shaw watched Baz make a motion to cut his flat hand. "You've been picking rock lately."

Baz snickered. "I *knew* you'd assume that."

"C'mon, bro—you're the one with the sweet tooth. You should do this one."

"Fuck outta here." Baz gave him a friendly shove. "You lost."

Shaw rolled his eyes then took a deep breath and reluctantly walked toward the makeshift stage that was set up for him and three other participants.

"Alright, alright!" The woman coordinating the contest got on a microphone. "I'm going to run through the rules, we have some of Tacoma's finest out here with us today competing in our First Annual Pie-Eating contest!" She introduced the contestants. In addition to Shaw—who was given a few feral cat calls when he was introduced—there was also a Tacoma FD firefighter, an EMT, and a member of the city council.

"I'm doing you a damn favor since your ass won't hop on any of those dating apps." Baz looked around. "You're about to pick up quite a few date offers after this one," he whispered as the rules were laid out. He was assigned to stand in front of Shaw and supply new pies as he finished.

Shaw tapped his middle finger on the table to conceal his irritation but let his buddy know how funny his commentary was. Baz knew full well dating wasn't something he'd done in a long while. When his eyes lifted for a dirty look toward Baz, he noticed, right across the street, Tinsley on the sidewalk in front of her shop smiling at a small group of kids who were patiently waiting for cotton candy. He wasn't at all surprised to see Brindle right next to her and then both of them playfully arguing with their animated gestures.

Shaw didn't want any part of Baz's apps, but he'd seriously done some reconsideration on the topic of dating since meeting Tinsley—he just hadn't made a real move with her yet.

"I can't tell you how much I wish this was a hot-dog-eating contest." Brindle reached for his cell phone.
Tinsley shook her head with a smirk on her face. "You are ridiculous."

"Lucky for you, we're about to see firsthand how quickly that man can eat a pie." Brindle held up his phone and zoomed all the way in to Shaw.

Tinsley's face turned red and she swatted her best friend. "You need professional help."

Brindle puckered his lips and then sassily bobbed his head around. "Depending on how Shawberry performs, I think we'll have finally found the professional help *you've* been needing, Boo."

Tinsley dropped her head and grabbed the bridge of her nose, trying her best to ignore her suggestive friend.

"Don't embarrass me, fam!" Baz coached Shaw up as the countdown began for the contest to start. "Got four you've gotta eat out of here. I'll do apple first, cherry, strawberry rhubarb, and then blueberry."

"Put the apple last, I can get through the others quicker." Shaw put his hands behind his back and leaned toward the table in anticipation for the whistle. "You're still a dick for making me do this, by the way."

Baz laughed just before dropping the cherry pie in front of Shaw when the shrill of the whistle blew.

"Hon-EY!" Brindle jumped up and down. "I'm about wetting my pants watching this, I cannot imagine how you're feeling."

Tinsley gave him a harsher-than-normal nudge to his side. "There are children present," she reminded him.

"Whooooo! Go Shawberry!" Brindle cheered and moved closer to the contest, sure to be diligent with his video recording duties.

Tinsley watched her friend, but was sure to keep an eye on Shaw as well. For as ridiculous as he started to look with pie all over his face, she couldn't deny that he was still as handsome as he was the day she'd met him.

"Shit! Fam, you *had* that!" Baz could hardly speak through his laughter as the whistle went off again because the council member had been deemed the winner.

Shaw looked down and saw that he only had about a quarter of the apple pie left. He knew that pie would be the one he'd take the longest on—he'd never been a fan of that flavor.

Baz, in his stellar judgment, thought it would be funny to smear the rest of it on top of Shaw's head.

"You *dick*!" Shaw laughed.

"I told you not to embarrass me." Baz winked, knowing full well what he just did.

"Oh joy." Brindle rolled his eyes. "Here comes the damn Black Casper."

"Be nice," Tinsley encouraged, a little more open to dropping any grudges since Baz's apology.

"I see Shawberry too, so you know I'll be on my naughtiest behavior for my favorite beefcake. *Especially* after watching what he just did to those pies." Brindle dramatically sunk his teeth into his bottom lip.

Tinsley gave him a soft kick while they stood behind the cotton candy machine and then smiled as Shaw and Baz approached.

"Shawberry!"—Brindle did a little shimmy toward him—"that was quite the performance." He turned around and winked at Tinsley. "I think we *all* enjoyed watching that."

Tinsley's eyes went wide and she hissed at her best friend who was skating on thin ice. "Brindle!"

Baz joined the laughter but took the opportunity to suggest what was on his mind when he'd dumped the pie on Shaw's head.

"I was hoping you may have something to help my guy out." Baz grabbed Shaw's shoulder. "He got a little something in his hair and all they gave him was a paper towel to clean up."

"I wouldn't have it in my hair if it wasn't for you, asshole." Shaw shook his head but grinned.

Brindle picked up on the quick glance Baz threw his way and finally started to appreciate Baz instead of wanting to slap him.

"Shawberry, you've come to the perfect spot. Hair is our speciality." He walked over and clung to his shoulder, giving his muscles an obvious and appreciative squeeze.

Shaw didn't want Brindle cleaning pie from his hair. He looked at Baz wanting to kick his ass for the suggestion.

Then, to his utter delight Brindle suggested, "Tins has the best hands for scalps, she'll have all that out in no time." Brindle assured Shaw and then caught a quick, and for once civil, eye with Baz.

"We've got more than paper towels on hand." Tinsley said with a friendly tone, "If you want, or have time, you can sneak into the salon. I don't mind washing that out for you."

Baz gave Shaw a subtle push on his back to encourage him to take her up on her offer.

"I don't want to trouble anyone," Shaw admitted.

"It's no trouble." Not as subtly, Brindle more or less shoved his best friend toward Shaw.

"You're good being on patrol alone for a minute?" Shaw looked at Baz.

"Shit, got a dozen rookies out here too and I'm sure your luscious locks won't take an hour," Baz assured him.

"Maybe like fifteen-ish minutes?" Tinsley projected before her eyes met Shaw's.

"If you don't mind? I know you have a lot going on out here."

"Oh, Shawberry, I'd be happy to take over out here. She's got time." Brindle's thick, freshly laminated brows pumped at Shaw a few times.

Shaw followed Tinsley back into the salon, where it didn't take her long to turn around to him.

"I'd apologize for Brindle, but I know 'I'm sorry' isn't your favorite line, and also he does love you in the best kind of way. That's his really odd and inappropriate way of showing you, unfortunately." She grabbed a towel from her station. "But, he's a good cookie and despite his outward sassiness, he's got a heart of gold."

"I'm confident enough to where that stuff doesn't shake me." Shaw smiled and then kneeled down to give Harvey a sturdy pat-down. The dog hopped with his front half to see Shaw again. After he felt like he gave him a good enough greeting, he ran for his toy bin to bring Shaw a stuffed frog with missing eyes.

Tinsley grinned at her dog's fondness of Shaw. "Well good, because as you can tell it only intensifies over time." Her head bobbed toward the sinks at the back wall of the salon. "You ready to get that apple pie out of your hair?"

Shaw wrestled the frog from Harvey and gave it a toss before following Tinsley. "Yes, please."

He tried to redirect his eyes when he inadvertently looked right at her backside. While the jeans he'd previously seen her in had been tight, she was in a pair of yoga pants now and her shirt barely met the top of her pants.

Tinsley patted her hand on the chair for Shaw to take a seat. "Are you going to be comfortable leaning back with your vest and all that on your belt?"

"I'll make it work," he assured her with a smile before settling into the seat.

Tinsley leaned Shaw back in the chair until his head was in the sink. Once she got him exactly where he needed to be she turned the water on and then carefully ran her fingers through his sticky hair a couple of times.

"Is the water temperature alright?" Tinsley asked after testing it on his scalp.

"It's perfect." Shaw tried to concentrate on his duty belt digging into his back, because Tinsley running her fingers through his hair to wet it down was the most intimate touch he'd felt in a long time.

"You know," Shaw started, "this might be the first time I've had my head in one of these sinks. The barber usually just uses a spray bottle for my cuts."

"Absolutely *not* around here." Tinsley laughed. "It's full service or bust. Plus"—she giggled while pulling a small chunk of apple from his scalp—"I don't think a spray bottle would stand a chance against this apple filling."

"Yeah, I really appreciate you getting all that out—apple pie isn't my favorite. Baz is such an asshole sometimes." He only half-joked, realizing his best friend may have actually had an ulterior motive for what he'd done.

"Well, we'll get the smell out too then so you aren't reminded of it all day," she assured him with a smile.

Once Tinsley had his hair completely soaked and he was free of any more apple chunks, she turned the water off and reached for the shampoo. Again Shaw tried to focus on the lingering irritant of his baton pushing on one of his bruises because Tinsley's chest was only inches from his face. It was even harder to concentrate once her fingers worked on his scalp. She wasn't simply washing his hair—full service was a full on scalp massage. Not only did she work her hands through the shampoo in the best kind of way, but she gave his neck and the base of his head a firm massage as well. Shaw's eyes were closed but removing that sense only heightened the others, including smell. He was completely surrounded by the scent of Tinsley. It wasn't a perfume he was familiar with, but it unraveled him and made him want to open his eyes to just take her in. He didn't detect any strong floral notes, but it was a warm, almost tropical, and definitely welcoming scent.

Tinsley turned the water on again. "I know you're used to just the spray bottle, Officer Shaw," she said with a short giggle, "but are you okay with conditioner too?"

"I can put my manhood aside and enjoy the full service, ma'am." He was grateful for the comedic break because he was afraid of getting too lost in her hands working on him.

Tinsley chuckled. "For every 'ma'am' I get you're going to catch an 'I'm sorry' in return." She turned the water off after the shampoo was cleared from his hair. "And for the record, conditioner isn't only for the girls and Brindle. While your hair is perfectly healthy, a little conditioner treatment from time to time is a nice addition. *And* it'll help with any lingering apple scent."

"I'll take the word of the professional," Shaw agreed. He tried to discreetly take a controlled breath when Tinsley repeated her massaging sequence with the conditioner.

She was soon drying his hair with a towel, gently working over his ears and then putting her hand just below the base of his neck to help him up from the sink.

"I'll keep your manhood intact and not wrap your head in the towel to walk over to my station."

"I appreciate that. I was beginning to question it myself because I think I not only prefer the sink over the spray bottle, but I may be a fan of the conditioner too."

"I won't tattle, tough guy." Tinsley giggled at him as he sat down. She put one of her hands on his shoulder as the other was softly running through his wet hair. "So, is your manhood alright with me using the hairdryer too?" She smiled at him through the mirror at her station.

Shaw put his hands up while grinning back. "I'm here for the full service."

Brindle looked through the front window multiple times to check on his best friend. She was smiling with Shaw in a way that he'd never seen before. She always exuded a friendly attitude at work, but her eyes were different around Shaw.

"Your boy seems to be a much better person than you are. Can you confirm he's not going to pull some ghosting-ass bullshit on my boo like you did?" Brindle stared at Baz who hadn't ventured too far from the front window either. He didn't wait for a response because he had more to say. "I know all about you cutting ties with her when she left to be with her *disabled* dog at the *emergency* vet all night."

"I get it. I fuckin' messed up treating her like that," Baz admitted. "You know what though? It was probably for the best—Shaw's a really great fuckin' guy."

"If that's only based on your standard, I'm not sure I'm sold'" Brindle's icy tone shot back.

"Listen." Baz chuckled and put up his large hands. "If something develops between them, you and I'll be seeing a lot of each other. We could attempt to make this civil. I already admitted I messed up."

"Probation." Brindle crossed his arms. "You're on probation in my book, Black Casper." He flung his arms to his sides and walked away to help Lacey with the face painting station.

Baz continued to laugh, he already owned his mistake and if nothing else he could appreciate Brindle's protective nature. After shaking his head again he tried to discreetly look through the salon window. He watched his partner laughing while Tinsley worked her hands through his hair, a large smile on her face as she told him something. Baz didn't want to stare, but he was glad to see his little apple pie routine had worked out exactly how he'd hoped it would.

"Officer Shaw, I don't mean to keep prying about the bruises, but it seems like you have some new ones." Tinsley worked pomade through his hair after drying it. "I'm getting a little worried you and Baz may have some DV situation going on in that patrol car."

Shaw laughed. "If anything, I'd be kicking *his* ass." He shook his head. "Just a few good marks from the job is all. And honestly, they've been looking better since that ointment you gave me."

"I told you, that stuff's magic." She wiped her hands on a towel to get the pomade off.

"It didn't exactly have a label on it though. I was trying to see where you get it. I do think I'll need to add it to my daily skincare routine." He smirked.

"I knew you were a full service kinda guy." Tinsley smiled. "Your secret's safe with me, Officer Shaw." Tinsley took the cape off of him and then opened one of the drawers in her workstation. "Here." She held out another container of the ointment.

"I can't just keep stealing your stock." He held his palm up. "I can pick it up. I just need to know your secrets on where it comes from."

"You're lookin' at where it comes from," she happily admitted. "This is my super-secret blend of witchcraft and sorcery for managing bruises."

"Well, what can I pay you for this then?"

"You're not paying for that," she declined with a giggle. "I'm pretty sure I owe you anyway for finding a bunch of my stuff *and* for the coffee." Tinsley leaned her backside on her workstation, facing Shaw. "You just come by when you need refills while I work on a bucket of it for you—you seem to get bruises far more than I do. Who knows? Maybe I'll figure out a way to put it in a bathbomb for you."

Shaw laughed. "That's probably not a bad idea for me. And to clarify, you don't owe me. The coffee was a gift, and being able to return at least some of your things was a pleasure."

Tinsley didn't have time to respond besides the flirtatious grin on her face when they were interrupted.

"Fam"—Baz popped his head into the salon—"Unc wants us down the block, some photo opp bullshit."

"Oooo! Shawberry, looking *so* delicious." Brindle shouldered past Baz through the door next.

"Yeah he is!" Baz laughed just before smacking his lips at his partner.

Shaw shook his head, looking down to hide the blush, and then stood up. "Thank you, Tinsley." He waved the ointment at her. "For the entire full service."

"Anytime, Officer Shaw."

"She's free tomorrow," Brindle offered.

"Brindle!" Tinsley held the bridge of her nose.

"So's Shawberry," Baz added with a smirk.

Brindle sauntered over to the cash register and then made his way to Shaw. "This is her card—that's her cell on there." He pointed.

"I'm so sorry." Tinsley covered her mouth and blushed while looking at Shaw.

Shaw didn't consider it long before he flashed his smoldering smile. "Ma'am." He tipped his head while sticking her card in the pocket of his vest. "Bye, Harv." He was sure to reach down and give Tinsley's dog a quick parting scratch.

Baz gripped his buddy's shoulder before they both walked out of the salon.

"Brindle, do you ever just mind your own damn business?" Tinsley was still flush with pink in embarrassment.

"Not when I feel a connection. Boo, that's all you—you two need to knock off the damn dance and go for it."

Tinsley turned around to tidy up her station. "That's not my department." She shook her head.

"We're not in the dark ages," he reminded her. "You're welcome to take charge in this situation too, you know."

"Ball's in his court." She shrugged and wiped down her station.

CHAPTER
Twelve

Later in the day, Shaw and Baz were patrolling the street and closing in on the salon. Shaw considered what he would do with Tinsley's phone number. Tinsley's appearance and personality already had him thinking about her more than he'd like to admit, but it was her sweet touch that day that sent him over the edge and had him in a chokehold now. As they got closer to the salon he noticed Tinsley's mom standing near them and then he watched as a young girl ran to Tinsley and jumped into her arms.

∞

"Hey, Laura Loo." Tinsley pecked the little girl's cheek as she held her in her arms. "How's auntie's favorite girl?"

"I thought I was your favorite girl?!" Brindle joked just before he rubbed Alaurra's back.

"Brindle Boo!" Alaurra laughed and reached over to hug him.

"Sorry we're late, honey," Colette said. "Your brother got called into work last minute, so I had to make a little detour." She leaned in and hugged her daughter.

"It's okay, you guys are still here in plenty of time to enjoy a few things." Tinsley pecked her niece one more time before setting her down.

"Girlfriend, you can't be running around the carnival without some facepaint." Brindle slapped the seat where he'd been painting faces. "Come let Brindle Boo get you right."

Alaurra scampered over to him and selected a butterfly design because it had the most glitter on it.

"I'm going to go get Harvey all set to walk around with us." Tinsley made her way back into the salon before her mom stopped her.

"Honey, are you sure? Didn't he just have an episode not too long ago?" Colette asked.

Tinsley didn't want to be reminded, but she felt like Harvey had been doing really well lately. "He's been doing really good, Mom. And we aren't going far." Tinsley didn't entertain the conversation anymore, she wouldn't put him in any kind of danger. Brindle was talking a million miles an hour catching up on the life of his favorite six-year-old when Tinsley walked back into the salon.

"Hey, Handsome Harv." Tinsley kneeled down to rub her dog's face. "You've been a good boy. Why don't we go take a walk?" She smiled at him when he nearly knocked her over from spinning in anxious anticipation for his favorite 'w' word. Once his harness was on he trotted over to his toy bin to select something he could bring along with them. Harvey had a tendency to hang onto a support stuffie when he couldn't contain his emotions. Tinsley adoringly shook her head at him when he came back with a balled fleece style bat. It wasn't exactly the season for that one, but at least this one wasn't missing any pieces and still had all of its stuffing.

"Let's go, buddy."

"Look at this little bombshell!" Brindle shouted and clapped his hands as Alaurra got up from the seat to look in the mirror, awed at the butterfly masterpiece that covered the entire top half of her face.

Colette, Tinsley, and the rest of the girls joined Brindle in the cheering.

"Auntie Tins, can we go play some carnival games now?" Alaurra asked with the biggest smile on her face now that she was what Brindle deemed to be 'carnival ready.'

"Let's go, Laura Loo." Tinsley held out her hand.

Alaurra squeezed Tinsley's fingers and kept an excitedly tight grip as they made their way down to a bookstore at the end of their block that had all the carnival games out front.

"I saw you lookin' that way, fam." Baz bumped into Shaw. "You bout to go talk to her?"

"She's busy." He shook his head.

"Don't start fucking reaching for excuses. You have the digits and you need to use them… Sooner than later."

"I'm not making excuses, she's just with family. I don't want to interrupt."

"How do you know she's with family?"

Shaw took a deep breath, he wasn't sure how Baz would react. "The lady she's walking with is her mom." He gestured toward them. "I met her when I dropped all Tinsley's stuff off the other day."

"Shit, fam!" Baz laughed. "You already met Mama, what the fuck are you scared of?!"

"I'm not scared." Shaw rolled his eyes.

"Then fucking pull the trigger."

Shaw didn't answer him. He knew what was holding him back and he didn't want to say it out loud. He felt like the attraction was mutual, but he needed to be more than sure before potentially dragging Tinsley through any kind of emotional damage because of some deep-rooted reservations he may develop if they got too close, too soon.

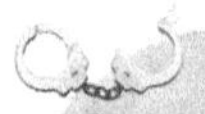

Alaurra collected quite a few fun treats while the small, multi-generational group made their way down the opposite side of the block from Tinsley's salon. Her face was properly painted, she had a sleeve full of temporary tattoos, plastic brightly-colored bracelets covering half of her arm, and to top it off she carried a bag of kettle corn almost as tall as she was. Tinsley and Colette had divided the rest of her goodies between the two of them because Alaurra's arms just weren't big enough for her entire loot.

"Did you guys already get your safety pack?" a woman asked as Tinsley and her family walked by the Health and Safety station.

She looked down at Alaurra. "Do you want to get one of these?" Tinsley pointed toward the drawstring backpacks they were handing out.

"What is it?" Alaurra was interested.

The woman in a Metro Parks shirt, brought Alaurra over to a table where kids were filling out emergency cards with a couple of Tacoma Police Officers.

"Maybe we'll see your officer *friend* over here?" Colette nudged her daughter.

Tinsley shook her head, trying to ignore the comment, but also hoping she may see Shaw again. Just when she started thinking about how much she'd enjoyed the simple task of washing his hair earlier, she heard Baz's distinct loud laugh and knew Shaw would be close.

"Yeah, where do you need us?" Baz's voice sounded closer.

"Uh, you guys can squeeze in with the kids over there," the photographer suggested. "And then maybe a few action shots helping them with their fingerprints."

"Hey, Harv." Shaw walked up behind them and gave Harvey a healthy pat to his side while tugging on his bat. "Tins." He smiled up at her while still hoovering over his biggest four-legged fan.

"Officer Shaw." She returned his smoldering smile while her dog jumped around his new favorite friend.

Shaw reached his strong hand across Tinsley. "Colette, nice to see you again."

Colette put one hand in Shaw's and the other on her chest. "Remembered my name and everything."

"Okay, Officer Shaw, can we get you to stand behind the kids over there?" the photographer interrupted.

"Which one's yours?" Shaw whispered at Tinsley.

She chuckled. "My niece is the beautiful little butterfly back there."

Shaw confidently walked over to the little girl and started asking her about the project she was working on.

Tinsley was finding it difficult not to classify Shaw as completely perfect. There wasn't a single thing about him that she didn't find absolutely swoonworthy. Nevermind the fact that he looked the way he did because on top of that he seemed like a genuinely wonderful man. Just as she was trying to come out of the trance Shaw put her in, her mom bumped her shoulder.

"Look, even your niece likes the officer." Colette pulled out her phone and snapped a few pictures of her own while Shaw and Alaurra made their way to a fingerprint station. "Honey, he's *so* good looking."

"Can you please stop being so obvious with the pictures?" Tinsley begged. She had no idea her mom and Brindle had such similar tactics for knowingly, or unknowingly, embarrassing her.

It looked like the photographer had finished with her ideas so she worked her way through the crowd to focus on more shots of the event. Tinsley noticed Shaw was still helping Alaurra though, photographer or not. He made sure her entire emergency card was filled out before she skipped over to the arts and crafts station that was next.

"Honey," Colette noticed a landscaping vendor not too far from them. "I'm actually going to go talk to those people. Your father and I have been looking for someone to make some updates to our front porch area."

Tinsley was thankful her mom hadn't caught on to the fact that Shaw had just parted ways with Alaurra, so she nodded to confirm she'd wait for her niece.

"I was asked to bring this to Auntie Tins to keep safe." Shaw presented Alaurra's emergency card to her with a smile.

Tinsley looked down at her niece's adorable handwriting and noticed her fingerprints looked a little off.

"What happened here?" Tinsley smiled as she pointed to the right hand pinky print that looked to have a couple of extra smudges on it.

Shaw chuckled at the inky blobs that were actually partial prints from his thumb and index finger. "It's been a while since I've done prints." He wiped the bottom half of his face. "Not to mention, our perps usually have much larger hands. You have no idea how hard it is to print someone with fingers as tiny as those."

"Thank you for helping her with all this, you didn't have to do that."

"She's a sweet kid." He shrugged. "It must be a familial trait, huh?"

Tinsley blushed and she was grateful for Harvey who was persistent with wanting Shaw's attention. He nudged him a couple of times with his now wingless bat.

"Whatcha got down here, Harv?"

"It was a bat when we left the salon." Tinsley laughed. "It's a burnt potato now."

"That's what Harvey Dent's supposed to do to bats." Shaw ruffled the top of his head and yanked on the toy with the other. "Good boy."

"EWW!" a young boy's voice screeched from the table where Alaurra was crafting. "What happened to that dog?! Look at his face!"

Tinsley looked right at her niece who was sitting next to the little boy, her happy face vanished immediately. Tinsley softly shook her head and tried to smile at her to let her know it was okay. Harvey was obviously not aware of people staring at him, but Alaurra was clearly getting upset as the boy continued to make comments about her beloved canine. It didn't take Alaurra long to run over to Tinsley, where she threw her arms around her aunt's waist. Shaw looked at Tinsley but was still entertaining Harvey.

Tinsley lowered herself into a squat so she could look her niece in the eyes. "Laura Loo, what did Auntie Tins tell you about bullies?"

Alaurra nearly cried out her response, "That they say mean things because they're mad they're not happy like us."

Tinsley held onto her shoulder and nodded. "That's right, and so how do we help them?

"We try to give them some of our smiles."

"Yep." She rubbed her shoulders. "So, let's wipe those tears before you smear your butterfly and we're going to put on a kind smile." Tinsley carefully dabbed Alaurra's face.

"But if that doesn't make me feel better then we tattle to Brindle Boo, right?" Alaurra sniffled.

Tinsley laughed. "Absolutely. Brindle Boo will tell him a thing or two. And that little bully said it in Harv's broken ear, so he didn't even hear him being so mean." Tinsley gestured toward Harvey who was still focused on trying to get his toy back from Shaw. "We just owe Handsome Harv extra cuddles now and that's not so bad, right?"

Alaurra nodded while Tinsley gently dried up the rest of her tears. The little girl gave Harvey a hug and then bravely went back to the table to finish her art project. She did exactly what they had discussed and she smiled at the little boy before she looked back at her paper.

Shaw was absolutely enamoured with Tinsley now after watching her with her niece. It was obvious Tinsley had talked the little girl off the ledge a time or two, and had the sweetest damn tactics to be the bigger person without telling her that's what she needed to do.

"Brindle's shit list isn't one I'd wanna be on. That bully has no idea what he's in for," Shaw whispered with a smirk once Tinsley stood back up.

She gazed up at him with a smile in her eyes. "Yeah, Brindle has been kindly asked to not chaperone any more field trips after he let a little kid have it for being mean to Alaurra last year. I try to take a different approach but also remind her she's got a feisty warrior on her side."

They both looked down at Harvey, who was getting tired from his attempts at freeing the bat from Shaw. He finally gave up and sat with his back leaning on Shaw's leg.

"Plus, it's a good reminder for me to be nice because my poor Handsome Harv gets that reaction more times than I'd like to admit."

Shaw bent down and rubbed Harvey's chest, taking a long look at the cane corso who panted heavily with his tongue hanging out from the side of his mouth, returning Shaw's gaze with his one eye.

"Harv's a good guy. Aren't you, buddy?"

The dog agreed with his entire body when he wiggled around Shaw.

"Takes one to know one, I suppose," Tinsley offered.

Shaw stood up to reply when they were interrupted by Colette.

"Well, I think we've found our new landscaping crew," she said, happily joining them with a business card in one hand and her phone in the other. "Look, honey, this water feature is almost exactly what your father wants and this company did this one."

Tinsley nodded, admiring the obnoxiously large waterfall style pond with lighting and colorful fish swimming around in it. "Oh, so Dad does want pets now?"

"Well, minus the fish." Colette held her phone out in front of Shaw for him to see as well, assuming he'd be interested. Shaw politely nodded.

"Grandma! Look what I made!" Alaurra ran over with a new drawing. She didn't want to color in the picture they'd given her of a seal balancing a ball on his nose—she had flipped the page over and made her own drawing.

"This is so good, honey. Tell grandma who all is in the picture."

"That's me, that's Brindle Boo, and that's Handsome Harv," Alaurra said proudly.

Shaw looked down at the picture and had to suppress his smile when he noticed she gave Brindle a rainbow t-shirt with his mid-section showing and he was wearing high heeled shoes.

"I'm going to give it to Brindle Boo because he painted my face for me."

"That's so sweet of you." Colette hugged her granddaughter.

Alaurra nodded, excited to put this masterpiece on Brindle's refrigerator. She grabbed her grandma's hand and began to pull her toward the salon.

"Looks like the two of us are on the move." Colette waved. "It was nice to see you again, Officer Shaw."

"Colette." He offered a friendly nod.

"Bye!" Alaurra turned around to wave at Shaw. "Thank you!"

"Bye." Shaw waved. "It was nice to meet you."

Tinsley looked down at her dog who was now mostly on his back. He had landed on Shaw's foot that he was politely allowing him to lay on.

"Harv, are you comfy down there, bud?" She smiled.

"Do you need to get back to the salon?" Shaw asked, really hoping she didn't.

Tinsley shook her head with a small grin on her face. "It's best I give them a head start. I'll be chopped liver for a bit; when Alaurra and Brindle get together the rest of us are just living in their world."

"Brindle's like that all the time already, isn't he?" Shaw joked.

Tinsley laughed and then followed her dog when he finally got up and gave himself a good shake. "You're not wrong. He tends to steal the show."

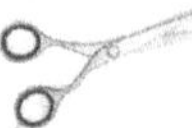

"Officer Baz!" A new photographer tried to get his attention. "Can I get you and your partner to join me down by the fire trucks with the other first responders for a few more shots?"

Baz looked around and saw his best friend talking to Tinsley. He didn't want to interrupt them with this, it was likely the pictures wouldn't even be used. He wanted Shaw to have a little one-on-one time in hopes he'd actually ask her out.

"Uh, I'll head down there, and I can grab another patrolman on the way down if it can't just be me," Baz assured her. He watched as Shaw and Tinsley started walking down the street in the same general direction as he and the photographer, so he made a move to at least cross the street to give them a little space.

"Oh, Harv." Tinsley fondly shook her head at her dog who was demanding they cross the street toward a fine-smelling vendor. Tinsley saw another dog at the tent patiently waiting for a treat from the marketer. Harvey made his way next to the Sheepadoodle and sat patiently, hoping he'd be rewarded as well.

"*Two* happy new friends, huh?!" The vendor beamed at both dogs.

Harvey drooled as if Tinsley had forgotten to feed him for a week straight.

"These are homemade, all natural dried salmon treats. I have a full line of over a dozen different proteins over here," the man continued along with his sales pitch.

Harvey wasn't interested in the speech, he made his way around the tent showing Tinsley all the things he needed to taste test. The Sheepadoodle and his handler left after their sample, but Harvey was still shopping.

Shaw leaned over and picked up the bat that Harvey had discarded in favor of the treats around him. Tinsley noticed and immediately offered to take it.

"Oh, thank you." She smiled. "Here, I can hold that gross thing."

"I don't mind at all; you're about to have your hands full anyway." He laughed watching Tinsley collect basically everything her dog drooled on.

"Uh, you're done, sir." Tinsley told Harvey as he attempted another circle around the tent. "I think we have plenty to sample here." Harvey tugged on her again and she gave him a firm sit command, which he did, but not before giving her a look and then letting out a large huff as if he paid the bills.

Shaw chuckled. "Oh, a little attitude, huh?"

"You have no idea." Tinsley shook her head and then asked the vendor what she owed him.

"Here, let me take him, you've got a lot going on." Shaw reached for Harvey's leash as he saw Tinsley struggling to manage everything.

"Thank you." Tinsley watched Shaw confidently take over—he even put Harvey back in a sit when the cane corso tried to take advantage of Tinsley not completely paying attention.

"Do you want me to walk him?" Tinsley offered after paying for all Harvey's selections.

Shaw smiled at her. "I don't mind, if you don't." He reached down and ruffled the top of Harvey's head.

"I just don't want you getting into any trouble, Officer Shaw," Tinsley teased.

He shrugged and opened his mouth to respond just as his radio went off.

"Hey Romeo, not that I actually wanna bug you right now, but Unc is demanding both of us meet down on the corner of 56th."

"I'll head that way in a minute, asshat," Shaw responded and then started to blush as he battled a smile and shook his head at Baz's name-calling.

"Hey, I tried, fam. Trust, I wasn't trying to pull you away when it looks like your balls have finally dropped." Baz laughed.

Tinsley looked down the entire time, biting her lip to hide a bashful smile herself.

Shaw lowered the volume on his radio and looked over at Tinsley. "I'm sorry, Tinsley, I—"

"If I don't get to apologize, then neither do you." She cut him off before reaching for Harvey's leash with a blush face.

Shaw chuckled. "Fair enough." He grazed her hand when he passed Harvey's leash back to her. "Thank you again for earlier." He gestured toward his hair.

"No problem at all. Any time, Officer Shaw." Tinsley couldn't get her smile in check so it continued to glow at him.

Shaw reached down and teased Harvey with his bat torso until he took it from him. "You hang on to that, big guy. Your mama's carrying plenty of your stuff already." He gave Harvey a firm pat to his side and then stood straight up to look at Tinsley.

"It was really good to see you again, Tins. I enjoyed hanging with you."

"You too, Officer Shaw," Tinsley admitted with a giddy demeanor. "Maybe we'll see you around?"

Shaw let a flirtatious grin take over his face and then tapped his front pocket where she knew he had put her card. He turned around to head toward Baz, so Tinsley started walking in the opposite direction back to her salon. They only got a few steps away from each other before both of them turned around for one more look, not knowing they'd catch eyes again. Tinsley was beet red when she got caught trying to get another glimpse of him as he walked away, so Shaw winked at her before he turned around to meet up with his partner.

CHAPTER
Thirteen

S HAW DIDN'T DO A LOT OF TEXTING. IT WAS MOSTLY LIMITED TO HIS family and Baz—he certainly hadn't texted a woman in years. Sure, he had met and spoken with Tinsley multiple times now, so texting shouldn't be awkward, but there was just something about it that seemed so cold. Not to mention, he had no idea what to say.

He also considered that it wasn't Tinsley who'd even given him her number—Brindle had. Of course he'd gotten it during their initial meeting when he was taking her report from the salon vandalism and robbery, but not for social use. She'd already been on his mind since meeting her, but after spending more time together at the carnival, Shaw was consumed with the mere thought of Tinsley.

No. He erased that text. *Can I sound like an even bigger tool…?*

Oh God, that may be worse. He laughed at himself and quickly cleared that text as well.

He slapped his forehead this time. *Yeah, no greeting or anything, just straight for the damn jugular.* He hit the back button until the text was blank again.

Communicating under the disguise of Baz while he chatted it up with women on his dating app was so much easier. Those instances were for his friend, so Baz didn't sound like a complete dog in *all* his messages. This was different though—this was Tinsley. He started to wish that she was aware of his involvement in her extended conversation with 'Baz' on the app before their date—most of that talking had been Shaw. He'd love nothing more than to simply pick up where they'd left off.

Who am I?! He couldn't erase the emoji fast enough. *A damn emoji?!* He laughed and hit his head back on the headrest of the driver's seat where he sat in the parking lot of his gym. Texting Tinsley was much more difficult than he imagined. They had no trouble talking when they were around each other, but the first text after—what he took as—establishing mutual attraction? That was an important one.

He finally set his phone down in the cup holder and put his truck in drive. Brindle said Tinsley was free today so he didn't think she was working, but he decided to drive by the salon anyhow. He knew he'd be able to use his actual words if he could just have the conversation in person instead of having to text her.

He wasn't surprised when he didn't see her 4Runner anywhere. He checked in front of the salon and around the alley just to be sure. The thought of driving by her house crossed his mind for a millisecond before he realized what a stalker move that would be. He sat in his truck across from Grit City Pretty and considered how he should attempt the next step with Tinsley. If he couldn't bring himself to send the appropriate text, he needed to try catching her in person again.

His mind flashed an image of the stolen items he'd recovered for Tinsley. She didn't outright say the book he found was hers but she surely accepted it. He did a quick google search and found out it was the first book in what appeared to be a series. Shaw flipped open his maps app to find the nearest bookstore and headed that way.

He figured he could stop by the salon next time she was at work, a much easier and more personal way of asking her out versus a likely corny text message. Plus, any guy would think to bring flowers. This angle was more thoughtful and would show her he paid attention and how genuine his feelings were.

CHAPTER
Fourteen

"**H**i, Officer Shaw." Farrah was with a client when he walked into the salon the next day. He was in full uniform this time instead of the gymwear she'd initially seen him in. She'd already classified Shaw as a hunk in that outfit, but she saw exactly why Brindle and even Tinsley had been so giddy and bragging about meeting him once she saw him in his uniform. The videos Brindle had taken didn't do him the justice he deserved.

"Good morning." He looked around and didn't see Tinsley or Harvey, noticing how quiet it was which likely meant Brindle wasn't around either.

"Lookin' for Tins?" Farrah predicted.

"I am—I didn't realize she wasn't in today." He gestured toward her station. "I can leave this here, not sure she'd want an old coffee though." He'd stopped at her go-to coffee shop to also bring both her and Harvey their favorite drinks.

"She's around—she should be back soon actually. She and Brindle do a free service thing and breakfast at a nursing home once a month."

As if Shaw wasn't already attracted to Tinsley, he had yet another reason to try and set aside any reservations he'd built up about dating.

"She wasn't expecting me. I can just drop this off and try back another time."

"Are you sure? She doesn't have a client for about an hour and really, they'll be back any minute. They usually get here right around noon."

"My partner's right next door, I'll grab lunch with him and pop my head in when we're done." Shaw left both the bag and the drinks on Tinsley's station. "Thank you."

"Sure thing." Farrah decided to divulge a little more about Tinsley's schedule. "She'll be here late tonight too—working on inventory… So, no clients." Farrah smiled. "But have a good one." She waved as Shaw gave her an appreciative nod for the extra information.

Shaw sat down next to Baz who was already digging into the short ribs that he ordered.

"Damn, fam—that was quick. She busy?" Baz asked Shaw when he joined him.

Shaw shook his head. "She wasn't there. They said she'd be back soon. I just left the stuff on her workstation."

"Hell no, fam. You didn't want to wait for her?"

"I can check in after we eat." Shaw took a drink before scooping rice onto his fork.

"You *can*, or you *will*?"

"Come on, bro."

Baz shook his head. "Shaw, fam, I've known you way too long. I know exactly what's going through your head right now and you need to knock that shit off."

"What are you talking about?"

"You're sitting there doubting your decision now over some dumb shit." Baz shook his head. "Her not being there isn't some sign from the universe that you're doing something wrong."

Shaw didn't say anything.

"There's a genuine damn spark there and you know it." He continued to shake his head at Shaw. "I'll never let you hear the end of it if you let that fizzle out because you're too chicken-shit to ask her out."

"We'll go over there after we eat to see if she's back," Shaw finally agreed. If he was being honest with himself, he had to admit that Baz was spot on. Shaw was genuinely attracted to Tinsley, but his past still haunted him. The last thing he wanted was to take a shot and end up hurting Tinsley if he figured out he wasn't ready for dating.

Almost as if Baz read Shaw's mind, he blurted out, "I've already told you you're ready to get back in that dating pool, fam. I wouldn't say that if I didn't believe it." He leveled his gaze at his partner. "Tinsley's the one worth getting back in for."

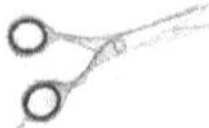

"What's this?" Tinsley set her purse down and watched Harvey sniff at the bag and his drink on her workstation.

Farrah smirked at Brindle before looking at Tinsley. "That's from Officer Shaw who was just in here like five minutes ago looking for you." She pumped her perfect eyebrows.

Brindle screeched and flung his arms in the air, scurrying over to look inside the bag.

"Brindle!" Tinsley scolded him for being so predictably nosey.

Brindle pulled out a dog toy and then dug back in the bag to pull out a book. "Girl!" He shook the book and then jumped around. "*This* book though?!" Brindle had recommended the series to Tinsley on multiple occasions and she had only just started reading the first one very recently. He'd vowed not to give her any spoilers, so he simply continued to squirm and hug the book to his chest.

Tinsley tuned out whatever else Brindle was saying, reaching Harvey's treat out for him to take to his bed. She carefully examined what Shaw had brought. The toy was nearly identical to the monkey Harvey loved so much that she'd thrown it out two days earlier because there was only a torso left after Harvey had dismantled the rest of it. When Shaw had brought Tinsley the items from her stolen purse, Harvey had his monkey and Shaw had played with them—he was only missing his legs at that point. The book he'd left her was the second book in the series. The first book in that series was the one Shaw had also recovered for her… He paid that much attention to know how to bring her such thoughtful gifts.

She felt guilty when she internally questioned how Shaw could be flawed. He seemed absolutely perfect from what she'd been subjected to so far. He was—hands down—the best looking man she'd ever seen, he was funny and easy to talk to, and now apparently was also the most observant and thoughtful man she'd ever known. *And* he was single? Something had to be wrong with him somewhere, and it almost scared her to think of what it could possibly be.

Baz decided to give his buddy a break and not follow him into the salon, so he waited outside the restaurant they'd just left. Shaw walked into the salon and saw Brindle and Farrah working on clients while Tinsley sat in her barber chair, fully engulfed in the conversation around her. He noticed Harvey was running around tossing his new toy in the air and chasing it down to slide across the floor when he caught it under his front paws.

"Brindle, you're going to Hell for being *so* mean!" Tinsley had her head back laughing at her best friend who was obviously unbothered by her prediction.

"AH! Shawberry!" Brindle squealed.

Shaw smiled and put his hand up to acknowledge his biggest, and most flamboyant fan. "Brindle."

"Hi, Officer Shaw." Tinsley smiled and sat up in her chair. "Sorry we missed you this morning." She stood. "I have something for you."

Shaw grinned at her and then reached for Harvey when he came barreling over with his new monkey in his mouth.

"Hey, buddy." Shaw grabbed the toy and they played a little game of tug-of-war. Harvey gave a couple of friendly growls as he shook his head to try to pry the toy from Shaw's grip.

"Your new best friend loves his monkey, thank you for that." She laughed. "You must've noticed how loved his last one was."

Shaw managed to wrestle the toy from Harvey and then tossed it across the salon for him to chase. "Yeah, his friend looked like he'd seen better days."

Tinsley agreed with a nod and a giggle. "And thank you for the coffee and the book. This was all really sweet, and so not necessary."

"You wouldn't let me pay for that magical bruise cream, so I figured a gift for a gift." He shrugged with a broad grin on his face.

"You brought *gifts* though." She laughed. "So, I guess it's fitting that I have another batch all set for you and a surprise." Tinsley walked toward the back. "I've got it back here, you can come along or wait here."

Shaw didn't even consider it, he followed her so they were at least out of Brindle's range since he wanted to talk to Tinsley with a little more privacy.

"You know this just means I'll be back with gifts for you if you don't let me compensate you for all this magical cream, right?" Shaw playfully warned her as they walked into the kitchenette area.

"I'm sure we can work something out now that the tough guy is hooked on the healing powers of this special ointment." Tinsley flirted back. "I wouldn't want you to have to purchase another one of those books."

Shaw was almost embarrassed. "I just found out the book that was stolen from you was actually from a series so I figured you may want the next one… I have no idea what it's about." He rubbed the back of his neck, now very unsure of some unknown message he may have sent and possibly regret.

Tinsley laughed. "Honestly, it's not all that bad. But that series is known for being a little smutty—it's a fantasy, well romantasy thing."

Shaw's face turned a bit pink. "I had no idea… And now I don't know how to take the cashier's comments when I picked up that book. She told me I look like a guy who would enjoy the fifth book."

Tinsley shrugged while giggling. "I obviously haven't gotten to that one yet—but I can't wait now. You can always ask Brindle, he's read this series at least three times. I will say, he *only* reads smut and his favorite is the one you just picked up, closely followed by the fifth one…"

Shaw couldn't help but chuckle as his face heated up even more. "I don't think I'll be asking Brindle about those books," he admitted and was overly grateful when Harvey came over with his toy, demanding Shaw grab a hold of the other end.

Tinsley opened a cabinet and pulled a few things out. Shaw let Harvey win this round so he could give his attention back to Tinsley when she walked to him.

"Truly, it was really nice of you to pick that up for me. I was definitely planning to get it once I'm done with the first one." Tinsley looked up and for the first time they both truly lingered on one another's eyes with what was an obvious and genuine fondness. Harvey interrupted them when he nudged Shaw's leg with his toy. Shaw reluctantly reached down with a smile and grabbed the toy again, which broke their eye contact.

"You're welcome," he replied. "I just really appreciate being able to bounce back from these injuries and I can't let you just keep supplying the good stuff with nothing in return."

"Well, I have a few containers for you this time." She smiled. "You can keep these little ones on you and then the big one maybe at home." She pointed out the bag she had with the rest of the ointments. "And, I can't say if these'll actually work, so there are only a couple, but I did manage to get them in a bath bomb form… no promises though." She laughed. "You'll have to let me know how they work out."

"You truly didn't have to do that." Shaw's smile took over his entire face.

"And *you* didn't have to remember what book I was reading and go get the next one in the series after already having found some of my stuff from the stolen purse. *Or* get us coffees, not to mention getting my menace of a dog a new toy." She rolled her head around while matching his smile. "But here we are."

Shaw was enamored with the sweetness that Tinsley exuded, he simply couldn't get enough of her. Baz was right to call him out for having any kind of doubt, Tinsley was more than worth taking a chance on and there was no denying they had more than a spark going on.

"I did also come to apologize," Shaw continued.

Tinsley started to laugh. "Oh, it's okay for you to say sorry, huh?" She shook her head. "No shot, Officer Shaw. Not only is that just not allowed, but I can't imagine what you'd possibly need to apologize to me for."

Shaw countered with a grin. "*Valid* apologies are always appropriate." He scrunched his brows. "Who said you get to make the rules anyway?" He chuckled.

"I'm thinking it was the same guy who gave you the green light to be laying down any rules around here."

Shaw had to restrain himself from taking another step toward her and put her in his arms at that moment. Tinsley had completely captured his heart, any doubt or reservation he had in his mind were currently floating away.

He finally took a step to at least shorten the distance between them. He was thinking of reaching for her hand. "Tins, I've been wanting to—" Shaw was interrupted by his radio.

"Shaw, Baz, we need an immediate response at the corner of 62nd and Adams. Multiple reports coming in of a possible carjacking in progress—"

Shaw didn't let dispatch finish before he made his move.

"I'm so sorry, Tins." He reached for Tinsley's hand and gave it a gentle squeeze. "I've gotta run. Thank you though, I'll see you again soon."

He didn't wait for a response before he ran for the exit of the salon. Baz had already come through the salon door to make sure his partner heard the call.

"Be safe…" Tinsley still said even though Shaw was long gone. An actual violent crime in progress turned her stomach. She didn't love the thought of Shaw running toward danger, which she quickly realized was ridiculous given he was a police officer. Not to mention, they weren't dating—probably friends at the very least at this point, but nothing romantic yet. Given their recent interactions, they were maybe headed there, but she didn't really know. She *did* know she wanted something more.

She thought about how carefully aware he was and the fact that he said he'd see her soon. Whatever his definition of soon was, she hoped to see him again later that day.

"So." Baz looked over at Shaw while he was blazing down the street toward the call, lights and sirens on. "You ask her out?"

"Was getting to it." Shaw let out an irritated breath and kept his head on a swivel in hopes they'd actually capture the degenerates who had been coordinating the recent carjackings. They were escalating at this point because this was the first incident in the daylight. The ring's typical M.O. was preying on people with cover from the darkness of the night.

"Shaw, Baz, be advised shots have been fired."

"Shit. Eyes up, fam." Baz mindfully sped through a red light.

"Yep." Shaw prepared to hop out of the car if he needed to.

They'd had their fair share of chases, stand-offs, and shootouts—they knew the risks. Shaw was on edge more so than normal because he'd narrowed down the ring's likely chop shop location, and one of the spots was just blocks from the call.

As they rounded a corner they saw two people in the middle of the street. It looked like a man lying on his back and a woman seated next to him screaming for help. Baz pulled up right next to the couple and Shaw was the first to make it to them.

"Help us!" she sobbed, her entire body shaking. "My husband! They shot him!" She had his head propped in her lap and was clinging to him by his neck while the man attempted to hold his abdomen.

When Shaw kneeled down, he noticed two gunshot wounds to the man's torso under all of the blood and he was struggling to breathe. Shaw attempted to help with the man's efforts to put pressure on his wounds.

"Baz, call it in, we need EMTs *now*." Shaw tried to get the woman's attention. "Ma'am, what type of vehicle were you in?"

"I don't know, I d-didn't see th-them," she stuttered and held her husband even tighter. "We were just stopped at the sign there, I don't know where they came from!"

"*Your* car, ma'am," Shaw tried again, gentle but firm. "What type of vehicle were you and your husband in?" He wanted to be able to put out an alert to locate their vehicle so they could hunt down the carjackers.

"A Hyu—" she started but wailed when her husband began coughing up blood.

"Here, Shaw." Baz kneeled down with them and offered Shaw a clean bandage to help hold the man's wound. After handing off the supplies he tried to console the wife and get more information from her while Shaw offered as much triage care as he could until the EMTs arrived.

"Sooooo…" Brindle sang loudly and shimmied his shoulders when Tinsley joined them again. "That was too quick to be gettin it on back there, but did you two *finally* make some plans for a date or what?!"

The rest of the salon noticed Tinsley blush as they waited in anxious anticipation for her answer. She didn't offer anything vocally and instead simply shook her head while sitting back down in her barber chair. Harvey didn't wait long before he shoved his new monkey into Tinsley's lap. She scratched the top of his head and gave the toy a few good shakes.

"What the fuck?!" Brindle flung his round brush in the air. "Boo, I'm sure he was planning to before they got hurried outta here. Big ol' Black Casper came busting through the door like the damn world was ending."

Brindle and Farrah exchanged a look.

"Boo, give us a recap of the convo," Brindle encouraged.

The salon dissected the conversation and all genuinely agreed that Shaw had been headed toward his date proposal—and they weren't just saying it to make Tinsley feel better.

Either way, Tinsley was grateful to have seen Shaw that day. Each of their interactions had been positive and she didn't harbor any hard feelings that he hadn't asked her out yet. She knew, once he got around to hopefully asking her out, she'd happily accept any time with Officer Shaw that he'd be willing to share.

"Fuck!" Shaw kicked the tire of their cruiser when the ambulance left. He was thinking back to the last few nights he'd gone out hunting. If he had just checked the last four locations he suspected for the chop shop he could've potentially prevented the death they'd just witnessed. He decided right then and there he wouldn't sleep after his shift until he marked every single possibility off his list. Baz grabbed his shoulder.

"Fam…"

"This fucking bullshit has to stop."

"I know, fam." Baz took a large, extended breath and squeezed his partner's shoulder once more before he reached for his buzzing phone. "It's Unc." He took the call and walked toward the back of the cruiser to give Chief Haywood the recap.

Shaw felt the anger surge throughout his body. His shift couldn't end soon enough—there'd be hell to pay the second he was off the clock.

CHAPTER
Fifteen

HARVEY BARKED WHEN HE HEARD KNOCKING ON THE SALON DOOR later that night. He and Tinsley were still at work trying to take inventory to restock any supplies they needed—her least favorite thing about being the owner. She was startled a bit because Brindle would've used a key and this was still way too early for him to be home from his date.

Tinsley looked up at the clock and saw it was just before eleven, they'd been closed for hours. Harvey was still barking but then the knocking stopped. She thought maybe whoever it was left when they heard Harvey's deep barks, but just as she sat back down, there was another round of knocking. It wasn't a loud pounding, but it was almost unnerving that the knocking was so calm.

She made sure she had her phone and crept to the front window to pull back one of the curtains to see who was in the doorway. She immediately recognized Shaw, who looked to be in distress. She ran to the door and quickly opened it.

"Holy shit." Her eyes widened and then she noticed blood all over his abdomen. "Officer Shaw, are you okay?!"

He stumbled into the salon and Tinsley quickly shut and locked the door behind him. Shaw managed to make his way to Tinsley's station and flopped down onto her chair.

"Tinsley," he gritted through his teeth. "I'm sorry, I didn't know where else to go…."

"The hospital!" She scrambled for her purse. "Come on." She tried to put herself under his arm to help him up.

"Ahh!" he grunted out in pain. "No, I can't go there." He was short of breath and removed his hand from his midsection. It was only exposed for a second, but once the pressure was removed the blood stain spread like wildfire on his charcoal shirt.

Tinsley watched as blood dripped from the back of her chair now too—and it didn't appear to be from his abdomen.

"Officer Shaw…" Tinsley held onto his forearm and started to cry. "You need help, we have to go to the hospital."

"I just need some towels. Do you have any towels?" he managed to ask despite the life-threatening injuries.

Tinsley ran to the back of the salon and returned with a handful of towels.

"What happened? Where all are you hurt?" She only watched him struggle with his jacket for half a second before she assisted him out of it. While the gash on the front of his body looked bad, she was now exposed to the stab wound in his lower back that appeared to be soaking the bottom of his shirt and pants. Tinsley grabbed a towel and lifted his shirt to hold it on the wound. "Officer Shaw…"

Shaw was able to collect himself enough to focus on her. Her face was still so beautiful, even despite the tears and the worry that now lived on it.

"I just need a minute." His breathing was shallow and he struggled to finish his sentence. "I can't go to the hospital because I can't have any reports about this."

"What about Baz? Do you have your phone? Can I call him to help?"

"No…" Shaw couldn't even shake his head. "Baz can't find out either…" He closed his eyes.

"Officer Shaw?" Tinsley kept pressure on his back but reached her free hand to cup his cheek. "Officer Shaw, open your eyes." She started to sob when his head turned into dead weight against her palm. "No no no no, Hunter!" she frantically yelled with tears racing down her face. "Hunter! Look at me!"

Shaw dug deep and opened his eyes to roll his blurry gaze toward her.

"There you go, tough guy." Tinsley choked out a sigh of relief through her tears. "Stay with me, Hunter." She nodded at him. "I'm calling for help. Please just stay with me, okay?"

Shaw weakly reached one of his hands up and gently held her hip as she carefully released his head to grab her phone from her back pocket.

"Come on, come on…" The worry in her voice was obvious as she waited while the phone rang. "Vance! I'm calling *Broath* and I need you at the salon as soon as possible with medical supplies." There was a short pause. "No, I'm not joking and yes—official Broath. Please hurry, Vance," Tinsley cried and then ended the call so she could hold Shaw's head again as he'd let it fall while she was on the phone.

"Tins, you alright?!" Vance shouted when he rushed through the back-door of the salon.

"Out here!" she frantically responded to her brother. "Vance, please help—I don't know if he's okay."

Vance noticed his sister was crying, but his attention zeroed in on the muscular man slumped in his sister's barber chair, covered in fresh blood.

"He's still breathing, but he won't open his eyes anymore. I didn't know what to do—he has at least two stab wounds on him and the blood just keeps coming."

Vance immediately reached over and put his fingers on Shaw's neck to find a pulse. "How long have his eyes been closed?"

"Maybe like two minutes after I hung up with you."

Vance put on a pair of gloves and continued to do an initial inspection. "He's definitely still alive, he's just lost so much blood that his pulse is weak. Tins, he can't stay in this chair, I need him flat somewhere. Where can we put him? Is Brindle home?"

"No, and Brindle can't know." Tinsley looked around. "Can he be in a car?"

"It's not a great idea, but honestly the quicker we get him somewhere stable, the better." Vance motioned to his sister to move her hand from the towel on Shaw's stomach so he could look at the wound. "What's the move, Tins? We gotta decide right now."

Watching Shaw's life slip away in front of her, she didn't think twice when she responded, "Can you help me get him to my house?"

Vance took a deep breath. "Get your car ready and as close to the back door as you can, okay?"

Tinsley wasted no time in running to follow her brother's directions, Harvey dutifully behind her as if he could sense the urgency of the movement.

When she came back into the salon, Vance had Shaw's arm draped around his shoulders and was working on getting him moved, struggling under the weight. Tinsley ran over to Shaw's other side to help her brother, and they got his unconscious body into the vehicle as gently as possible.

CHAPTER
Sixteen

"Tins..." Vance rubbed her shoulder. "I know I'm not supposed to ask any questions since you called an official Broath, but is there anything you want to tell me?"

Tinsley looked down at Shaw who was breathing a little more steadily now. She didn't really have any information to tell her brother—it wasn't like Shaw had told her anything.

"Honestly, Vance, I don't know what happened to him. He showed up at the salon tonight and obviously needed help. He didn't say who did this."

"You know him at least, right? He's not just some random stranger who stumbled into the salon tonight?"

"No." She shook her head. "No, he's not a random stranger; yes, I know him. Well, we met a few weeks ago anyway."

"A *few weeks*? Tins—do you know what this guy's into?"

"I don't know what he got into tonight, I'll admit that much. But he's not a threat." She glanced down at Shaw again. "He's good people, Vance."

"He's down and all, but I'm not sure I should leave you. He's gonna wake up, and be in a lot of pain. Are you comfortable alone with him?"

"I promise, it's okay." Tinsley nodded. "I'm telling you, Vance, there's more to whatever happened. He's not a bad guy."

"Is your phone charged and nearby?"

"In my pocket." She gestured toward the back of her jeans.

"Will you call me when he wakes up?"

Tinsley nodded.

"I need to get more painkillers and antibiotics for him, so I'll be back later today. I think I should grab more blood just in case too. You probably shouldn't be giving anymore—you'll be the one needing medical attention next if we tap into your supply again."

"He's not a fan of painkillers." Tinsley remembered.

"Well, when he wakes up he'll be damn thanking us for deciding that he needs them."

Tinsley put her arms around her brother and squeezed. "Thank you, Vance."

"Let's just hope I don't lose my fucking license." He returned her hug just as tightly.

"No one's going to say anything, he can be trusted."

"Call me if you need *anything*." He leveled his eyes at his sister. "I'll be back though."

"Okay, thank you." She nodded and allowed Vance to let himself out so she could stay with Shaw.

Tinsley grabbed a throw blanket and added it to the one that already covered Shaw's lower half. She gently tucked the blanket around his shoulders. Tinsley's eyes lingered on Shaw's calm and handsome face. She wondered what had happened to him that night and why, of all places, he ended up coming to her for help—she had never even told him her brother was an ER doctor.

She'd been physically attracted to Shaw since the second she saw him, but he'd always seemed just distant enough. Very respectful and even at times thoughtful, but he hadn't given her a firm indication that he was romantically interested. She continued to wonder if it was because Baz told him they'd been on a date. Whatever it was or wasn't, her heart felt settled that he was safe. She hesitated but ended up gently running her fingers through his hair for a few strokes hoping it would comfort his sleeping body.

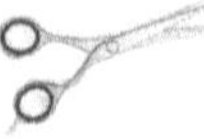

Shaw's mind picked up on the sound of an unusually loud snore and he slowly opened his heavy eyes. It took him a minute to adjust to the dimly lit room that he'd never seen, but when he did he found Tinsley sleeping near his waist. She was seated in a chair but had her top half on the bed. The side of her face was planted against an open book and one of her hands rested gently on top of his leg, just above his knee. Shaw didn't move, he took comfort in the feeling of her hand and the sight in front of him.

After the sound of fluttering jowls, he noticed the culprit of the snoring that woke him was Harvey, whose stocky body was curled up right behind Tinsley's chair. His face cracked a smile at the scene.

His entire body was sore. He knew it was bad, but then he noticed a different soreness in his hand and glanced down. He was hooked up to an IV that hung on the bed frame above his head. Somehow going to Tinsley's that night was exactly the right move to make. He had no idea his desire to just catch a final glimpse of her was actually going to end up saving his life.

Shaw watched Tinsley sleeping peacefully beside him. She was in what looked like an oversized sweatshirt—the most dressed down he'd ever seen her—but couldn't see what kind of bottoms she wore. Her hair was twisted up in some kind of messy bun and he had an urge to reach for the loose piece of hair that partially obstructed her face. Ultimately he didn't want to wake her, unsure if she was a light sleeper. Instead, he did set his hand on his leg near hers in hopes she may end up holding it when she woke.

He looked around at what he assumed to be her bedroom. It was tastefully decorated in a similar modern floral glam-style that he'd noticed at the salon. It was also the most feminine room he'd ever slept in. Tinsley's furniture looked to be a matching set—everything was black. He was lying on sheets that looked similar to the wallpaper she had at the salon with a mural of large peonies on a black background. Her comforter, that was bunched down around his waist, was a cream-color that complemented the lighter shades of the pink peonies on the sheets.

She had about six large sleeping pillows in addition to various accent pillows around him. He smiled at the impractical options she had, like the mauve lips and the white, ball-shaped pillow that looked like a polar bear had been skinned to make it. She must have been a fan of that material because the black throw blanket near his feet was the same style. Tinsley didn't have a television in her bedroom and the only photograph he noticed was a framed portrait of Handsome Harv on the large dresser against the wall opposite of the bed. It looked like she'd dragged the chair she slept in from the corner of the room. It didn't look completely uncomfortable, but he still felt bad that she'd resorted to the tufted leather armchair while he was in her bed.

Despite his injuries, Shaw felt very calm and welcome in Tinsley's bedroom; it fit her perfectly and her scent lingered in the air which brought him even more comfort. He was surrounded by *her* and against his previous judgment, he reached out. Very gently, he picked up the loose piece of hair that had covered part of her face and carefully placed it behind her ear. She didn't move. Shaw watched her until his eyelids grew so heavy that sleep once again claimed him.

Tinsley felt a harder-than-normal surface under her head when she woke up. Her brain quickly reminded her what happened the night before and encouraged her to open her eyes. She swiftly lifted her head off her book to see if Shaw had woken up.

His eyes were still closed, but he did look like he'd moved a little. His hand with the IV rested on his exposed chest since the blanket Tinsley had covered him with was now pushed down to his waist. She studied his chest. It was visually appealing to her given his muscle mass, but her brows furrowed when she saw all the bruising on his body. It wasn't just fresh bruising from whatever had happened to him the night before—the markings that covered his torso were in varying stages of healing.

She realized she'd placed her hand on top of his quad, and instead of removing it she rubbed her thumb softly back and forth. Her comforter was a barrier between his leg and her hand that remained a respectful distance from his inner thigh. As she looked at him her hand soon started to rub his leg with more than just her thumb—it was a soothing caress instead of anything suggestive.

She reached for her book to quietly close it and set it to the side when she noticed Shaw's eyes were open.

Tinsley quickly removed her hand from his leg. "I'm sorry," she said, bashful as she put her hands in her lap.

Shaw's mouth curled into a smile. "You're apologizing again, *ma'am*."

His response evoked a bright grin on her face and they stared at each other for a moment.

"I'm really glad you're still with us, Officer Shaw."

"Here I was thinking we moved beyond the Officer Shaw routine."

That elicited a soft giggle from Tinsley and she rested her arms on the bed.

"So, you did hear me when I had to pull a solid *Hunter* or two out on you, huh?"

"I did." Shaw reached toward her until he found her hands. "Thank you, Tinsley."

She matched the soft squeeze he gave her and couldn't help a few tears that dropped before she was able to suppress her emotions. "You're welcome."

"I know I owe you an explanation…."

Tinsley was already shaking her head and she quickly wiped her eyes. "Why don't I get you something to eat before you start worrying about anything like that?" She didn't want to, but she let go of his hand and stood. "I'll grab you some water too."

He gave her a grateful sigh before he watched her make her way toward the kitchen. He lightly chuckled at her dressed-down look. She was in baggy joggers and a sweatshirt that also looked to be at least two sizes too large, which was the complete opposite of the skin tight clothing she wore to work.

She returned in no time and Shaw tried to scoot himself up in the bed.

"Oh, careful. Here"—Tinsley set the food on the nightstand—"don't be tearing any of those stitches, my brother will kill me." She put a few extra pillows behind Shaw once he was sitting. "I'm supposed to be doing more good than harm until he comes back to check on you." She chuckled.

"I guess I owe two explanations then." Shaw took a long drink of water.

Tinsley shook her head again. "Nope. Vance isn't going to ask any questions or say anything to anyone. I declared Broath, so he can't. You can tell him whatever you're comfortable with, but he won't demand an explanation."

"I know I don't deserve to be asking any questions, but do I get to know what a 'Broath' is?"

"I mean, I'll just leave it super surface level until I get a few questions answered myself." Tinsley smiled. "It's the Brother Oath. Part of that is he's not allowed to ask any questions."

Harvey made his presence known when he plopped his head onto the bed as he stood next to Tinsley. His face pointed toward Shaw and his wiggling body begged for any kind of affection or acknowledgment.

"Hey, bud." Shaw reached over and rubbed the side of Harvey's head.

"I think Harvey's happy you made it too." Tinsley patted Harvey between his shoulder blades and he wiggled even more now that he was getting attention from all sides. "You really scared me there for a minute."

"I'm sorry, Tinsley," Shaw sincerely apologized.

"Oh," Tinsley smirked. "So, that statement's still okay coming from *only* you, huh?"

"Remember the rules, it's okay when it's valid." He gave a small grin before continuing with a more serious tone, "and I do really mean it. I'm sorry for bringing this to your doorstep and scaring you."

"I'm glad that you did," Tinsley admitted. "And you can feel free to apologize to me by not dying." She hugged her dog around his head when he set his chin on her lap. "Do you have a cat or anything I should go feed for you? Any plants that need watering?"

Shaw smiled at her. "No, I don't have anything like that."

"I know you didn't want to call anyone last night, but what about today? Do you need to check in anywhere? I charged your phone, it's on the nightstand over there. It's got a pretty gnarly crack, but seemed to take the charge, so I think it's working."

"I'm not scheduled to work today or the following two, so no one's gonna be looking for me." Shaw shook his head before taking another drink of water. "I'm actually not feeling all that bad, I can probably head outta here pretty soon."

Tinsley started giggling. She inadvertently reached out and touched his leg again for the slightest moment before putting her hand back down on the mattress. "Officer Shaw, I know you're a tough guy, but I wasn't asking all that to hint that you need to leave. Not only are you more than welcome to stay, but you're not going anywhere until my brother signs off."

Shaw mindfully picked up her hand and covered it with his when he placed it back on his leg. "I thought we discussed the whole Officer Shaw thing?" he spoke softly and rubbed her hand with his thumb.

Tinsley looked down at their hands, her face began to blush and she could feel her heart beat faster just before their moment was interrupted.

Harvey scrambled to his feet and ran to the back door when he heard it opening. Shaw looked toward the hallway and then at Tinsley.

"That would be my brother." She affectionately squeezed his quad before getting up.

Even after Tinsley left the room, Shaw could still feel her hand on his upper thigh. He'd tried to fight any genuine feelings for her, but, life-saving rescue or not, being around her felt right. Tinsley felt right.

"Hey there." Vance awkwardly waved when he walked into the room. He got closer to the bed and reached his hand out. "I'm Vance, or Dr. Adams—this dweeb's big brother." He gestured toward Tinsley. She was already rolling her eyes and had her tongue sticking out toward him.

Shaw smiled at them and carefully reached his hand toward Vance. "Shaw."

"Nice to formally meet you, Shaw." Vance nodded and returned the handshake. "This one just texted that you were up, glad you're still with us."

"Me too, man, I really appreciate it."

"I'll apologize." Vance looked at Shaw's chest. "I cut up your shirt, so that's gone."

Shaw shook his head and raised his hands. "I'm not worried about that at all."

"The pants, however…" Vance turned to Tinsley. "You'll have to talk to Tins about that."

Tinsley turned every shade of red and she struggled to find words. "I… they…"—she shot a friendly glare at her brother—"I washed them because I didn't want them to stain…" She focused on Harvey instead of anyone else in the room. "I would've put something besides a blanket on you, but I don't have anything that would fit you."

Vance's eyes narrowed at his sister while he smirked. "The homeless, tent-sized clothes you're wearing right now wouldn't have fit?"

"These aren't homeless clothes." She defended her comfortable outfit. "And no, not everyone has your feminine figure, Vance. Plus, jeans aren't comfy to sleep in, I was just trying to help. And you were here when I did that," she was sure to remind her brother.

Shaw tried to fight a grin watching her justify and explain why she had removed his pants.

"It's okay, I noticed I still have the final layer on."

Vance shot out a quick chuckle before collecting himself.

"I'm not sure if my truck's here, but I do have a bag in there with some things that'll fit me."

Tinsley was finally able to look at Shaw again. "Actually, we put you in my car, so your truck isn't here."

"Boxer briefs and a blanket it is." He shrugged.

Tinsley needed air, she could feel her brother about to explode from the inside out with a full-on belly roar. "I can go grab your bag, I already have your keys. I just need to know what kind of truck I'm looking for. Do you need anything else?"

Shaw smiled at her squirming. "It's a black Ford Raptor, it should be a few doors down from the salon. And I just have a black gym bag behind the passenger's seat. You don't have to go get it, but I do have a fresh pair of clothes in there."

"I don't mind at all. I'll go get that while Vance is checking your injuries." Tinsley quickly turned to leave the bedroom.

"Are you taking Helen with you?"

Tinsley spun and narrowed her eyes at Vance. "I told you to stop calling him that. You're such an asshat." She slapped her legs a couple of times. "Come on, bud—I won't make you stay here with your mean uncle."

"Yeah, get on out, Helen Keller. I don't wanna hear your big ass down there mouth breathing anymore." He stared at the cane corso who had sprawled out next to the bed.

Harvey excitedly got up and leaned on Vance's leg for a scratch or two before he ran to his own bed to grab a ball. He set it up next to Shaw and then wagged his nub of a tail in anxious anticipation. Shaw smiled at him before giving the ball a toss toward the doorway so he'd follow Tinsley.

"Helen Keller, huh?" Shaw tried not to have too big of a grin on his face while he shook his head.

"She's my little sister—if I can't give her a hard time then there's really no point in keeping her around."

"That's fair," Shaw agreed with a slow nod and a smirk.

"How're you feeling? Any concerning pain anywhere?"

"Nothing besides the obvious. And really, the pain is mild at best."

"You either have an extremely high tolerance to pain, or that micro dose of meds are kicking in a little extra." Vance shook his head and continued, "Any lightheadedness or nausea?"

"None at all."

"I know this isn't the traditional medical treatment, but I do want to be open with everything I did."

Shaw nodded for Vance to elaborate.

"Tins said you aren't a fan of painkillers, but I did put you on a few for the cleaning and stitches. I lowered the dosage after all of that though, so it can be adjusted if you change your mind. And I'm sorry to have done that without consent, but I wanted to be sure you'd stay still enough while I was working on you and not be woken up and thrashing around in pain."

"No, I get it—and I really appreciate it. I don't have an addiction problem or anything, I've just never been a fan of using them." He wanted to assure Vance he wasn't just looking to get high.

Vance nodded before he continued, "I've also put you on an anti-biotic, which is being added to your system intravenously. I'll have pills you'll need to keep taking once this IV's out though."

Shaw nodded and watched as Vance removed the bandages from his stomach wound to inspect it.

"I also had Tins go through your wallet to see if we could find any-thing about your blood type. Luckily you and Tins are compatible. She's got that rare, good stuff that can be donated to anyone anyway. I did a transfusion. Tins is clean, so you're not going to be getting anything from her."

Shaw wasn't worried about getting any diseases from her, he was more shocked at the lengths they'd taken to keep him alive without taking him to the hospital. He didn't have bonds like that aside from Baz—and they'd known each other forever. Tinsley also hadn't men-tioned any blood donations to him, making him wonder what all had happened after he'd passed out.

"I can't thank you enough, man," Shaw finally spoke. "I know Tins said you wouldn't say anything about this or ask me, but if you'd like an explanation I'm happy to give it to you."

Vance nodded with pursed lips before he responded, "I owe it to my sister to uphold the Broath. But I'll admit, it would make me feel a hell of a lot better if I had an idea of how this could potentially have a negative impact on her. I like to give her a shit time here and there, but she's still my baby sister."

"That's completely understandable and I swear to you, I mean her no harm."

Vance simply looked at Shaw, hoping he'd share more.

"I met Tinsley a few weeks back when her shop was broken into. I'm a cop with the Tacoma Police Department."

Vance nodded. "A cop who apparently can't be seen at the hospi-tal… Not sure this story is giving me the warm fuzzies I was expecting."

"I absolutely deserve that." Shaw held up his hands. "To make a very long story short, I've been investigating a string of crimes where I'm definitely not a part of the official task force, and I may have stepped into a little something that I can't have anyone at the department finding out about yet. I know it looks bad, but I'm not doing anything completely illegal and there isn't anything I'm bringing to Tinsley's doorstep. I wouldn't put her in danger like that."

"So… you're out there doing good—in the middle of the night—but don't want anyone at work to know about it? You just met my sister a few weeks ago, who's not medically trained in any kind of way, but you still chose to find yourself on her doorstep when you got stabbed?" He studied Shaw for a long moment before continuing, "Are you guys dating or something?"

Shaw shook his head. "No. Like I said, I just met her a few weeks ago. We've only really interacted a couple of times. So, I'll admit it looks bad that I ended up there… It's just… complicated."

"I see."

"I swear to you, if she wants me gone, I'll get out of here. I'd never mean her any harm. Your sister seems like a very special lady."

Vance took a deep breath. "Yeah, well, we don't like to lie to her about that." He collected all the garbage from the bandages. "If you're able, I'm going to have you roll to your side so I can look at the one on your back too." He waited for Shaw to ease onto his side. "And I'm not a mindreader, but if my sister wanted you gone she wouldn't have brought you here in the first place, that's for sure. Her home is her sanctuary— Brindle's ass isn't even welcome here all the time and those two are the best of friends."

Shaw grinned. Brindle did seem to have a completely different energy than Tinsley's.

"You can also thank your trainer or whatever the hell you do. These could have been a lot worse if you didn't have all that muscle mass. This one isn't going to take too long to heal, it's the one on your abdomen that I'd like to keep an eye on."

"How long do you think I'll have to have these stitches?" Shaw asked as Vance inspected his back wound.

Vance rolled his head around. "This one on your back? Maybe like seven to ten days. The other one is hard to say right now. I sincerely don't believe it grazed any organs in there, you were very lucky. For as deep as it appears to be, it's really in a great spot. You'll need to try to limit your activity for at least a week and a half—maybe two weeks. I don't want you tearing any of these, especially the abdomen. If you've got leave, I'd suggest taking it."

Shaw kind of snorted a laugh, he had more leave than he knew what to do with. He was never sick, never took vacation, and did nothing but sign up for overtime. His life truly revolved around work and work alone the last couple of years.

"Yeah, I've got some days I can take."

"Good." Vance nodded and then finished on Shaw's back. "Limited activity means not working out, obviously, but also not even lifting anything more than ten pounds right now. I wouldn't recommend sudden movements or reaching beyond what's comfortable—mostly just the obvious. But do you have specific questions about certain activities?"

Shaw shook his head. He'd dealt with stitches before, just nothing this serious.

"I figured I may be telling you things you already know." Vance gestured toward Shaw's torso. "It looks like you get your fair share of injuries on the job."

"Yeah." Shaw lifted his arms. "It's definitely not my first rodeo."

"You typically work on injuries yourself?" Vance looked him in the eyes, having noticed a few poorly healed scars he would have half a mind to report whoever had closed him up if it'd been done by any kind of licensed medical professional.

"I consider myself somewhat of an expert at this point, so yeah. Obviously I wouldn't have been able to take care of these alone."

"I mean, you're still here, but I have to say it anyway. You should consider being seen by a professional when you have more serious injuries. A few of these scars look like you may have needed to seek some assistance. That's just my two cents though." Vance held up his hands.

"I get it." Shaw nodded. "I really appreciate everything, Doc. I owe you."

CHAPTER
Seventeen

"**O**h! You're up?!" Tinsley's face was both shocked and lit up with glee when she got back to her house and watched Shaw slowly making his way to the bathroom with Vance monitoring nearby. She tried not to completely stare at him in his boxer briefs. Injured or not, she couldn't deny he had an incredible body.

"I tried telling him to just milk it, but he insists on being all manly about it." Vance exaggeratedly rolled his eyes.

"Wait, should he not be walking around then?"

"He's doing fine, Tins."

"Yeah, ready for a goddamn triathlon in a sec." Shaw tried to laugh but instead let out a large exhale when one of the wounds shot a quick stab of pain throughout his torso.

"I'll go ahead and strongly advise against that one." Vance shook his head, grinning.

Shaw held the back of the couch so he could turn to face Vance. "Would you advise against a shower? I know I shouldn't get the stitches wet, but how about if I'm just careful?"

Vance took a deep breath. "I suppose if you're really careful. They're all bandaged up too, and I'll check them again before I leave. So, now would probably be a good time if you wanted to shower. Are you going to be okay in there alone, or do you want some help?"

Shaw continued slowly making his way to the bathroom. "Thanks Doc, but I think you've helped plenty." He chuckled at the thought of Vance helping him wash.

"Not me!" Vance barked out a laugh. "I figured you'd prefer Tins for any assistance in there. I mean, she already took your pants off, why not the rest of it?"

Tinsley smacked her brother with Shaw's gym bag while his back was to them.

Shaw tried to swallow his laughter, just before he responded, "She doesn't have to do that—I should be able to manage. But, Tins, if you don't mind putting my bag in there, that would be helpful."

Tinsley gave her brother another firm shove when she passed him and then turned to stick her tongue out at him for good measure.

Shaw made it to the bathroom doorway shortly after Tinsley had gone in. He noticed, thankfully, the shower didn't have a tub, it was a walk-in style. Tinsley had just set the bag on the vanity and was taking off her socks.

"I'll get the water started for you. I think this'll actually work out well because the hose will reach the bench seat in there so you won't have to stand if you don't want to." She walked into the shower and made all the proper adjustments for Shaw to easily manage. The water was already steaming up the mirror when she opened a cupboard to grab him a few fresh towels and a washcloth. After she set the washcloth on the bench in the shower she came out and was met with Shaw's inviting green eyes.

"Thank you, Tinsley." He reached out and held her elbow.

Tinsley was momentarily paralyzed. She didn't know how to play this cat-and-mouse game she seemed to be in with Shaw. Not with her brother in the house, and *especially* not with a nearly naked version of the best looking man she'd ever seen standing just inches from her.

She snapped herself out of her thoughts and warmly replied, "You're welcome… Will you let me know if you need anything?"

"I will." Shaw gently squeezed her elbow before he removed his hand, then watched her leave the bathroom, shutting the door behind her.

"So," Vance took a seat at the breakfast bar. "A cop, huh?"

Tinsley confirmed with her head and then rolled it around knowing her brother hadn't even scratched the surface of his obnoxious comments yet.

"Has he told you anything about what happened?"

"No." Tinsley shook her head. "He told me he knows he owes me an explanation, but I stopped him and told him he needed to eat first. He hasn't been awake all that long yet, so I'm sure it'll come up."

"You know I'm not going to keep pushing you on all that, *but* I do think there's a little loophole for some other questions I have." Vance had a smirk on his face that Tinsley knew only showed its ugly face when he wanted to tease his sister. "Is the officer a *gentleman caller* of sorts?" He pumped his eyebrows.

Tinsley threw her head back smiling. "Oh my gosh!" She grabbed her face with both hands. "How can you be such an amazing and annoying brother all at the same time?"

"It's a gift." He shrugged and reached for an orange from the fruit basket on the breakfast bar.

"As far as I know, we're simply friends." Tinsley tried to hide her face. "And I'd like to leave the conversation at that for now." She finally looked up at her brother with narrowed eyes. "Plus, you aren't supposed to be asking for *any* information—you know the rules."

"You'd like to leave the *conversation* at that... not the friendship status at that..." Vance's eyes dramatically doubled in size as he peeled the orange. "I see."

Tinsley playfully shoved her brother and then got up to get herself a drink.

"On a more professional note, while your cop *friend* seems to be doing okay getting around, I'd say he needs at least a day or two lying low. Honestly, if you're both okay with it, you should just have him stay here tonight too. After that, he'll obviously still need to mind those stitches, but otherwise, he's an adult and can decide how much he wants to push that recovery process. I gave him the best advice I can, but it'll be his choice."

"Yeah, he's a tough guy for sure." She chuckled.

"Oh, I'm sure he's not going to take much convincing to stay here tonight." Vance pumped his eyebrows again.

Tinsley gave him another friendly shove and then looked down at her buzzing phone.

> **BRINDLE BOO**
> Boo! I just got home FYI.
>
> #itchwasscratched

Tinsley knew that hashtag was reserved for dates in which Brindle ended up with a physically pleasing experience, but didn't see any future dates with that beau. He had a handful of hashtags he'd use as code with her so she knew it was actually him texting and not one of his dates who'd taken him against his will.

> LOL—not planning to U-Haul after your sleepover, huh?? 😂 😏 Happy for you, but not sad that you're still on the prowl. That guy gave off icky creeper vibes.

> **BRINDLE BOO**
> Ur so damn picky. I got mine so idc.
>
> Wanna do lunch or drinks today?

> Hanging with Vance. 😬 😬 Raincheck??

Tinsley could live with that white lie. She technically was hanging with her brother at the moment. She didn't want to explain anything else, Brindle would've driven over to her house immediately if he knew Shaw was there.

> **BRINDLE BOO**
> If ur lucky!

I guess I'll go fishing instead.

We all know there's another fine ass man out
there wanting to entertain me this evening.

Be safe, send pics and let me know your plans so
I can be sure you don't get kidnapped. 😉🖤

BRINDLE BOO ⭐
Will do Boo 😉

"Miss Popular these days, huh?" Vance leaned over toward her phone. "A guy at the house, a guy on the chatline…" He assumed after watching his sister laugh while looking at her phone.

Tinsley rolled her eyes and turned her phone to him. "It's Brindle."

Vance slowly nodded and shoved a piece of the orange in his mouth. "So, we *are* exclusive with the officer, huh?" He smirked.

"You were adopted and no one likes you." Tinsley tossed him a sarcastic glare before she got up to put fresh sheets on her bed.

Shaw watched Tinsley walk into the bedroom that night wearing another surprisingly baggy outfit that was the sexiest version of adorable he'd ever seen. She was in a pair of thin cotton joggers that were a blush pink but had various hairdressing tools all over them and her long-sleeve black top was oversized and hanging off one of her shoulders. She took a seat on the armchair next to the bed with her legs curled up and then started to blush when she noticed Shaw staring at her.

"What?" She smiled brightly.

Shaw took a deep breath and then let it out slowly. He wasn't entirely sure what to say to her, he'd just wanted to admire her. He had a compliment sitting on the tip of his tongue but held back. "Are you all ready for bed?"

"Well, I've got the jammies on." She held out her arms.

Shaw grinned at her. "I can go to the couch." He started to get out of the bed, moving slowly he tried to discreetly suck in a breath when the stab wounds sent sharp pains through his torso.

"No." Tinsley shook her head. "No, the bed is much better for you."

He stopped and looked her in the eyes. "Tins, you're not sleeping in that chair again and I'm not about to have you out on the couch while I'm hogging your bed."

"Are you tired?" She cocked her head to the side.

"Not entirely," Shaw admitted.

Tinsley grinned. "Then why can't I just sit here and chat for a while? You can lose our argument about sleeping arrangements when we're ready to go to sleep."

"What makes you so confident about winning that one?" He smirked.

"You might be a tough guy, but something tells me you've also got a soft side." She bit her bottom lip but didn't look at him.

Shaw chuckled. "You might be right." He reached for her and gently stroked her hand a couple of times until she finally looked up at him. "I don't let just anyone see that side though."

Tinsley felt her heart skip a beat. Shaw had been running through her mind the last couple of weeks and each time she saw him she craved even more. The previous uncertainty of his intentions were becoming very clear and while she hated having watched him almost lose his life, she was grateful the universe had found a way to cross their paths.

As they'd chatted away for the last couple of hours, Harvey had found his way up on the bed next to Shaw while Tinsley held strong to her spot on the chair. She'd brought in several midnight snacks for them to enjoy and she felt like they'd established a good enough mood to try and dive into the explanation Shaw had offered when he'd first woken up.

"So… Any chance you wanna tell me what happened last night?" Tinsley took a sip of her water and then decided to join him on the bed. She sat criss-cross applesauce facing him, but slightly to his side as he was sitting up with his back against the headboard. He didn't move away from her, the proximity was welcome. He was now sandwiched with Tinsley on his right and Harvey snoring comfortably on his left.

Shaw sighed, almost embarrassed. "I made a rookie mistake with an investigation I've been conducting, and it nearly cost me my damn life." He reached up and rubbed his neck before continuing, "I have this… urge… to work off the clock from time to time." He checked her expression. "I'm still working through something that happened a couple years back, and the way I do that is by going around like some fucking idiot." Shaw shook his head while taking a long breath. "I revisit perps—and any other low-life degenerates Baz and I come across on a daily basis—when I feel like the law doesn't exactly carry out the justice it should."

Tinsley carefully held back her expression, she just listened.

"I think bad people should be held accountable for their actions. It fucking sucks when good people get hurt." Shaw felt his fists clench so he shook his head again to loosen up. He gazed at Harvey who'd made himself very comfortable by lying his head on Shaw's leg as he snored. He gave his new four-legged friend a good neck rub before he started again. "So, last week, Baz and I responded to a call from a lady who heard her neighbors fighting. We get there and the woman is just completely beat to shit. She's already bruised on every inch of her body, her face is bleeding so much I can't even tell where her injuries started and the man's hands are just busted up."

Tinsley could feel a cold sweat creeping up on her.

"The fucking lady ended up begging us not to do anything. She said she tripped—it was a whole fucking thing. We looked for every goddamn excuse to get her out of there and she didn't want to. She actually ended up smacking Baz to get us to leave; we left her with the EMTs to treat her injuries. I was fucking pissed when we left that house."

Tinsley watched as Shaw stroked the side of Harvey's large head.

Shaw's gaze was aimed at the corner of the bed and he didn't blink when he continued "I went back there that night and I beat that man to within an inch of his life with a baseball bat."

A tear fell down Tinsley's face and she tried to discreetly stop anymore from falling.

"I go out almost every night and that's what I do. I try to correct the wrong—or what I think is wrong anyway. I'm not saying what I do is okay, but it's been a way for me to live with some of the things that've happened." He shrugged and couldn't bring himself to check Tinsley's reaction after his admission. "So, I chase the next bad thing. Once that's handled, I look for the next one. It's sickening that there's an endless supply of terrible people out there."

The room was quiet, aside from Harvey's snoring, for a long moment.

Tinsley understood why Shaw was constantly covered in bruises now.

"Last night I wasn't after a specific person. There's been a string of violent carjackings lately, I'm sure you've heard." He finally glanced at Tinsley, but he wasn't able to read her expression. "That was actually the reason Baz and I had to haul ass out of the salon," he informed her. "I've been trying to pinpoint who's behind it for weeks. I truly thought I was onto something last night, and then I lost my fucking head." Shaw's face went dark. "I watched a man die when we responded to that call yesterday… I wasn't in the right mindset to be out doing what I was last night."

"Officer Shaw… I…" Tinsley rested her hand on his leg for a split second before taking it back. "You don't have to tell me about this if you don't want to," she offered in a soft and shaky voice.

"You deserve to know." He picked up her hand to set it on his leg again and then covered it with his. "I was at this chop shop that I'd staked out a few nights before. Based on the cars I saw there, they'd definitely been using it as their homebase for at least a week. I have no clue how the task force hasn't stumbled on it yet. While I was watching them, I saw someone I recognized."

"Baz?" Tinsley guessed with a hesitant tone. She remembered how adamant Shaw had been about not calling him for help and saying 'Baz can't find out either.'

Shaw shook his head. "His cousin… the Police Chief's son."

Tinsley's eyes widened.

"I couldn't process what I was seeing, but I got the fuck out of there before he could see me. I'm still not sure what to do with that information. I was about a block from that building and could see my truck in the distance when I heard some lady crying for help. I ran back toward the chop shop to see what was happening, but someone must've seen me lurking around earlier because it was a fucking set up." Shaw's brows were angry as he shook his head. "The second I knelt down to help the woman on the ground, she was shoving a knife in my stomach."

Tinsley's hand involuntarily tightened around his leg.

"I didn't even have time to stand all the way up when that second knife went into my back."

"Shaw…" Tinsley had a steady stream of tears now as her hand gently rubbed his leg.

"Tins." Shaw reached for her face and wiped a few tears with his thumb. "It's okay, I'm okay." He looked into her eyes. "You saved me."

Tinsley leaned in and hugged him. Her arms reached around his neck as she nestled her head next to his. Shaw didn't think twice when he wrapped his strong arms around her and held tightly. So close, he was fully engulfed in her scent with his nose in the thick of her hair.

"When I made it back to my truck I headed straight for you, Tinsley. At first I didn't know why." He rubbed his hands up and down her back and spoke softly into her ear. "But then I realized it was because if that was it for me, all I wanted was to be able to see your beautiful face and feel your sweet presence one last time. I can't tell you how grateful I am that you were there."

He felt and heard Tinsley sobbing, and couldn't seem to hold her tight enough.

Once Tinsley was able to calm down enough to speak, she moved her mouth closer to Shaw's ear as they clutched each other. "I'll always be right here for you, Officer Shaw," she whispered.

Shaw backed up far enough to lift his hand to hold the side of her face. He looked into her watery brown eyes before slowly moving his lips toward hers. The second their mouths touched they both felt an immediate sense of relief and overwhelming release. Shaw had been so hesitant for this moment and now that it was happening he regretted every second he'd wasted not pursuing Tinsley.

Their mouths moved as if they'd known each other for a lifetime. Pressing their lips against one another's wasn't enough, and they were soon letting their tongues explore. Shaw's hand massaged the back of her head, gripping on to her hair, perfectly in sync with their mouths. She didn't want to stop—kissing Shaw felt more natural than she could've ever imagined.

While he was gentle, there was a fierceness behind each movement that made Tinsley feel like Shaw was solidifying some bonding destiny determined by the stars long ago.

There was a natural slowing of their mouths and Shaw was the first to speak when they separated.

"So, the Officer Shaw thing is here to stay, huh?" A sly grin started to appear on his face.

Tinsley tried her best to fight her own smirk from taking over. "I quite like Hunter, but the full name seems like it should be reserved for when you're in trouble. I need a single syllable option for everyday use… Can I call you Hunt?"

Shaw had his arms around her while Tinsley had one hand lightly scratching the short hair on the back of his head and the other gently set on his bare chest. He smiled widely at her. "You can call me whatever you want, sugar."

Tinsley's face lit up at Shaw's pet name for her and she moved toward him to peck him this time. She lingered near his lips before saying, "Well, *Hunt*, how can we fix things so you stay much safer now that I know I can't lose you?"

Shaw took a large breath and pulled Tinsley's head toward his chest to hold her there. "Tins, how much of that do you want to unpack tonight?"

"All of it." She stayed nestled against Shaw's strong chest while he brushed his fingers through her soft, chocolate hair. "I'm ready to show you my skeletons and I'm not afraid of any of yours."

"Okay," he agreed. Shaw pecked Tinsley's head before he began. "Almost three years ago now, I was engaged with a baby on the way."

The rhythm Tinsley had started on his pecs never faltered. She felt the rising of his strong chest as he took a full, healthy breath before continuing.

"I met Baz in high school. We became like brothers almost immediately after meeting, so his family basically became my family. I was at a Haywood reunion right after we graduated and that's where I met

Sloane. She was a friend of one of Baz's distant cousins… I don't even remember anything else that went on that week, just that I met Sloane and we were going to spend our lives together."

Shaw paused for a moment to be sure this was something Tinsley was still okay with him sharing. While Shaw thought about her daily, he hadn't actually talked about his late fiancée in a long time.

"We got engaged about five years ago and a couple years later—knee deep in wedding planning—we found out she was pregnant." Shaw started to rub his hands up and down Tinsley's back as he held her. "At that point we didn't see a real big reason to keep waiting, so we decided we'd do a smaller thing so we could be married before the baby was born. About a month before the wedding, Baz and I were on our normal route and he got a call on his cell… I knew it was something bad, but I had no idea the severity. Baz hit the sirens and hauled ass without saying a word. When we got to the scene and out of the car he grabbed me. I basically blacked out when I saw the stretcher coming out of that convenience store. It was Sloane… She was covered in blood and had an oxygen mask over her face."

Tinsley felt tears running down her face again and she only broke her rhythm on his chest to give him a comforting squeeze before she went back to gently rubbing him.

"I was in the ambulance with her when she flatlined… She never woke up again."

Shaw was quiet for a long moment. Tinsley noticed him remove one of his hands from her to stroke Harvey's head.

"She had four separate through-and-through gunshot wounds from two guns—all to her back. She was probably trying to run from the shooters. They told me our baby likely died from what they believed was the first shot."

Shaw leaned his chin down to kiss Tinsley on the top of her head. His voice was even, as though he'd lived through and repeated this nightmare every day since it happened.

"After I gathered enough of my head to register what happened, I fell into my little vigilante bullshit and haven't stopped since. It was a pair of fucking kids who basically stopped my world. Both seventeen-year-olds who were holding up a little convenience store for the $411.19 that was in the fucking register. The judge decided to treat them like children and allowed them bail so they could be in their beds at home the *next fucking day* after they killed my family… I couldn't live with that."

Silence took over for a long minute. Tinsley wiped her eyes and Shaw felt a couple of her tears hit his chest. He rubbed her arm again before he offered anything else.

"I didn't even think twice about it when I was following them the next week and took both of their useless fucking lives…"

Tinsley felt Shaw's grip on her tighten for the slightest moment before he took another deep breath.

"Baz is my brother… I didn't intend for him to find out about what I did, but I know he knows and that man protected me from facing any of the consequences. He'll take my secret to the grave. And whether or not they actually know, Baz's family did everything to make sure those murders didn't come back on me. If his family—Chief Haywood really—wasn't so well connected within the system, I'd be behind bars—I'm sure of it. I was on administrative leave for over six months before I could go on patrol and carry a weapon again. They spun it to where I was in an emotionally damaged state over my family, which was the damn truth—just not all of it—and needed medical leave. I've never even asked Baz what anyone else knows. He told me we don't have to speak of *that* ever and hasn't said another word about it since." Shaw swallowed hard and rubbed his hands along Tinsley's shoulder.

"I don't know if it makes it better or not, but I haven't killed anyone since then… Yes, I do some shady shit to people who deserve it, but I'm not out there taking lives. Baz doesn't know about my extracurriculars either. He definitely doesn't know I've been lurking around the carjacking ring."

Tinsley let the air in the room go still before she lifted her head off of Shaw's chest. She wiped the remaining tears from her eyes before looking at him. Her heart hurt for him and she was sorry for what he'd been through, but she didn't want to say she was sorry. So, she reached for the side of his face and settled on the next, most genuine sentiment she could think of.

"You are *such* a good man, Hunt. I wish you never had to feel that kind of pain." She gently rubbed the side of his face and looked deep into his eyes. "I don't think less of you, and I certainly don't judge you for what you've done."

Shaw moved in and connected their lips for a long moment. "I'm not sure I deserve the title of a good man, but I do try."

"If nothing else, that effort proves my point." Tinsley was still close to his face so she leaned in and softly pecked him again. "Thank you for trusting me with your past… I'm not going anywhere because of that— I'll still be here for you." She reinforced the statement with another kiss before lying her head back on his chest.

They sat holding one another in silence. Neither thought about any feelings of regret, they just felt connected to each other.

Shaw had never talked to anyone about his late-night vigilante activities and only the people who personally knew Sloane knew about that tragic side of Shaw's life. After those deeply intimate disclosures and Tinsley whole-heartedly accepting him, Shaw felt weightless. He'd never imagined a scenario where he could be so vulnerable and in return feel nothing but unapologetic acceptance. For the first time in a long time, he could feel his heart beating again. Tinsley felt right.

Tinsley acknowledged that Shaw had owed her an explanation, but he'd offered quite a bit more from his closet, so she figured she should reciprocate his trust and disclose something to him. She would tell him everything, but decided it was most appropriate to come clean about Baz first.

Before she was able to say anything, her phone rattled off a few text messages. It was after two o'clock in the morning.

"I'm sorry. I'm sure it's just Brindle." Tinsley lifted her head off Shaw. "But girl code demands that I at least check… And then I'll put my phone on silent."

Shaw rubbed her shoulder as she leaned over to grab her phone, smiling at her claiming 'girl code' for Brindle.

> BRINDLE BOO
> Bitch!

This guy is MARRIED!!

WTF!?!! He brought me over to his damn house!

He's got a wife and kids in his picture frames!

I'm safe but outtie.

#goinghomehorny

"Is he okay?" Shaw noticed the texts were one after another.

Tinsley nodded after a quick, deep breath. "Brindle always does the rapid text style—which drives me nuts—but he's just leaving what sounds like a failed date night. We have a rule about checking in to stay safe out there." Her fingers raced across her screen. "So, he's just letting me know he's heading home."

Oh man!! 😅 🫠 Drive safe, love you and stop texting me. I'm sleeping—we'll chat tomorrow. 😘 🖤

BRINDLE BOO
Kk love you goodnight

"I'm sorry." Tinsley set her phone back down.

Shaw's mouth curled into a grin. "Don't apologize, ma'am." He reached for her hair and put a piece of it behind her ear. "Brindle's lucky to have a friend like you."

"Yeah, he is!" she agreed. "Damn drama queen texting me at all hours because *he's* a ho."

Shaw laughed but kept it light to avoid disturbing his stitches.

Tinsley looked into Shaw's eyes and knew she needed to tell him about Baz. She reached for his leg and held her hand on him, watching her gentle touch hoping she'd find the courage to look in his eyes.

"I appreciate you being so open with me… I feel like I need to tell you something about Baz."

Shaw chuckled and rubbed his thumb along her arm. "Honestly, you might be surprised at what I may already know." He figured he'd help her out on this one since he was just as guilty and wanting to confess a few things himself.

Tinsley's head shot up and their gazes met. "I have a feeling this is going to be one of those *Hunter* moments…" She narrowed her eyes at him with a smile.

"Why don't you start, since you said you have something to tell me?" he suggested with a wide grin taking over his face.

"That's entirely unfair since it sounds like the two of you have already had a little chat."

Shaw couldn't help but give her what she wanted, he was already wrapped around her finger. He planted another kiss on her forehead this time and squeezed her. "I may already know he met you on a dating app."

Tinsley's face turned red and she covered it with her hands.

"And in my boy's defense, he *did* feel like shit when he realized you legitimately left for an actual emergency. It was me who told him to just let you be—he was going to try to apologize."

"You didn't want him to say sorry at the very least?!" She laughed but had a hint of disbelief hidden behind it. Baz had in fact apologized—weeks after the date, granted—but nevertheless he did. It didn't appear he'd informed Shaw about that though.

"Well… don't repeat this to him, that's my brother." Shaw looked into her eyes.

Tinsley made a cross motion over her heart before closing an imaginary zipper on her mouth.

He smirked at her and then continued, "He wanted to apologize to fix things after we left the salon that day we met. I told him the ship had sailed, but that may have also been because I know he had…" Shaw rolled his head from side to side considering his word choice. "A lady friend he wasn't willing to give up in the meantime. I love him, I always will—and he's not a pig or anything—but after meeting you I knew you didn't deserve to be placed in some roster-style mindfuck."

Tinsley was still a little red in the face when Shaw kept going, "Plus, how fair would that have been for me to encourage him to think he had a shot when it was so clear you had a big fat crush on me the second you saw me?"

"What?!" Tinsley's head fell back, giggling. "*I* was crushing on *you*, huh? That wasn't you getting down on one knee in front of me and asking me to touch you the second we met?"

"Well, for full transparency, I may have technically met you before meeting you…" Shaw held up his hands.

Tinsley's eyes shot up to him again. "I'm afraid to know what that means," she admitted.

"I swear, it's not some game or anything like that either, so just know that please. And honestly, you seem to have yourself a little side-kick while you're scrolling through those dating apps as well—"

"Oh, I see." She rolled her head around with a grin on her face. "You have to help your friend match with girls, huh? I'll have you know Brindle and I exchange app stories for safety reasons. Well, that's why I share with him anyway. I think he takes great pleasure in someone having to listen to all his boyfriend escapades."

Shaw scrunched his face and looked at her with accusing eyes. "You were relying on *Brindle* to protect you from someone like *Baz?*" he laughed.

"Well, like in the way that he'd definitely do some digging and have zero shame in finding out what happened to my body if I went missing."

"Okay, that's fair." Shaw wholeheartedly agreed with that explanation.

"And you boys don't need to feel guilty about playing any games on those apps or anything because one or both of you were basically chatting with Brindle that night Baz and I were going back and forth for hours."

Shaw made a little choking noise. "What?!"

"Not the whole chat, obviously." She giggled. "But initially, I wasn't even going to message Baz back. That was Brindle who convinced me that he'd just sent a message that wasn't a completely cocky douche-bag follow-up invitation about how lucky I'd be to touch him or what-ever." She shook her head. "I'll go out on a limb and assume that's when *we* met."

Shaw only smirked.

"*If* that's the case, your first couple of messages were with Brindle. I wasn't convinced Baz wasn't gearing up for another run of the mill piggy pick-up line, so he did the initial exchange after I put Baz in chatline timeout. I mostly had the phone after that, but anything super late that night was 1000% Brindle taking my phone after I fell asleep."

"Well, then that was Baz and Brindle going back and forth." Shaw howled with controlled laughter, holding his injured torso. "I did initially have the phone that night, that was us talking about your ideas to expand the salon—and that was also my cultured ass going toe to toe on all the movie quotes."

Tinsley smiled widely at Shaw. "So, what I'm hearing is you and I really enjoyed talking to each other and so did Baz and Brindle."

They laughed together for a long time thinking about how Baz would feel if they ever told him he'd been flirting with Brindle all night. Shaw had to try and stop himself several times because the laughter literally tore at his stitches.

"I actually have one more confession on the whole dating app thing."

"Oh no." Tinsley lightly hit her forehead with her hand. "I'm scared."

"So, all the girls Baz talks to have nicknames…"

"Oh Jesus, I'm not sure I want to know." She covered her face. "And perhaps it's actually Brindle's nickname—depending on how the nickname developed, that is."

"I have to tell you, I'm usually the mastermind behind the nicknames." He checked her expression. Tinsley simply waited in anxious anticipation of what they'd been calling her.

"Well, let's hear it." She closed her eyes, giggling.

"I thought your profile and the things you were saying were just so damn sweet—you seemed like the good girl type… So, I started calling you Tickle-Me Tinsley." Shaw suddenly realized exactly how ridiculous and embarrassing that actually was.

"What?!" Tinsley held onto his hand and laughed at him. "That was the best you guys could come up with?"

Shaw's face flamed red. "I didn't want Baz to end up telling you before me. I'm thinking this was a terrible idea now."

"I'll certainly *never* let you live that down." Tinsley shook her head. "But you earned yourself a little nickname too, so I guess we're even. Although, I'd say our team is better at coming up with names—being deemed Shawberry Beefcake by Brindle is pure gold."

"Don't get me wrong, I've had my share of… fans. Just never any quite like Brindle."

Shaw looked over at a small antique-style clock Tinsley had sitting on a shelf in the corner of the room. "Do you know what time your brother's coming back?" It was almost three o'clock in the morning.

She shook her head. "He said he's on-call at the hospital today, so he's planning to come by whenever work doesn't need him. Are you feeling okay?"

Shaw reached for her face and brushed his fingers through her hair. "More than okay."

"And you don't mind that I snuck up on the bed with you?"

"Honestly?" Shaw smirked. "I was hoping you would."

"I didn't want to have to argue about sleeping arrangements." She giggled.

"Are you ready to go to sleep?"

"I'm actually not even tired," she admitted.

"Neither am I." Shaw cupped her face, his thumb gliding along her cheekbone. "I'm really enjoying your company."

"I've been thinking the same about you."

They stared at each other for a long moment before Shaw pulled her head toward him to connect their lips. Shaw's tongue played with Tinsley's in a way that made her crave even more.

"Damn," Shaw murmured as they separated. "We should've started this weeks ago."

She grinned. "I don't like pointing fingers, but I think that was a mishap from your department, not mine."

Shaw exhaled a chuckle. "Oh, trust me—I know that and I've thoroughly learned my lesson about wasting any more time fighting my feelings for you."

Tinsley caught her bottom lip on her teeth to suppress her smile. She was doing a terrible job so she decided to hide her face instead when she curled up closer to Shaw. She laid her head on his shoulder and pulled a blanket over them. Shaw rubbed her arm as he placed a soft peck on her hairline.

"We didn't finish our conversation about the Broath," he said, curious. "Vance did say he owed it to you to 'uphold the Broath.' It seems legit, whatever it is."

He noticed Tinsley's body language tense. She said she was ready to share her secrets, but perhaps this wasn't one she was referring to.

"You don't have to tell me if it's just between you guys," he offered.

"No." Tinsley slid her hand along his chest before putting it back in her lap. "It's not a secret like that."

He gave her a comforting squeeze but waited for her to elaborate.

"It's pretty deep…" Tinsley peered down at her hands. "I, in a way, saved my brother's life. Since all that, he's felt guilty, and I think he'll always feel like he owes me… The Broath happened right after Alaurra was born." She shrugged while shaking her head. "Having her really changed Vance—how he saw family anyway. He pulled me aside that same day and he created what he called the 'Broath,' or the Brother Oath." She sat up a little taller. "Which might seem odd, because you'd think a big brother, six years older and all, would just automatically take care of his little sister whenever. Vance was never a big brother bully or anything like that, but he certainly took his role with me much more seriously after having his daughter, like she made him realize how much he loved me or something. The Broath is deeper—like a vow or covenant type of thing."

"That's why he was so eager to help me out?"

"He's not allowed to say no—whatever I ask of him, he'd do. I could call Broath and tell him I need him to streak at the Superbowl and he'd do it, no questions asked."

Shaw smiled, but knew she was only procrastinating telling the rest of the story.

Tinsley took a deep breath. "I actually had a criminal record when I was just a kid… My parents paid a ton of money for it to be expunged, and I spent a lot of time in a specialized detention center of sorts when I was younger."

Shaw was at a complete loss for words. Nothing about Tinsley had given any indication that she'd been a delinquent as a child. She was the sweetest person he'd ever met, well put together, and had a successful business—this disclosure didn't track at all.

"I remember we were on a family vacation one summer," Tinsley started to explain and reached for her dog to stroke his head as she continued. "It was like a whole group vacation with a few of my parent's friends and their families too. They rented this really cool compound-type place right on the Sound that used to be a summer camp or something. There was a main house and then a bunch of cabins scattered." Tinsley could still smell the salt water and vividly remember the sand and gravel beach peppered with random driftwood where they'd all enjoyed bonfires until their final night of their stay. Up until the end, it had been the dream vacation.

"My brother brought his girlfriend on that trip, Delilah, who's actually his wife now. My parents have always loved her. They were both nineteen and I was a couple months away from turning thirteen. To Vance's *utter* delight"—Tinsley projected sarcasm in her voice and her eyes—"I stayed in the same cabin as him that week." She shook her head. "He did everything to get me out of there most nights so Delilah could sneak in—she was supposed to be in another cabin area with the other girls. I was so in love with my brother and Delilah though, and I thought I was like the coolest kid on the trip getting to hang with them. The cabin was like a quad-style set up, so it was like four small cabins all connected with a communal space in the middle. He managed to kick me out to the couch in the shared space more nights than not, which wasn't the worst. There were eight other kids on the trip with us, so I wasn't like completely alone. No one else slept in that communal space though, usually. On the last night we were there..." She paused.

Shaw watched as tears started silently falling down Tinsley's face. "Tins"—he wiped a few of them away—"You don't have to tell me what happened."

"It's okay," she tried to assure him. "I, uh… in the middle of the night, Vance came out to where I was sleeping and screamed at me to get up. He held Delilah's hand and yanked me out of there too while there were flames just *everywhere*." Goosebumps prickled along her arms. "Everyone was just screaming everywhere all around us. It was all us kids in that cabin and I didn't even know if our parents knew what'd happened yet since they were all in the bigger house across the yard."

She had to stop for a moment so she could wipe her face and collect her voice. Shaw's large hand rested on her leg as it offered a comforting rhythm of squeezing and rubbing as she continued.

"I finally started to hear something other than the screaming—it was my brother and Delilah. They were freaking out because they'd had candles in the room. They started the fire. They, obviously, hadn't been paying attention and by the time they noticed, the flames were just too wild. Those cabins were so old and that summer was so dry, it just started and spread quicker than anyone could've stopped it. So, being the doe-eyed little sister I was, I told Vance I'd say it was me who was playing with fire in the cabin."

Shaw wrapped his arms around Tinsley and held her against his chest before pressing his lips on the top of her head. Tinsley's tears were flowing freely, she hadn't talked about that night for years. She had never admitted to anyone else that it hadn't been her.

"Vance asked me ten million times during the commotion of all the parents running down and searching for their kids and I just kept telling him it was okay. I couldn't imagine I'd get in as much trouble as he would. I mean, he would've had to tell my parents he and Delilah were in the room together when they weren't supposed to and plus I was just a kid—kids do dumb stuff. I told him over and over it was okay. I didn't realize what I had signed up for though."

Shaw's brawny arms pulled on Tinsley so she was tucked even deeper into his embrace.

"I really thought Vance might own up to it, but he didn't—he told our parents he had no idea what happened. My parents were so grateful for him, they couldn't praise him enough for getting us out of there. I just remember bawling that whole time—I had so many emotions going through me, watching everything around me… I finally blurted out that I was afraid of being in the dark."

She shook her head. "I've never seen my parents so heartbroken. I stuck to my story, that I was scared of the dark and Vance was sleeping so I had lit a candle. I owned that fire and my brother and Delilah watched me do it. I just thought I'd be in trouble for accidentally burning down the place, but then I heard a sound I'll never be able to get out of my head… My mom's friend let out what sounded like a suffering wild animal, it shook me to the deepest parts of my damn soul. That's when we…" Tinsley swallowed hard and fought back tears. She held her face for a long moment while Shaw continued to press feather-soft kisses against her forehead.

"That's when we realized one of the kids wasn't outside with the rest of us."

Shaw let out a noticeable exhale from the pain in his heart for Tinsley—he couldn't hold her tight enough at that moment.

"Honestly, the rest of that night and the following weeks were such a blur." Tinsley wiped her eyes again. "I didn't start school that fall. My parents decided it was best for me to go to a highly specialized school for other delinquents. It wasn't like a correctional facility per say, but it was certainly not any type of finishing school or a mainstream academic establishment. They thought they were doing what was best for me. I couldn't go to any Gig Harbor school with the rumors of what I'd done swirling around me, and I honestly think my parents felt guilty about not seeing like cries for help or whatever they thought I was going through at that time to possess me to light a fire that ended up killing one of our friends."

"Oh, Tins." Shaw kissed her head.

"I was only twelve, and they obviously didn't find any premeditation or anything like that, but my story of lighting a candle to battle off the darkness obviously held when they investigated."

"What did Vance do when they sent you away?"

"Vance and Delilah were already back in school by the time most of the punishment was handed out. They left less than two weeks after the fire. He had a scholarship, a whole life ahead of him… If he confessed he would've been tried as an adult."

"Tins, you gave up your childhood… *your* life for him."

She shook her head. "I didn't realize the full impact of that decision back then. I mean, I turned out okay."

"You turned out perfect."

Tinsley looked up and met his eyes. "Honestly, besides the obvious of losing a friend, I don't know what the worst part about that decision has been. It likely feels the same to have people *think* you killed some-one versus if I had actually done it. For a long time I felt like it *was* me who'd killed her. I know my parents love me, and they're really wonder-ful people, but they haven't looked at me the same since. Vance has done his best, and Delilah… well, she's never acknowledged it. I think she sees it as a Vance deal and not hers. I still don't know which one of them actually lit the candles in the first place, we've never spoken of that night… It took me a very long time to feel like I could emotionally do the whole family gathering thing. My family has never treated me with outright cruelty or anything even close to that, but you can just tell Vance and his family are the trophy kids. I mean, he's a doctor, she's a teacher, they have a perfect kid, they live in the perfect house… and then there's me." She shrugged.

"I just found something I hate more than you apologizing." Shaw held her head with both of his hands and gazed into her eyes. "I don't ever want to hear you discredit yourself. Tinsley, you are *incredible*."

"Are you saying you'll accept all of me? Skeletons and all, Hunt?" Tinsley asked as a tear balanced on her eyelid.

He shook his head. "Not only do I accept every last bit of you, sugar, but I welcome it." Shaw didn't spend any more time discussing it, he connected their lips as he pulled Tinsley toward him. She was more mindful of his injured midsection than he was, but they found themselves in another passionate embrace, souls bared to one another and hearts open.

CHAPTER
Nineteen

AT SOME POINT IN THE EARLY HOURS OF THE MORNING BEFORE THE sun came up, they'd fallen asleep in Tinsley's bed clinging to one another.

"Tins." Shaw gently rubbed Tinsley's side and whispered, "Your phone's going off." He handed her the phone she had left on the nightstand.

She rolled to her back and her hand covered her forehead, taking a deep breath when she saw it was Brindle. She could've sworn she'd put her phone on silent after his texts earlier. "I have to pick up Brindle's call or he'll come over here."

"That's okay, I don't mind if you need to talk to him." Shaw gave her side one more gentle squeeze before she swiped to answer the FaceTime call.

"Hey, Boo!" Brindle more or less shouted into the phone. "Are you still in bed?! What the hell? It's literally two o'clock in the afternoon."

Tinsley shrugged at him. "I was just reading." She made sure to hold her phone in a way that Shaw wouldn't be seen in the frame. She wasn't embarrassed to be with him, she just didn't want to have to explain everything to Brindle.

"Well get your juicy little ass outta bed because you're gonna come pick me up."

She huffed a laugh. "Do you see that I'm still in my pajamas?"

"You can look like a troll, I just need a ride. That shadow daddy lookin' thing wants to catch drinks at Point Ruston and I'm not paying to park, nor am I letting him pick me up."

"Uber!" Tinsley suggested with a smile. "You aren't really going to make me get up because you're too cheap to Uber, are you?"

"Bitch, I need you to bring me a top too—I know you have that mesh thing and it'll look so damn good on me with this." Brindle set his phone down and then backed up for Tinsley to see the full outfit.

"Okay, Brindle—you're a baddie queen." She pumped up her friend, who did a couple mock hairflips for the camera. "You don't need anything else, you look perfect."

"I know I look good, but didn't you hear me?! I said the *SHADOW DADDY* is taking me out. I can't fuck it up by not looking my best."

Tinsley giggled. "Did you not provide me with the proper definition of shadow daddy or something? I thought you said they were supposed to be buff and tough with questionable morals. That guy is definitely not giving any of those vibes—maybe like your weak little shadow second cousin or something. And anyways, I thought you were going to be all butthurt about your date from last night? What happened with all that?"

"*First* of all, bitch, we'll talk about that asshole at work tomorrow. Secondly, maybe sometimes I have the urge to be the man." Brindle shrugged and cocked his head from side to side. "Or maybe we don't all want to have a brute of a man giving us a backwards shoulder ride like you do."

"Brindle!" Tinsley slapped her forehead all too aware of Shaw's silent chuckling next to her. "I've *never* said that."

"Please." Brindle flicked his wrists around, rolling his eyes before his hands flailed about, in sync with every word. "You can see that desire in your eyes, Boo. You're on board for a shadow daddy for sure. Big ol' damn muscles, strong enough to hold you up by your thick, sexy-as-hell thighs to go all *Tinsley Down Under* on you."

Tinsley laughed and thoroughly regretted the fact that she hadn't gotten up and away from Shaw hearing this entire exchange. "I need you to stop talking."

"What the fuck for?" Brindle threw up his hands. "No one's listening. I *wish* your damn phone was tapped right now because you know exactly who I'm talking about with those fuckin' fine-ass muscles. He needs to be taking notes. Hopefully he read that book he got you."

"I'm hanging up on you now." Tinsley could have melted from the heat radiating from her face.

Brindle started dancing—he twerked his bubble butt and then flung one hand in the air and grabbed his ankle with the other. He didn't wait long before he started to sing an improv song: "Shawberry, *uh uh*, Shawberry—that beefy cake ma—"

Tinsley quickly hung up on Brindle and then dropped her hands to her face.

"I swear to God, I want to crawl under a rock right now." She mumbled through her fingers and considered pulling the comforter up over her face.

Shaw was in as much of a belly roar as he could manage while holding his midsection to avoid damaging his stitches. He tried to suppress his volume and his movements when Tinsley's phone rang again. She reluctantly held the phone up over her face before she swiped it to answer, knowing full well it would be worse to have Brindle just drive over to her house.

"Bitch, you hung up on me?!"

"I told you I was going to." Tinsley massaged her temples.

"I was just sayin', Boo." Brindle shook his head.

"You don't need to say anything." She was smiling and giddy but still irritated with her best friend.

"What?! Did he call you?!"

"No!" Tinsley laughed. She wasn't lying either, Shaw had never called her. He'd slept in her bed the last two nights, but hadn't called her once.

"Well, what the hell?" Brindle was putting on eyeliner. "The sexual tension is real, Boo. I need him to move a little quicker before I have an actual chat next time he comes in here claiming to be doing or needing anything other than asking my girl out on a date."

"Brin, why don't you worry about your own date tonight and how you'll be getting there because it's not with me. I'm staying in bed, you know I have an early morning tomorrow, not to mention a long day."

"So, *no* on the mesh top then?"

"I'm not bringing that to you," she shook her head, chuckling. "*Or* driving your lazy self to the waterfront. You can do better than the little shadow friend anyway. I won't sign-off on him, he looks like the type who would chew his own toenails."

"Bitch, ew! You're always so damn critical and have shit to say—it's a wonder you've managed to stay so damn single." He whipped his head around.

"Yeah, well I have to be the critical one since you're willing to let anything touch you these days. You're going to end up with herpesyphilidous or something if *you* don't start being more picky."

"Please," Brindle rolled his eyes. "I'm an educated gay man—not some feral fucking liability. I spread love throughout my community, not disease."

Shaw couldn't help his smirk. Tinsley's speech was similar to that of the thousands he'd given Baz on countless occasions. Brindle seemed just as unphased as Baz did listening to the ways in which he should care more about his health.

"Let me know when you get there and when you get home."

"What if I end up at his place?" Brindle pumped his eyebrows.

"Then definitely don't FaceTime me," she advised.

"Fair." He nodded. "Just know, when you make it to Shawberry's place, you can *definitely* FaceTime me. In fact, I demand that you FaceTime me from there."

"You're the worst." Tinsley hung up.

Tinsley took a deep breath after she tossed her phone to the side of the bed. Both of her hands immediately covered her face again to avoid having to make eye contact with Shaw.

"I'm so sorry," she grumbled.

She didn't even have time to move when Shaw had already rolled to his side and was nearly on top of her.

"Sugar, I've told you—you don't need to apologize."

Tinsley slowly moved her hands and was met with Shaw's smoldering green eyes. He only waited for a split second after her lips were exposed before he leaned down to kiss her. Tinsley put her arms around Shaw's neck and was gently scratching her fingers through his hair when he reached for her leg. He placed it over his hip so they were both on their sides, fitting together like two pieces of a puzzle. Tinsley let him caress her backside a few times before she started to slow down.

"While I'm fully appreciative of every last bit of this, I don't want to mess up your stitches."

Shaw let out a semi-defeated sigh but then shot her a devilish grin. "You're right. I need to not only take you out on a proper date first, but I'd like to have these heal up a bit before the real fun starts."

"Hunt, what kind of girl do you think I am to agree to sleep with you on the first date?" she teased him with a smile.

"The kind who already let me sleep in her bed *twice* now." He winked.

Tinsley blushed. "So, you're gonna take me on a date, huh?"

"That's been my plan. I've just been a pansy-ass about asking you."

Harvey's head popped up and he let out a short, low bark because he'd heard a car pull up next to the house.

"That's probably Vance." Tinsley smiled and motioned to get out of bed.

"Hang on." Shaw lightly tugged on her to stay close.

Tinsley's entire face lit up and Shaw wasted no time in reconnecting their lips.

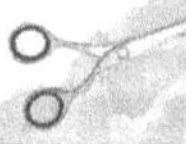

"Are you hungry? Should I make some dinner?" Tinsley offered shortly after Vance left. He strongly encouraged Shaw to stay away from work and any other activities that would require him to move quicker or lift more than an infant would be capable of, no matter how 'fine' he felt.

Shaw sat up taller where he sat on the couch and by the movement, Tinsley could tell his torso was still tender.

"Tins, you've done so much already. I can get out of your hair if you have a routine you need to get back to before work tomorrow."

Tinsley exhaled a brief chuckle. "Has the food I've been serving you been just barely edible? You're ready to run for the hills?"

"No!" Shaw laughed. "No, that's not what I was saying at all." He reached over and rubbed her leg. "Besides almost dying and now these damn stitches, I've been *thoroughly* enjoying myself. I just wanted to be sure I'm not wearing out my welcome."

"Hunt, you're more than welcome to stay again if that's what you want to do." Tinsley held his hand. "You're nowhere near wearing out your welcome."

Shaw leaned closer to Tinsley's face—their mouths nearly touching. "If you're sure about that, then I'd love nothing more than to stay the night with you again."

Tinsley closed the miniscule gap between them and softly pressed her lips against his. Shaw held the back of her head while he escalated their kiss, sliding his tongue along hers. It was his smirk that inevitably slowed their kissing.

"You're more than welcome to come take a seat on my lap," he flirtatiously suggested.

Tinsley giggled as she pulled back. "Well now, Hunter, are you trying to skip some steps and get out of that first date you were teasing me about earlier?"

"I wasn't teasing, sugar." He gently placed a piece of her hair behind her ear.

They looked into each other's eyes for a long moment before Tinsley spoke again.

"You didn't answer me about dinner, tough guy."

"Any chance you wanna take me to get my truck? I can pick us up some dinner once I grab some fresh clothes from home."

"I can bring you to your truck, but you don't have to pick any-thing up."

"Tins." Shaw hooked a finger under her chin and tilted her face up to meet his gaze. "Like I said, you've done a ton. Can't I do this one little thing to help? I promise, I won't count take-out as our date." He grinned.

"Oh, I know—you're too much of a gentleman for that." She winked at him.

Tinsley was putting the finishing touches on her client's beach waves the next day when the salon door opened. She didn't even have to turn around to know who it was when she heard Brindle's welcome screech.

"Ah! Shawberry!"

Harvey galloped over to Shaw as well and encouraged him to bend down when he leaned up against his leg.

"Hey, bud." Shaw lowly bent over and gave Harvey a few healthy pats to his chest and then looked up at Brindle. "Brindle." He tilted his chin down.

Tinsley's cheeks flushed pink when she saw the bouquet Shaw held.

"Good morning." Tinsley smiled.

"Hi, Tins." Shaw stood upright and Tinsley could tell he was still moving a bit slow.

"Ooh, *Tins*." Brindle did a little shimmy and folded another piece of foil onto his client's hair.

"I don't want to interrupt." Shaw raised his free hand.

"Oh, no—you're not interrupting." Tinsley shook her head. "I'm just about to finish up, do you have like two minutes?"

"Absolutely, me and Harvey can hang out." He tilted his head toward the small but chic waiting area in front of the window that was next to Tinsley's station and Harvey's bed. He loved watching her giddy face as she tried her best not to look at him or the flowers he'd brought. He specifically bought the most obnoxiously large bouquet he could find that also had an oversized ribbon attached to the vase. His mind still lingered on Brindle's FaceTime conversation and he wanted to put on a full production for his official date invitation.

Tinsley gave her client a few more tousles of her hair before she walked her to the register to cash her out and schedule her for her next appointment. She waved to her client and walked over to Shaw who was playing a mild game of tug-of-war with Harvey, who didn't even bother to get off the ground.

"Well, what a pleasant surprise, Officer Shaw." Tinsley smirked before catching her bottom lip under her teeth.

Shaw wanted to kiss her right then, she was sweeter than anything he'd ever known. "I'm sorry I got run outta here the other day. I've really been meaning to come by and ask you something, ma'am."

Tinsley was immensely grateful her face wasn't exposed to Brindle, she could feel his eyes on them and knew he was listening to every last syllable. She smiled with her eyes up at Shaw, holding his gaze as the air between them thickened.

Shaw held the bouquet out to her with a knowing grin.

"These are absolutely beautiful." Tinsley admired the blush-color themed arrangement that smelled like she'd been transported to an enchanted garden. She had to hold the vase with two hands because it was so heavy. "Thank you for these."

"You're welcome. I was going for something that could have a chance to compliment that amazingly bright and beautiful smile of yours."

"Ugh!" Brindle squeaked in the background and slapped the back of his hand to his forehead in the most dramatic fashion before he started to fan himself.

Tinsley giggled and couldn't take her eyes off Shaw.

"What time are you off tonight?" Shaw asked, even though he was fully aware when she planned to leave work that night.

"I should be outta here around seven-ish." She smiled.

"I'd love to come pick you up for dinner if you're free… If you're interested."

"I'll take the dog!" Brindle couldn't get the words out fast enough. "I'll watch Harvey, you can go—you're free."

Tinsley and Shaw both laughed, but she didn't turn around to her best friend. "Looks like I'm available."

"And you're interested?" Shaw couldn't help himself, and to make her smile even brighter he flashed one of his very own before reaching for her hand to gently hold it.

She looked down at their hands for a quick second to suppress the gleeful giggle that started and then she looked up at him. "Only if you are, Officer Shaw."

Shaw gave her hand a soft squeeze. "Can I pick you up here, or at your place?"

"Here!" Again, Brindle answered for her. "You can get her from here around eight—she'll be ready."

Tinsley *did* turn around this time. "Brindle!" she playfully scolded him.

"That works for me if you're okay with that, Tins." Shaw reached over and tucked her hair behind her ear.

Tinsley heard Brindle do another fake fainting episode and she flirtatiously rolled her eyes at Shaw, but was unable to stop beaming.

"I'll see you here at eight then."

"I'm looking forward to it."

Shaw wrapped both of his arms around her—pinning the vase between them in a warm embrace. As if Brindle hadn't already been sent over the edge, Shaw doubled down and pressed his lips to the top of Tinsley's head. Before he left the salon he gave Harvey a quick scratch behind his ear and then waved to Brindle who was still picking his jaw up off the floor. Tinsley watched him until she couldn't see him through the window anymore, she didn't even turn all the way around when Brindle was quite literally screaming.

"What the fuck just happened?!" Brindle skipped over to Tinsley with almost enough energy to hit his head on the ceiling.

When Tinsley finally looked at Brindle she still had her bottom lip captured under her top teeth and her face was flushed with color. "I guess I have a date tonight."

CHAPTER
Twenty One

"Y**ou're gorgeous.**" Shaw lifted Tinsley's hand and twirled her when he walked into the salon to pick her up for their first official date. She was in a bohemian smocked midi dress that had a square neckline and short, ruffled sleeves. It was a grayish denim color and while it was flowy overall, it showcased the appealing curves of her body. He shook his head because he'd simply never be able to get over how damn sweet she was.

Tinsley giggled. "Thank you. I knew you'd show up looking all handsome, so I had to be sure to dress the part." She glanced down to the nude slip-on block-heeled strappy sandals she wore.

Shaw drew closer to her face and whispered, "Is Brindle around or do I get to kiss you before we leave?"

"He'll be down any minute," Tinsley warned with a smile, but didn't back away from him.

Shaw gently held her chin and placed a quick peck to her lips before he winked at her.

"Hey, buddy." Tinsley turned around when she heard Harvey galloping into the salon. He ran to her and didn't stop in time to avoid slamming into her leg. Tinsley winced at the feeling of his shoulder ramming her thigh. "That's exactly why I always have that ointment around."

"Oh, big guy, you gotta be careful." Shaw rubbed the top of Harvey's head. "You alright, Tins?"

"I'll be totally fine, it's for sure going to bruise though." She chuckled and gave Harvey a quick scratch on his head. "Where's your Uncle Brindle? You should be off terrorizing the cat."

"Is Shawberry here?!" Brindle sauntered into the salon with his cat in his arms. He had a long-haired all black cat. "Oh!" Brindle gave Tinsley a suggestive look before he gave Shaw a once over. "Uhm, okay, Mr. GQ—is there anything you don't look good in?"

Shaw's face turned red before Tinsley even had time to scold Brindle. Brindle had never seen Shaw in jeans, but he was thoroughly appreciating him in them now. Not to mention his simple, black pocket tee offered the best display of Shaw's muscular chest that Brindle had ever seen.

"You know, I have a photographer friend." Brindle swayed back and forth with his cat now climbing up his shoulder. "Have you ever thought about any modeling? Maybe like an underwear ad or something?"

"Brindle!" Tinsley swatted him this time before covering her face.

Shaw dragged his palm over his mouth, trying not to laugh but failing miserably.

"What?" Brindle shrugged as if what he was suggesting wasn't completely inappropriate. He watched as Shaw reached over to rub Tinsley's lower back. He gawked at his best friend who didn't seem surprised by the touch at all—she looked very much at ease with the placement of Shaw's hand. He'd unpack that later. "Now, let's go over the ground rules for this evening." Brindle set his cat down and then put his palms together. He shot Tinsley a grin that was all mischief and no apology then turned to Shaw.

"Brindle." Tinsley squinted and shook her head.

One corner of Shaw's mouth tipped up as he continued to rub Tinsley's back with the same comforting pace. He waited for Brindle's speech.

"Now, where are you taking my boo? She refuses to share her location with me."

"We have reservations at El Gaucho."

Brindle put his hand on his chest and yelped out in shock. "What?! Shawberry, I had no idea you were so sophisticated." He nodded and glanced at Tinsley. "I knew I shoulda called dibs on this one the second I saw him."

Tinsley rubbed slow circles above her temples and didn't even bother with the typical 'Brindle' groan.

"No offense, Brindle"—Shaw put his hand up—"but I wouldn't have even noticed if you did call dibs that day because Tins eclipsed everything else." He watched as Tinsley turned pink but ended up resting her head on his shoulder. Shaw put his arm around her waist and didn't even think about it before he was leaning down and placing a kiss on the top of her head.

"Did I miss something?" Brindle put his hand on his hip and narrowed his eyes as he pointed back and forth between the two of them. "This isn't looking like date number one behavior in front of my fine-ass eyes."

"Any other ground rules you'd like to embarrass me with?" Tinsley hesitantly asked.

Brindle gave them both another once over with suspicious eyes. "It seems like you've got this all more than handled, Shawberry. But, if you're having trouble with a dessert option, Tins would like an Australian-themed dessert back at home… If you know what I mean." He pumped his eyebrows and looked just below Tinsley's waist.

"Brindle!" Tinsley reached out poked him this time.

Shaw didn't further embarrass Tinsley with a response to Brindle. Instead, he held Tinsley's hand and looked down at her with a smile before he turned his attention to her bestie.

"We'll see you later, Brindle. Thank you for watching Harvey."

Shaw led them out to his truck and Tinsley flipped Brindle off behind her back as they walked away.

"You know what's so nice about all this?" Shaw rubbed Tinsley's leg under the table as they were just about finished with dinner.

"Mmmm?" Tinsley bit her lip and smiled with her eyes at him before answering, "That I get to be here with hands down the most handsome, thoughtful, dreamy date imaginable?"

Shaw chuckled. "Sugar, if I was going down that route I would've just told you it's because I'm here with the most gorgeous, sweetest damn woman imaginable." His hand squeezed her thigh. "But I was going to say it's nice we don't have to have that awkward moment at the end of our date tonight where you're gonna try to kiss me for the first time."

Tinsley slowly shook her head with a smirk. "Our first date must not be going all that well then. I didn't know our date would be ending this evening. I assumed you'd want to be sleeping in my bed again." She shrugged.

Shaw's head fell back and he laughed. "Tins, are you skipping the first date kiss and going straight to an invitation to sleep with you?"

She leaned in closer to Shaw and spoke softly. "If you'd like to sleep in my bed tonight, Hunt, you'll have to be a gentleman and give me a proper first date kiss."

"Oh, it's gonna be the best first date kiss then," he assured her. "Awkward as fuck for sure *and* there will be absolutely no tongue." He put his hand down on the table to gesture that his ruling was final.

"That all tracks." She giggled. "But then you'll have to tell all your friends it was the best first date kiss and lie to them about totally getting all kinds of sloppy tongue action."

"Please." He scoffed. "I'm telling my friends we went all the way."

"You're not going to just tell Baz you got limited to a nice little tickling?" She tried to bite her smile.

Shaw laughed and had to hold his midsection. Once he was able to calm himself down, he looked into her eyes. "Goddamn…" He shook his head. "You're so damn sweet."

He reached his hand out and caressed the side of Tinsley's face with his knuckles. "Is this the appropriate time to be asking you about a second date?"

"You don't want to see how that first kiss feels before you offer up a second date?"

Shaw shook his head. "I already know I'm gonna love it." He reached over and dragged her chair toward his.

Tinsley's eyes widened. "Hunter! You should *not* be putting all that pressure on your stitches."

Shaw smirked. "I think I'm gonna like getting in trouble with you." He put his arm around her.

"I'm being serious." She leaned into him now that they were practically sitting in the same chair.

"And so am I—about you, Tins."

Tinsley was still leaning against Shaw's shoulder but she gazed up at him while placing her hand on his strong thigh.

His face moved in closer to hers and he said softly in his deep voice, "So, how about we do this again and see where it leads?"

"I would really love that, Hunt."

"Good, what are you doing tomorrow night?"

Tinsley scrunched her face. "I actually won't be leaving the salon until around ten tomorrow night. We do this monthly event where a few families from local low-income schools come out and get free hair cuts." Her hand lingered on his leg, thumb tracing the seam of his jeans.

"That's okay." Shaw kissed the side of her head. "You still have to eat dinner—I'll happily bring that to you. I can keep Harv entertained while you finish up work and then we'll hang out at home after your long day."

Tinsley giggled. "Oh, so you think I'm just going to sleep with you all the time now, huh?"

"Hey, you're the one fussing over these stitches. It's obvious I need a night nurse."

"I'll admit, I may have blamed the stitches…" She smirked before their eyes locked. "But I quite enjoy having you in my bed, Hunt."

That disclosure was music to Shaw's ears. He too had enjoyed sleeping with Tinsley the last couple of nights—even if it was truly limited to sleeping and conservative cuddling.

"It was worth every stitch to have me end up with the privilege of sharing a bed with you, sugar."

"Should we head home?"

"Let's go get your car and Harv, then we can all go home." He lifted her chin and softly pressed his lips against hers, grinning when he felt her squeeze his leg a little tighter.

Shaw followed Tinsley up to the apartment above the salon. She had a hold of his hand and all he could focus on was her sweet backside as it swayed side to side while she climbed the stairs in front of him. He had half a mind to reach for it and give her a few playful squeezes, but he thought better than to do that before going in to see Brindle. Harvey barked the second they knocked.

"Oh, Harv—chill your tits," Brindle said as he approached the door to unlock it. "It's just your mom." He opened the door and a huge smile spread across his face. "Oh, and *daddy's* here too." Brindle did a little clapping routine.

Shaw cringed. He not only hated that term as a sexual pet name, but there was also something about it being said by Brindle that made it even worse.

"Brindle." Tinsley sighed and kneeled down to greet Harvey, "Hey, baby boy." She scratched his ears and looked up at Brindle. "Did he do okay tonight?"

"Well, we didn't have any…" Brindle started jerking his body around and violently shaking his head.

"You're definitely going to Hell." Tinsley shook her head and stood. She paused when she saw someone sitting at the little breakfast bar between Brindle's kitchen and living room. "Oh, company?" She blazed right by Brindle with a bright smile on her face.

For the first time ever, Shaw saw what looked like embarrassment cracking on Brindle's face.

"Hi!" She confidently strode over to the nicely dressed Latin man who she was sure Brindle had never sent her pictures of. "I'm Tinsley." She held out her hand.

"Bitch," Brindle mumbled under his breath and then waved Shaw inside.

"Victor," the date replied in a surprisingly deep voice while shaking her hand. Her best friend didn't always go for the more-masculine types.

"Brindle, you didn't tell me you were having company over." She grinned at Shaw, overly excited to have the opportunity to try and embarrass Brindle for once instead of getting the butt-end of all of his inappropriate jokes. "Victor"—she gestured toward Shaw—"this is Shaw."

"Shawberry," Brindle corrected her.

Shaw reached out his hand. "It's nice to meet you."

"You too." Victor eyed Brindle for a split second, making it clear Brindle had already bragged about Shaw and his date was confirming he was as good looking as Brindle's description.

"Would you guys like to join us for a glass of wine?" Victor asked but looked only at Shaw.

"Thank you—" Tinsley started but was cut off by Brindle.

"Normally I'm sure my wine loving girl would take us up on that, but this is their first date. I'm sure they have *other* plans this evening." He suggestively fluttered his eyes at Shaw.

Shaw tried not to laugh when he reached out and put his arm around Tinsley who looked like she wanted to smack Brindle.

"I appreciate the offer, Victor. Maybe next time." She gave her best friend a sickly sweet smile. "I know Brindle would prefer we leave you two for the plans he has."

Brindle sliced her with his eyes but she just kept the smile plastered on her face and waved at both of them.

"Come on, buddy." Tinsley scratched the top of Harvey's head to encourage him to follow her and Shaw out of the apartment. "Thanks, Brin—see you in the morning still, right? Or will you be sleeping in?"

"Bye." He hurried her to the door and gave her a final glare.

They didn't even get halfway down the stairs when Tinsley's phone rattled off text notifications.

Tinsley giggled and held her phone out to Shaw to read. As he was reading, more texts popped up.

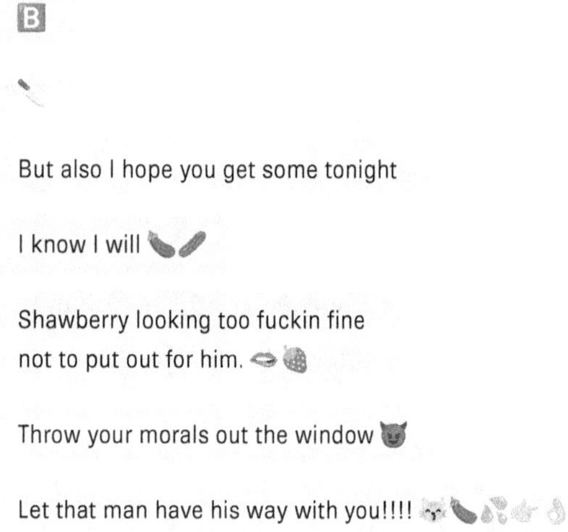

"Oh my gosh!" Tinsley blushed when she realized he'd sent more and Shaw was gleefully reading it. She shoved the phone in her purse and walked out of the building, her face now a special shade of scarlet.

Shaw massaged her shoulder with a devilish grin. "I'm thinking maybe Brindle's not so bad."

Tinsley put her arm under Shaw's and leaned her head against his strong shoulder as he walked her and Harvey to her car. Tinsley's face was hidden from Shaw, but she knew she was projecting the infatuation that was growing for him. Brindle was definitely *that* bad, but she knew what Shaw meant and she loved his sense of humor—in fact, she was loving virtually everything about him lately.

"Should we have our awkward first date kiss right here?" Shaw turned to her and held both of her hands once they reached her 4Runner.

"How about we kiss here, but let's save that awkward first date one for my porch—that seems more fitting. Don't you think?"

"I get *two* kisses?!" Shaw dramatically shook his head. "I'll definitely be telling all the guys."

Tinsley closed the gap between them and fell into the now familiar feeling of Shaw's strong body against hers as their tongues danced.

Once they had their teeth brushed and were in pajamas, Shaw and Tinsley got comfortable in her bed. They were still giggling about the awkward kiss they'd shared on the porch—it exceeded any predictions and expectations they'd had for the perfect first date kiss. In their dramatics, with closed eyes, Shaw ended up running his mouth into the bridge of Tinsley's nose and then she'd practically spit on him from the laugh she had tried to suppress when it happened.

"Now I don't have to lie to all my friends when I let them know I made it to your bed on our first date." Shaw put his arm around Tinsley as they laid on their sides facing one another.

"I'll allow it." She tilted her head up and pecked him. "But only because that first date kiss was obviously the best I've ever had. I can't wait to tell Brindle—he's gonna be so jealous."

Shaw laughed. "He has his own company to brag about tomorrow."

"Honestly, I was a little surprised by his friend," Tinsley admitted. "Not only is this the first time in a year he hasn't sent me a picture and screenshot of the profile for any guy he's ever met up with, but he invited him over to his place—which is rare. *And* he seemed a bit too… normal? I don't know the word, but definitely not Brindle's usual type."

Shaw started rubbing his hands up and down Tinsley's back as he held her. "Oh yeah?" He chuckled. "What's Brindle's usual type?"

"Besides you, Shawberry?" Tinsley teased.

Shaw squeezed her and gently nibbled at her neck to showcase his playful irritation for that comment.

"No," she giggled. "Brindle usually dates the eccentric types—you know, wild clothes and crazy different aesthetics. Plus, I don't think I've met any that don't have a voice at least eight octaves higher than Brindle's. This one seemed all put together and such. So, I'm actually hopeful. Usually I'm telling him ten different reasons his dates aren't for him. I wouldn't have been able to say one thing about Victor. He seemed nice."

"How long have you known Brindle?"

"We've known each other for around six years now—we met at beauty school." She smiled up at Shaw. "He was the little emo looking hot mess who decided I was going to be his best friend and he hasn't let me escape since."

"I guess I could see him rocking the emo look." Shaw decided with a smile on his face.

Tinsley laughed, remembering how far Brindle had come with establishing his current style. "He was a frail little thing that was out, but not out-out. His parents have never fully accepted his lifestyle, so I met him when he was teetering on the decision to appease them or to simply embrace the unique and mostly wonderful being that he is."

"He must've seen what a sweet soul you have and knew you'd be worth capturing." Shaw placed a kiss on top of Tinsley's head.

"I think we needed each other. Brindle and I had a drunken night early on after we met where we dished out most of our secrets. I was technically living with my parents at that time, but stayed with Brindle in his tiny apartment more often than not. Before starting at the salon academy, I'd just come back from a transition facility of sorts that my parents were convinced I needed to be in just to make sure I wasn't going to be a menace to society. It was nicer than the place I spent my high school years, but it was a little sketchy because I'd just been a naive kid who confessed to arson and I was surrounded by people who were legitimately recovering from drug and alcohol addictions. I didn't want to go. I had graduated from a barber program while I was still in high school classes, but my parents weren't buying all that as a suitable life-style for me and sent me off again."

Tinsley took a moment to gather her thoughts and then said, "So, after that, I managed to convince them I wanted the career I have now and they let me enroll at the academy where I met Brindle. Once I was there I realized how much I needed to not be around my parents all the time—I needed to figure life out kind of on my own without their constant suggestions. I told Brindle about my childhood. I just left out the part about how I wasn't actually responsible for the fire—so he doesn't know all of it. That night he vowed we were broken besties and would be together for life."

Tinsley snuggled closer to Shaw so her head was on his chest just under his chin before she continued. "Brindle was in a prison of sorts himself as a kid because he comes from a very Catholic family who tried to send him off a few times to 'cure the gay,' as he puts it. In the six years that I've known Brindle I've only met his parents three times—they didn't even come to our graduation. I'm sure they aren't fans of mine because I encourage—well, mostly encourage—Brindle to be who he is. He could use a good filter on his mouth from time to time as I'm sure you've noticed, but he truly is a good person and I admire his confidence and zest for life. Not to mention you'll *never* find a better hype queen."

Tinsley's fingers flexed and released Shaw's sturdy chest. "He does have the dopest aunt and uncle around, but I know his relationship with his parents still hurts him."

"I'm glad your paths crossed." Shaw gave her a gentle squeeze. "I'm sure meeting each other really helped both of you."

"I know he's a lot sometimes, but that's the feistiest bestie you could ever hope to have in your corner. He's also a reminder of sorts that even if you start in a tiny little pot, in the darkest shadows, with the worst kinda dirt, you can still grow into the most beautiful flower in *allllllll* the gardens." She smiled.

"I already told you, I don't think Brindle's so bad." Shaw smirked and gently placed a piece of Tinsley's hair behind her ear. "You didn't have to convince me he's a good one. I'd be okay if he *never* referred to me as daddy again, but otherwise he's alright."

"Trust me." Tinsley laughed. "I was ready to puke in my mouth when he said that tonight and that was *nothing* against you. I don't get the whole daddy thing. It grosses me out and Brindle is constantly using it with his dates."

Shaw smiled, relieved he'd likely never have Tinsley attempting to turn him on with his least favorite pet name.

"Plus," Tinsley continued, "I think Shawberry is here to stay—it's just too good."

"I'm confident enough to roll with Shawberry from Brindle," he assured her. "I also think I can rely on you to save me if he ever gets too aggressive."

"Yeah." Tinsley's arm slid its way along Shaw's side so she could hold him as she leaned into him. She spoke just as their lips were about to connect, "I don't think I'd do well sharing you."

"That's okay, because I have no interest in sharing when it comes to you." He closed the tiny gap she'd left and pressed his lips to hers. They grew more heated, consuming each other when Shaw reached for Tinsley's leg to pull it over his hip.

Tinsley giggled against his lips. "Hunter, we've talked about this…"

"Just making sure you didn't change your mind." A sly grin took over his face before he lowered his head and kissed the base of Tinsley's neck.

She held her breath, trying to rein in the tingling fervor making its way through her body when his tongue explored her collarbone. "The only thing that hasn't changed is the status of those stitches."

Shaw took a deep breath and put a little distance between their bodies, fondly looking into Tinsley's eyes as he held her face. "Let's try to get some sleep then."

"Deal."

"Sweet dreams, Tins."

"Goodnight, Hunt."

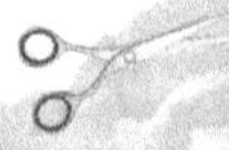

Harvey poked his head over the bed and set his chin on the mattress. It was well after four in the morning. It didn't take Tinsley long to sense her loving four-legged companion softly wagging his short tail to wake her up for a bathroom break. She slowly opened her eyes and was met with Harvey's handsome, one-eyed stare.

"Hey buddy," she whispered with a smile. "Do you need outside?" She rubbed the side of his face.

Tinsley felt the arm Shaw had draped around her waist as it gently squeezed her. "I'll get up with him, sugar—you stay warm and cozy."

She reached down for his hand and intertwined their fingers. "I appreciate that, but I don't mind. This is a pretty normal thing for him." Tinsley turned her head to brush her lips against Shaw's before rolling out of bed.

Harvey was circling one of his many favorite spots in the backyard as Tinsley watched from the deck when Shaw joined them. He walked up behind her and put his arms around her waist to hold her from behind.

"You didn't want to stay warm and cozy?" She smiled as she put her hands on top of his and leaned into his embrace.

Shaw smiled and leaned down to whisper in her ear, "I can't be cozy if you're not in there. Plus, I don't like you out here in the dark alone."

"Harvey's out here," Tinsley assured him, but loved that he had such a protective nature.

"He's preoccupied." Shaw kissed her neck as he massaged her hips.

Tinsley giggled. "Seems like both of you are preoccupied." She only let him continue his sequence a couple of times before she spun around to face him. Shaw pressed his lips to hers even before she was able to get her arms around his shoulders. They went back and forth with their mouths dancing a few times before Tinsley slowed.

"This is getting pretty dangerous." She smirked and hovered over his lips.

Shaw grinned back lazily as he grazed her lips again. "You know I'm not afraid of a little danger."

Tinsley reached up and lightly ran her nails through the short hair on the back of his head. "Oh, I know, tough guy—that's part of your appeal." She quickly bit her bottom lip.

Just when I thought she couldn't get any damn sweeter, Shaw thought as his heart swooned. He reached down and cupped her plump backside. "How can I manage this danger then? I need you to feel safe with me."

"I do feel safe with you, Hunt." She peered up at him before she hesitantly continued. "The danger is in falling for you… It's only our first date and I'm starting to expect this every night now. You staying with me, waking up in your arms, kissing you throughout the night…"

"Sugar." Shaw hooked a finger under her chin and tilted her face up to meet his eyes. "We're just getting started."

Tinsley's face lit up just before she reached on her tiptoes to connect their lips again. Shaw took the opportunity to lift her by her backside. The attempt had Tinsley immediately squirming and she stopped their kiss.

"*Hunter!*" She giggled. "Let's not rip out all your stitches—you've got some healing to do."

"Ah shit…" Shaw let out a frustrated breath and agreed to set her back down. "These damn stitches are gonna be the death of me." He grabbed a lock of Tinsley's hair. "You have any magical ointment to speed up this healing time?"

Tinsley leaned in close enough to graze his lips. "I sure wish I did."

"You're not making this any easier, Tins," he accused and went back to fondly squeezing her cheeks.

CHAPTER
Twenty Two

"**S**PILL THE DAMN TEA, BITCH! YOU HATER-BUTTONED ME TWICE last night! I almost drove to your place, you're lucky I was trying to be nice." Brindle was full of energy and wanted every last detail about Tinsley's date.

Tinsley laughed. "Let's start with *your* evening—tell me why I found a nice Latin man in your apartment who you've never mentioned."

"Shawberry stayed the fucking night! Didn't he?!" Brindle excitedly hopped up and down, completely ignoring her question about his date.

Tinsley's face flushed and she noticed Farrah was also hanging on to every last word. "Brin, you know me better than to be touching cookies on a first date situation." It was the most honest thing she could say out loud without having to disclose that Shaw spending the night had been a pretty regular thing as of late and their first official date night was no exception.

"Something is *severely* wrong with you if you didn't bend the rules for Shaw-fuckin-berry!"

Farrah shook her head laughing. "Tins, I'm with Brindle on this one."

"See, bitch!" Brindle slapped his hands on his thighs. "*Tell* me you gave him *something*! Or fucking got something!"

Tinsley was setting up her station and leaned down to give Harvey a good scratch when he made his way over to her to see if there was anything he'd be able to help with. Her face was more pink than *Barbie's Dreamhouse,* but she bravely turned and faced Brindle. "We kissed… a lot…" She giggled.

"Ahh! Boo!" Brindle skipped over to her. "Okay, that's a start. I know you're a little more reserved than I am." He patted her on her shoulders. "I'll give you that, but you need to dive in head first with this one."

"Tins, Brindle's right." Farrah shook her head with a wistful grin. "Men that look like Shaw are a rarity—hang on tight to that one, girl."

"Is he a good kisser?" Brindle bit his lip.

"No." Tinsley shook her head and then beamed with a bright smile. "He's a *phenomenal* damn kisser." She laughed as her friends squealed.

"Shawberry!" Brindle sang when he walked through the salon doors seconds after their giddy laughter had subsided.

"Brindle." Shaw raised a hand like he always did to wave at his biggest fan. He was stopped by Harvey who danced around his feet, knowing full well what Shaw had in his hands. "Hey, bud." Shaw held Harvey's treat down for the dog to take. After Harvey was well on his way to his bed, Shaw looked up and saw Tinsley watching him.

"Good morning." She smiled.

Shaw closed the gap between them and then cupped the side of her face before he kissed her forehead. "Good morning. I figured you may not have had time to pick up your coffee before work."

"You'd know if she didn't have time to get her coffee this morning. Didn't you two just wake up together?" Brindle was going to get the information one way or another, even if he had to play a little dirty.

Shaw had been developing a good game plan to deal with Brindle and his outspoken personality so he just shrugged. "Brindle," he said as he leveled his gaze. "I'm a gentleman."

"Oh, I see." Brindle rolled his eyes. "You assholes already practiced your story."

Tinsley rested her head on Shaw's chest as he wrapped his arms around her. They both gave Brindle no more than matching smirks.

"Shawberry, you're lucky I like your beefcake ass." Brindle situated a few tools on his workstation to prepare for his first client of the day.

Shaw squeezed Tinsley and then placed a kiss on the top of her head before he responded. "Actually, Brindle, how'd *your* date go last night?"

Tinsley and Farrah tried to suppress their squeals while they stared at Brindle for his answer.

Brindle whipped his head around and then shook a round brush at Shaw. "Like hell if you get to know all that when you won't even admit you slept over at my girl's place."

Shaw shrugged and diverted his attention back to Tinsley who was still clinging to him from under his arm. "I'll be back with dinner later, sugar."

"Thank you." She smiled up at him.

"Text me with what you guys feel like eating and I'll grab it."

"Have a good day, tough guy."

"You too, Tins." Shaw held her chin to give her a parting kiss.

"Bye, Farrah." He waved before catching Brindle's attention. "Brindle." Shaw smirked.

"Shawberry." Brindle cocked his head and offered a wiggling fingers-style wave.

Brindle didn't even wait for the door to shut before he started in on Tinsley. "BOO!" He grabbed her shoulders. "Pet names already?! I swear, I missed something…" He narrowed his eyes at her.

Tinsley didn't offer any indication on her face that she'd be sharing. "Let's talk about Victor," she suggested with a smile.

"Oh, that's gonna be my next boyfriend for sure." Brindle flung his hand around nonchalantly and squatted for product from a bottom shelf in his station.

"What?!" Tinsley whipped her head around. "*I'm* the one who missed something, clearly. Boyfriend?! Brin, you never even sent me his pic. Did you meet him on the app?"

"Nope." Brindle sassily shook his head. "He works with Uncle Frank. So, we exchanged numbers and all of a sudden he's driving down to hang with me."

"For the night?" Tinsley smirked.

"Wouldn't you like to know, you gatekeeping bitch."

Tinsley laughed and left it at that because she wasn't willing to say anything else about whether or not she had her own sleepover. She'd give him any other detail of their date, but he was right—she'd gatekeep the sleeping arrangements.

Hey Tough Guy 😈🖤 why don't you let me know what you want and I'll call the order in so it's ready when you get there? Brindle's order is OBNOXIOUS 🙄🙋 I'd hate for you to have to repeat it lol. 😷 🤡

🖤Hunt💪
Whatever you wanna do. But I'm still buying.

That's sweet of you 😈🖤 but you do realize that means Brindle is going to be bragging about how his fave beefcake bought him dinner, right?? 😷 🤡

🖤Hunt💪
Everyone already knows who I have a crush on. And anyways I've got enough confidence to buy another man dinner and not feel any attachments about that. Lol

I hope it's me you're crushin' on 😍🖤 I've got bruises all over from falling so dang hard for you Hunt 😆🖤

🖤Hunt💪
I've got some ointment I'll happily rub all over you. 😏

Goddamn, she's got me using fucking emojis now. Shaw laughed at himself but felt the emoji was appropriate.

When are those stitches coming out again?? 😷 🖤

🖤Hunt💪
LOL damn. Not soon enough sugar.

It was organized chaos when Shaw stepped into the salon that night. It was pretty crowded—he counted at least twenty different school-aged children and about a dozen adults, but Harvey still managed to run around like a small puppy playing with a few of the kids. There were extra chairs scattered throughout the salon and three stylists cutting hair that Shaw had never seen. He looked around and noticed Tinsley was at the sink washing a little girl's hair. She had her back to him and hadn't seen him walk in yet, but Brindle sure did.

"Shawberry!" Brindle waved as he worked on taming a young boy's shaggy hair. "Thanks for dinner." He winked.

Shaw turned red, he didn't want everyone in the salon thinking he'd brought his boyfriend dinner.

"No problem." He shook his head. "Should I just put this all in the back?"

"Your girl's over at the sink, you can ask her what she's doing with hers, but mine's okay to put back there though."

"Hey, Hunt." Tinsley had just wrapped a towel around the little girl's hair when she noticed Shaw walking up to her. "Honey, you want to hop in my chair and I'll be right over?" Tinsley rubbed the girl's shoulders before she nodded and followed Tinsley's instructions.

"Hi, Tins." Shaw leaned down and pecked her. "Do you want me to stick all this in the back for now?"

"Would you mind?"

"Not at all," he assured her.

"Are you hungry now?"

"I can wait and eat with you, is there anything I can help with?"

Tinsley chuckled. "Not a lot I'd actually ask you to do. Harvey could probably use a bit of a break, do you mind seeing if he wants to go outside? We've been a bit busier tonight than usual."

"I've got him, you just get back to your patient little client over there and I'll catch up after taking Harvey for a walk."

Tinsley squeezed his forearm. "Thank you." She waited for his lips to reach hers again and then got back to work.

Shaw watched as Tinsley treated each of the kids she had in her chair like her most important, highest-paying clients. He loved seeing the smile on her face, he could have sat and watched her radiant beauty all night. The seemingly endless rotation of clients finally dwindled and the only stylists left were Brindle and Tinsley—and Brindle had just finished up a buzz cut.

"Shawberry." Brindle lowered his voice when he approached Shaw, who was sitting on a blush velvet chair in the waiting area with Harvey's head in his lap. "I need to chat at you for a second." He glanced back to be sure Tinsley was still preoccupied with the cut she was doing.

"Sure, what's up?" Shaw nodded and prepared himself for another suggestive and likely inappropriate string of comments that Brindle always managed.

"Not sure if you know, but it's my girl's birthday in sixteen days."

Shaw whipped his head toward Brindle. "Oh shit, thank you—I didn't know that."

"Bitch is about to be twenty-eight. So, not a milestone, but still worth celebrating."

Shaw grinned and looked over at Tinsley who was now beginning to curl a red haired girl's freshly-cut locks. Tinsley was giggling along with the girl and fully immersed in whatever she was telling her.

"I like to take her out for a little ladies' night and all, but that's always the day *after* her birthday. Now I figure I need to ask the boss what he has planned for her…" Brindle set one hand on his hip and gestured the other toward Shaw. "Seeing as you didn't even know her birthday was coming up, I suppose you don't have a plan yet."

"I'm guessing you'll help me a bit, huh?" Shaw flashed the winning smile he used when the chief made him and Baz do social media campaigns.

Brindle rolled his eyes. "Only because you're such a damn beefcake."

Shaw's face blushed the same color pink as the chair he sat in—like it always did when Brindle offered compliments that Shaw didn't actually want.

"I'm plenty capable of doing something special for my girl, don't get me wrong, but are there any traditions I need to be mindful of when I'm planning?"

"The parental units always insist on a stuffy dinner out somewhere on her actual birthday." Brindle's lips pulled to one side as he grimaced. "So, don't get any ideas of taking her to dinner that night. Also, she's scheduled to work on her birthday this year because it's on a Friday and she never takes her actual birthday off unless there's a good reason. I already checked the books and she's got a couple clients that day—she won't cancel."

"Does she ever take trips with Harvey? Or does he need to stay close to home?"

Brindle put his hand on his chest with a dramatic gasp. "Shawberry, are you really considering a getaway?"

"Too much?"

"Taking her away means my girl's *definitely* in for a little birthday sex, huh? She's been one stingy bitch on the topic of where you two slept last night." Brindle pumped his eyebrows before plopping his elbows on the table and resting his chin on his fists. "At least I know who the weaker link is now. She put out on the first date, didn't she?

"Brindle." Shaw tried not to laugh at Brindle's expressions—he wanted to be sure to establish a clear boundary for him.

"Oh my." Brindle clutched his imaginary pearls. "So, we really haven't given my girl a little pickle-tickle yet, huh?"

Shaw lost it and cracked up trying to be mindful of his torso compressing on his stitches. He wasn't sure if Tinsley disclosed the whole 'Tickle-Me Tinsley' story to Brindle.

"You and I won't *ever* be having any kind of girl talk," Shaw finally managed to say.

Brindle huffed. "I thought we were becoming friends."

Shaw chuckled. "We are, but I'm a gentleman. You wanna have any of those details you'll have to pry them from Tins."

"Like I said, she's been a stingy bitch with those details." Brindle rolled his eyes.

In any other scenario Shaw would be more or less violently demanding an apology for the continued 'bitch' references toward Tinsley, but Brindle didn't say or mean it in a way that Shaw needed to worry about—it was said with an odd sort of affection. He let their quirky love fly and only shrugged at Brindle.

They both watched Tinsley with the final client of the night. She knew this child was likely headed straight for bed when she got home but it didn't stop her from curling every last strand of her thick red hair.

"You said she's a big fan of wine, right?" Shaw remembered Brindle's comment in front of Victor the night before.

Brindle dramatically rolled his head around indicating that she was. "Yes, but she's not a red girlie. I mean, she'll try them, but they don't really do much for her. Her faves are in the pinot and riesling families but she'll also happily take a good chardonnay and the occasional rosé."

"Thank you." Shaw nodded, taking mental notes of all Brindle's insights. "And what about Harv? Is he okay with extended car rides?"

"You *are* thinking of a getaway?!"

"Shhh." Shaw checked to see if Tinsley was looking at them, which she wasn't.

"Sorry!" Brindle made a zipping motion over his mouth. "Harvey is a road warrior though."

Shaw nodded again, his mind racing. He had a few ideas already and couldn't wait to get started.

CHAPTER
Twenty Three

SHAW AND TINSLEY CONTINUED PLAYING HOUSE THE NEXT COUPLE of days. She didn't mind that he'd slowly been bringing a few things over to her place, or that he spent time at her house while she was at work. He was pretty limited to what he was able to do since the gym and visiting criminals were his normal go-to activities when he wasn't working. With Vance's recommendation, he wasn't able to do either of those things.

The last thing he wanted to do was prolong the stitches because Tinsley was insistent he fully heal before their physical relationship progressed from its current state. He reluctantly agreed, understanding how upsetting it'd been for her to see him injured the night he'd shown up at the salon. The stitches didn't stop him from suggestively offering more virtually every time they touched though.

Shaw had already bored himself beyond all belief by going to the gym and slowly walking on the treadmill as if he was a few decades older than he was. Despite his better judgment, curiosity got the better of him and he'd picked up the book Tinsley was reading. He was *definitely* embarrassed he had purchased the second book when he read a few of the smutty parts the first one had to offer. He could only imagine how the next one would escalate if it was Brindle's favorite. As he cracked open the second book his phone notified him of a text so he sat up on the couch to grab it off the coffee table.

He wasn't surprised Baz reached out. In the last couple of days, Shaw managed to reduce text topics with his buddy to general sports commentary. That tactic crumbled because Shaw hadn't called in sick to work for years and he'd been out for two days now beyond their weekend. He knew his initial excuse of being exhausted wouldn't last all week.

Baz was clearly gleeful at the thought of his celibate friend having anything like that. But it certainly wasn't like him to call off work two days in a row.

Baz
Oh shit! Is that why ur "sick"?!?! 😆

Baz
Okay I see you Shaw!

Good for you fam. That's my fuckin boiiiiiii 🖤

But also ur a dick for leaving me with Crusty Karl.

This mother fucker is getting his flaky skin all over
our damn car. Ur cleaning that shit when you come
back now that I know ur not on your deathbed.

Don't get me fuckin started on the number of
times I got stuck with him when you couldn't get
out of some chick's bed, including Big-Titties.

Baz
Oh so ur really not sick?! Just tired from all that time
you been spending getting tickled in bed huh?

I JUST started talking to her. Be real bro.

Baz
Like ridin a bike fam just gotta get on. 🚴

You know I'm a gentleman. Not like your horndog ass.

Baz
Trust me ur gonna be changing your tune real
damn quick.

I won't call her Tickle Me anymore though. 😆

Better fuckin not because I'll admit it's that official.

B_{AZ}
Shiiiiiiiiiit. Let's goooooo!!!!!!!!!!

You let me know when I need to stop
referring to your "friend" as Big-Titties

B_{AZ}
I was hoping to see you at work yesterday
cuz we did officially go on a date.

How'd that go?

B_{AZ}
Going on another one tonight. So I guess not that
bad huh?

I'm sorry about the Big-Titties comment earlier then.

B_{AZ}
I don't give a shit lol You do need to meet her tho.
She's fun

Well damn I'm sorry I was so opposed to you
taking her on a date. I'm happy for you bro.

B_{AZ}
Pump the goddamn brakes lol I said she's fun.
We're having fun.

Okay I'm happy your big ass is having fun then.

B_{AZ}
Since your ass isn't actually sick do you wanna link up?

I thought you had a date tonight?

B_{AZ}
Not tomorrow tho she works

Yeah lemme talk to Tins

Baz
Oh you got a boss already?! 🙂

Fuck off lol

She works tomorrow but not tomorrow night. Actually
let's do brunch then ur off tomorrow anyway.

Baz
Fam I got a date with her TONIGHT I'll still be in her bed
around the brunch hour

Okay look who has a damn boss already.

Baz
Big Daddy can't be leaving that bed to meet a buddy.

I don't wanna hear that shit.

Baz
😈

I'll see your big ass at 2 then. Meet at the Loose Wheel?

Baz
Deal

CHAPTER
Twenty Four

"Hey, fam," Baz greeted Shaw when he sat down at their usual Loose Wheel table.

"Hey." Shaw reached his fist out in return.

"So." Baz smirked as he clasped his hands and looked at his partner. "How's the tickling?"

Shaw tried not to laugh and offered a hand gesture in response.

"Fam." Baz leveled his gaze across the table. "You missed a week of work, you're not taking *any* O.T. that I saw, and you're still gonna sit there and act like you ain't done shit?!" He barked out a disbelieving laugh. "Were you fuckin' pulling my leg that you've even talked to her?!"

"No!" Shaw laughed. "We've definitely been seeing each other."

"So?"

"So, what?"

Baz rolled his eyes. "Alright, this is the mature, private, and *sprung* Shaw then. I see you. You don't wanna tell me *anything* about what's been goin' down though?"

"I stopped by the salon a few days ago and asked her on a date." Shaw shrugged with a grin. "We've been hanging out since."

"Hanging so much she's at work right now but your ass still can't show up? Fuckin' leaving me with Crusty Karl all goddamn week."

Shaw wasn't ready to tell Baz the truth about why he hadn't been at work. He knew it was a conversation they needed to have sooner than later, but he held his tongue on that subject.

"Why don't you tell me about you and *Tilly* since she's so much fun these days?" Shaw dodged the topic of him and Tinsley for now.

Baz took a deep, reluctant breath, but then smirked before he began. "We've been *hanging out*," he mocked, creating air quotes with his large fingers. "Obviously a lot of the same shit we been doin', but I started taking her on dates."

"Is this the mature, private, and sprung Baz?" Shaw teased, mocking him right back.

"Fuck no." Baz chuckled. "She's *fun*."

Shaw nodded before taking a drink.

"Where'd you take little Tickle M—Where did you take Tinsley?" Baz corrected.

Shaw smiled at the lingering nickname that would likely follow his interest for a while. "Our first date was El Gaucho."

"What?! Damn, fam." Baz took a few healthy nods. "You better fuckin' hop back on some overtime soon."

"Please." Shaw's brows furrowed but he shook his head, laughing.

Baz eased up on the topic of Tinsley and instead commented on the game that was playing across from them on a large screen near the bar. The best friends were happy to spend time with one another again.

"What're you doin' under there, tough guy?" Tinsley got home after work that night to find Shaw under the sink in the mudroom.

Shaw waited for Tinsley to pop her head under the cabinets. He flashed his smile when he finally caught her gaze.

"Well, the sink was dripping, but then when I got under here to fix it I noticed you had a bit of a leak in the pipe and some drywall missing too."

"Hunt." Tinsley kneeled down next to him. "You don't have to do all this." She smiled and set her hand on his leg. "But thank you."

"You're welcome. I can't imagine you hang out under here a ton." He finished slapping a bit of mud on the wall before he slid out from under the sink. "I'll finish it up tomorrow after this dries."

Tinsley leaned in to press her lips against his and as she did she lovingly tightened her hold on his leg.

Shaw took the opportunity to prolong their kiss and was soon holding the side of her head. He leaned her back until they were on the floor with half of Shaw's body lying on top of her. Tinsley giggled when she felt Shaw's hand rubbing along her sides and catching the bottom of her shirt.

"Is this the form of payment you accept for these repairs, tough guy?"

Shaw chuckled. "Sugar, you never have to pay me for anything like this."

"I'd like to though." She continued sliding her tongue against his and lightly tugged on his shirt.

"I can think of a few forms of payment I'd like to try out, if that's the case," Shaw spoke softly just above her lips.

She was giggling again before she replied, "Oh, Hunter." She blew out a breath and ran her nails up and down the back of his neck. "What am I going to do with you and those stitches of yours that are ruining all your plans?"

"Again"—his devilish grin curled higher—"I can think of a few things."

Tinsley turned to her side and continued to gently roll Shaw so he laid on his back. She bit her bottom lip and straddled him for a split second before placing her hands on either side of him to help push herself up off the ground. She stood, reaching down to help him up.

Shaw wiped his hands on his face, chuckling at the *almost* progression he'd been begging for.

"Well, now I know you've got a sour side too," he jested. "I prefer my sugar sweet, just so you know."

"I'll try to keep that in mind once those stitches are out." She winked as he gripped her offered hands and allowed her to help hoist him up to join her.

Shaw pecked her forehead and rubbed his hands up and down her back while Tinsley took comfort in resting her head on his chest.

"How was your day?" she asked.

"Pretty good… Significantly better since you got home though."

Tinsley lifted on her tiptoes to place a soft kiss on his lips.

"How was yours?"

"Long." She chuckled. "But this is my second favorite part of the day so far."

"Oh yeah? What was your favorite?"

She gazed up at him. "Waking up next to you."

He couldn't resist connecting their mouths again. He caught her bottom lip between his and tugged gently. They went back and forth a few times before Shaw slowed down.

"I've got a little something to tell you." He reached for her backside and gave her a few flirty squeezes.

"Something to compete with my favorite things from the day?" She guessed, a smile taking over her face.

"I do think I've got something that'll be a worthy favorites competitor." He brushed her hair behind her ear. "Do you have plans for your upcoming weekend?"

"Like the actual weekend or like my work weekend?"

"Your work weekend—the one before your birthday." He winked.

Tinsley's head fell and lightly hit his chest to hide a smile.

"Yeah, I know all about that special day coming up." He kissed the top of her head. "And if you and Harvey are up for it, I'd love to take you guys somewhere for a couple days."

"Hunt?" Tinsley peered up at him. "Are you serious?"

"Of course I am." He reluctantly removed his hands from her perfect rear-end to slide them up and down her back. "I heard you've already got birthday night plans *and* post-birthday plans so I figured I should slide in there with pre-birthday plans. I want to be the first to celebrate you."

"And Harvey can really come?"

Shaw laughed and his hands gravitated back to his favorite spot. "Absolutely, I've made sure he's going to be more than welcome." He gently swayed them as they held each other.

"Thank you." She stood on her tiptoes again to meet his lips. "That's so sweet of you and I'm already so excited. What can I help with?"

"Nothing." He grinned against her mouth. "You just pack your bags, sweetcheeks. We leave Sunday and we'll be back Tuesday."

TINSLEY SAW HER PHONE LIGHT UP AS SHE WAS WORKING ON A BLOW-out a couple days later. Her client was the type who didn't mind phone interruptions, since she had plenty of her own, so Tinsley checked it.

Brotherrrr

Hey Tins, have you seen your officer "friend" lately?

Maybe… Why?? What's up??

Brotherrrr

I just wanted to check in. I should probably see if I can remove those stitches on his back. Assuming he didn't go and do that himself already. 🤨

I also have to assume he's gone back to work. Which wouldn't be at my recommendation, but I can check him if he wants.

Thank you Vance—I'll text him. Are you free tonight??

Brotherrrr

Yep. Just let me know.

Tinsley put her phone down and decided she'd reach out to Shaw once she was finished with her client.

"Sir…" Shaw held the bridge of his nose, irritated that they were still on this call. He and Baz had been monitoring and unsuccessfully trying to resolve a dispute between neighbors for nearly twenty minutes. "My partner and I don't want to have to take you in, put the box cutter down."

The neighbors had been arguing about where each of them was entitled to park between their houses in poorly-defined driveways. When Shaw and Baz showed up the two were already wrestling each other; they'd had to physically intervene to get them to stop. It hadn't taken much, they'd simply grabbed each man by their collar and were able to restrain them from one another.

The men were taking turns shouting at each other and then one of them brandished a weapon. The man had pulled a blade from a pocket in his cargo shorts. Just as the man considered putting his small weapon away, the other man pulled a pocket knife from his pants.

Baz eyed Shaw when the man was waving it around and they both had to bite back their smirks. The knife looked more like a nail file than any kind of threatening weapon.

Shaw gave Baz their unspoken signal that he'd had enough of the shit show, but before Baz could begin his tough cop routine the men were going at each other again—this time with a glorified nail file and a worn down box cutter.

"You got blue jeans?" Baz asked Shaw.

"Yeah, you take sweatpants over there," Shaw confirmed.

The men were swinging wildly at each other and somehow in their complete lack of any combat skills they both ended up on the ground again. Another squad car pulled up as Baz and Shaw separated the men again.

"Dammit!" Shaw grabbed blue jeans with a little more force after getting grazed by his crusty box cutter.

"Officer!" The man immediately dropped his box cutter, stunned. "I didn't mean to, I'm sorry." He scrambled for words, now in fear of being arrested.

"Quit fucking squirming around and lay your ass face down on the ground." Shaw spoke with a stern harshness and put the man in cuffs.

"You good, fam?" Baz asked as he restrained the man they'd called sweatpants.

"Yeah, just a damn cut."

"I'm sorry," the man begged from the ground now.

Shaw inspected his bleeding forearm, it wasn't too deep of a cut but enough that a regular band-aid wasn't going to cover it.

Two additional officers walked up to the scene. "Everything all good over here?"

"Fucking lover's quarrel." Shaw rolled his eyes.

Baz gave a deep chuckle as he held the other man in place. "Go get that cleaned up, fam. We got this," he encouraged Shaw.

Shaw was already irritated and getting cut only increased that feeling. He took his partner's advice and headed for the patrol car to wipe the knick clean and at least cover it. When he got to the car he felt his phone buzz.

Pump the brakes tough guy! He said the ones
on your BACK.

A guy can dream.

Well, dreamer, he also said he hopes you're not
back at work yet. Can't wait until he finds
out you're not only at work, but you got hurt again.
I need to see this new cut because I'm starting
to think you want to stay in stitches.

HELL NO do I want any more damn stitches!

And you know good and well why not sweetcheeks.

Well, the doc will be lookin at the new one too. I'll
see if he can just come by tonight. Is that okay?

Tell him to be ready to take both sets of stitches out.

Be safe tough guy, I wanna see you at home later.

Nothing will ever keep me from coming home to
you sugar. I gotta go deal with this damn idiot who
just cut me though. I'll see you in a few hours.

Shaw put his phone back in his pocket along with the wrappers
from the bandage he'd just applied to his arm. He was excited to find
out at least one set of stitches was likely coming out tonight. He had
a couple more days before he would go ahead and take the other ones

out himself, whether the doc signed off or not. There was no part of him that planned to have those when he took Tinsley for her birthday celebration to a wine resort.

"Fam, what do you wanna do with this joker?" Baz pointed at the man who Shaw had cuffed and was still on the ground. The other two officers escorted the second man to his house to have a talk with him.

"I don't fuckin' care, man." Shaw squatted down to the man who cut him. "You have an exciting afternoon?"

The guy had tears in his eyes. "I'm sorry, I didn't mean to cut you. That guy's a prick though, I would've cut him."

"Over a damn parking spot?" Shaw shook his head.

"He parks on my property! I'm sick of it!"

"You two are gonna have to figure that out." Shaw stood up and looked at Baz. "Let's just run him for warrants, and if he's good just let him go. I don't wanna deal with this shit."

CHAPTER
Twenty Six

"**A**UNTIE TINS!" ALAURRA CAME BURSTING THROUGH THE BACK door that evening.

Tinsley was in the kitchen and turned around to her niece the second she heard her. "Hey, Laura Loo!" She opened her arms. "I didn't know I was going to get to see you tonight." She hugged the excited six-year old before pecking her on the head.

"I told Daddy I wanted to come see you because I made you something." She beamed when she held out the bracelet she'd strung together.

"Oh my goodness! Did you make this all by yourself?!"

Alaurra hopped in excitement. "Yes! And it says BESTIES." She swayed her body back and forth while smiling with all her teeth.

"I love it! Thank you." Tinsley put on the bracelet and gave her niece another hug. "Are you hungry?"

"Alaurra, I told you to knock first." Vance walked through the back-door with a small medical supply bag in hand.

"Vance, please—she's never knocked." Tinsley grinned and rolled her eyes before she turned around to Alaurra, who scampered to the breakfast bar next to Shaw.

"Well, I didn't know." Vance suggestively looked at his sister who just stuck her tongue out at him.

"I remember you." Alaurra climbed into the high barstool next to Shaw.

He smiled at her. "You do, huh? I remember you too. Except last time I saw you, you looked like a butterfly."

"That's because Brindle Boo painted my face!" she threw her head back and giggled.

"Do you remember his name?" Tinsley asked as she opened the rice cooker when the timer went off.

Alaurra covered her smiling face, embarrassed to have to admit she didn't remember.

"That's Officer Shaw." Tinsley helped her out.

"I know." Alaurra fibbed. "But he doesn't have cop clothes on." She looked at her aunt, now a little confused.

"You can just call me Shaw then," he assured her.

"How about Uncle Shaw?" Vance whispered to his sister as he creeped up behind her and helped himself to the crockpot contents.

Tinsley gave him a friendly elbow to his ribs.

Harvey charged into the kitchen with a toy and went straight for Alaurra.

"Good thing you've got an officer here. Helen isn't much of a watchdog to be letting us get all settled in before he bothered to check on things."

"Vance, you're such an ass." Tinsley shook her head. "He was *obviously* trying to pick out the perfect toy before he came in here." She watched her cheerful dog as he shoved his plush chicken on Alaurra's lap for her to play with him.

"Harvey!" Alaurra squealed and then hopped off the stool to play fetch in the living room.

"I was going to offer you dinner, but maybe you don't deserve it being so rude to him."

"Oh, I'm having dinner—when have I ever passed up your kalua pork?!"

"I just have to finish the mac salad."

Vance threw his head back, groaning in anxious anticipation. "You're about to have your tastebuds transformed." He glanced at Shaw.

"I don't offer my sister many compliments, but she kills it with this dinner. Every. Single. Time."

"Oh, I've been here smelling it for an hour." Shaw smiled. "I'm more than ready to try it."

"What happened to your arm there?" Vance noticed the fresh bandage on Shaw's arm. "I can't turn my back for ten seconds and you're already getting injured again?" He laughed.

"This one's minor." Shaw shook off the teasing with a chuckle. "I was able to clean and bandage this one all on my own."

"Well, do you mind if I take a look at your back?"

"Sure, thank you. I'd love to get these stitches out."

"We'll take a look and see what we can do," Vance assured him as he walked over to the breakfast bar to join Shaw.

"Auntie Tins!" Alaurra's frantic cries rang out right before they heard a lamp crash to the floor.

Tinsley knew what had initiated the call for help and she scrambled for her dog. Harvey was on his side flailing around while his eyes flickered uncontrollably. Tinsley shoved the coffee table away from him and threw a pillow in front of the hard leg of the couch that Harvey was near. She didn't reach for him yet and reminded Alaurra to give him space. Vance picked up his daughter and Shaw stood by cautiously waiting to see how he could help. Harvey wasn't in his seizure long before he stilled and then his large chest gasped for air to fill his lungs. When Tinsley saw him open his eyes she slid in right by his head and put both of her hands on him—one hand was on his ribs while the other caressed the side of his face.

"Oh, baby boy." She tried not to cry. "You alright, buddy?" She gently held him down when he tried to get up. "Let's take a minute, you just catch your breath, bud." Tinsley encouraged him by rubbing her hands along his body and leaning down to kiss the side of his face. Tears steadily streamed down from her eyes but she wasn't sobbing. She was thankful this was a quick one that he likely wouldn't take too long to recover from.

"Tins…" Shaw knelt down and rubbed her back. "What can I do to help you guys out?"

She shook her head. "That one was pretty mild, he's gonna be alright." She wiped her eyes. "But actually, can you get his water dish, please? I don't want him to have to go too far and he'll likely want a sip when he sits up."

Shaw affectionately gripped her shoulder and leaned down to kiss her head before he walked into the mudroom for Harvey's water bowl. Vance gave him an appreciative look when he passed them on his way to the kitchen.

Tinsley was kissing the side of Harvey's face when Shaw walked back into the living room with a fresh bowl of water for Harvey.

"You did a really good job, buddy," she praised him and Harvey reached up to lick the side of Tinsley's face as she was still leaning over smooching on him. "I know, bud—we don't like those."

Shaw picked up the fallen lamp and put it back on the side table before he set Harvey's water bowl near him. He took a seat next to Tinsley and gave Harvey a loving rub to the side of his head.

"Thank you." Tinsley didn't take her eyes off her dog but she did momentarily move one of her hands to squeeze Shaw's leg before holding Harvey's head again.

"You're welcome." Shaw pecked the side of Tinsley's head. "Are you guys okay?"

"That was a pretty normal one, nothing he has to rush to the vet for… as long as he doesn't have any more tonight, anyway."

Tinsley turned to her niece who was still in Vance's arms, her eyes wide and a little scared. "Laura Loo, thank you for looking out for Handsome Harv. Do you want to show Daddy his special treat that makes him feel better?"

She nodded, excited at the chance to help, so Vance took her into the kitchen.

Shaw lightly massaged Tinsley's shoulders. "Are you okay, Tins?"

Tinsley leaned toward Shaw and rested her head just under his. "It's always hard to watch him. I know he has no clue what's going on, but it scares me every damn time. He's such a good guy, I don't like that he has to deal with these."

"He *is* a really good one," Shaw agreed. "Handsome Harvey is a

tough guy—and I would know about being tough." He placed a prolonged kiss on the side of Tinsley's head.

She exhaled a quick laugh.

"Auntie Tins, I did it just like you taught me—and Daddy helped."
Alaurra and Vance walked back into the living room.

"That is the *best* looking ice cream. Did you make the heart on top?"
Tinsley smiled.

Alaurra's chin tilted down as she smiled. "Yes. That was Daddy's idea
but I made it."

"Well, I love it and I know Harvey will too."

Tinsley took the ice cream from her and put it next to Harvey's
water bowl, he quickly sat up after smelling his routine post-seizure
treat. She carefully watched him stand and was relieved to see he didn't
seem to have any wobbles or trouble with that task. She noticed Shaw
intently watching the slightly dazed dog.

"It's vanilla ice cream topped with honey." She stroked Harvey's
back as he consumed the small sweet treat. "It just helps with his
blood sugar after a seizure," she informed Shaw. "His post-seizure
routine is the treat, a little protein if he'll eat it next, watching to
be sure his temperature doesn't get too high, and then really just a
ton of monitoring—like making sure he's comfortable and not going
into another one. His last bad one was not only about two minutes
long, but then they clustered—just one after another. So, that's what
landed him at the emergency vet. These short ones are more normal
and he should be okay." She nodded, reassuring herself more than
Shaw.

"Harvey's lucky to have you, Tins." Shaw put his arm around her
and Tinsley completely leaned into him. They didn't stay like that for
long as Harvey was making his way to the back door.

"I guess he'd like to be let out now." Tinsley squeezed Shaw's leg
before she got off the floor to follow her dog. Vance reached out and
gripped her shoulder as she walked by.

"You want me to take a look at those stitches now?" Vance asked.

Shaw was still sitting on the floor but he looked up and nodded
before standing.

"Thanks, man." Shaw walked over to the breakfast bar where Vance and his medical bag were waiting.

"It'll probably be easiest if you just take off your shirt—if you're comfortable with that," Vance instructed.

Shaw removed his shirt and then turned so his back was to Vance.

"Yep, this set's ready." It didn't take Vance long to decide.

"What happened?" Alaurra asked when she saw her dad expertly removing stitches from Shaw's back.

Shaw wasn't sure what exactly to tell her, but her dad was ready and beat him to it.

"Remember? Shaw's a cop. He chases bad guys and sometimes the bad guys do extra naughty things like this and hurt the cops."

Alaurra's eyes were big as she watched the stitches coming out of Shaw. "Does that hurt?"

Shaw shook his head. "Not anymore, your dad fixed me all up."

Tinsley and Harvey walked back into the kitchen, he was all wiggles following Tinsley to the refrigerator.

"Let's see what we've got in here, buddy." She searched around for a quick meat treat for her excited dog.

"I'm not comfortable taking these stitches out yet," Vance said while he inspected Shaw's stomach. "I'd say another few days oughta do it though.

"What happened to your tummy?"Alaurra asked. She had perched herself onto one of the barstools next to her dad to watch as he worked on Shaw.

"I got a cut and your dad stitched it all up for me." Shaw smiled at her.

"No, why does it look like that?" She pointed.

They were all confused, but it was Tinsley who finally asked. "What do you mean? Why does the cut look like that?"

"No, those lines by your belly button. My daddy's tummy doesn't look like that."

Tinsley slapped her hand over her mouth trying to hide her laugh while Shaw's face burned with embarrassment—Alaurra wasn't used to seeing defined abs.

"And my daddy has hair allllll on his whole tummy and up here." She patted her chest. "Your hair is just down there." She pointed toward Shaw's belly button where he did in fact have a happy trail.

"Laura Loo." Tinsley tried to swallow her chuckles while she finished mixing the mac salad. "Everyone has different bodies."

Shaw didn't waste any time putting his shirt back on once Vance was done with his examination. "I really appreciate you taking those out. Well, really for everything."

"It's not a problem." Vance eyed Shaw. "Let's not make those a habit, please. Seems as though my sister would like to keep you around."

Tinsley smiled but didn't disagree or scold her brother.

"Yeah, I'd like to stick around for a while… if she'll have me." Shaw smirked.

Her face was turning red now. She bent down and pet Harvey on the head before encouraging him to go lay on his bed. Changing the subject, she held up the bowl of mac salad. "Are you guys ready to eat?"

"So…" Shaw flashed a mischievous grin when he got into bed that night. "My stitches are out." He rolled on his side to face Tinsley who was already curled up on her side.

"*One* set of stitches was removed." She laughed. "You've still got a bit of healing, tough guy."

"A couple more days is what the doc said." Shaw slid his hand up and down Tinsley's torso and hips before he reached back and cupped her cheek. "I've taken stitches out before, I'll be evaluating these ones daily. The only reason I waited for my back is because I couldn't see or reach those ones."

Tinsley slipped one of her legs in between Shaw's and put her arms around his shoulders. "As long as you're healed, you won't hear any arguments from me."

"I'm healed *now*," Shaw declared.

Tinsley's leg put slight pressure on him and she smirked. "I wish you were, but we're going to be very careful about that wound."

"I thought you liked my tough side?" Shaw practically begged while massaging her cheeks.

"Oh, I do." Tinsley pushed up against him, leaving no space between them. "But this waiting will also be a good reminder for you to be much safer out there."

Shaw blew out a defeated exhale, trying to suppress his excitement. "I think I need to go get a second opinion on these damn stitches."

Tinsley giggled and backed off of him a bit. "Goodnight, tough guy." Tinsley kissed the base of his neck.

Shaw sucked air in through his teeth and smiled at her; reluctantly agreeing it was best for them to try to sleep instead of any of the activities running through his head.

"Sweetdreams, sugar."

CHAPTER
Twenty Seven

"I'VE NEVER ACTUALLY BEEN ANYWHERE ON THE COLUMBIA River," Tinsley admitted as they walked into their room. It was a standalone building; inside was a luxurious one-bedroom condo that featured views of the Columbia River Gorge and nearby vineyards. A set of floor-to-ceiling windows and a sliding glass door showcased a private patio off the back of the unit.

"I've never been this far south on it." Shaw rubbed her hand with his thumb before turning to her to hold the side of her face. "I made us some reservations in a little less than an hour for dinner."

"Hunt," Tinsley melted into his touch, "you've done too much."

"Nothing's too much for you, sugar," he assured her and then leaned down for a quick kiss. "Harvey can join us too."

Tinsley threw her head back. "Can you be any more perfect?"

Shaw smirked, he wanted to respond but had to be very careful to avoid them missing their dinner reservations. "I'm gonna go throw some jeans and a nicer shirt on."

"Oh, so I shouldn't wear my yogas to dinner?" she teased with Shaw's favorite smile.

"You can wear whatever you'd like, you're gorgeous in everything."

He swatted her butt before he made way to his suitcase. "I just don't want to be in shorts anymore."

Shaw brought Harvey outside to explore and take care of business while Tinsley got ready. He walked back into the condo when they had about fifteen minutes before their fire pit dinner reservation.

Tinsley's wrap maxi dress had a natural high slit in it because of the style. It was cream with a deep golden floral print that nearly brought Shaw to his knees because of how sweet she looked.

"Oh, sugar," he managed to say past his awe. "Can you be any more beautiful?"

"Stop." Tinsley giggled and hid her face by putting her arms around Shaw to bury her head in his sturdy chest.

"Let's go have some dinner." He reached for her hand and walked her and Harvey out of the condo.

They were shown to a concrete patio that had four separate fire pits. Each of the fire pits had several wooden adirondack chairs around them but all were situated to look over a cliff that had the Columbia River in the distance. The hostess directed Shaw and Tinsley toward the fire pit on one of the ends because they had Harvey with them. The end spot was perfect as it offered slightly more privacy than the middle ones.

"Here's our wine menu." The server handed it to Tinsley. "And the pizza menu—we have award winning wood-fired pizza," she informed them with a smile as Shaw took the second menu. "Can I interest you in our seasonal flight to get you started?"

Shaw looked at Tinsley to see if she wanted to start with wine; she didn't help when she simply smiled.

"What selections are in that flight?" Shaw asked.

"Mostly whites—" she didn't even finish when Shaw agreed. "Very good, I'll go get that and be back shortly to take your order." She peered down at Harvey. "We also have water, treats, and a mat if you'd like any of those items for your friend here."

"Yes, to all of those things, please," Shaw requested before Tinsley could.

They watched the server make her way to grab everything.

"It's *so* beautiful out here." Tinsley looked toward the river. "I *cannot* believe how big that river is."

"We can go take a closer look tomorrow if you'd like—we get to enjoy the moonlight tonight." He gestured to the sky that was beginning to darken, there was only a sliver of pink left on the horizon.

"Hunt." Tinsley reached for his hand. "Thank you for planning all of this."

"You're welcome." He squeezed her hand and looked deep into her brown eyes that were glowing from the fire in front of them. "Your birthday deserves a big celebration."

The server came back with their flight and Harvey's things, resulting in an uncontrollable nub spin.

They'd been enjoying the fire pit for almost an hour when Tinsley hesitantly said, "you know, I haven't sat in front of a fire in like fifteen years. I almost forgot how good s'mores are… And I've never heard of this whole meat and cheese roasting thing, but I'm a big fan now." She smiled and inspected the gouda and pepperoni masterpiece she made before sliding it onto a cracker.

Shaw felt his chest tighten at the thought of something as simple as a bonfire being absent from her life for so long. Her face gleamed from the excitement she felt living in the moment and enjoying a carefree evening.

"I'll give it to them…" Shaw reached for another slice of cheese. "This is pretty genius, but I have to think they may have resorted to another roasting element because they don't know much about s'mores."

"What do you mean?" Tinsley cocked her head.

Shaw inspected the tray once more. "I don't see any Reese's out here—only rookies leave that off the s'mores spread."

"I'd agree, Reese's are top tier." She giggled. "Is that your favorite candy?"

"I don't really have a sweet tooth." Shaw rolled his head before he leveled his gaze and shot a sly grin at her. "When we're talking food anyway." He winked as Tinsley blushed. "But you've never had a s'more until you've done it with a Reese's—they're called 'graham crappers' and they'll change your life."

Tinsley attempted to suppress her giddiness to Shaw's suggestive behavior by biting her bottom lip. The butterflies rushing through her body finally settled enough to tell him what was on her mind. "I'm thinking my life has already been changed… for the better, of course."

Another hour passed and they still had pizza left because of all the appetizers and wine they'd indulged in. Two fire pits away there were three couples enjoying the late night, otherwise the patio was quiet. Harvey had been a perfect gentleman with his manners all evening and was comfortably lying between Tinsley and their fire pit, lazily soaking up the heat.

The server had just dropped off another flight of wine when Tinsley gazed over at Shaw. He gave her a sly smirk and reached for her hand which she happily accepted.

Tinsley loved the feeling of the cozy fire in front of them, it was the most romantic evening she'd ever had. She let Shaw rub her hand with his thumb a couple of times before she stood to join him on his chair. She didn't give him any consideration for the fact that they were out in public when she slid directly onto his lap.

He was a little surprised, but welcomed her with open arms as her cheeks sat comfortably against the front of his pants. He had been getting more comfortable caressing her backside and they had cuddled every night for the last couple of weeks, but this was the first time he felt the full weight of her on him and he was instantly addicted. He momentarily closed his eyes at the feeling.

They shared sips of a pinot before Tinsley leaned over and set that glass down to pick up the chardonnay that was also part of their current flight. After she handed the glass to Shaw, she reached down and gave Harvey a light scratch to the top of his head. Shaw wanted to go back to the condo the second she bent over. When she was done giving Harvey a few pets she picked up another wine glass and leaned back onto Shaw's chest. He put his arms around her and she nuzzled her head next to his.

Tinsley watched the fire dance and crackle in front of them before speaking softly to Shaw, "You truly are an amazing guy, Hunt."

She propped her feet up on a small stool that wasn't too far from them, causing part of her wrap-style dress to fall to the side, immediately exposing her entire leg almost to her panties. Tinsley tried to catch it but ended up slapping her leg instead. It was Shaw who took hold of the fabric and covered her thigh for her. He left his hand on the dress and her lap to keep her from being exposed to anyone.

"Thank you." She giggled a little breathlessly.

"You're welcome." His hand slid slowly up and down her thigh. "And I know it's early and all, but Happy Birthday, sweetcheeks." Shaw kissed Tinsley's cheek.

"I've never been so spoiled—birthday or not." She turned her head to him. "So, if I forget to tell you later, I've had a really great time already."

"I'll never stop spoiling you. You have no idea how much I love watching your sweet face enjoying life."

Tinsley softly pressed her lips against his. When she opened her eyes and looked at Shaw, she fell even harder for him. He'd let his facial hair take over a bit the last few days and she loved the look. He had a face that allowed him to basically try and pull off anything he wanted. The scruffiness really elevated his tough guy status in her book. Seeing him in uniform would never get old or keep her heart from swooning, but she was getting used to his off-duty style as well. Shaw was very fashionable for a man who claimed to not care about those things. It helped that his body was built like a Greek god. Tinsley took a sip of wine and then tried to settle back in by leaning further into Shaw and resting the side of her head against his. Shaw's hand rubbed her leg while still maintaining a hold on her dress to keep her appropriately covered out in public. She could feel her body pulsing for him each time his hand made it ever so slightly higher along her thigh. Tinsley noticed part of her dress drifting down again and instead of picking it up, Shaw laid his hand flat on her bare skin and tried to reach as far onto her inner thigh as possible while her legs were crossed. Tinsley's breath grew shallow, she wanted his hands to explore. Gently, she pressed back into him with her hips and didn't have to wait long for Shaw to suggest their next move.

"Tins, sugar, you're gonna need to pick a wine or two so we can order a couple bottles to bring back to the room." Shaw made another tantalizing pass of his hand up her exposed leg, his slightly calloused fingers causing goosebumps in their wake. "We need to move this behind closed doors," he whispered.

"Of all the thoughtful and meticulous planning my tough guy has done to make this the most special birthday I've ever had," Tinsley teased and pressed into him again before turning her head to look him in the eyes, "he's not confident enough to pick a wine?"

"I've got nothing *but* confidence, you oughta know that by now." Shaw pulled her by her hips to be even closer to him before he continued in a quiet voice, "I just need to be sure we have what you want."

Tinsley softly rolled her hips before leaning back to whisper in his ear, "Hunt, I think you already know exactly what I want."

Shaw didn't hesitate, he firmly held her around the waist and got them out of the chair. Once they were both standing he kissed her neck and reached down for Harvey's leash, who had been startled awake by Shaw's sudden movement.

He quickly grabbed the attention of the server. "Excuse me, can we get a bottle of this pinot and that first chardonnay we had to-go; and then charge our tab to the room, please?"

Harvey stretched and then shook off a bit before looking up at Shaw.

Tinsley spun on the ball of her foot and wrapped both of her arms around Shaw's shoulders. She was as close to his lips as she could get without making contact. "I would've picked the pinot too." She softly pecked him. "Seems like you and I may want all the same things tonight."

Shaw barely grazed her lips and then moved his mouth to her ear to whisper, "You'll be getting things you didn't even know you wanted. Having those stitches only gave me more time to contemplate all the ways I'd be worshiping your perfect damn body."

Tinsley wanted to continue whispering in his ear but the server came back with their bottles.

"Here you are, Mr. Shaw." She smiled and held the bottles out to him. "Thank you for dining with us tonight."

"Thank you," Tinsley and Shaw said nearly in unison before they began speed walking to their condo.

CHAPTER
Twenty Eight

SHAW SET THE WINE ON THE FIRST SURFACE HE SAW WHEN THEY entered their room. He reached down to unclasp Harvey's collar and the cane corso trotted to his bed, excited for the bone he'd left there earlier. Tinsley was slipping off her light jean jacket when Shaw walked her backward until her spine made contact with the closest wall, reaching one hand to hold her head. He gazed into her eyes for a long moment before he leaned down to connect their lips.

They'd become very familiar with their lips and tongues playing with one another. The first couple weeks of their relationship had limited them to their mouths, but now that Shaw's stitches were gone, so were any of the rules they'd established.

Tinsley smirked and let Shaw continue to explore with his hands. She knew he was looking for a zipper to remove her dress. He'd never find the zipper because her dress was a wrap-style and didn't have one. She let him run his fingers along her back again before she slowed their lips and opened her eyes. When he met her gaze she smiled at him and put her hand on one of his to guide it to the bow tied on her hip. She gently urged him to hold on to the end of the bow and then helped him pull. When he realized it was loosening her dress, he grinned triumphantly at her and continued to untie the knot.

Once the dress was completely undone he waited a moment before opening what now looked like a robe hanging on Tinsley's body. Tinsley took the opportunity to reach for his chest before he did anything else. She had both of her palms placed firmly on his strong pecs and she bit her lip before sliding her hands to the bottom of his shirt. Shaw smirked before removing his shirt for her, allowing Tinsley's hands and eyes to roam until he couldn't take the fact that their lips weren't touching. He held her head with both hands and tilted it up, catching her bottom lip between his and tugging gently before crushing his lips to hers.

Tinsley's soft hands made their way slowly but firmly up and down his muscular back as they kissed. As she pulled him closer with each stroke, her dress began to expose more of her. She wanted as much of their bodies touching as possible so she slid her hands down his back a final time and then moved them along his hips, tracing the deep-grooved muscles on his obliques until they met the front of his jeans. She worked on the button and loved the tickle from the hair Shaw had forming a trail from his belly button down.

"I'm so glad I'm conscious this time so I can experience you taking off my pants," he teased with a gentle voice that hovered just above her neck.

Tinsley couldn't help but be embarrassed, but she giggled her way through it and pulled his jeans off when he helpfully stepped out of them.

"I would have to agree—this is a much better experience," she managed.

Once his pants were cast aside, Shaw's hands dropped to her cheeks and pulled their bodies closer together. Tinsley's whimper encouraged Shaw to grab the back of one of her thighs and pull her leg around his waist so they could get even closer before he thrusted toward her. Tinsley's dress opened completely and she lost all control of maintaining their kiss as her head rolled back to lean against the wall.

Shaw watched Tinsley's face, her blissful expression ramping up his own excitement. Her eyes were closed and he noticed her brows trying to connect as she exhaled a short moan when he pushed toward her and then lightened into a giddy smirk when he pulled away. He loved the sequence but knew he wouldn't be satisfied simply watching that all night, he wanted more. They *both* wanted more.

Shaw occupied himself with kissing and nibbling on her neck before he made any other moves. His rhythm on Tinsley's entire body had her gripping his head while she sucked in tiny gasps to try to catch her breath from all the pleasurable sounds that were escaping her mouth. Her dress was now barely clinging to her, hanging on her elbows—and she was essentially in her bra and panties. Shaw slowed his movements so he could take a small step away from her to take in the view.

"You are so damn gorgeous, Tins." He barely had to tug on the dress before it hit the floor, then he scooped her up into his arms, supporting her by her cheeks to hang securely around his waist. Shaw carried her to the bed and gently laid her down before crawling on top of her. He softly pecked her chest a few times while moving her legs to either side of him.

"I'm gonna need you to stay stitch-free from now on, tough guy. I can't be waiting this long again."

Shaw exhaled a light chuckle. "You and me both. I finally have a reason to be much more careful at work. I won't disappoint you again because I've been waiting *years* to find you, sugar." He reached behind her and unclasped her bra, losing his breath and his train of thought when he was finally fully exposed to her perfect breasts. "Holy hell." He wasted no time in massaging a hand under one of them and putting her nipple in his mouth.

Tinsley fought her body's natural reaction to arch her back so Shaw didn't lose his placement and ran her nails through his hair as gently as she could. Goosebumps formed down his spine from the touch and he lifted his head, his tongue immediately finding itself inside her mouth as he reached down between her legs. He didn't even have to go under her thong to feel she was more than ready for him.

"Holy shit." Shaw massaged her through the fabric but felt her soft, welcoming skin underneath.

Tinsley bit her lip and looked into his eyes, her chest heaving. "Round one might not last all that long for me… But I'm willing to go multiple rounds with you tonight, Hunt."

Shaw chuckled again. "I already know I'm gonna need extra rounds." He slowly began sliding her thong off of her hips. "I've been thinking about this for weeks, Tins."

"Oh, I contemplated testing those stitches *multiple* times," Tinsley disclosed as she reached down and gently tugged on Shaw through his boxer briefs.

He huffed out an appreciative exhale before looking into Tinsley's eyes. The blissed-out expression on her face coupled with the placement of her hands encouraged him to strip her even quicker before he raced to get his own bottoms off.

Shaw held himself directly on top of her and planned to go slow, but the second their skin touched he felt how ready they both were. He barely grazed her entrance when he felt Tinsley's hips shift toward him and he didn't make her wait any longer. As he steadily made his way into her, her fingertips gripped his lower back with one hand and his scalp with the other.

Tinsley whimpered at the feeling of fullness as he sank into her. Shaw immediately let out an appreciative groan. As his hips worked on a comfortable rhythm, Tinsley's hand slid to the back of his neck and pulled him to meet her lips; their tongues dancing the second they connected. He felt the intensity rise as their mouths moved in sync with one another. He didn't realize his thrusts had sped up as much as they had when Tinsley's lips separated from his and her head rolled back with a breathy moan. She pressed into the pillow with more force as her back arched and hips welcomed him. Shaw couldn't resist placing a hand on her exposed breast eliciting an even sweeter sounding moan while Tinsley hooked her leg around his to help pull him deeper into her. He lost control of the rhythm he established and gave her what her body begged for.

"Tins…" Shaw groaned, knowing he had mere seconds left.

Tinsley's leg lost its grip because her mind was fully consumed by the feeling of Shaw racing to the finish line. His lips met hers as he gave her one final thrust before he couldn't hold on any longer. Their lips vibrated as Tinsley whined at the feeling of him releasing all he'd built up in the weeks since meeting her.

"Mmmm, tough guy," Tinsley's sensuous voice tickled Shaw's ears, "you were definitely worth the wait."

Shaw couldn't help but chuckle. He leaned down to place a firm kiss on her lips and gently pressed himself deeper before he lost all the blood flow below his waist. Her hips jerked and she giggled at the sensation before he eased his way out of her.

"Sugar, *you* were worth the damn wait." Shaw laid on his back while pushing his arm under Tinsley's shoulders. "I won't be disappointing you again." His arm curled to roll her into his chest.

Tinsley wiggled around and adjusted the covers to get comfortable next to him. She placed one of her legs in between his and rested her head on his shoulder. Her mind and body were still completely captivated by the sensations from Shaw when she decided to confirm his promise of not disappointing her again.

"Hunt…" she said in a soft voice as her fingertips gently tickled his strong chest.

"Yes, sugar?" He pecked her forehead.

"Can we talk about work?"

Shaw shot out a quick chortle through his nose. "That's what you'd like to talk about right now? I'll try not to take that personally." He continued to smile, tucking a piece of Tinsley's hair behind her ear.

Tinsley looked into Shaw's addictive green eyes and he immediately picked up on her sincerity. "I was hoping I'd be able to talk you into giving up your second job… I understand why you do what you do, and trust me when I tell you, your intentions are admirable and damn if that morally gray compass of yours doesn't make me fall even harder for you." She looked at his chest where her fingers still lovingly traced his muscles. "But, Hunt, the more time we spend together, the more I know I don't want—well, I *can't*—lose you."

Shaw didn't hesitate, he pulled Tinsley on top of him to fully engulf her in his arms. He laced his fingers through her hair to hold her firmly against his body.

With her head now next to his, he whispered in her ear, "Tins, I can't lose you either." He felt her entire chest relax as she blew out the breath she'd been holding.

"I'm not trying to just change you, that's not it." She shook her head as best she could squished against Shaw. "That tough guy in you is pretty dang hot."

Shaw chuckled, sending a slight vibration through his chest to hers.

"It just scares me for you to be out there alone when no one has your back or knows where you are… Not to mention, I feel like a lot of why you're out there doing that is coming from a place of pain. It kills me to think of your heart being anything but happy." Tinsley shoved her hands under the pillow Shaw's head rested on so she could hold him. "You deserve a happy heart, Hunt."

Shaw's hands released their grip around Tinsley to hold her face until she met his gaze. He didn't say anything, he pressed their mouths together and slid his tongue past her lips. Their exchange was languid and unhurried—mutual passion and understanding that they were both in this and neither wanted to lose the other.

"Tins, sugar…" Shaw said after separating their lips, "my heart's been nothing but happy since I met you." He watched her face light up before he continued, "You've given me a reason to want to come home after work. I haven't had that in a long time and I'll *never* take that for granted. You still get to keep your tough guy, but I promise you I'll come home to you every night after work—no more vigilante bullshit."

"Thank you, Hunt." Tinsley lightly scratched the top of his head with one of her hands. "I promise, Handsome Harv and I are going to do everything we can to keep you happy."

"I'm not worried about that at all." His hands moved down to grip Tinsley's plump backside. "I'd say we're doing a pretty fantastic job of making each other happy."

"You've got no complaints from me, tough guy." Tinsley kissed Shaw's neck. "In fact"—one of her hands drifted down to his waist—"I need to be playing catch up to get to your level."

Shaw laughed. "While I'm sure I'd *thoroughly* enjoy you taking that approach, you literally saved my damn life, sweetcheeks. If anyone owes a debt, it's me."

"That was Vance," she countered.

Shaw shook his head. "You made the call… And it's not Vance's blood I've got running through my veins."

Tinsley's head immediately shot up and looked at Shaw.

"Yeah, I know all about that—your brother's a snitch for sure." Shaw smiled. "My heart literally beats because of you *and* for you, Tins." Shaw maintained Tinsley's adoring gaze as his hands rubbed up and down her bare back. "I have to admit though, at some point I'll need to tell Baz about his cousin… I can't walk away from that one and I don't know what that'll end up looking like."

Tinsley took a moment before she responded, "But just telling him, right? Not going out alone to investigate more?"

"Tins, I promise—no more solo, dark, vigilante-style outings." He grabbed a lock of her hair. "You know better than anyone where I've been every single night for a while now." He held her head and continued, "I don't have any intentions of changing that routine, *especially* now." He gave her a few suggestive squeezes with the hand that still cupped the bottom of her cheek.

Tinsley smiled and slid her right leg out from between Shaw's legs so she had one on either side of his waist. She moved her lips toward his and led with her tongue while she better aligned their pelvises.

"You must really enjoy watching me struggle to keep my composure." Shaw chuckled but wholeheartedly welcomed her on top of him with his hands on her lucious rear end.

"What?" Tinsley asked in a playful tone. She sat on him, slowly circling her hips as he laid on his back.

Shaw gripped her backside a few times and couldn't help but squirm with each pulse of his hands as she continued to grind on him. "I lose all fucking control with this perfect goddamn peach of yours, Tins." He watched as a smirk made its way across her face when she felt him hardening under her. "Plus, the view of your flawless fucking rack." He exhaled heavily before one of his hands momentarily left her backside to grip her left breast. "It's not just the build up from the last couple of weeks. You're damn sexy and I want every last part of your body."

She leaned down so their exposed chests touched. "Lucky for you, tough guy, I want you to take every last part of my body."

Shaw couldn't flip her fast enough.

Tinsley's squeal turned into a giggle once she was on her back. "I thought you liked my peach? Why would you go and cover it up?"

"I'm trying to keep my goddamn composure for a little longer." His mouth pressed into her stomach just below her belly button before he began slowly placing soft pecks up her torso and around her breasts.

Tinsley felt her entire body form goosebumps in response to his calculated lips as he continued playing.

Once Shaw made it to her neck, he gently pressed himself between her legs to tease her as he was ready for their second round. He grinned when he felt her short, manicured nails try to tickle his side. Shaw reached down for her hand and intertwined their fingers before placing their hands over her head.

"I don't think so, little Ms. Tickle-Me," he whispered into her ear, smirking. "I'm doing work right now." He pressed their pelvises together again but didn't penetrate her.

Tinsley squeezed his hand as she tried to settle her hips that were begging him for more. Her smile took over her face and she slowly opened her eyes to find Shaw waiting for her gaze.

"So, I just have to lay here while you tease me?" She bit the corner of her bottom lip.

"Sugar, you've done enough teasing for the both of us these last couple of weeks," he flirtatiously accused. "You can go ahead and let me return that favor for a few minutes." He didn't release her hand when his head went back down to help his lips reconnect with her neck.

Tinsley closed her eyes to enjoy the feeling of Shaw completely consuming every inch of her body. She could hardly manage the squirming in her hips from each pleasurable touch he made and she giggled when she felt her body shudder after his tongue made its way around her breast and delicately landed on her nipple.

She tried to maintain a steady pace as she rubbed her thumb on his strong hand that was still interlaced with her own. Tinsley's other hand rested on Shaw's waist, patiently waiting for the right time to start roaming around his perfect physique again. Once she was able to collect herself enough, she slowly slid her hand to the front of his hip and held it there for a split second while she sucked in a breath when Shaw's lips lightly sucked on the base of her neck. The moment her breathing returned to normal her hand continued its journey below his waist.

Shaw slowed to a complete stop when he felt her gently holding on to him with her soft hand. He sat up on his knees and smiled down at her before putting his hand on top of hers.

"You've got Hunter for me, should I be pulling a firm *Tinsley* when you're in trouble?"

She giggled in return as Shaw carefully took her hand off him and placed it with the other one he'd been holding. He now covered both of her hands with one of his as he went back to working his mouth on her body.

Tinsley only let him work for a few seconds before she moved to her next attempt. She bent her leg and caressed the outside of his hip with the inside of her knee before she hooked her leg around his. She simultaneously slid her hips and put pressure on his backside to try to better align herself for what she truly wanted in addition to everything his mouth was doing.

"You're lucky you're so goddamn sweet." Shaw blew out an appreciative chuckle before completely giving into Tinsley. He held onto the back of the thigh she already had wrapped around him and slowly thrusted into her. "But don't think that means you'll always get your way, sweetcheeks," he warned with a devilish smile as he mindfully slid in and out of her.

Tinsley freed one of her hands and reached for his jaw to gently bring him closer so she could meet his lips with hers.

Shaw maintained a slow and steady pace with a firm grip on her leg and everything he was doing had Tinsley's mind completely lost. Her free hand found the tricep that held her leg and she gripped the solid muscles that flexed and pulsed as he maintained his hold on her. She felt him nearly pull all the way out of her but realized he was just changing his angle.

As he worked his way back into her, he reached up to grab the headboard to pull himself deeper.

Tinsley moaned when he hit a slow and perfect rhythm. "Oh, Hunt," she cried out as her back arched off the bed.

"Oh, fuck." Shaw slowed his movements and slid out of her before a soft chuckle took over. "Not yet you don't—you almost had me with all that though." He leaned down and pressed his lips against hers.

"Hunter." Tinsley tried to catch her breath in between their lips crushing against one another. "Why… why'd you stop?" She nearly pouted.

"Sugar, don't you worry." Shaw leaned down to whisper in her ear, "We've got all night… I owe you a longer round this time." He smirked while sliding his hand between her legs.

"I do have a few things planned out for us tomorrow… but, they're all things we can skip if we find ourselves unable to get out of this bed." Shaw kissed the top of Tinsley's head as he held her from behind.

"I'm more than content being assigned bed rest with you forever." She smirked. "But, I know Handsome Harv will want out for a bit, and I wouldn't mind sitting in front of another cozy fire with you. Not that I don't love cuddling in bed," she clarified, "but I feel like I'd be a big fan of bonfire cuddling too."

"We did cut that a bit short tonight, didn't we?" He lightly chuckled.

"For good reason," Tinsley flirtatiously pointed out.

Shaw kissed her neck to agree and they both laughed when Harvey poked his block head over the bed and wiggled his nub.

"Is he waiting for an invitation up here or is he informing us we forgot to let him out before bed?" Shaw smiled at his favorite canine.

"Both." Tinsley's lighthearted sigh left her body just before she tossed off the comforter, attempting to get out of bed.

Shaw pulled her back toward him. "No shot. If anyone's going out in the middle of the night, it's me." He kissed the back of her head and got up.

Harvey took a few steps to follow Shaw but came back to the bed by Tinsley and stared at her.

"You wanna go outside, buddy?" Shaw held up his leash.

Harvey took a couple of quick trots toward him but again came back to let Tinsley know they were all going. She chuckled and rolled out of bed.

"Oh, I'm still not to be trusted, huh?" Shaw playfully scoffed at Harvey. "That actually hurts—I thought we were bros." Shaw threw a pair of sweats over his boxer briefs and then tried to coax Harvey again.

"He just wants to be sure we're all going." Tinsley smiled and watched Shaw pull on a shirt. She reached for a hoodie of Shaw's that he'd tossed over a chair.

Shaw got Harvey all hooked up with his harness and then looked at Tinsley who joined them while wearing his hoodie and some tennis shoes.

"Besides your birthday suit, that may be my favorite damn thing I've seen you in, sugar." His eyes lit up at the sight and he leaned down to kiss her.

Tinsley giggled and then wrapped her arms around his strong bicep for him to lead them outside for a short walk.

Harvey hopped around near Shaw's side and excitedly grabbed at his hand with a friendly growl.

"See, you *are* his bro." Tinsley smile seemed to take over her entire face. "He just isn't used to leaving me out of the equation."

"I forgot about that—Harv prefers company over comfort." He smiled back and shrugged. "I guess we'll just always have to drag you outta bed with us then."

"As long as you promise to always drag me back in."

Shaw snaked his hand down between them and squeezed one of her cheeks. "Oh, you'd need me to drag you?"

Tinsley giggled. "Not even close." She stopped them and put her arms up around Shaw's strong shoulders.

He didn't hesitate at all in pressing their bodies tightly together and connecting their lips. His concentration on holding Harvey's leash faded until the trusty dog tugged him toward a new sniffing spot. Shaw loosened the leash a bit more and slowed his lips.

"I can't promise you we're gonna get much sleep tonight." He winked at Tinsley.

"I'm more than okay with that. We've got some catching up for lost time we need to take care of." She returned his wink and then intertwined their hands so they could follow Harvey on the impromptu late night walk he decided they needed.

CHAPTER
Twenty Nine

"Y**OU OFFICIALLY HAVE MY PERMISSION TO CLAIM MY HOODIES** as your own any damn time, sweetcheeks." Shaw watched Tinsley reach for a cup in an upper cabinet while wearing his hoodie the next morning.

She giggled. "Thank you. I did bring my own, but I sure prefer the feeling of yours."

He winked before he put his arms around her. "So, I noticed that not only do we have a little fire pit on the patio out there, but there's also a grill." As Shaw held her from behind he walked them to the slider. "I happen to be a grillmaster. Do you wanna stay close to the room tonight and have dinner here? I looked up a few places around and I'm more than happy to take you out instead—it's your call, Tins."

"I'll be able to wear your most favorite outfits if we stay close." Tinsley squeezed the arms Shaw had wrapped around her. "Why don't we go explore for a bit today and then come back here for dinner and a fire?"

"Deal," he agreed while planting his lips on her temple.

ॐ3

"Is he alright to be off leash?" Shaw asked as they made their way along the bank of the Columbia. He sensed Harvey was very much ready to bolt into the distance to chase all the new smells he was being exposed to.

"Normally I'd be totally fine with him off-leash, but the wildlife and whatever else I can't see before he does makes me nervous."

Shaw nodded. "That makes sense."

"Have you ever had a dog?" Tinsley glanced up at Shaw while they walked hand in hand.

"Besides Harv?" He flashed his dashing grin her way.

Tinsley returned the gesture and playfully bumped the side of her head into his shoulder.

"Not since I was in high school." He reached down for Harvey's tailbone. "We always had a random mutt when I was growing up. No papered pedigrees or anything—my mom was always a fan of adopting from the Humane Society."

"I like her already." Tinsley smiled. She considered asking if Sloane liked dogs, but she wasn't really sure how much he wanted to talk to her about his late fiancé. She decided to divulge about herself instead.

"My parents were never a fan of pets, so Handsome Harv is actually my first."

Shaw grinned. "Go big or go home, huh? You decided you'd get one of the biggest dogs for your first?"

Tinsley walked a few steps, keeping her eyes on her dog, before she said anything.

"I'd never really been alone." She shrugged. "Growing up I was certainly never left alone. Even with my parents' crazy work schedules, Vance was always at the house with me. And then when I got sent away there was never a moment of quiet in that place. So, it was a super rough adjustment for me at first. I actually lived above the salon with Brindle for a while too—even after buying my house I'd stay there sometimes." She looked up at Shaw and rubbed his hand with her thumb. "I just didn't want to be by myself. Handsome Harv is always down to be around—so I haven't worried about that in a couple years."

"You won't have to worry about being alone around me, sugar." He caressed the side of her face.

"Please don't ever pinch me, Hunt. I'm quite happy in this dream and want to stay here with you."

"You're not dreaming, Tins—I'm building a new reality for you."

CHAPTER
Thirty

Shaw and Harvey were out on the patio preparing the grill for dinner while Tinsley cut up fruit and made a couple of sides in the condo kitchen. Harvey didn't have a leash on and minded Shaw perfectly fine without it.

"Hi neighbor!" A couple of women walked by and stood a respectful distance from Harvey but were closing in.

Shaw offered a wave and a slight tilt of his chin.

"What a cutie!" one of the women gushed. "Can I say hi?!" She continued moving forward.

Harvey cocked his head at the women but his nub twirled in every direction.

"Sit, bud." Shaw gently held his collar until he sat.

"What's his name?" The woman made lip smacking motions at him and called her other friends over.

"This is Harvey." Shaw noticed the women were in very tight and suggestive clothing. He realized it was a bachelorette group when a woman in a white bodycon dress sauntered her way toward them. As she got closer he saw all the obnoxious paraphernalia her bachelorette party accessorized her with—including the tiara covered in colorful penises.

Based on the sash she was wearing, their theme appeared to be *One Dick for Life.*

A small herd of women stood around Harvey, most clearly using him as a pawn to get closer to the handsome guy behind the grill. One of them not so subtly took a picture of him and he tried to ignore her—he was no stranger to the ogling, he and Baz got it all the time.

"And what about you? Do you have a name?" The same woman who asked for Harvey's now bit her lip suggestively at Shaw.

"I'm Shaw." He held his hand up to gesture a cordial wave.

"Shaw." She elbowed the woman next to her. "We're heading out in a bit but have a few Jell-O shots we need to finish—would you and Harvey like to join us?"

"I'm okay, thank you ladies," he politely declined.

"C'mon, please?" the woman practically begged. "We literally have the three houses around you. We want you to feel comfortable coming by *anytime.*"

The bride added to her campaign speech, "Yeah, I even have this whole scavenger hunt thing." She dug into the small phallic-shaped purse that was hanging around her shoulder. "I think you could help me check a few of these items off the list."

Shaw maintained a neutral face while reading her list of '*To-Dos Before I Do.*'

The bride tapped the bottom of the list that included multiple sexually explicit activities.

This wasn't his first rodeo, being subjected to pushy and inappropriately suggestive women. He wasn't interested in taking her, or any of the women around him, up on any of the offerings they were likely prepared to give. He and Baz had posed for pictures and very appropriately participated in bachelorette shenanigans while on the job before—well, Baz was always the one to push the line of what was appropriate in those situations anyhow.

Shaw was never interested in entertaining the attention of women while he was with Sloane, and the last couple of years he'd been shut off from any type of romantic connection. This was very different and he wasn't sure how Tinsley would feel about him offering attention to a bachelorette party. The last thing he'd want to do is hurt her in any kind of way, especially given the recent progression of their relationship. The bride's list contained a couple items both he and Tinsley could help them with though, so he decided to suggest just that.

"Actually, I can probably help with the list just a bit. One sec." He snapped his fingers at Harvey to follow him and walked into the condo. "Sugar, come save me," he almost whispered, projecting his signature grin.

"Save you?" Tinsley stood at the kitchen counter but turned around smiling when she heard him. "What happened?" She made her way to Shaw, soon noticing the unfamiliar guests gathered on the patio.

"We need one of those bottles of wine too." Shaw intertwined their hands and then plucked the chardonnay off the counter. His thumb caressed Tinsley's palm, smiling at her, he led them to the porch.

"Tins, these are our neighbors." Shaw gestured to the bachelorette party.

The woman who had offered Shaw Jell-O shots gave Tinsley an unfriendly once over with a snarled lip.

"Oh, congratulations!" Tinsley excitedly offered the bride.

The bride's momentary high, anticipating Shaw would agree to something fun on her list, didn't look amused to see him with a woman.

"Thanks," she curtly replied before whipping her head to Shaw. "Is this your sister?"

A quick chortle shot out of Shaw's nose. "Not at all"—he rubbed Tinsley's lower back, reaching out the bottle of wine to the bride—"you were looking for some help with that scavenger hunt of yours. You can cross off having a stranger buy you a drink."

The bride reluctantly accepted the bottle and then looked at her friend.

Her overly flirtatious bridesmaid's deceiving grin landed on Tinsley. "We actually have room for one more to join us tonight"—her venomous gaze moved to Shaw—"are you interested, Shaw?"

Tinsley didn't hesitate—Shaw had asked her to save him, afterall—she answered for both of them.

"That's such a kind invitation, but the twins will be calling soon, honey." Tinsley smirked up at Shaw, her hands working a circular motion on his strong chest. "You know Baz and Brin will be so disappointed if *Daddy* doesn't answer their post-game FaceTime."

Even while teasing him with his most hated pet name she still managed to be the sweetest damn thing he knew. Shaw's hand caressed Tinsley's side, sliding down her waist to land on the bottom of her cheek. A smile threatened upon his reply.

"She's right"—the knuckles on Shaw's free hand gently swept down her cheek—"it's tradition and our daughter Brindle is already so sensitive—we can't miss that phone call."

Tinsley couldn't help but giggle, leaning into her impromptu baby daddy. "We're going to be here all night though. If you guys need us to take any group photos for you later, please let us know," she spoke to the girls but couldn't take her eyes off Shaw, interlacing their fingers.

"Actually, that's on your scavenger list too. We'd be happy to take your group 'before' photo for you," Shaw added while squeezing Tinsley's hand.

"Can you take a group one for us now with the sunset in the background over there?" a different member of the bachelorette party requested.

"As long as one of you takes a picture for us in exchange." Shaw placed his lips on Tinsley's forehead.

"Sure," the woman agreed.

With Tinsley's hand in his, he followed the bachelorette group.

Tinsley gently tugged Shaw's hand. "I need to grab shoes."

"Hop on, sugar," Shaw encouraged her to climb on his back, which she did with no hesitation. "Come on, Harv." He couldn't leave out his favorite four-legged companion.

They all took a short hike several yards away from the condos to get a few photographs. Tinsley suggested poses she knew would be a hit and the women loosened up on her. Some were appreciative of Shaw and Tinsley for the perfect angles and capturing pictures on multiple phones.

While the group scrolled through the photos to approve them, Shaw set Tinsley on a patch of grass to fix the Maid of Honor's hair.

The bride took some convincing from her friends to change her attitude when Shaw declined multiple requests to be in their pictures. He did his best to chase the party away by pushing the socially acceptable line of PDA for the pictures he had requested. Tinsley giggled along and happily played into his affection until the women informed them they would be late for their reservation.

While perched on Shaw's back, Tinsley held her phone out so he could see the dozens of pictures they took. They claimed each picture as their favorite and Shaw made a friendly threat he wasn't going to share anything from the grill until she AirDropped him all the pictures. Their lips playfully argued against one another until they finally sat down for the dinner they prepared.

CHAPTER
Thirty One

Later that night Shaw noticed their private fire needed another log. He squeezed Tinsley's leg before getting up from their comfortable cuddling position on the patio to tend to the fire. Shaw set two additional logs on the flames, while poking around to ensure proper airflow he started singing.

The corners of Tinsley's mouth curled. "You do *not* know all the words to this?!" She chuckled along in awe and adoration.

Tinsley had connected her phone to the patio's bluetooth speakers. She'd been playing throwbacks for them to enjoy and Shaw sang along to *MMMBop 2.0.*

"Listen, this may be a different version, but the song's the same." Shaw smiled and pecked the side of her face. He filled Tinsley's wine glass, handing it to her as he sat back down with his hand on her leg.

Tinsley lifted the blanket to share, Shaw took the opportunity to place his hand on her bare leg.

"There's this Filipino patrolman that Baz and I have known for a few years. If you didn't know, Filipino people fucking love karaoke. Sometimes we join his family for karaoke nights." Shaw's thumb strummed along Tinley's thigh, he took a swig of his beer before continuing, "Baz and I have a few famous duets." He raised his eyebrows at Tinsley who adoringly giggled along to his story. "We happen to be professional karaoke kings," he proclaimed.

"Oh, lawd." Tinsley playfully rolled her eyes, but craved to hear more. "I would actually love to see the two of you in action. I can only imagine what you guys think you're really good at performing."

"I'll have you know, he and I took home gold one night because of our *Grammy*-worthy performance of *Proud Mary*."

Tinsley nearly spit her wine, bursting into laughter. "Stop it! No you didn't."

"I swear, sugar, on everything." He shook his head laughing. "Baz has some pipes."

"So, he's the Tina to your Ike then, huh?"

Shaw quickly clarified, "I never said I didn't help. He might have a larger range with the vocals, but we *both* put in work when it comes to our choreography."

Tinsley smirked behind her wine glass. "Oh, I'm aware of what your hips can do, tough guy." She pumped her perfect eyebrows. "I would never question whether or not you can dance."

Shaw briefly caressed the side of Tinsley's face just before pulling her chin close enough to connect their lips. After a sensual peck, he spoke softly to her, "just think, I've only had a couple opportunities to show you what I'm capable of."

Tinsley led the next kiss, her tongue diving into Shaw's mouth. Her hand found itself sliding along his inner thigh before she slowed her lips.

"I fully intend on allowing you an endless amount of opportunities to keep showing me." Her mouth teased him as it brushed over his.

Shaw gently shoved his hand under Tinsley's thigh to bring her over to straddle him.

She was on her way toward his lap when she pulled back giggling and readjusted the blanket to hide her bottom half that was now partially exposed.

"Hunter!" she flirtatiously scolded him, "I don't have any pants on."

Tinsley had joined him on the patio wearing only his hoodie, a thong, and the blanket she had kept over her bottom half.

Shaw conceded, letting her sit next to him to cover herself up.

"You're right, I'm not trying to share that view with anyone."

He leaned his back against the side of the wicker couch they were on and then encouraged Tinsley to make her way between his legs.

She happily leaned herself against his chest before covering them both up with the blanket.

"You've shown me about a dozen new favorite things in just like the last twenty-four hours alone. Are you ready to maintain my increased level of expectations there, tough guy?"

Shaw massaged Tinsley's chest as she reached up behind her to lightly scratch the back of his head.

"I'm sure that I am, but why don't you let me know what's on that list, sweetcheeks."

"Obviously, I'm immediately and blindly including your karaoke skills to my list."

Shaw's masseuse hands didn't break their rhythm. He smirked, waiting for her to continue.

"And I'm not sure if you're aware, but you're even hotter than normal when you're at the grill with a beer in your hand." She giggled in anticipation for her confession. "I almost had to bring you back inside for a little bit when I caught a glimpse of you out here earlier."

"What?!" Shaw chuckled in her ear and gave her breasts a suggestive squeeze. "For future reference, you come get me next time you have those thoughts running through your head—I don't give a *damn* what I'm in the middle of."

"Not only were you out here making me blush, but I'll *fully* admit, you, sir, are a grill master. So, basically, *one* of my new favorite things is you grilling us dinner."

"I'll be making it a priority to get us set up for that when we get home then. I'll be your personal grill master *anytime*, sugar," Shaw promised with a smile.

Tinsley's hands drifted from Shaw's head to his legs, she made circular motions on both of his thighs.

"I've also fallen completely in love with this whole getting to cuddle with you in front of a fire kinda thing."

Shaw's hands descended along her torso and gripped her hip bones to pull her closer to him.

"That's another item I'll happily add to the priority list," he whispered into her ear before placing a couple of soft pecks on her neck.

Tinsley responded by moving her hips back to press into the front of his shorts as she squeezed his thighs.

Shaw's mouth played on her neck while his hands firmly pulled her hips toward him again.

Tinsley exhaled a pleasurable sigh as her head rolled back toward his shoulder.

The soft sound triggered excitement so Shaw's hands made their way along the inside of Tinsley's legs. He only stroked her inner thighs a couple of times before one of his hands reached the front of her thong. His fingers made passes along the material and her delicate skin as she tried not to squirm under his enticing touch.

"Hunt," she whimpered.

Shaw attentively and sensitively glided his hand under the scanty thong so he was free to explore. His fingers slid around in a rhythm that elicited a matching movement in Tinsley's hips.

Her head turned to find his lips just as he was mindfully pressing his fingers into her.

Tinsley exhaled a soft moan into his mouth when his fingers curled. She reached up with one hand, gently rubbing his ear. Shaw's very capable hands were making Tinsley lose control as she felt them coming out of her to circle her clit.

She tried to swallow another moan when she jumped from a woman who let out a loud laugh that sounded almost like a scream.

Shaw's arms instinctively wrapped around Tinsley as he whipped his head toward the noise.

Harvey shot up as quickly as he could when he heard the voice, now growling at the edge of their patio.

"Harv!" Both Shaw and Tinsley called him, almost in unison.

Harvey grumbled a bit more before turning around to check-in while they sat on the small couch.

An endless rumble of cackling and screeching echoed as the bachelorette group stumbled toward their condos.

Shaw placed a gentle kiss to the top of Tinsley's head and made sure the blanket completely covered her torso and legs as the women got closer.

"Oh, it's Harvey!" The bride changed her route and headed toward the cane corso who obediently sat near Shaw and Tinsley, watching the group with his nub flying all over the place.

"Ooh, and Shaw!" She shimmied. He sat facing the door of the condo with his back to the edge of the patio so he didn't see her dancing approach.

A couple of the women followed the bride, and they soon spotted Tinsley cuddling on Shaw's chest.

"Oh, we're interrupting." One of the women spit out a drunken chuckle.

"Ladies." Shaw nodded while rubbing Tinsley's arm.

Tinsley offered a quick wave to the bride and two of her friends who joined her on the small patio.

All three women took it upon themselves to sit in the empty chairs across from Shaw and Tinsley. The bride sat on her friend's lap as there were only two chairs.

"Isn't this the coziest little setup?" the blonde woman commented. "Perhaps you'd like to come light our fire?" She pumped her brows at Shaw.

"I'm a one fire kind of guy." He lovingly squeezed Tinsley before instructing Harvey to lay down.

"I'm confident you could manage," she barely vocalized before hiccups took over.

Tinsley stayed silent, she wasn't a fan of how forward the group had been. Not to mention, they interrupted her perfect moment of thoroughly enjoying Shaw's phenomenal touch that still had her heart pounding and private areas pulsing.

"What kind of guy would I be disrespecting my wife and the mother of our twins if I managed multiple fires?" He shrugged. "My boy Baz is at an age where he needs a respectful father figure to teach him how to treat women."

The corner of Tinsley's lip curled—even though they'd spun a ridiculous story for these strangers it was funny to hear him making likely realistic connections about his best friend.

"Oh yeah? How old?" the bride asked.

"They'll be twelve in a few weeks," Shaw answered while plucking his beer from a side table.

"Twelve?! How old are you two?"

"Tins and I were high school sweethearts." He hooked her chin and gazed into her amazing brown eyes before placing a soft kiss to her lips. He winked at her and finally finished answering the bride, "That stereotypical jock and cheerleader turned prom royalty love story that drove us into parenthood on prom night."

"Wow!" The most sober of the trio shook her head with wide and disbelieving eyes. "You don't see that work out too often these days."

"We're actually celebrating our tenth wedding anniversary this year." Tinsley continued to spin their imaginary life, her hand firmly gliding down Shaw's torso.

He took a deep, adoring breath and looked at Tinsley who was still comfortably perched on his strong chest. "Yep, fifteen together, nearly ten married."

"Married?" the bride scoffed. "I haven't seen a ring on *either* of you."

Tinsley smiled. "I'm getting an upgrade for our ten-year, so it's with the jeweler."

"I typically don't wear mine because of work." Shaw squeezed Tinsley and pecked her head. "My wife knows I'm always a gentleman with or without my ring though."

"What are the gentleman rules surrounding bachelorette parties?" the bride inquired. "I still have a few items on my scavenger hunt here." She struggled to open her purse, fighting the fancy clasp that held it shut.

"If the last fifteen years have taught me nothing else, I know better than to participate in any more of the items on that list than we already have," Shaw declined. He released a baffled chuckle that these women were still pursuing this nonsense, especially with Tinsley literally lying on him. "I'd never do anything to risk my marriage in the slightest."

"What if your wife signs off?" The bride pumped her brows, leaning her elbows onto her thighs and squeezing her breasts together in the process.

Shaw opened his mouth to respond but Tinsley provided a response first.

"I don't force my husband to do things he isn't interested in. And I can assure you, I'm not the sharing type." Tinsley smiled, but her eyes projected a more serious tone.

The friend the bride sat on decided it was best if they left. "C'mon, girl, we have an early appointment at the spa tomorrow. We should get to bed."

The bride reluctantly stood and drunkenly swayed, trying to balance in her heels. "There's no expiration on that offer, Shaw." She finally got pulled from the patio by her friends.

"My my, Officer Shaw, you sure like to hit the gas." Tinsley giggled just seconds after the bachelorette party finally left.

"What the fuck?!" Shaw laughed and made her look at him. "I give an honest and genuine denial to those voracious women and you're back on the Officer Shaw routine?" He pecked her forehead.

Tinsley's head fell into his chest and she continued to giggle. "I was talking about how I've always known us to have a non-traditional relationship. You know, full on tongue action for our first kiss, closets cleared on our first meaningful conversation, sleeping over before our first date—it makes *total* sense that we haven't even left our first getaway and we've been married for ten years with twins."

Shaw rolled his eyes back, grinning from ear to ear, he pulled her in tighter.

"I mean, where do we even go from here?! Are we to be grandparents soon too?!" Tinsley exaggerated her tone.

"I fuckin' hope not!" Shaw choked out a laugh. "Baz isn't even close to being ready for kids." He kept it at that, not wanting to divulge his opinions about Tilly being wrong for Baz.

Tinsley reached down and scratched Harvey's head before she settled comfortably against Shaw's strong body again. She laid on her side, leaning into his chest as they allowed the allure of the crackling fire to consume their gaze.

"I have an idea on where we can go from here." Shaw's hand slid down the side of her body, he lifted Tinsley's top and gave her exposed cheek a suggestive squeeze while still under the cover of their blanket.

She tilted her head up and was immediately met with Shaw's lips. Rather than stretching, she twirled her body to face him and within seconds, straddled him as they continued to let their tongues play with one another.

"Before we were so rudely interrupted I was going to also let you know this progression is another one of my new favorite things." Tinsley leaned down to whisper in his ear, "this stitch-free version of my tough guy is *exactly* what I've been craving."

Shaw pulled Tinsley in by her cheeks as he thrust to leave no room between them, she soon joined his rhythm but wanted more. As their lips mutually slowed on one another, Shaw's hands ascended under his hoodie she wore.

"While we're on the topic of favorites, I'd like to get you into my other favorite outfit of yours." He lifted the back of the hoodie but didn't remove it, his hands instead reached for her thong and tugged on the back of the band.

Tinsley slowly but firmly pressed her pelvis against the front of his shorts before she placed her mouth near his ear again.

"Hunt, you'll have to bring me inside if you want to see that outfit."

Shaw didn't hesitate. He got his hands out from under the blanket and secured it against Tinsley before lifting both of them off the couch.

"C'mon, Harv," he encouraged the dog to follow them. Shaw set Tinsley down right inside the condo so he could lock the slider and pull the blinds shut. He tugged on the blanket that covered her and flung it to the side before lifting Tinsley again.

She wrapped her legs around his waist and reached her soft hands to his scruffy face.

"This"—she gently rubbed his facial hair—"really elevates your tough guy status. I'm a *big* fan."

"You'll have to let me know when it reaches the perfect tough guy status." He walked them to the bed. "Because I'm *very* interested in giving you every damn thing you want." He set her down and reached for the bottom of the hoodie to remove it.

"I just want you, Hunt."

"I'm all yours, sugar," he whispered before gently connecting their lips and leaning her back onto the bed.

CHAPTER
Thirty Two

"Should I head back to my place, or do you want me to stay here tonight?" Shaw asked as he pulled into Tinsley's driveway the next evening.

The corners of her lips quivered down. "Do you not want to stay with us?" She stared at him with sad eyes as he parked.

"No—I do!" he quickly assured her, shaking his head. "I just don't want to wear out my welcome is all. I realize I kind of barged in and haven't given you any kind of break from me." He chuckled.

Tinsley reached over and held the inside of Shaw's leg. "I'm sorry I gave you any indication that I needed a break from you—*especially* after this weekend."

"Ma'am." Shaw leveled his gaze at her, the corner of his lip curling slightly. "We've talked about those apologies."

"You know what else we've talked about, *Officer Shaw*?"

Tinsley put her elbows on the center console to reach for him, he met her halfway for their mouths to connect.

"What?" He smirked after their lips separated.

Tinsley caught her bottom lip with her teeth before responding, "how much I love waking up next to you."

He touched their foreheads and then tucked a loose strand of hair behind her ear. "That feeling's *more* than mutual, sugar."

"Then don't feel like you have to pump the brakes on us, tough guy. I'm more than happy and the last thing I need is a break from you."

They had only just pressed their lips together again when Tinsley's phone rattled off texting notifications.

> **Brindle Boo**
> Bitch!
>
> Are you home yet?!
>
> I NEED getaway deets ASAP!
>
> How many times did you put out for Shawberry?!
>
> How many OOOOOOOs did my girl get?!
>
> It's time to share!!
>
> Is he as big as I think !?

"Brindle?" Shaw grinned, knowing full well no one else sent Tinsley rapid fire texts quite like her melodramatic bestie.

"I don't even have to look to confirm." She laughed.

> **Brindle Boo**
> Are you home?
>
> Drinks tonight?
>
> Did you get ANY pics of that man's body you'd be willing to share?!

"You sure he's okay?" Shaw tilted his chin with a crooked grin while Tinsley's phone continued to sing.

Tinsley dug through her purse for the noisy phone, her eyes widened but she giggled and confirmed Brindle was more than fine.

"Any texts you'd like to share?" Shaw's curiosity peaked watching Tinsley read Brindle's texts.

Tinsley immediately shook her head. "Mmmmm…" Sounds of amusement crept through her voice. "He wants to know if I snapped any *revealing* pics of you that I'd be willing to send his way." Her brunette brows pumped suggestively.

Heat rushed to Shaw's face and he shook his head before holding the bridge of his nose.

Tinsley placed her hand on his vein-popping forearm. "Don't worry, even if I did snap any photos of you like that, I certainly wouldn't share them—*especially* not with Brindle. I told you"—her thumb made passes on his forearm—"I'm not interested in sharing you, tough guy."

"*Zero* interest in sharing you in any capacity either. You're all mine, sugar."

Shaw hooked her chin to peck her before getting out of the truck and helping Harvey jump from the back door. The excited cane corso sprinted for the wooden gate while Shaw gathered everyone's bags. He thought about how effortless it had been with Tinsley—besides his initial ask. He smiled to himself, nearly embarrassed about how hesitant he'd been to ask her out. She'd been nothing short of perfect and their getaway only intensified his feelings for her. Phantom sensations of loving on her flawless body all weekend ran through his mind, making his heart race. He wasn't surprised she'd exceeded his expectations in every single way imaginable.

He'd already been completely captivated by the fact that she was sweet, gorgeous, brilliant, resilient, funny, and kind; but now that they'd broken all the physically intimate barriers intact while he had stitches, Shaw was infatuated. The mere thought of her brought overwhelming joy to his heart. He leaned further in the truck to grab another bag when he felt Tinsley's hands slide around his waist until she had them wrapped around his torso from behind.

She laid her head on his back before telling him, "I had an amazing time this weekend—thank you for *everything*, tough guy." Her fingers, spread wide, moved up and down his chest and abs after giving him an adoring squeeze.

He felt a rush of warmth from her loving embrace. He caught one of her hands and brought it to his lips for a quick peck before spinning around. They held one another's gaze and Shaw gently swayed them just before pressing his lips against her forehead.

"You're welcome, sugar."

"Not that I want to sound ungrateful," she clarified with a smirk, "but any chance you'll take me one more place before our week-end's over?"

Shaw chuckled and gently grazed her cheek bone with the back of his fingers. "Anywhere. Where're we headed next?"

"I think it's about time you take us to bed, Hunt." She placed both palms on his strong chest as her sultry eyes lingered on his.

Shaw's hands gravitated to Tinsley's backside and he lifted her up. She hooked her legs around his waist and her arms around his shoulders.

"I'll get all this later." He closed the back door of the truck and carried Tinsley to the house.

CHAPTER
Thirty Three

BOTH SHAW AND TINSLEY HAD WORK THE DAY AFTER THEIR RETURN. Shaw got up predictably right when his alarm went off and adoringly smiled over at Tinsley who didn't move an inch at the sound. A large part of him wanted to wake her up because he'd never be able to get enough of her. She looked so peaceful in her sleep that he decided to shower first. He swung his legs over the side of the mattress and heard Harvey stretching to get out of his bed just before the sound of his nails clicked on the hardwood floor.

"Wanna go outside, bud?" Shaw stood, stretching while the cane corso trotted to him just before shaking his entire body, jowls slapping the sides of his face.

"Oh, I'm good enough to take you out alone at home, huh?"

He reached down and gave him a few good scratches on his rear-end.

"Come on, buddy."

They walked to the backyard where Shaw stood on the deck while Harvey took care of his morning duties. He thought about Tinsley's new favorite things she'd disclosed over the weekend. Her large yard offered plenty of room for him to bring those to life for her. Once he had an overall plan in place and Harvey completed his business, Shaw went back inside to shower and get ready for a long workday ahead.

"So." Baz smirked at his partner, wiping his beard with his thumb and index finger as they started their patrol.

Shaw stared through the passenger window, offering no verbal response and restraining a smirk of his own.

Baz's heavy hand quickly reached over to swat Shaw's chest.

"You don't wanna tell me how many *new* ways your ass got tickled this weekend?"

"Come on, bro." Shaw failed to conceal his crimson complexion, but covered the smile that consumed his face.

"We're still gonna gatekeep, huh?" Baz chuckled and flicked on the blinker. "I get it. Don't think I'm not in the know though. I know you been fuckin' living with her. I just wanted to be sure she took care of you a little extra considering your grand damn gesture of a weekend getaway."

Shaw and Tinsley had both taken very good care of one another given their new found freedom with the removal of all Shaw's stitches. Baz didn't have any idea about that injury though and Shaw had been very cryptic when it came to any details related to what exactly he'd been doing with Tinsley. Of course, his partner made his own assumptions that Shaw had never confirmed or denied.

"You know"—Shaw finally turned his head to look at Baz—"you're starting to sound like your boy, Brindle."

"Fuck you, fam." Baz laughed out loud, slapping the steering wheel. He pulled into the parking lot to pick up their morning coffee and got out of the cruiser. He looked at Shaw over the hood. "Can you at least tell me if you had a good time or not? I'm genuinely fuckin' asking how your weekend was." Baz's palms tilted towards the sky, his elbows near his hips.

Shaw headed for the coffee shop, unable to wipe the smile from his face thinking about Tinsley.

"It was an *unbelievable* time, honestly." He had to shove down the memories of the more intimate details of their weekend to avoid a deeper interrogation by Baz. "Tins is..." He shook his head, cheeks raised as the corners of his mouth reached for his ears. "She's such an amazing woman. And *so goddamn* sweet." He looked sideways at his best friend and asked, "Who knew the biggest fumble in your life would be the reason I want to wake up every morning and make it home every night?"

"Fuck off." Baz delivered a healthy, lively shove as they walked into the shop. "I'm okay being the villain in that story to see this little spark in you again, fam." He patted Shaw on his shoulder before tickling his earlobe with his oversized fingertips.

"Get the fuck off me, bro," Shaw batted his hand away, smiling and trying to whisper as there were kids within earshot.

"Uh oh, she spin you a little too tight this weekend?" Baz teased with a final tug on Shaw's earlobe before greeting the barista.

"Hi guys, how're you two doing?" the barista asked, interrupting their bickering.

"Livin'," Baz responded for both of them.

Shaw's head still shook at Baz when his phone buzzed.

"Uh oh, boss already checking in," Baz continued to torment his twitterpated partner.

Shaw rolled his eyes but mostly ignored Baz as he read Tinsley's text.

> SWEETCHEEKS
> The girls are here bright and early on their day
> off today. They would like me to give them
> a play by play of our entire weekend…Brindle
> even rescheduled his first client.

"You and Brindle are two damn peas in a pod." Shaw shot a chuckle through his nose, smirking at Baz before he replied to Tinsley.

> Baz would be pissed to know he didn't get the
> invite. His big ass just started hounding me.

> SWEETCHEEKS
> We're surrounded by giddy pervs

"Did I lose you?" Baz asked as they walked back to the cruiser.

"What?" Shaw looked up from his phone.

"Shit, fam. Do I need to take the phone?" He laughed. "I told you fuck you for the Brindle comment and then I asked if I lost you."

"No, bro, I'm here." Shaw slid into the passenger's seat and secured his coffee in the cupholder. "Brindle apparently cancelled his first client today because he wants Tins to tell him all about the weekend. So, like I said, two fucking peas in a pod."

Baz flipped off his partner.

Shaw put his phone back in his pocket and took a drink of his coffee.

Baz reached over and gave him a few knowing pats to his leg before he rolled out of the parking lot.

"You're done fucking gatekeeping!" Brindle threw his hands around like a crazed conductor but managed to stay seated with crossed legs. "You've been cryptic since he came in and finally asked you on a damn date!"

The salon girls cackled but agreed with Brindle. They *all* wanted details.

"*And* we all fucking know that we missed some kind of critical damn piece of information after what I witnessed when he picked you up for that first date, bitch." He slapped the arm rests of his barber chair.

Tinsley pulled out her phone since her last text to Shaw. She donned a smirk on her face but hadn't offered Brindle a verbal response. Her fingers scrolled around her phone a bit before she stuffed the device in her back pocket and then smiled at her client, Brook.

"Let's get your hair washed," she urged her to follow her to the sinks.

"You bi-" Brindle started until his phone signaled a text. He looked at the screen to see that Tinsley had sent at least a dozen photos to the salon group chat. His shoulders settled as he leaned into his chair, settling on the fact that they'd all get to look at those while Tinsley washed her client's hair.

Tinsley knew they'd all received her text when a collective squeal rumbled throughout the salon.

At no surprise to anyone, Brindle offered an inappropriate comment.

"Ahhhh!" he screeched. "How many times did Shawberry take you in front of this fire?!"

Tinsley's face burned as she helped Brook lean back into the sink.

"What would we all do without Brindle?" Brook asked.

Tinsley quickly replied with a smile on her face, "obviously, we'd all be cringing a lot less."

Brook opened one of her squinted eyes. "Well, good for you to have someone who's putting such a big smile on your face, Tins."

Tinsley had to agree, "Hunt's been doing a *phenomenal* job in that department for sure."

After washing Brook's hair Tinsley stayed behind to rinse the sink. She got lost in thoughts of her perfectly dreamy weekend with Shaw. He'd taken long enough to finally ask her out, and then of course they were quite conservative before his stitches were removed, but he'd absolutely been worth the wait. Everything with Shaw, since their very first meeting, had felt undeniably right. She wondered how her heart ever managed without him.

Her growing heart melted even more when she walked toward her station and Brindle had the television projecting a screen mirror of his phone. They all gawked at one of the pictures Tinsley sent—the shot that was actually her phone's screensaver now too. It was a picture of their hike along the Columbia River and Shaw had lifted Harvey to pose for this photo. He had the one hundred-twenty pound dog suspended in his muscular arms like a baby in front of him and Harvey's tongue happily hung out of his smiling mouth. Shaw's green eyes were piercing, his expression smoldering, and the arm visible behind Harvey showcased his brawny bicep.

"Damn!" Brook turned to Tinsley. "*That's* your boyfriend?!"

Tinsley gleaned with pride and adoration while looking at the photo. "That's Hunt."

"Tins! Boo! I *love* this for you!" Brindle did a few excited hops, clutching his phone to his chest with a pouting look on his face while Tinsley combed through Brook's wet hair. "Shawberry's got it goin' on." He zoomed in on Shaw's bicep before moving to the front of his pants.

"Brindle!" Tinsley scolded him.

Brindle reluctantly zoomed back out and then flicked to the first picture she sent so he could go in order while they looked at the pictures Tinsley was willing to share of the weekend.

"Shaw. Fucking. Berry." Brindle enunciated when he stopped on a dreamy photo of Shaw sitting by the private patio fire. "Tins, you lucky bitch!"

The cackling hen style conversation reverberated throughout the salon. The girls asked a thousand and one questions about the weekend as they slowly rolled through the photos Tinsley sent.

"So quit fucking playing games with us." Brindle stood and made a full rotation of his sassy arm before landing it on his hip. "We want real answers—it's been *weeks, and* you guys just went on your first damn trip. No more gatekeeping! One to ten, exactly *how good* is our favorite beefcake?" Brindle trapped his bottom lip with his eyes rolled to the back of his head.

All eyes now on a blushing and giddy Tinsley.

She took a deep inhale, trying to tame her smile and attempting to keep her thoughts of Shaw loving on her body at bay so she could think straight.

Tinsley bit her bottom lip as her mouth morphed into a smile. Her gaze slowly lifted to her friends. "Whatever's in your head right now about how perfect he is, Hunt *infinitely* exceeded that fantasy the *entire* damn weekend."

Everyone squealed and Brindle gripped his chest talking a million miles an hour on all the things he would've happily allowed Shaw to do to him.

CHAPTER
Thirty Four

Shaw and Baz stopped at a flower shop later that week during their morning route so Shaw could pick up a birthday bouquet for Tinsley. Baz watched his partner hand select a few of the peonies he wanted the florist to add to the already overflowing arrangement.

"Damn, fam." Baz spun on his heel, shaking his head and smiling. "You've fallen pretty fuckin' hard. A goddamn getaway wasn't enough? You're gonna buy out the stock of flowers here too, huh?"

Shaw wasn't embarrassed at all about his feelings for Tinsley. If anything he was kicking himself for having been so hesitant. He shrugged at his partner during his reply, "What can I say, she's damn perfect."

"Fam." Baz swatted his best friend's chest. "You ever think about how Tins wanted me first? Maybe she'll always have a little lingering desire for Big Daddy?" He projected a devilish grin as he caressed his own chest.

"You fucking *wish*!" Shaw laughed but still flipped off his buddy. "If you remember correctly, she liked talking to *me* on the app. I revitalized that damn conversation for you. Not to mention, I've seen your profile—she left because your ass catfished her."

Baz threw his head back and let out a belly roar. "I only filtered *one* of my photos, and it's not even that much of a stretch," he defended himself before continuing, "and you can't deny that she likes how I look in a suit." He leaned toward Shaw and winked.

"You better watch your fucking self." Shaw smiled at his best friend as he scratched his chin with his thumbnail, considering how long he'd let Baz continue his dumbass little speech.

Baz took pleasure in getting Shaw riled up, but he decided he'd done enough for the day so he took a different direction. "I'll be telling everyone at the wedding it was my failure that brought you so much happiness." Baz flexed a bit. "Can't wait for my Best Man toast."

Shaw gave his partner a little friendly shove. "Shouldn't you be getting flowers soon too?" He narrowed his eyes at Baz. "Don't act like you haven't been spending much more time with Tilly lately. Not to mention, you haven't called her Big-Titties in a while. Sounds to me like someone else is getting serious."

"I don't know about *serious*." Baz's head rolled to the side and he looked at Shaw from under his brows.

Shaw chuckled. "Bro, you haven't been taking any overtime lately either. You clearly don't even stay at your place every night. Don't forget, I caught your big ass trying to act like you'd been parked there all night when I picked you up the other day."

Baz laughed before he dug into his buddy, "Your ass probably hasn't stayed at your place in weeks either!"

"I'm not the one in denial. I'll fully admit I've been sleeping at her place," Shaw reminded him with a friendly shrug. "I'm also not discouraging you, I'm just sayin'—don't act like you're not working toward getting yourself all boo'd up."

"Maybe." Baz swiped his meaty hand across his mouth, if nothing else just to cover and try to clear the smile from it.

Shaw reached up and grabbed his large shoulders. "Don't shy away from that spark, big guy," he teased.

"Fuck off," Baz laughed.

"Happy Birthday, sugar." Shaw confidently pressed his lips against Tinsley's in front of her entire salon.

Tinsley gushed when they separated as memories of their steamy morning flooded her mind.

"Thank you." She looked at the oversized arrangement he carried that was nothing but various shades of pink peonies. The bouquet was enormous, the floral notes consumed the lingering chemical scent of the salon.

"Hunt, these are *beautiful*. You've done so much for my birthday already." She fondly shook her head at him, sliding her hands around his waist to squeeze him.

"And I'm not done yet." He pecked the top of her head and then reached for Harvey who had been begging for his turn.

"Happy Birthday, Tins." Baz walked over and gave her a hug.

"Thank you." She smiled at him before noticing Brindle roll his eyes at the exchange. Tinsley shot her best friend a light warning glare, reminding him to be nice.

"Shawberry, you better be careful spoiling her like this," Brindle warned, shaking his head with his best duck face projecting toward his favorite beefcake.

"C'mon Brindle, are you trying to say my girlfriend's not worth this level of spoiling?" Shaw was still in a squat greeting Harvey but looked sideways up at Tinsley. That was the first time he used the official girlfriend title with her.

Tinsley hid her bashful, blushing face while Brindle squealed. Her chest pounded as each beat of her heart surged at Shaw's proclamation.

"We better head outta here." Shaw stood and pulled Tinsley into his strong arms. He would never pass up an opportunity to show her affection, but he also wanted to offer her a moment of hiding her face. "I'll pick you up after work." He hooked her chin with his index finger, smiling down at her as he pressed his lips against hers. "Have a good day, gorgeous."

Tinsley giggled in his arms and managed a giddy response. "Be safe out there today, boyfriend."

Shaw couldn't help but kiss her again with glee-filled satisfaction of her returned affection. He'd barely taken a step from her when Baz grabbed the back of his vest as Brindle squealed like a schoolgirl.

"Let's go, loverboy." Baz laughed, ushering Shaw out of the salon. They missed Brindle and the girls screeching and rushing toward Tinsley. The taller of the duo put his arm across his buddy's shoulders. "Fam, that makes me damn happy to see that smile on your handsome mug."

Shaw was smitten. He wiped his face before looking at Baz who'd just removed his large arm from him. "Alright, I may owe you for fuckin' it up with her." He laughed before narrowing his gaze at Baz. "But don't ever be an asshole to her again." His friendly warning ended with a firm jab to his partner's arm.

Baz held his belly as his head fell back laughing. "I haven't even called her Tickle-Me in weeks!"

"I know," Shaw admitted with a grin.

CHAPTER
Thirty Five

THE ESTABLISHMENT SLATED FOR THE BIRTHDAY DINNER RESERVA-
tions Tinsley's parents made was semi-formal. Shaw had a few suits
on hand that he'd wear to court. He ran home after work to get
ready for Tinsley's birthday dinner. He selected a tailored denim blue
suit with a simple white button up that wasn't clasped all the way to
his neck.

Tinsley threw her head back in enchanted awe when Shaw walked
into the house that evening to pick her up. "How do you look so hand-
somely delicious in *everything* you put on?" She hurried over to throw
her arms around his broad shoulders. She thought his uniform would
always be her favorite look, but watching this suit hug the rippling muscles throughout his body, she contemplated sliding the police uniform
to a runner-up spot.

"Me?" Shaw chuckled with her in his arms. "Look at your drop
dead gorgeous ass!" He twirled her to get a full view of her ensemble.
His eyes made an appreciative pop at the view from behind that was just
as good as the front.

Tinsley's hair was always perfect, but she created an elegant half
up-half down style to pair with her dress. She wore the tightest, full

length bodycon dress that accentuated every curve on her body. The dress was a dark cobalt blue with a halter style neckline. She decided not to accessorize with a necklace or any bracelets—just a set of very simple, silver dangle drop earrings.

"I just need to go get my shoes." She pecked him before heading to her closet. Tinsley reentered the living room about four inches taller, but still fit comfortably under Shaw's arm.

"Can I give you your birthday gift now, or do you want to wait, sugar?"

Tinsley whipped her head toward Shaw, blowing out a chuckle. "Wait… a birthday gift? An entire trip, one helluva sexy wake up round this morning, beautiful flowers, *and* agreeing to dine alone with my parents wasn't enough?" Her palms started at the bottom of his ribcage and grazed the length of his torso before interlocking her fingers behind his neck.

"I told you I wasn't done." He tilted his chin down to initiate a passionate kiss, leading with his tongue. They went back and forth until hearing Harvey's favorite babysitter bursting through the back door.

"Boo!" Brindle shouted, as they slowly separated before he was visible. "You better have the blue one on or I'll be going as Shawberry's date instead of you." He walked through the mudroom and to the kitchen where he lasered in on Tinsley and Shaw standing in the living room with their arms wrapped around one another.

"Damn!" Brindle set his bag down and pulled his phone out. "How fucking amazing do you two look?!" He snapped a few photos, not allowing them any time to pose. "I'm surprised you're still agreeing to go out after seeing him looking like that." Brindle appreciatively gestured toward Shaw.

Tinsley shook her head, smiling as her brows furrowed. "What?"

"Bitch, I'd be taking that man to bed. Dinner my ass! Ditch the parentals, I'll go home, and you two go to bed."

Tinsley and Shaw laughed, they both knew that's how their night would end, but they could manage to spend a few hours beforehand with the company of others.

"So." Tinsley affectionately rubbed Shaw's leg over the center console of his truck as they headed toward Bellevue to meet her parents for her traditional, fancy birthday dinner. "How long have we been girlfriend-boyfriend?"

Shaw picked her hand up to kiss the back of it before he looked at her with a smirk. "So, you *are* okay with those titles? You weren't just agreeing in front of the girls to avoid embarrassing me?"

Tinsley giggled, caressing his hand with her thumb. "I accepted that with my whole heart, Hunt."

"I couldn't be happier, Tins." Shaw gently let go of her hand and opened the middle console to pull something out. "Happy Birthday." He smiled and held out a small bag.

"Hunt." Tinsley beamed and her head lightly fell against the leather headrest. "You've already done *way* too much for my birthday."

Shaw grinned with a slight shrug. "First of all, it's never too much when we're talking about what you deserve. But fine, this one isn't a birthday gift then, it's just a regular old girlfriend gift." He finished with a subtle tilt of his head

"Well, that's not fair because I didn't get you a boyfriend gift," Tinsley playfully protested.

"Oh, my damn boyfriend gift's coming, sugar." He gave her a suggestive look up and down. "The second we get back home—actually, the second Brindle leaves— I'll be getting my boyfriend gift."

Tinsley squeezed the inside of his leg, eyes smiling and heart swelling. "Deal. Even though that's a gift for both of us."

Shaw reached across the console, trying to place his hand between her legs but the dress didn't allow it. He settled for a gentle grasp on her thigh, his thumb and fingers making a valiant effort to orbit her leg.

Tinsley briefly caressed the back of his hand before directing her attention to the small bag he'd given her. She pulled a piece of tissue off the top of it and uncovered a small box inside—a jewelry box. Tinsley gasped upon opening it.

"Hunt." She looked at him, eyes widening and struggling for words. "I… y-you…" She shook her head in disbelieving gratitude and took a quick breath. "Hunt, are you sure? These are gorgeous!"

"More than sure, Tins." Shaw smiled at her and rubbed the side of her gorgeous face with his knuckles.

Tinsley took off the dangling earrings she wore to put on her new diamond studs. "I'm going to owe you like a billion boyfriend gifts when we get home." She secured the second one and then leaned over to kiss the side of his face. "You are so thoughtful and amazing, tough guy. Thank you."

"I know I'm in the dark a bit on what diamond earrings you got stolen from you, but figured a gorgeous, classy lady like yourself likely had some studs."

"Well, I didn't *officially* have a stud until today." She winked at him while Shaw rolled his head back smiling.

"But you're right. I *did* have my studs stolen that day. They weren't *this* big though." Tinsley pulled down the mirror on the back of the visor to look at the shimmering diamonds.

"Hunt"—she looked at him while closing the visor—"are you sure? Like these are—"

"Sugar," he interrupted her worry with a quick chuckle. "You're more than worth it, and I wouldn't have gotten them if I couldn't."

He could still see the concern in Tinsley's eyes, despite the smile she projected. He reached his hand over the console to interlace their fingers.

"As my official girlfriend, you're just gonna have to get used to the fact that my job is to take care of you in every capacity imaginable." He kissed her hand. "That includes an outrageous level of spoiling."

Tinsley melted from his touch and couldn't help but get lost in simply staring at her perfectly thoughtful boyfriend.

"Hi, honey!" Tinsley's mom greeted her. "Happy birthday!" She held her daughter and firmly rubbed her hands on her back. While still in her welcoming embrace, she looked up at Shaw right behind Tinsley and offered him a greeting as well.

"Shaw." Smiling, she walked over to hug him. "It's so nice to see you again."

"You as well, Colette." Shaw returned the friendly gesture.

When Colette backed away she gave her daughter a suggesting look with her eyebrows raised at how handsome Shaw was in his suit. She stole the introduction from her daughter when she held a hand, palm up, toward her husband.

"Shaw"—she held his strong bicep—"this is my husband, Rick." Colette laughed and rolled her eyes. "*Dr.* Rick Adams." She knew her husband preferred when people were made aware of that title during initial introductions.

"Dr. Adams, it's a pleasure to meet you, sir." Shaw extended his reach to shake hands with Tinsley's dad.

The dark-haired, clean-cut, lean man chuckled. "Rick is just fine too, Shaw. It's nice to meet you." Rick looked toward his daughter before hugging her. "Happy Birthday, sweetie."

"Thanks, Dad." Tinsley gently pulled a lock of her hair that got caught on her dad's jacket.

A hostess showed them to a round table almost directly under the massive glass chandelier that hung in the middle of the restaurant. Shaw pulled out a chair for Tinsley before he took a seat next to her so he had a view of the entrance.

Everyone browsed the dinner menu when Shaw made conversation with Tinsley's mom.

"Colette, what is it that you do? Are you in the medical field as well?" Shaw asked before taking a sip of the one glass of wine he planned to have during dinner.

"I am," she proudly confirmed. "I've been a labor and delivery nurse for over twenty years." She shook her head and plucked her glass off the table. "I can't handle the emergency room like my son does and my husband's pretty specialized with his work. Being around sweet babies is where I like to be. More often than not it's a happy experience for families."

Shaw nodded in agreement. "I can understand that."

"Now, Shaw, how long have you been a cop?" Rick asked, attempting to find out more about this man his daughter seemed to be spending a significant amount of time with.

"About eight years now." Shaw readjusted himself in his chair to square his shoulders towards the doctor.

"Do you have any ambitions for a different position within law enforcement?"

Tinsley looked at her dad. She didn't want to have a typical 'what are you doing with your life' conversation projected on Shaw. She was sure hers would come next, her dad always managed to bring it up.

"I've been presented with multiple opportunities, but my partner and I work really well together and enjoy what we do," Shaw spoke steady in his response. "For now, I'm not really sure I'd want to move around. I have all the credentials for a detective position, but I feel like I still have an itch for patrol. There's always room for advancement or switching gears to a tactical team, but I haven't taken any of those offers either."

"Isn't there more money in advancement?" Rick wasn't subtle about the point he wanted to make.

Tinsley's eyes widened, projecting her disapproval of the questioning.

"Yes and no." Shaw rolled his head around. "Obviously any advancement would come with a higher base salary. But I think you'd be surprised what officers get paid. Plus, the overtime alone is enough to make those other positions less desirable in terms of money."

"Speaking of pay"—Rick moved his focus to his daughter—"Tinsley, did you look at that price model I sent you this morning?"

"I took a quick look at lunch today." She nodded.

"You need to consider increasing your pricing across the board. We discussed the incremental profit margins when you opened that salon and you haven't done it. Not to mention, the CPA just informed me this week that not only are you still doing the senior breakfasts, but you're also doing the low-income events *monthly*. I thought we already discussed this? Tinsley, you're losing money each time you do those things.

You need to at least consider running that through a well-established non-profit so you can have a tax write-off."

Tinsley slowly nodded, this wasn't the first time she'd heard this speech—and it wouldn't be the last. She needed *some* encouragement to appropriately price her talents. But it was *her* business, it'd been that way since the start.

"I know, but I can't just pull the plug on those events. And they've always been free, I won't start charging people now. They really need that… And I like doing them."

"We discussed this when you opened that business. The bottom line is more important than how someone will feel about you doing what's best for your business. Tinsley, if you can't make those changes yourself, you need to outsource the financial side of your business to someone who can."

"Rick, honestly"—Colette shook her head, placing her hand on Rick's forearm—"we can't have a nice dinner without talking shop? Tinsley and the salon are doing perfectly fine." She smiled at her daughter.

"Someone has to watch the books there. If you're not going to charge Brindle more for living at the salon you need to significantly increase the price for your services. You provide a highly trained, professional service, with a well-established pool of clients. People, especially women, expect to pay a premium for that." He looked up from his glass at his daughter. "Vance tells me Harvey's going to the neurologist again soon. If nothing else, you need to charge more to cover the kind of money you'll be spending with that specialized care. I called around. Starting consultation fees are a standard five-hundred dollars and that fee doesn't include any of the labs or tests they'll be running or recommending. Not to mention, medications they may prescribe him. I'm also going to assume his most recent stay at the emergency hospital was—"

"Rick," Colette said with more firmness to her tone as she reached over and covered her husband's hand. "It's Tinsley's birthday, the only thing we'll be discussing about our Harvey tonight is how handsome he is." She stared at Rick for another long moment. "Give our only grandson a break." When she decided he'd drop the topic she rubbed his hand before setting hers back in front of her and then fondly smiled at Shaw.

"Tinsley, honey, did you hear Delilah is a final candidate for the assistant principal position at her school?" Colette gleaned with a hand on her heart. "We're so proud of her, she's worked really hard for that."

"Vance didn't mention that last time I saw him." Tinsley looked up at her mom. "But that's really great for her, I know she really wants to get into administration."

"Your brother is looking to get out of the emergency room soon. He has multiple offers at a couple local hospitals and medical centers right now," Rick made sure to add.

"Vance doesn't want to join you up at Harborview anymore?" Tinsley asked.

"I think with Alaurra still being young and them talking about another, it'll suit them best to stay near Tacoma." Colette's voice projected hope, she didn't want to be separated by Alaurra more than she already was living a whole fifteen minutes apart. "And I'll do anything to encourage that over them leaving right before a new baby in the family."

"Your brother and Delilah know what they're doing." Rick nodded and then looked at his wife. "They'll make the right choice for their family and we don't need to pressure them, Col."

Shaw couldn't help but catch Rick's choice of words. Despite what Tinsley had said about her parents always loving her and not treating her cruelly, he wasn't a fan of how her dad essentially talked down to her. He gave Vance and his wife so much credit when it was Tinsley who'd sacrificed everything so they could have that life. He wondered what Rick would think if he knew the truth about that fire. Shaw put his arm on the back of Tinsley's chair and rubbed her between her shoulder blades. When Tinsley reached over and put her hand on his lap he immediately picked it up with his free hand to interlace their fingers.

"Oh, Shaw, honey," Colette started. "Have you been able to meet Vance or Delilah yet?"

Shaw assuringly rubbed Tinsley's hand with his thumb and responded, "I did meet Vance, but not Delilah."

"Delilah's been in the family for almost twenty years now, we love her so much," Colette gushed.

"Their daughter's adorable." Shaw smiled at Tinsley, putting a loving squeeze around her hand. "Alaurra sure seems to love Auntie Tins quite a bit."

"Yes, at this stage—especially with Vance and Delilah so career focused—it really helps to have Tinsley available for all the fun stuff," Rick pointed out.

Shaw couldn't help but feel some resentment toward Tinsley's dad and all the digs he picked up on. He had to believe Tinsley felt each and every one of those. Her dad was out of his mind to not see how truly wonderful his daughter was, despite having the childhood he knew of. He knew the first meeting, on her birthday, wouldn't be the time to challenge him. He would definitely be making his feelings known—in a respectful manner—the next time her dad felt the need to put Tinsley down. For tonight, however, he'd simply observe and continue to assure Tinsley he was there for her.

"From what I've seen she's been learning some wonderful life lessons while spending all kinds of fun time with Auntie Tins." Shaw squeezed Tinsley's leg.

"Excuse me," Rick commanded the attention of the server. "I'd like to order my daughter here a slice of the tiramisu for her birthday after our dinner is served. But please, no candles." He held up his hand, palm facing the waiter.

Shaw's gaze landed on Tinsley who'd shamefully lowered her head. He noticed her hands fidgeting under the table so he placed one of his over hers to calm them down. She turned her hands over and squeezed his hand in return. She clutched his thumb with one hand and the rest of his fingers with the other. Shaw leaned over and pressed his lips to the top of his girlfriend's head to ease her into the rest of the evening. Once Shaw's mouth disconnected from her head, Tinsley lifted her chin and projected a smile toward her dad as if she wasn't upset at all.

Colette noticed Shaw's demeanor change when Rick declined a candle for Tinsley's birthday. She changed the subject to focus on Shaw. "Shaw, honey, what do your parents do? Are they in the Tacoma area too?"

The arm he had around Tinsley's shoulders landed on the back of her chair, but he maintained a hold on her hands with the other. "They used to live locally, I grew up in Tacoma, but they moved away a little over five years ago now. My mom stayed home with me and my brother when we were growing up and my dad's always had an itch to get out of the big city and back to a slower paced life in the country somewhere."

"Are they retired?" Colette took another drink of her merlot.

Shaw sipped his water and swallowed while shaking his head, smiling. "Quite the opposite. They moved to Idaho—which is where my dad's from—because he bought a small practice out there. I guess my mom's looking into buying the town bakery now too. So, they don't plan to retire anytime soon; they love it out there."

"What kind of practice? Is your dad a lawyer?" Colette asked.

"No, he's a doctor. It's just a general practice that he bought though. He wanted a more traditional schedule."

One of Tinsley's soft hands gently rubbed his forearm. Her boyfriend was a much more humble man than what her dad had shown that evening.

"Doctors all over the place," Colette chuckled and reached out for her husband. "That sounds like a very relaxing and rewarding life they have out there though. Did your brother move with them?"

"No." Shaw grinned. "My brother hasn't lived near family since he left for college. He's in Bellingham—he went to Western and once he met his now wife, who's from there, it was over."

The server came back with everyone's dinner order and at that point the topic of Shaw's family was lost.

Colette made sure there wasn't any awkward, dead air during dinner. She knew her husband would fill in the silence with his business-centered talk and didn't want that going on anymore during their daughter's birthday dinner. She was anxious to catch up on all the salon gossip and find out more about Shaw since it appeared he and her daughter were very much involved with one another these days.

Rick decided to observe. Tinsley had never brought a date to her birthday dinner and while Shaw had an established career, Rick wasn't sure if he was exactly the kind of man he'd prefer his daughter end up with. Tinsley, in her dad's mind, needed a man who would lead and manage her like he always felt the urge to. She reinforced her dad's worries that night when she more or less admitted she wasn't making any financial changes to her business model. Shaw telling him he was content being on patrol didn't offer much confidence that he would be able to make Tinsley's situation any better or lift any of the micro-parenting burden from Rick. He continued to worry, watching his wife also become enamored by this apparent love interest.

"Thank you for coming tonight, Hunt. I'm sorry about my dad." Tinsley shook her head as they walked, hand in hand, to his Raptor. "I probably should've better prepared you for meeting him."

"Tins"—Shaw slowed them down and put her in his arms—"you don't have to be sorry about that. The only thing that bothered me was his tone toward you a few times… And the candle thing. I'll be correcting that this evening."

Tinsley smiled up at him, a sparkle in her eyes.

"I'm confident enough to where I don't care what anyone on the outside thinks of me or my career. Plus, your dad's supposed to hate me right off the bat—I'm the boyfriend." His crooked smile lingered in her gaze before winking.

"I don't think he hates you, you'd know if that was the case," she assured him.

"He seemed more concerned about my ability to take care of you financially than anything else." Shaw reached down to hold her hand and continue leading them toward his truck. "I'm not trying to be an asshole, but money isn't an issue for me. I have no debt whatsoever, have been pretty damn smart about the money I do have, and like I told him, overtime opportunities are stupid with the department. Baz and I have been working pretty non-stop for a few years. Money is the very least of my worries."

"I've been noticing you don't have an issue spending." She shook her head before smirking at him. "I was really hoping it wasn't because you were out there doing something strange for some change."

Shaw leaned back and laughed out loud. "Sugar, my days of hookin' ended the day I met you."

"Good. I didn't want to be the one to have to ask you to give that up." She fondly squeezed his hand, looking down at the cracked side-walk as her heels clicked along the pavement. "I'm sure the conversation about my business was awkward too."

"That would be one example of the tone of his I didn't like—yeah," Shaw confirmed.

"I'm not like drowning in debt, upside down in my business, or leeching off my parents to keep me afloat. I feel like that's how he made things sound."

"Tins, you don't have to explain anything to me." He rubbed her hand with his thumb.

"My parents don't have any kind of stake in my business, it's 1000% mine. I *do* use their CPA—which is becoming more of a problem than anything I guess since he's apparently such a snitch. My dad just worries. He acts like I haven't purchased a home and been at least successful enough not to lose my business in the timeframe that most statistically fail. If I would've turned out like the rest of my family I'm sure he wouldn't give me such a hard time."

"Tins, you're doing amazing. You shouldn't let your dad's opinions stop you from doing what makes you happy. Don't forget, you and I chatted about your plans to expand the business." He winked, remind-ing her that it was him who had command of Baz's dating app the night she disclosed her plans for the salon. "You have some amazing ideas and I know you work hard."

"I'm honestly really happy with what I do. I know I can make more money, but I make enough to be able to take care of Harvey and do community events—that's really what matters most to me. Not to mention, I love my clients, my hours, my shop, my co-workers… And those free events… I know I do nothing but lose money, but you have to be able to feel good about yourself. So, I don't want to cut that ser-vice off."

Shaw's face brightened. "You have no idea how much I loved watch-ing you at that low-income event. Sugar, you can tell how much it means to you to offer that to families. You should definitely keep doing them if they light you up like that. So what if you lose a little bit of money? Things will always work out how they're meant to. Everything you want will happen in time, Tins."

"Thank you, Hunt." Tinsley turned and put her arms around him.

Shaw held her tightly and placed a few kisses on the top of her head before his strong hands slid down her back to land on the bottom of her cheeks. "And you're out of your mind if you think I'm gonna stand here and watch you do all that alone. We're a team, sweetcheeks."

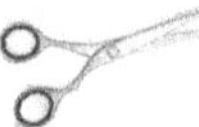

"What are we doing?" Tinsley smiled when Shaw parked in the lot in front of the Metropolitan Market once they got back into town. She only shopped there on occasion for specialty items because it was an upscale grocery store that made Whole Foods seem like it was for the poor.

"I won't let you end your birthday without a damn candle on a cake. How else are you supposed to make a birthday wish?" He reached over the console and rubbed the side of her face.

Tinsley gazed into his mesmerizing green eyes and moved toward him, their lips met and softly made a few exchanges. She only backed up enough to offer her reply.

"Hunt, baby, you don't have to do that for me." She brushed her nose against his. "I don't need a birthday wish because I already have everything I'd be wishing for."

Shaw felt the pounding in his chest escalate in response to everything that just came out of his girlfriend's mouth. He adoringly shook his head and a loving smile stretched across his handsome face.

"I'll say it until I'm blue in the face. You are *so damn* sweet, Tins. I don't think I'll ever get enough of that." He held a lock of her hair, gently tugging for their lips to meet. "But, I'm still getting you a dessert of your choosing this evening. *And* there *will* be a candle because I'm going to properly celebrate my girlfriend. Your dad got his final candless cake tonight—it won't happen again."

Tinsley leaned in to his gentle touch as he held the side of her face.

"I'll admit, I don't even like tiramisu." She glanced at the combined 'MM' logo on the building. "You must be a mind reader though because *The Cookie* here is hands down my favorite dessert. So, if you were going to suggest we have that tonight for a birthday treat, I'll be more than happy with that selection."

The corners of Shaw's mouth raced to his ears. "*The Cookie* is one of the only sweet treats I'll crave from time to time," he admitted and then got out of the truck.

"Hey, Boo! How was dinner?" Brindle gave Tinsley a hug that made Shaw notice he likely knew how those birthday dinners usually went.

"Oh, you know." She shrugged. "How'd Harvey do tonight?" She changed the subject with a deep breath.

"Perfect angel, obviously." Brindle rolled his head around and drew a halo on top of his head. Leaning his elbows on the kitchen island his focus turned toward Shaw who squatted to greet Harvey. "How was meeting *Dr.* Adams?" He pumped his bushy, but well-maintained eyebrows.

"I think I nailed it being the unimpressive boyfriend who could be better in a few categories." He smiled while tossing a toy across the room for Harvey to chase.

"Shut the *fuck* up!" Brindle laughed and swatted Shaw's strong chest with the back of his flimsy hand. "You must've picked up on his pompous-ass comments that I'm sure he peppered you both with. The only way he'd even be interested is if you had *doctor* in front of your name. You *do* know that's the only career anyone can have to find financial stability around here, right?"

Shaw's laugh only escaped through his nose, Brindle definitely knew exactly what Shaw had gone through that night. It wasn't the worst encounter, but Shaw could tell there were more judgments coming from the doc than any kind of welcoming sentiments about him being with his daughter.

"That's why we started our *post*-birthday tradition"—Brindle put his arms around Tinsley again—"right, Boo?" He pecked the top of her head.

Tinsley nodded against her best friend's chest as they hugged and let him rock her in his arms.

Brindle rubbed Tinsley's shoulders after pulling away from their hug. He put a hand on his hip and flicked the other wildly through the air. "You've got her tonight, Shawberry. Enjoy that time because she's mine tomorrow night." Brindle winked at Shaw. "You may be giving her some things I *never* will. Mainly, some wild birthday sex. But you also won't be crashing our post-birthday tradition."

"Brindle." Tinsley held her forehead.

"Shawberry." Brindle pumped his eyebrows and snagged his bottom lip with his teeth.

Shaw tried to wipe his grin. "You and I don't do girl talk, remember?"

Brindle rolled his eyes, lips vibrating on the breath he blew out. "I'll get outta here so you two can get started." He swung his Prada cross-body over his shoulder and strolled out the back door.

"He just leaves everything for you to clean up?" Shaw examined the mess Brindle had made of the kitchen. It looked like he fixed himself dinner and didn't bother putting anything away. The counters were a wreck, he left dirty dishes out and sauce sitting on Tinsley's stovetop.

"Yep." She looked up at him. "Heaven forbid he ruin his manicure with a little cleaning."

"I'll help you out with that, but not right now." Shaw swung Tinsley firefighter carry style into his arms because the tightness of her dress wouldn't allow him to pick her up with her legs around his waist. "We've got other business to tend to." He walked them to the bedroom.

"See, I told you I didn't need a candle for my birthday wish to come true." Her tongue played on Shaw's neck before lightly sucking on his collarbone.

"I'll be granting that wish *multiple* times, sweetcheeks," Shaw grinned.

"*After* I give you some boyfriend gifts," she corrected the order of events.

"Yeah, we'll see about that…" Shaw gently laid her on the bed.

CHAPTER
Thirty Six

"Tins, Sugar, your phone's going off." Shaw called out from the kitchen the following night. He and Harvey made themselves a few snacks in the kitchen while Tinsley got ready to go out with Brindle and the girls.

"If it's Brindle will you please pick it up? I'll be right there!" she hollered from the master bedroom.

Shaw slid the screen to pick up the call but didn't even have a second to answer because Brindle shouted into the phone.

"Boo, we're on our way! Can we take the 4Runner though? You don't have to drive, but we're not all fitting comfortably in my car." Brindle finally diverted his eyes from a mirror to the phone screen. "Ah! Shawberry!" he squealed.

"Hi, Brindle." Shaw's comfort level steadily improved with Brindle over time—he didn't turn as red when his biggest fan was dramatizing and drawing out 'Shawberry'.

"I'm excited we get to see your beefcake ass before we go out tonight. I have a pre-funk bottle, so we'll just come inside when we get there. My boo better be ready though! Pictures will be happening right away." He snapped his sassy fingers.

"She's always picture ready," Shaw informed him.

"UGH!" Brindle slapped the back of his hand on his forehead and pretended to faint. "You're *such* a lady killer!"

"Bye, Brindle." Shaw rolled his eyes, grinning.

"See you soon, beefcake!" Brindle smacked his lips.

Shaw happily ended the call and laughed to himself.

Harvey rose off the runner in the kitchen at the sound of Tinsley's heels clicking down the hallway. Shaw's heart skipped a beat when he saw her. Her clothes were skin tight, which wasn't unusual for her, but he'd never seen her in the boot and skirt combination that she had on. Her black suede, high heel boots came up just over both of her knees, she had on black nylons and a ridiculously short black skirt. Her forest green long sleeve top looked like spandex on her and it was tucked into her skirt. Shaw loved her hair in beach waves, she had it parted down the middle tonight.

Shaw blew out an appreciative and noticeable exhale as he walked toward his girlfriend.

"Hmmm, I don't know about letting you leave the house tonight, sweetcheeks." He smirked as he closed in on her and dipped her back for a juicy kiss.

Tinsley giggled while dangling in his arms after their lips separated. "Hunt, baby, if I was dressing to go out with you I wouldn't have put on nylons and please believe my top wouldn't be up to my neck."

"I'm pissed Brindle's already on his way." Shaw nibbled on her ear. "I don't even have time to give you a nice little goodbye to send you out with the girls," he teased into her ear.

She gently scratched the back of Shaw's head before pecking him. "Good thing we didn't miss our opportunity this morning… or this afternoon."

Shaw smiled at her before pressing their lips together as he lifted her upright again. "As per usual, you look *gorgeous*, Tins."

"Thank you." She reached around and gave his backside a quick squeeze. "Are you sure you're okay hanging with Harv tonight? I can always bend the rules since it's *my* birthday celebration and all. I think it's more than okay for my dreamy boyfriend to join us."

"I appreciate it, sugar, but you should enjoy a night out with your friends. Not only is it a birthday tradition, but I've got some things around here I wanna finish up. I'm more than okay having Handsome Harv for company tonight until you come back to us. Plus, I might get myself into trouble tonight if I had to be around if anyone thinks it's okay to even glance in your direction."

Tinsley giggled. "Oh, Hunter, you know the only eyes *and* hands I want on me are yours." She pecked him. "I can't be having you get into trouble." One of her hands moved from his hip up to gently hold his chin. "Are you hiding some chocolate over there, tough guy? I feel like I just had a little taste of chocolate."

Shaw smiled widely. "I may have been eating off one of those cookies we still have," he admitted. "I just popped it in the microwave too, it tastes fresh."

Tinsley scurried into the kitchen to pluck a piece for herself. She didn't quite make it to the sweet treat when she felt Shaw behind her.

"I didn't think those damn cheeks could get any sweeter, but this skirt…" Shaw squeezed her lucious rear end then spun her around to kiss her. They went back and forth a couple of times before Shaw reached down and picked up Tinsley by her cheeks to set her on the kitchen island. He was pleasantly surprised when her skirt was flexible enough to allow him to be in between her legs.

"I may have to call and cancel tonight." Tinsley giggled in between kisses.

Shaw backed off, grinning. "You don't have to do that because I'll be here waiting for you." He grabbed a chunk off of the cookie to offer to his girlfriend.

"Mmmm"—she rolled her eyes back—"that does taste fresh."

"Told you." He shrugged and took a bite for himself.

Tinsley watched as melted chocolate ran down Shaw's finger. She pulled his hand to her mouth and didn't hesitate before slowly and suggestively sucking the chocolate right off his index finger.

Shaw's heart thundered and mouth gaped watching her lips around his fingertip while she gazed at him. He had trouble containing himself at the gesture so he grabbed the side of her face to send his tongue into her mouth. Their lips vibrated when Tinsley giggled at Shaw's hastiness.

After the first couple of exchanges his hands gripped her backside to pull her closer to him.

Tinsley fought a smile so their mouths didn't have to separate as she felt more pressure from Shaw's hands *and* the front of his pants. She put her arms around his shoulders and hooked one of her legs around his. Just as she ran her fingers through the back of his hair, Brindle made his presence known.

"OWW OWW OWWWWWW!" He clapped and quickly tapped his feet on the kitchen floor. "Did we come at a bad time, or just in time?" Brindle gawked at his best friend who buried her face in Shaw's neck. Lacey and Farrah were right behind Brindle only getting the tail end of the show, Brindle continued jumping around like a maniac.

"Brindle… always a grand entrance, huh?" Shaw took a deep breath that was one part irritation and one part an attempt to calm the blood flow in his pants. "Hi ladies," he greeted Farrah and Lacey.

"Shawberry." Brindle put his hands on his hips and the tip of his tongue traced his top lip. "If I didn't know any better I'd think you *wanted* us to walk in on all that. I'm only upset that you're not in some gray sweatpants right now."

"Brindle!" Tinsley and her blush face scolded him.

Shaw couldn't be more grateful to still be in jeans because the gray sweatpants definitely would have given Brindle and the girls an outline of how he felt about Tinsley. He kissed Tinsley's forehead before helping her down from the countertop.

"I wasn't sure if you were still coming, this is a pretty late start to get all the way down to Olympia." Tinsley still hadn't looked at her best friend yet.

"Oh, Boo! Change of plans, we're going downtown instead." Brindle walked over, arms out like a zombie with loose wrists, and hugged Tinsley.

"Yeah," Farrah jumped in, "ask him why we're staying in town?" She nudged Brindle's shoulder.

Tinsley looked at Brindle with accusing eyes. "Oh, let me guess, *your* boyfriend gets to come along to *my* birthday, but not mine?"

Brindle helped himself to the kitchen cabinet that stored all

Tinsley's shot glasses. He shrugged with his back still turned, collecting enough shot glasses for everyone. "I don't have a boyfriend."

"Shut the fuck up!" Farrah squealed as Tinsley and Lacey also chirped back at their delusional friend.

Brindle ignored their accusations and simply set up shot glasses along the kitchen island. "Shawberry, would you like to join us for this shot?"

Shaw rubbed Tinsley's shoulder. "Maybe just one, but I don't want to get caught up in all the girl talk. What are you guys shooting?"

"*We're* drinking vodka like actual party girls." He gestured toward himself, Lacey, and Farrah. "This feral bitch prefers tequila." Brindle pulled a bottle of Tito's from his leather wine cooler and set it on the counter. "We grabbed your nasty ass anejo shit." He revealed a small bottle of Don Julio out of the bag next.

"You're still the worst for railroading plans to meet up with your boyfriend tonight." Tinsley hugged Brindle. "But I'll accept this apology gift."

"This is a bit of a surprise," Shaw admitted with a smile. "Anejo, huh?"

"It's obviously so I don't have to share drinks with Brindle." Tinsley winked, sliding under her boyfriend's arm and gliding her hand around his waist.

"Shawberry, which one do you want?" Brindle poured the clear liquid into three glasses for he and the girls as he waited for a response.

"If you're sharing your apology gift, I'll drink with you, sugar." Shaw stood behind Tinsley and wrapped his brawny arms around her before kissing her beach waves.

"Of course." She pulled their shot glasses toward her and filled them with the tequila.

"Happy Birthday, Boo!" Brindle raised his glass to clink it with everyone.

They all joined his sentiment and then touched glasses before throwing their drinks back.

"Another, Boo! You've got catching up to do." Brindle twirled his finger in the air.

Shaw tried not to be too pushy about it but cut in anyway. "Who's driving you all this evening?"

"Me"—Lacey reluctantly raised her hand—"I have a bridal shower I'm helping with in the morning, so I can't be drinking all night."

Shaw watched her prepare for another shot. He didn't want to be in complete cop mode and stifle their fun, but he also didn't want his girlfriend in any type of danger. The bottle Brindle brought over wasn't fresh either, so he made the assumption they'd started before they got to Tinsley's.

"Well—" he looked at Brindle—"since you guys are just heading downtown, why don't I drop you off?" He held his hands up. "Don't worry, I'm not trying to join all night. I just wanna be sure everyone's safe. Plus, I have to stop by Home Depot, and I'll be awake until my girl's home anyway. You guys can hit me up whenever you want to be picked up."

"Shawberry, you're the best!" Brindle slammed into him for a hug, his arms wrapping around Shaw like he prepared to slide down a pole.

Tinsley smiled at Shaw's reaction—he wasn't ready for the hug but accepted it anyway.

"We can load Harv in the car too, he can go for a little adventure with me." He rubbed Tinsley's shoulder and pecked the top of her head.

"Let's take another." Brindle pushed the glass in front of Shaw again.

"Just one for me," Shaw politely declined but grabbed another chunk off the cookie that sat in front of them. He noticed Tinsley watching him so he reached out a piece to her which she happily accepted. They were eye flirting, both wanting to get back to what they were doing just before Brindle and the girls interrupted them.

"You two still with us?" Brindle snapped his fingers at the couple.

Lacey scolded Brindle this time with a quick swat to his arm. "Jealous bitch"—she laughed—"Let them be."

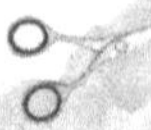

Harvey wasted no time in hopping over the back seat from the cargo area when Brindle, Lacey, and Farrah filed out of the 4Runner.

"Tins, have fun but be safe tonight, okay?" Shaw held her face when she turned to say goodbye to him. "If you need anything just call me."

She leaned over the center console and pressed her lips onto his. Shaw returned more than just a peck when his tongue dipped into her mouth, sweeping its way through familiar territory.

"Thank you, baby. I'll be calling you to bring me home tonight because I can't wait to go to bed with you."

"You and me both, sugar." He grinned. "Be safe."

"I will." She pecked him once more before turning around to give Harvey a quick kiss. She linked arms with her friends but turned to blow a kiss at her boyfriend before he pulled away.

"Boo!" Brindle put his arms around her. "You're in *love*."

Tinsley giggled but didn't offer a verbal response as Brindle dragged her into the club.

CHAPTER
Thirty-Seven

S HAW HAD JUST SAT DOWN FROM A LONG NIGHT OF WORKING IN THE backyard to bring his vision to life for a new outdoor area when he heard his phone signaling a text. He rubbed Harvey's cropped ear before reaching over him to grab his cell from the arm of the sofa. He smiled upon opening the message.

SWEETCHEEKS
Do you want a hot dog Officer Shaw?!

WTF I leave you with the girls for one night and we're back to the Officer Shaw routine?

SWEETCHEEKS
Hunt baby you know I'm teasin. I've been missing you like CRAZYtonight.

Are you ready for me to come pick you guys up?

SWEETCHEEKS
I'VE BEEN READY!!!!!!!!!!!!!!!!!!!!!!!!!!!

Lacey and Farrah already left.

I'm getting in the car now. You still at The Stone
or do you want to just share your location?

Shaw loaded Harvey into the back and started the 4Runner, his phone rattled off three more notifications.

SWEETCHEEKS
Yes and yes

Tinsley shared her location with Shaw even though she knew they'd likely be standing in the hot dog line outside of the club when he got there.

Thank you tough guy can't wait to be home
with you.

Same sweetcheeks I'll see you soon.

Shaw wasn't sure what was going on when he rolled up, but he wasn't settled with what looked to be unfolding near the hot dog cart. He watched a man give Victor a firm shove that sent him into Brindle and Tinsley. Brindle's hands flew around wildly as both he and Victor yelled. Shaw threw the 4Runner in park, he didn't care that cars waited to go around him. His determined footsteps quickened around the truck and onto the sidewalk where he heard yelling.

"Tins, you alright?" he asked as he made his heavy approach.

She whipped her head around, a tsunami of relief slamming into her to see him. She didn't vocalize a reply, her eyes quickly diverted to the two men who'd been causing trouble.

Shaw immediately put himself in the middle of the commotion and faced the men. "Is there a problem here?"

"Push along pretty boy." The taller one flicked his wrists in an attempt to shoo Shaw away.

Shaw remained expressionless, his stance didn't falter.

"These guys are the problem!" Brindle's high pitched voice projected his anger. "Malibu's Most Wanted can't take no for an answer. Been following us around the club all damn night! Fucking stalkers!"

"Calm down RuPaul, we aren't interested in you," the other man scoffed.

"It doesn't look like any of them are interested in you either," Shaw's tone sliced through the air, sharp and threatening.

"Like I said, push along." This man was roughly the same height as Shaw, but he stretched his neck to make his forehead a little higher than Shaw as he moved toward him. The man only had another half step before they'd end up bumping chests.

"You get one fucking warning. I'd suggest you don't get even an inch closer." Shaw stood eerily still besides his fists that were now clenched.

The people in line behind the men started to make room in fear of whatever was about to unfold. Even Brindle made an uncharacteristic decision to keep his mouth shut while stepping further away.

Tinsley knew better than to reach for her boyfriend, she didn't want to be inadvertently hit or be within reach of the creeps. Anything else from them would undoubtedly set Shaw off.

"Warning for what?" the second man spat out and rolled his eyes. Despite Shaw's muscular build, the man figured he and his buddy wouldn't have a problem—neither of them were anywhere close to the size of Shaw, but he'd be at a disadvantage having to manage the two of them.

"Which one's your girl?" the man closest to Shaw taunted but took the advice about getting any closer to him when he stayed in place. "Or perhaps you're here with the boys?" His wicked smile curled.

Shaw didn't offer any kind of reply, he waited for them to make the wrong move. His job had taught him the composure he honed in on; admittedly that composure was much more difficult with Tinsley behind him. They stood in silence for an uncomfortable second before the man decided to speak again.

"I see, just an empty threat hoping we won't call your bluff." The man took half a step toward Shaw and before anyone could blink Shaw hit him so hard that he instantly crumbled to the ground.

His buddy swung at Shaw who dodged him and then gave him a firm kick on his leg to knock him off balance before he caught an elbow to the side of the face, sending him to join his buddy on the ground. The first man looked uneasy getting himself back up when people around them gathered, making a scene now.

"That was a cheap fucking shot!" the man yelled as he stumbled.

Shaw laughed. "Cheap shot? I gave you a warning, you're the dumbass."

The man made another attempt at Shaw but this time Shaw grabbed his arm and yanked it up behind his back, shoving him toward a wall. He made sure the man made contact with his face before anything else as he slammed him against the brick.

Tinsley noticed a patrol car pull up next to her 4Runner. The officers approached the crowd to see what was going on.

"Hey!" one of the officers called out marching toward Shaw. The second officer checked on the man lying on the ground.

Shaw held the guy against the wall, but he hadn't hit him again. Once he noticed the cops he gave the man one final and firm shove into the wall and then let him go.

"Oh, shit"—the cop smiled at Shaw—"what are you doing here?"

Shaw still had a scowl on his face. "Trying to pick up my girl and these punks were starting shit." He looked up at the familiar patrolman. "So, I got out of the car to finish it."

The officer slapped Shaw on the shoulder. "Well, we got this. Is that your car?" He gestured toward Tinsley's 4Runner.

"Yeah, I parked there."

"No worries, man." He shook his head.

"I want to press fucking charges!" the man who got thrown against the wall yelled.

"Charges?" Shaw laughed and shook his head. "Yeah man, I'll be over here grabbing a hot dog. You let me know if I need to come back over here with a statement. I'm sure any one of these people will let you know what went down." He gestured toward the crowd before pointing at Victor. "If we're talking charges, maybe we can talk to this man who you put your hands on first."

The officer moved the man to talk with him and his buddy who finally sat up on the sidewalk holding his head.

Shaw confidently walked to Tinsley, immediately putting her under his arm. "Are you okay, Tins?" He hooked her chin with his finger, peering down at her beautiful brown eyes.

She squeezed him and reached her lips up which he met. "I am now. What about you, are your hands okay?"

"They're more than fine." He smiled. "Let's grab a hot dog."

She giggled at him just going back to business as usual after he essentially just beat two guys up.

"I think Harv deserves one too." Shaw's head motioned to the 4Runner where Harvey poked out his loveable face through the back window. "You guys all okay?" Shaw turned around to the group, looking at Victor who'd been shoved earlier.

"Yes, couple of hateful, creepy little fucks." He sneered at the two men who threw daggers at Shaw.

The hot dog vendor insisted on the group's order being on the house. Apparently he heard a few of the slurs they threw Victor and Brindle's way. He wanted the opportunity to show appreciation for what Shaw had done.

Hot dogs in hand, they made their way toward the 4Runner.

Shaw stopped, shouting to the officers, "Hey, you need me to stay, or am I good to go?"

Both officers waved Shaw off.

"Thanks—have a good one." Shaw offered a raised hand.

"Goodnight, Boo! And Happy Birthday!" Brindle hugged Tinsley. "We love you!"

Victor joined their embrace.

"Brindle, how are you guys getting home?" Shaw didn't want to leave anyone stranded.

"Victor drove."

"I'm good, Shaw." Victor held his hands up. "I only had one drink tonight."

Shaw noticed the men they'd had an issue with walking down the street, presumably to their car. "Hop in for now because I don't want you guys walking to your car with them around. I'll take you to your car."

Brindle gushed and scrunched his chin near his shoulder as he made his way to the truck. "Awww, such a gentleman, Shawberry!"

Tinsley stood at the back window greeting her excited dog who salivated for the plain sausage she passed to him. Shaw smiled when Tinsley turned around, he opened the passenger door for her and made sure she was comfortably in her seat before shutting her door. Victor wasn't parked too far away so Shaw got them to their car, watching them pull away before he made his way home with Tinsley and Harvey.

"I'm sorry, Hunt," Tinsley was soft with her words.

Shaw immediately shook his head. "No, Tins. You don't need to be sorry at all. You guys should be able to go out and let loose for the night. There's no fucking excuse for people to act like that toward you. You guys are totally fine. I'm mad, but not at you."

Tinsley reached for him and leaned her head on his shoulder. "Thank you, tough guy."

"You're welcome, sugar." Shaw put his hand on her inner thigh before pecking the top of her head. "Did something else happen in the club I need to know about with them? Brindle said they were following you guys around." He wasn't interrogating her with any thoughts that she was unfaithful; he wanted to see if he needed to reconsider his vigilante bullshit style of living for the evening.

Tinsley knew all too well what Shaw would possibly do if he thought she was put in an uncomfortable position at all, but she wasn't interested in lying to him either.

"They were following us throughout the night," she confirmed. "Like bringing drinks over and then trying to dance." Tinsley felt Shaw's hand as it stiffened. "Us girls have plans and rules in place for guys like that though. We don't accept any unwanted drinks that we don't watch the bartender pour *and* Brindle does the bumping and grinding on guys when they try to get too close to us on the dancefloor. He's no body-guard in the regular sense, but that method is pretty damn effective with those types of creepers."

The image of Brindle scooting close enough to those guys to be considered grinding had Shaw fighting a smirk.

"Hunt," Tinsley turned toward him and put her hand on the front of his pants. "I don't want you out on some dark mission this evening because of some basic-level creepers." Her hand rubbed him suggestively as she leaned closer to his ear. "I'd like you to take us home so I can spend the foreseeable future giving you endless amounts of boyfriend gifts." She softly pecked just behind his ear and continued down his neck.

Shaw's hand slid up her inner thigh and increased in pressure as Tinsley continued working on him. Both of her hands reached for his zipper and Shaw chuckled at her.

"Sweetcheeks, you're gonna need to slow down or I'm gonna need to pull over."

Tinsley smirked and put her lips in Shaw's ear to whisper, "Uh oh, tough guy, are you losing your focus?"

"Don't get it twisted," Shaw assured her. "I've got solid fucking focus on you, it's the damn road I'm losing focus on."

She captured his earlobe between her teeth before backing off him a bit. "My my, Officer Shaw, you must not have passed that distracted driving training by much." She slid back into her seat completely.

Shaw couldn't help but laugh. He turned his head and noticed she leaned down to fuss with something by her feet. "You alright down there?"

He watched her slide the zippers down on each of her boots and tugged them off.

"I'm making sure we don't waste any time once we're home." She reached up under her skirt to pull on the top of her nylons. "You better hope I'm not in your favorite nudey outfit before we make it home." She fought her nylons that gave her trouble on her left thigh. "Because I'm coming for your clothes next, *Hunter*."

"Brindle's *definitely* not so bad," Shaw shook his head with a permanent grin on his face. "He got you all kinds of tipsy, didn't he?"

"I'll try not to take it personally that you're thinking of Brindle right now." She finally managed the nylons past her knees.

Shaw barked out a laugh and slapped the steering wheel a couple of times. "Oh, sugar!" He took a deep, grateful breath and watched his perfect girlfriend who he couldn't get enough of. "You're getting punished the *second* I park this car for that one."

Tinsley rolled her head around when she leaned back into the seat. She bit her bottom lip and looked at him. "I'm looking forward to it."

Shaw couldn't get them home quick enough at that point.

CHAPTER
Thirty-Eight

As the days passed by, Shaw and Tinsley fell into a comfortable, domestic routine. Shaw rarely went to his apartment; most of the time it would be for a quick twenty minutes after the gym so he could shower and ensure nothing was amiss given he had two safes with quite a few firearms in them.

They'd also been out a few times with Brindle and Victor, but more often with Baz. One night, in fact, they had a double date where Tinsley finally met Tilly.

Shaw and Baz had moved the traeger from the apartment one day and Tinsley decided they should thank Baz by having him stay for dinner. Prior to Shaw entering her life, Tinsley hadn't really tried the red meat cuisine. That's all she craved these days though, she didn't know if it was truly the taste, or in the preparation since she got to watch her smoking hot boyfriend in his element.

After a grilled dinner, they made their way to a gazebo Shaw had constructed to enjoy drinks by the fire while visiting as the hours passed by.

"Tins"—Baz sat upright, lowering his voice almost immediately after Shaw got up from the outdoor sectional they were sharing—"I wanted to tell you something, just in case you didn't know." He took a deep breath, locking his hands together before he started, "Shaw went through some fucked up shit a couple years ago. There's an anniversary of sorts for that coming up and I just wanted to give you a heads up because he usually calls outta work and I'm not sure what he does all day. He doesn't even talk to me usually. I know things are new with you guys, I'm just making sure his behavior that day isn't taken personally—I think he's still healing."

Tinsley appreciated that Baz was so concerned and cautiously protective of Shaw. Initially, she wasn't sure if she should let him know all the details her boyfriend had already disclosed. She acknowledged Baz wasn't just a partner at work, Baz was family. Tinsley would confirm what she knew because ultimately, they both cared about Shaw's heart through that healing process. "Are you talking about Sloane?" she gently asked.

Baz's eyes widened before he collected himself. "You know about Sloane?"

Tinsley gravely nodded until her gaze fell to her lap. "Hunt told me he was engaged to Sloane, with a baby on the way, and they were both murdered a couple years ago."

Baz exhaled a painful sigh. "He was in a dark place with that for a long time. Even when he came out of the shadows, you could still tell he was hurtin'."

"I want to be as respectful as I can about that day. What day is it exactly?"

"Tomorrow." Baz noticed Shaw heading back out to the gazebo. He leaned back nonchalantly and grinned at his buddy. "Should we teach Tins how to play bones?" His tone light, masking the graveness of the conversation he just had.

"Obviously, I'll need to teach her so she has a shot at winning." Shaw teased, clearly having missed the entire conversation between Baz and Tinsley.

"Did you bring your domino set?" Shaw sat down and grabbed his beer off the table before resting his other hand on the back of Tinsley's chair.

"No." Baz admitted, realizing his diversion had a gaping hole.

"Well, how the fuck were you planning on playing?" Shaw laughed.

Tinsley placed her hand on Shaw's knee to hoist herself up. "I'll grab my set." She winked at him.

"What?!" Shaw grabbed Tinsley's hip before she got too far. "Sugar, you play bones?"

"Let's just say *I'll* be the one teaching you boys how to play if you're interested in winning."

Baz and Shaw both laughed as Tinsley made her way back into the house to get her domino set.

"Hunt?" Tinsley hesitantly started as they laid in bed that night.

"Yeah, sugar?"

Tinsley's fingertips made gentle passes across his exposed chest a few times. "Please don't get mad at Baz… but he told me about tomorrow."

Shaw didn't respond. His head rested on the locked hands he had behind it and he continued to look up at the bedroom ceiling.

Tinsley let the air sit for a moment longer before she continued, "Hunt, baby, I just want you to know that I'm here for you. Whatever you need, please just let me know. If it's space, that's okay too. There's no pressure from my end."

Tinsley wouldn't push the issue anymore than that if he didn't want to talk about it, she shared what was on her heart. She pressed a soft peck to Shaw's cheek before her head returned to his shoulder.

It took a minute before Shaw unclasped one of his hands to rub his strong fingers along her arm a few times, but he did it in silence. Tinsley decided that would be enough for her and she'd try to navigate his needs when they woke up. There was no reason to push him at that moment.

CHAPTER
Thirty Nine

Shaw's alarm went off two hours before Tinsley's was scheduled to alert her—as it always did on their mutual workdays. Tinsley felt Shaw roll over and silence the device. He was never one to hit the snooze, but she didn't say anything to him when he readjusted his position on the bed, putting his arms around her. Her pelvis pressed into him and she lovingly held onto his strong and familiar arms. They both drifted back to sleep almost immediately.

It was Tinsley's alarm that went off a couple hours later, she reached for the nightstand to silence it. She *was* one to hit snooze on occasion. Her yawn ended in a small chuckle when Harvey popped his head over the mattress.

"No snoozing in today, huh, Handsome Harv?" she whispered, smiling at his perfectly unique face.

The cane corso had his entire back end wiggling, his nubby tail hoping Tinsley would get up to let him outside.

"Okay, buddy." She carefully slid out from under Shaw's arm. Once standing, she reached down and gave Shaw's hand a loving squeeze before following Harvey out to the backdoor.

Harvey didn't want to be outside very long that morning, he kicked the door before Tinsley finished putting his breakfast together.

"You are a demanding little creature this morning." She smiled while opening the door, her happy dog trotting back inside with an empty bladder. Tinsley set his food bowl down and watched him take a few bites before she made her way to the shower.

She hadn't heard him come in, so she jumped and let out a short shriek when she felt sturdy hands slide across her soaked torso.

"You scared me!" Tinsley laughed when she saw Shaw standing behind her chuckling.

"I'm sorry, sugar." He grinned and moved closer to her to put his arms around his girlfriend and lean his chin onto her shoulder. It didn't take him long to lift his head and place a quick kiss on her cheekbone.

Tinsley moved so the water fell on both of them. "Here, come share the warmth with me." She looked up at Shaw when he stood straight with his arms still around her waist.

"Thank you." He smiled down at her, his hands exploring the length of her torso and pelvis.

Tinsley wasn't sure about picking up on the topic of the anniversary Shaw likely had on his mind. He still hadn't said anything to her since she brought it up the night before. Instead of pushing him again she decided to carry along as normally as she possibly could until his words or behavior indicated he needed her to give him something different.

"Did you come in here for a professional full service hair wash? I know you like those." She pumped her eyebrows, reaching for his shampoo. "I'll have you know, this would be a first for me offering *this* level of service. You're definitely a VIP for getting all this." She spun to face him before working a glob of shampoo onto his hair. "I'll be expecting a *ridiculously* big tip, sir."

"Oh, I've got much more than just a tip for you, sweetcheeks." Shaw reached his hands down to cup her plump backside.

Tinsley's head fell back as she laughed, Shaw wasted no time in nibbling on her neck. She let her nails lightly dig into his scalp before she worked her hands down to the base of his head and neck to give him a massage. She worked the tops of his shoulders when he turned his head so their lips could meet. Tinsley wrapped her arms up and around his neck to fall into a passionate embrace, losing focus on her washing duties. Shaw's mouth worked on her, wanting more with each sensual movement.

"Tins"—Shaw was the one who finally slowed their pace and then looked into her eyes—"Thank you. I didn't mean to be such a dick and just ignore you last night. I heard you, sugar. You have no idea what that meant to me." He held the sides of her face and pressed his lips against her forehead.

"Hunt, I meant every word." Her hands glided down to his strong pecs where her thumbs found a comfortable circular rhythm. "I won't stand here and pretend to have any idea what you're going through. But I'll always remind you how perfectly amazing you are and that you deserve to have a happy heart. I know you'll be forever scarred with the love you have for Sloane and your baby." She gently cupped his strong jawline with her soft hand. "You just tell me what you need from me today and it's yours, tough guy."

Shaw watched the tender sincerity in Tinsley's eyes and felt it projecting through her gentle touch. He knew if he could be vulnerable in front of anyone, it was her. If he was being honest with himself, he wasn't sure what he needed. He was no stranger to living with scars, his body was covered in them; he had never considered his heart could simply be scarred instead of shattered. He chased the degenerates in the night thinking darkness was all he had after the loss of Sloane and his baby, but since the day he met Tinsley, Shaw made an honest effort to not be broken. The more time he spent with her, the more his heart showed signs of life again. He knew there would always be pain, but the sweetness of the woman standing in front of him was enough to show him love was possible and he didn't have to live in the shadows anymore.

Shaw engulfed Tinsley in his powerful embrace. "I'd really love to drop you off at work this morning, sugar. I'll even stop at the coffee shop first." Droplets from the showerhead ricocheted on his face when he placed a kiss on her forehead. "I have a few things I want to do today, but I'd love to see you right when you're done with work and just spend time with you."

Tinsley's arms maneuvered around his hold to wrap around his neck again. "Absolutely whatever you want, tough guy." She brushed her fingers through the back of his wet hair.

Shaw picked her up by her cheeks so she could hang around his waist. "I don't need conditioner today. You still get a big tip without providing the full hair service." He smirked before reaching his lips to suck on her plump chest.

Tinsley's head rolled back, fingers tightening around his head, as his tongue played. Shaw created a trail of soft kisses up her neck when she looked down at him to confirm one final thought.

"Still no vigilante bullshit, right?" She held his jaw in place so their eyes could gaze into each other's.

"No vigilante bullshit, Tins," Shaw promised and sealed it with a juicy kiss. All he could do was kiss her while he held her around his waist so he suggested a change in venue. "Do you have time to go back to bed for your tip?" His devilish smirk begging for her agreement.

"I thought you were going to offer more than just a tip?" She grinned while brushing over his lips with hers.

"Oh, I am."—he reached for the faucet and shut off the water—"That's why I had to make sure you have time."

"You might have to run the lights and sirens to get me to work on time then." Tinsley giggled as Shaw rushed them out of the shower.

"No towel or robe?!" she complained, laughing as he walked down the hallway carrying her. "Hunter! It's *cold*!"

"Lights and sirens, sugar!" he joked before peeling the comforter back to put her in bed. Once he had Tinsley with her head comfortably on a pillow he climbed on top of her and threw the comforter over both of them.

"Tins…" Shaw started and gently rubbed her face but decided not to finish his thought, instead he moved his head down to hers and led with his tongue when their lips met.

Tinsley's hands worked from Shaw's backside all the way up until she ran her fingers through his hair again. Shaw had been ready when they left the shower, so he didn't spend much time before he slowly thrusted into his girlfriend. He felt her exhale into his mouth at the sensation as one of her legs bent to hold itself against his waist. Shaw worked on a steady rhythm but separated their lips so he could look at Tinsley. She slowly opened her eyes and smirked at him when he separated their chests—her bright face triggered a flutter in Shaw's heart. He found himself losing the rhythm in his pelvis when he began massaging her chest.

"I'd like to wash your hair *every* morning if this is the kind of tip you'll be providing." Tinsley managed while he maintained a focused and appreciative pattern with his hands on her breasts that perked for him.

Shaw's gaze slowly lifted from the nipple he gently held between his fingertips to her warm eyes. "You want me around every morning?"

Tinsley stopped all movement in her hips and reached for Shaw's face. "I do. Tip or not, Hunt. I love waking up to you every morning."

"Tins…" He ran his fingers through her hair. "I… Sugar…" He fumbled, unsure of vocalizing what was on his mind and his heart. Ultimately, he decided not to say it. "I can't think of anywhere else I'd rather be every morning than next to you."

CHAPTER
Forty

"Thank you for the ride, tough guy." Tinsley rubbed Shaw's hand as he pulled up to the back door of the salon.

"The one to work?" He put his truck in park. "Or the one before we left?" He winked and finished with a devilish grin.

Tinsley's head fell back and she hid her blush face, turning to look out the passenger window.

Shaw gave her a break and got out of the truck to help Harvey from his lifted seat in the back.

"Come on, Harv." Shaw encouraged the weary dog who carefully assessed the area he planned to land on. He was still getting used to the times he had to jump from Shaw's much taller Raptor compared to Tinsley's 4Runner. Initially Shaw had lifted him out of the truck, but Harvey was becoming an independent young man and didn't need help—just an extra few seconds from time to time to build up his courage.

Once Harvey's feet safely hit the pavement, they both walked over to the passenger door that Tinsley had open. He watched her gathering her coffee and purse.

Tinsley turned around with her drink in her hand and a smile still on her face.

"Both, obviously," she finally replied before hopping out of the truck and into Shaw's strong arms. "The first ride being, hands down, my favorite of the two."

Shaw pressed his lips against hers as his hand wandered to her backside.

"What time will you be ready to go home tonight, sugar?" he asked, both hands holding firm to her rear end as he swayed them.

Tinsley offered a soft smile and rubbed his chest with her free hand. "Hunt, why don't you just let me know when you're free later? I can hang with Brindle or even have him drive me home. I don't want you to feel rushed today."

Shaw took a deep breath while gazing into his girlfriend's sincere eyes. "Tins, I…" He reached for a lock of her hair considering his words for the millionth time that morning already. He waited a long moment before brushing his fingers through the hair on the side of her head. "I'll be here waiting for you at the end of your day because that's where I want to be, with *you*." He leaned down and pecked her forehead. "So, what time can I plan to come get you, sugar?"

Tinsley looked deep into his eyes. "My last client should be wrapped up by seven tonight."

"I'll be here," Shaw assured her. He held her head, tilting it toward his mouth to indulge in a final, juicy exchange before she needed to head into the salon for her first appointment.

"Call me if you need anything today, tough guy." Tinsley buried her head in his sturdy chest and gave Shaw a comforting and prolonged squeeze.

He kissed the top of her head before he let her go.

Tinsley turned around right after opening the salon door to get another glimpse of her handsome boyfriend.

"Have a good day, Tins."

"I'll be thinking about you all day, baby," Tinsley replied with Shaw's favorite sweet smile on her face.

Tinsley stood at the register, making another appointment for her first client when the salon doors opened and she watched Baz walk in.

"Good morning." Her voice was as warm and welcoming as her smile.

"Hey, Tins," Baz replied, stepping to the side so her client could exit the salon.

"Where's the hotter half of the duo?" Brindle asked but managed a smile toward Baz instead of his normal sassiness. Tinsley noticed Brindle had been trying lately—with *a lot* of encouragement from her and reassurances from Shaw that Baz wasn't actually the worst.

Baz and Tinsley exchanged an awkward glance between them.

Tinsley provided an answer before Baz could. "Oh, he said he was catching up on some things today."

"Shouldn't he only be playing hooky when the two of you can be *catching up* on some things together?" Brindle gave a few suggestive winks.

"Brindle." Tinsley rolled her eyes and then looked at Baz who tried wiping his smile. She encouraged him to follow her out front for a minute, assuming he'd prefer talking to her without Brindle as their audience.

"I'm sorry, I think you're always gonna catch shit from him. Hunt and I are trying, but Brindle's as stubborn as he is sassy," Tinsley explained when they stepped outside.

"Honestly, I don't know if I'll ever be able to hold it against the guy, that's loyalty right there. I gotta respect it." Baz shrugged.

Tinsley had a good idea of why Baz dropped by, but she asked anyway, "Is everything alright, Baz? Did you hear from Hunt or something?"

Baz shook his head. "No. That's not unusual on this day though, I let my boy be. He usually bounces back fairly quickly"—he rolled his head around—"as best he can anyhow."

Tinsley folded her arms while nodding. Shaw wasn't completely himself since Baz told Tinsley the significance of the day. She liked to think she would've noticed that change on her own, but it was nice that Baz had given her the heads up so she had time to think about what she could do to support her boyfriend.

"Have you heard from him today?"

Tinsley was surprised he asked something like that. Baz had surely known Shaw had been staying at her house at this point. Plus, he had left pretty late the night before and Shaw wasn't in a condition to be driving home.

"He dropped me off at work this morning. He said he'd be back tonight too."

"Okay, that's a good thing." Baz reached his oversized arm up and scratched the back of his head. "Look, I'm not trying to place any kind of doubt in your head about Shaw, he's a great fucking man. I just know he can get a bit dark sometimes, please don't take that personally."

Tinsley looked down, she knew exactly how dark Shaw could get, but he'd been flashing his bright light when they were together. If she was being honest with herself, she'd fallen completely in love with Shaw. She'd not only stand by him while he shined bright, but also brave every inch of the darkness that consumed him on occasion.

"I mean, I can tell he's a little off, but nothing completely horrible. He said he had some things he wanted to do today, but he said he'd be back to pick me up tonight." She shrugged.

Baz nodded. "Like I said, I'm not tryna place doubt or anything. Shaw's the best fucking guy I've ever known; I just worry about him. Tins, you've put real life back into my best friend and I just didn't want today to slow down what you guys are building. I know you mean a lot to him and I also know he wouldn't want to hurt you."

"I really appreciate that, Baz. And please just know that I… Uh…"—she looked down for a split second to get herself together—"Hunt means a lot to me as well." She swallowed a lump in her throat. "He's safe to have off days without me immediately running for the hills. I know what an amazing guy he is and if nothing else, he'll always have respect and grace from me."

"Thank you, forreal, Tins." Baz hesitantly reached for her, putting his arms around her.

Tinsley welcomed Baz's friendly gesture, gently returning the squeeze.

"Thank you, Baz." She finally backed up from him. "I know you guys are more than just partners at work and I appreciate who you are for Hunt. He's usually the strong and protective one in our duo, but please just know when it comes to his heart I'll be the one protecting that thing like there's no tomorrow." She smiled.

"I don't doubt that at all." Baz shook his head grinning back at her with his hands resting in his vest. "I'd put my money on you for that job any day of the week."

Tinsley chuckled. "I don't think Hunt knows what he's gotten himself into with the two of us now."

"The *three* of us." Baz pointed to the salon window where Brindle was very obviously spying. "Don't leave Shawberry's biggest fan out of the mix now."

Tinsley held her forehead like she always did in response to Brindle's antics. "I'll take full responsibility for that one."

"I'll let you get back at it." Baz reached in his pocket for a card. "Not to be awkward or anything, but I wrote my personal cell on the back there. If something pops up tonight just give me a call." He offered the card to her from between his index and middle fingers. "I mean, it's probably best you have my number anyway, we'll be seeing a lot of each other. Honestly, I'd do anything for Shaw and that extends to you now too."

"Thank you." Tinsley inspected the card while an obnoxious thought crossed her mind. A smirk formed as she shared the sentiment. "Be careful offering all that though, Brindle is kinda *my* partner, sooooo…"

"You and Shaw—two fucking peas in a goddamn pod!" Baz bent back, his distinctly loud laugh ringing.

"I'll text you when I get back in there so you have my number too," she confirmed and took a few steps toward the salon.

"I'll be sure not to block you this time!" Baz shouted.

It made Tinsley laugh but she only rolled her eyes at him just before walking back into work.

"Hey, toots." Shaw knelt down and cleared the dried-out contents of the vase near Sloane's headstone. He brought a fresh bouquet with two dozen white roses, an array of baby's breath, and scattered greenery accenting the exterior of the arrangement.

"I see the deer had their way with your flowers, huh?" He chuckled at the stems he removed. There were no remnants of the flowers or buds; it was likely the local deer had helped themselves to the last bouquet. "Looks like you deserved fresh ones anyway. I brought some baby's breath this time too because I heard the deer don't like those. Maybe they'll be a deterrent and help you keep the flowers a little longer this time."

Shaw stood, looking down at the aging headstone. He took a few deep breaths trying to clear his head. He was beyond lost when the funeral arrangements were made and certainly didn't have much to contribute to anything Sloane's family had decided on. Burying his fiancée and unborn child was never something he considered. Losing them so unexpectedly, and violently, didn't make it any easier when the family wanted to lay them both to rest. It was decided they'd be cremated together and share a headstone; Shaw wouldn't have objected even if he'd been emotionally present enough to help make that decision.

"I hope you and little man have been finding your way up there. I still miss you both and think about you everyday."

Shaw meant every word but somehow felt lighter than he did at any of his other visits. Time at Sloane's grave typically resulted in the darkest and most vengeful evenings. He'd leave the cemetery and spend the remainder of the night expressing his grief through handing out the most physically harmful justice imaginable—aside from actually killing anyone. Today he didn't plot out a nighttime vigilante tour, he already knew he wanted to end his night with Tinsley instead of that darkness.

"Toots, I have to tell you"—Shaw kicked a rock away from the vicinity of the headstone—"I'm sure you already know, but I've been living in the dark for a while. Well, not exactly living… I'll admit that much."

A flock of birds rushed out of a nearby tree, catching Shaw's attention for the moment.

"Life's been fucking tough without you. I never imagined it was going to be me who got left behind. If anything I thought I'd be the one who broke your heart."

He squatted down to the headstone and put his hand on it.

"I haven't been a good man since you left. I've done some real shitty things. I'm ashamed to have to admit that to you and I'm not wild about our son having that image of me. I really wanted to be a good father… and a good husband."

Shaw's throat tightened at the thought of how close he was to both of those things. He had his fist over his mouth when soft footsteps from behind interrupted his racing mind. He assumed it was someone visiting a loved one, so he took a breath and cleared his face.

"Hi, Shaw," a gentle voice greeted him.

Shaw turned around to see Sloane's grandma.

"Hi, Lenore." He stood and hugged the frail woman.

Lenore delivered a couple healthy pats to Shaw's back and then took a step away to look at him. "You're still as handsome as ever, dear."

Shaw grinned. "Trying to keep up with your lovely self."

Lenore looked at the flowers Shaw brought. "Those sure are beautiful. You always knew how to pick the perfect bouquet—some things never change." She bent down to add her bundle of seasonal flowers to Sloane's vase.

"If I knew I'd have the pleasure of seeing you today I would've picked something out for you too." Shaw smiled.

"If only I was about forty years younger, dear." Lenore shook her head chuckling. "Well, and single too," she added.

Shaw rubbed the old woman's shoulder, she still smelled like white lilies. It made him smile remembering the countless bottles of *Pleasures* her family, including him and Sloane, had gifted her over the years.

"This isn't exactly my favorite day of the year." She put her arm around Shaw's waist as they stood side by side. "I'm actually really happy to have run into you though." Tears formed on the old woman's eyes. "It's like we planned for them to get a visit from their all-time favorite people at the same time today, huh?"

Shaw nodded in agreement as the corner of his lips curled. "Hands down we've always been the favorites."

Their shared laughter slowed until they stood in silence.

"Besides today being a painful reminder, how've you been, dear?" Lenore looked up at Shaw and tried not to linger too long at the exhausted or sorrow-filled breath he took—she wasn't sure which it was.

"Still working at TPD with Baz." He shrugged. "Thankfully we've got it so good with the Chief—he somehow lets us still be partners."

"How's the family?"

"Sounds like they're doing good. Business is good anyway. I haven't been out there for about a year," he admitted.

"How 'bout you? You been stayin' outta trouble?" Shaw squeezed her shoulder and gave her a side grin.

Lenore wanted to circle back to what Shaw had been doing to enjoy life, but she'd answer him first.

"You know I'm not one to stay out of trouble for long." She smirked. "I've actually been working on a decluttering project in hopes that we can move this year. I want to get to a nice, semi-assisted living place while I can still be one of the younger residents, *and* before my kids put me in a home of their choosing," she only half-joked. "I just don't think we've got the energy to take care of an entire house anymore. It'll be nice to live with the royal treatment instead."

"I've got a truck. I'll grab Baz and we can help you guys move if you need it."

"You've always been such a good guy, Shaw."

Shaw wasn't sure how much he agreed with that sentiment, if grandma only knew what his last couple years had looked like.

Lenore let the air hang for a minute, finally deciding she needed to dig a little deeper into what Shaw had been doing since the loss of his family.

"So, you work; and you don't see your family too often these days… You see Baz at work." She looked up at Shaw, hoping to catch his eyes. "What've you been doing to live life to the fullest, dear?"

Shaw took another deep breath, shaking his head slowly before offering a shrug. The only hobby he'd managed to pick up in the last couple of years had been chasing down the bad guys virtually every night until his body begged him for rest. Aside from that, he wasn't sure if he should share about his relationship with Tinsley. He wondered if that would be in poor taste, especially given what day it was. He truly didn't have an answer for her.

"Still building all your fancy motorcycles?" She tried to suggest a topic that used to really get Shaw going.

He shook his head. "I sold everything when I sold the house." He truly meant everything. Shaw didn't keep furniture, vehicles, the house—nothing. He couldn't stand to be surrounded by the life he loved without Sloane there.

"Shaw." Lenore rubbed the back of his arm with her nails.

He didn't respond, he maintained his concentrated gaze on the headstone in front of him.

"Shaw, can this old lady offer you some words of wisdom and hopefully encouragement?"

Shaw nodded to assure her he wouldn't be bothered by the unsolicited advice.

"Dear, for as much as it hurts my heart to say this"—she took a quick breath—"they're gone."

She paused to see if Shaw would give any indication that she needed to stop.

"Of course they'll always be in our hearts and in our memories, but dear, that life is in the past and the only thing you can do now is be grateful for that experience and honor that love by finding happiness again." Lenore squeezed Shaw.

"I had a hard time when Sloane's grandpa passed away. I was in my sixties and starting over, it was *awful* and I still love him to this day." She shook her head. "But then I started to think about how disappointed Marty would've been to watch me shrivel away into my golden years. I owed it to him to be the spunky and fun girl he fell in love with."

While Shaw nodded, his face was expressionless. He wasn't exactly shriveling away, he'd turned into the coldest version of himself for a while and was inevitably running toward joining Sloane if he didn't find a way out of that chaos. The last few weeks he'd felt more alive than he had in the last three years, but that wasn't exactly showing today. The fact that he couldn't even offer any kind of enjoyable hobby was only further proof that Lenore was right.

"Sloane is already likely mad at you." Lenore gave him a side eye. "I remember her pestering you relentlessly to get rid of your death on wheels collection."

Shaw finally cracked a smile, holding his hand out in a chopping motion. "I still maintain the fact that she actually enjoyed riding those."

Lenore chuckled. "Shaw, don't let life pass you by. It's too short and we know that better than anyone, unfortunately." She reached down and held Shaw's hand.

He gave her hand an affectionate squeeze to let her know he heard her.

"You are young and handsome, dear. Despite how you may be feeling, we aren't meant to be alone. Don't shut everyone out of your heart forever. Some lucky lady deserves that amazing love you're capable of." She looked up at Shaw and waited for him to return her gaze before she continued, "you deserve a happy heart, Shaw."

Her last thought took Shaw by surprise and he felt his breath catch. It was exactly what Tinsley had been preaching to him. He couldn't help but think it was some kind of sign. Of all the things she could have possibly said on that topic, she specifically said he deserved to have a happy heart.

"I'll let you have some alone time with them." Lenore rubbed Shaw's lower back again. "It was really great to see you, dear. I hope to see a bigger smile on your face next time we run into each other though. Go live life, Shaw." She put her arms around him and squeezed before heading back to her car.

Shaw waited until Lenore was far enough to not be within ear shot.

He'd never run into any of Sloane's family or friends at her gravesite, not even on her birthday. He definitely took it as a sign from the universe—or Sloane herself.

Shaw smiled down at the headstone. "Did you send her my way, toots? I really needed to hear all that today," he admitted. "I was embracing the dark and gloomy for too long, it started to feel like home."

Shaw stood in silence for a while. His mind thought about a few of his favorite memories with Sloane. He could even pinpoint the exact moment in which he fell the hardest for her at that Haywood reunion. And despite what Lenore and everyone else assumed about motorcycles, Sloane *did* love a nice Sunday ride; she just didn't admit it around her family because of their opinions. His chest felt tight when he thought about the last time he saw Sloane before they parted ways for work that tragic morning.

He'd been running late and had just grabbed his lunch off the kitchen counter. He never left without saying bye to his fiancée, but he didn't see her in their master suite, so he'd searched the house. He'd checked the home office and the laundry room before walking into the nursery to find her. Sloane was still in her robe and definitely working her way toward being late that morning because she was happily hanging the tiniest clothes in the closet. He'd watched her for a long moment until she realized he stood in the doorway. That smile was permanently etched in his mind and on his heart. They didn't say a word, just an unspoken and heartfelt conversation with their lips as he'd held her swollen belly before he left for work.

Shaw had let that eat at him for months before he was able to live with the fact that he didn't even tell her he loved her. Sure, he showed her daily, sure she knew and had heard it from him an infinite number of times before, but he didn't vocalize the words that morning and it sat heavy on him. Even if he'd known that was the last opportunity to speak to her he wouldn't have known what to say, but 'I love you' definitely would have been part of it.

He thought about the mistake he'd be making if he didn't tell Tinsley. The words had been on the tip of his tongue multiple times now and he knew he'd felt that way for even longer. If he allowed himself to truly listen to his heart, it was guilt that held him back. He realized how ridiculous that guilt was because he wasn't cheating on anyone and his intentions weren't to erase Sloane from his life. The truth was, she was gone. A truth he didn't want to face for a long time. From the moment he'd met Sloane the world around them didn't exist without her; so when she left he allowed himself to simply exist in darkness rather than living in the world that was still there.

The universe always had a way of putting things where they were meant to be. The only time he wasn't a true believer in that was when Sloane was taken from him—he never understood it. Recently, however, it was like the universe was screaming at him to come back to the world that was still thriving around him. That same universe that stole his happily ever after and shattered his entire being was making amends by sending him Tinsley. Running into Lenore that morning— and the words she had to offer—only further solidified the message he needed to continue along, happily in love, with Tinsley. While he truly believed in his heart he had developed nothing but love for Tinsley, he still wanted to talk to Sloane about her. He figured the universe could let him know   by some force of nature or otherwise—if him being with Tinsley was wrong.

After terrorizing himself for long enough he knelt down to talk to Sloane.

"You might wanna start haunting Baz for what I'm about to tell you, toots." Shaw smirked. "While I've been dark and gloomy, your boyfriend number two has been a certified ho. He's dating app addicted these days." Shaw laughed at his best friend while shaking his head.

"Just be thankful I saved us from ever resorting to those things—they're awful."

Shaw waited until the chuckling subsided. It took a while considering the infinite number of girls Baz had connected with on his app. His best friend only had physical standards; beyond that, he was willing to spread the love.

"But Baz, uh… he, uh, kinda brought someone to me."

Both of Shaw's strong hands wiped his face from hairline to jawline.

"Well, she's not just someone"—he looked at the gravestone—"she's special."

He'd always been able to talk to Sloane about anything, but this was never a topic he anticipated bringing up with her. He spoke from his heart, the only thing that felt right at the moment.

"Toots, you know I wanted nothing more than a lifelong love with you—getting married, building a family, all of it. I was more than ready. And I'll *always* love you."

Shaw rearranged a few of the roses he brought, waiting for his chest to release the pressure he felt.

"I'm not just leaving and forgetting about you. You'll always be in my heart… I have to tell you though, my heart hasn't felt this good in a long time," Shaw admitted.

"I've changed, I know that much. But I think the universe sent me exactly who I needed to save me from that spiral I was in. She's been lighting up my world in the sweetest damn way possible lately. Tinsley's… she's… I love her." Shaw let out a large breath. "I never thought I'd be telling you I've fallen in love with another woman." He snorted a short chuckle. "But here I am. Trust me when I say I fought any attraction to her initially because you were on my mind, toots. Maybe grandma's right though, maybe we're not meant to be alone."

Shaw shook his head again with a smile on his face, scratching his jaw with the back of his thumb.

"Part of me thinks your ass had a hand in sending her to me anyway. You know how hard I fought for us to *not* end up with a son named Harvey of all fucking names. And damn if Tins doesn't already have a four-legged son named Harvey. Honestly, I thought I heard her wrong at first. I know you were never a fan of having a dog, but I think you'd love good ol' Harv. The name is even growing on me. I *still* wouldn't ever agree to giving a baby that name, but it fits this guy."

He looked around the cemetery, he didn't see anyone else on site, just a few cars parked at the far end of the property.

"Sloane, I think life's gonna start looking very different for me. Different in a good way, but I didn't want you to ever be shining down on me and think I still don't love you. That'll never change, toots. I'm going to take grandma's advice and live life. I know you wouldn't want that stalking in the night lifestyle for me. I know it wasn't sustainable and I got my wake up call loud and clear. Not only that, but I got the message—Tinsley's the future that I want, and I won't take that love for granted." He laughed at himself. "Assuming she loves me back, that is. I need to work on actually telling her that's how I feel. And it's probably weird to say, but I think you'd love her too."

Shaw took another deep breath and watched a ladybug land on the headstone. Red was Sloane's favorite color, the small bug made him smile. He finally sat in the grass next to the grave, the ladybug flew over and landed on his forearm once he settled.

"Alright, I definitely hear you, toots." He smiled and allowed the small insect to rest safely on his arm.

Shaw sat in silence for over an hour, however, his mind was anything but silent.

CHAPTER
Forty Two

"Boo, you wanna come have a drink?" It was just after six and Brindle had finished up for the day.

Tinsley's final client canceled on her last minute because of a sick kid, so she was done much earlier than when she told Shaw. The last thing she wanted to do was rush him though, so she figured she'd find things to occupy her time until he came back.

"I'm going to clean a few things down here and catch up a bit, but thank you."

Brindle could tell she'd been a little off that day, checking her phone but never actually texting on it, her tone, Baz coming by to see her without Shaw around—it was all a bit off.

"Are you good?"

"Oh"—Tinsley looked over at Brindle realizing that he was suspicious— "yeah, I'm totally fine. Just tired."

"Did something happen with Shawberry? Are you guys okay?" Brindle's suspicious tone exposed his worry.

"We're good." Her expression was neutral.

Brindle walked over and hugged her. "Boo, you've never been good at hiding your feelings from me. Just spill already."

Tinsley softly shook her head. "Brin, it's not my business to tell." She kept her head on his chest but looked at him. "But please just know Hunt and I are more than okay—it's nothing like that."

"You know I love me some Shawberry, if he needs anything you guys just let me know. I did think it was odd to see Black Casper today and then Shawberry just randoml—"

"I thought we talked about being nicer to Baz?" Tinsley cracked a smile.

"I *have* been!" Brindle defended himself while pulling a bottle of wine from the cabinet in the kitchenette. "If you're not partaking that's fine, but I'm having a glass. Victor's coming by to pick me up for dinner soon."

"So, when will you two be moving in together? Isn't he basically here every night now?" Tinsley smirked and popped her shoulder toward him.

"Bitch, don't come for me when you know that's *been* you and Shawberry—probably for longer than I'm aware too." His eyes narrowed.

"Don't be jealous"—she winked—"and technically speaking, he hasn't *officially* moved in."

"Get the fuck outta here!" Brindle poured himself a healthy glass of wine. "When's the last time you slept in your bed alone?"

Tinsley shrugged and turned toward the sink to hide her face and wash a few dishes they had used that day.

"Gatekeeping bitch!" Brindle laughed.

"You know"—Tinsley turned around—"in the time we've known each other, I don't think we've ever had a serious relationship at the same time."

Brindle was quiet for a moment before agreeing with her.

"I mean, have you and Victor confirmed titles? You're sure acting like boyfriends." She rinsed a cup and set it on a towel to dry.

"Oh, he's my boyfriend." Brindle sharply flicked his wrist before sitting at the small bistro table. "I don't know if he knows that yet, but we're boyfriends."

Tinsley chuckled. "Brin, just tell him that then. You are *so* stubborn sometimes. I seem to remember you telling me not too long ago that sometimes maybe you like being the man. So, man the fuck up with this one because he's a good egg and you know it."

He crossed his legs and took another drink of wine. "Yeah, well, *he* can be the one to man the fuck up in this case. I'm not gonna be the one messing anything up."

"Messing anything up?!" Tinsley basically yelled out, laughing at him. "What are you talking about?" She watched Brindle who got more serious and wouldn't look at her now.

"Brin… Did you fall in love?" She smirked. "You caught some real feelings this time and you're scared?"

"You can be a real bitch sometimes." He tried to hide his face behind his clear wine glass.

Tinsley rushed over to her best friend. "Oh, Brindle Boooooo!" she practically sang as she stood behind him and put her arms around his shoulders while pecking his cheek. "I'm happy for you!"

"I would normally tell you to get your hetero lips away from me, but since they've probably been *all* over Shawberry, I'll allow it."

"You're definitely the bitch in this duo." Tinsley laughed and gave him a friendly shove before walking back to the sink.

They both watched Harvey get up and run to the back door. He didn't get far before he turned around for the plush banana he'd been playing with.

Tinsley knew Shaw was there so she dried her hands off.

"Hey, bud!"

They heard Shaw before they saw him. Harvey let out a few friendly growls while he tried wrestling the banana from him.

"Daddy's here!" Brindle squealed.

"Brindle!" Tinsley hissed.

Shaw walked around the corner with a smile on his face but shaking his head at Brindle. He looked relaxed compared to the tired or anxious look Tinsley assumed he'd have.

"You know, Brindle, I looked up the term shadow daddy the other day." Shaw smirked. "If that's the type of daddy you keep referencing, I might be okay with it."

"Ahhhh!" Brindle slapped the table and squirmed in his seat. "Yassss! I can definitely see that, Shawberry. Tins, you lucky bitch!"

Tinsley smiled, she'd been reading the Brindle recommended series and was nearly done with the third book. They were right, Shaw *definitely* gave shadow daddy vibes. She smiled at her boyfriend who made his way to her. Tinsley threw her arms around his shoulders once he was close enough.

"Hey, tough guy. How was your day?" She ran her fingers through the back of his hair.

Shaw pecked her while rubbing his hands up and down her back. "It was a good day today, sugar."

Brindle cleared his throat. "Don't mind me."

Shaw pecked Tinsley's forehead before turning around.

"Tins and I were just talking." Brindle made sure to avoid looking at Tinsley and instead maintained his eyes on Shaw. "Are you two officially living together now, or what?"

"Brindle!" Tinsley held the bridge of her nose. "Why don't you take advantage of having a real man here and ask Hunt's opinion about *your* hesitating ass?"

Shaw laughed at them but kept his arm around Tinsley's shoulders.

"Trouble in paradise?" Shaw asked. "You and Victor seem great."

"He's pouting because he claims Victor is his boyfriend, but Victor hasn't established that yet. And Brindle—as we all know—is a stubborn ass."

"Listen"—Shaw put his hand up—"I'll admit, I don't know boy code for what you and Victor have goin' on. But what I will offer is this, I would've been more than fine if Tins had just started calling me her boyfriend, but I would've also felt like my manhood was in question if I wasn't the one to have asked her or claimed it first. So, I guess you need to figure out first and foremost if he's worth locking down and secondary to that if you want to be the swooner or be swooned."

"This is a hate crime what you two are doing right now," Brindle complained while both Shaw and Tinsley laughed. "Ganging up on me and pressuring me and shit."

"Brindle." Shaw laughed. "I'm truly just trying to help."

"Obviously, I'm the pretty one." Brindle's delicate fingertips touched his pec. "So, that's why *he* should be swooning *me*."

"Okay, well us guys aren't always the smartest. You'll save yourself a lot of heartache if you keep that much in mind. Sometimes we take a little longer than we should to do and say things." He squeezed Tinsley's shoulder.

The front door of the salon opened, eliciting a barking fit from Harvey.

"Harv!" Tinsley tried but the dog had already made his way to the front of the salon. "Brindle! I thought you locked the front door?" She followed Harvey but Shaw made his way in front of her because it didn't seem like they were expecting anyone in the salon.

"Hey, Harv!" Victor's friendly voice echoed throughout the salon.

Shaw relaxed when he realized it was just Victor.

"*Boyfriend's* here," Tinsley turned around and snickered to Brindle.

"Bitch," he mumbled back with his wine in his hand but quickly made his way to his beau and put his arms around him.

"Hey, Victor." Tinsley waved. "*I'll* lock the door since you can't be trusted to do so." She threw a side eye toward Brindle with her tongue out.

"Tinsley, good to see you." Victor turned to greet Shaw as well and they shared a friendly handshake.

"What are you boys up to this evening?" Tinsley asked after locking the door.

"Taking this one to dinner." Victor pecked Brindle and then reached for his hand.

"Ooh"—Tinsley shook her shoulder and smirked—"*swooning* Brindle Boo this evening?!"

Shaw smirked at the glare Brindle shot Tinsley's way.

"Celebrating anything in particular? Or does Brindle's pampered ass just always get taken to dinner?" Tinsley couldn't help herself once she caught Shaw smirking.

"You can shut the hell up about being a pampered ass." Brindle flung his free hand around. "I know damn well your *spoiled* ass hasn't lifted a goddamn finger around Shawberry."

Shaw put his arm around Tinsley once she was close enough. "As the *boyfriend*"—Shaw looked at Brindle—"I'm not ashamed at all to be spoiling her ass, you've known this." He turned his attention to Victor. "Victor knows. Us gentlemen happily provide the swooning when we have someone worth spoiling." He shifted his focus on Tinsley and lifted her chin to connect their lips.

Tinsley couldn't help but giggle through their kiss as they heard Brindle hissing at Shaw now.

"Shaw's right." Victor rubbed Brindle's hand with his thumb. "Are you ready to head out? Our reservation is for eight."

"A reservation?!" Tinsley pumped her eyebrows. "Where are you guys going?"

"Stanley & Seafort's," Victor replied.

Tinsley gushed but managed to keep her words at bay when she watched pink flood to Brindle's cheeks. She knew they liked going to the hole in the wall places to find all the hidden gems. An upscale and well-established restaurant wasn't really their preference; it was likely tonight could be a special occasion for them.

"Well, you guys have fun tonight." Tinsley silently smacked her lips at Brindle when Victor leaned down to pet Harvey.

Brindle flipped her off while she and Shaw chuckled. They all said their goodbyes before locking up the salon.

Tinsley hoisted herself into the truck when she heard her phone rapidly firing text notifications. They still rolled in when Shaw opened his door. They smiled at each other knowing it was Brindle.

Brindle Boo

HATE

CRIME

You BOTH are assholes

Tinsley leaned over and held her phone out so Shaw could enjoy the fit Brindle was throwing too.

Damn breeders always got some shit to say

Just wait

I'm going to get BOTH of you back

Oh Brindle Boo you know we love you

BRINDLE BOO
I'm serious .. ASSHOLES!!!!

... But also maybe thank you IF he does
end up calling me boyfriend tonight.

But still

Let us know!!

They returned home that night and decided to have a snack-style dinner, neither one of them wanted to cook. Tinsley picked cereal and Shaw dug into the meat and cheese arrangement he put together. Harvey patiently waited for Shaw to toss him something from his tray and they had *Lethal Weapon 3* playing in the background. Tinsley sat criss-cross on the couch with one of her knees resting on Shaw's leg. She watched him toss Harvey a piece of salami, he hadn't said much since they left the salon so Tinsley tried to talk to him.

"Hunt"—she put her hand on his leg—"do you want to talk about today at all?"

Shaw took a deep, visible breath. "Let's start with how your day was, sugar." He smiled.

"Well, getting ready for work this morning was obviously the highlight of my day." She rubbed his leg. "I survived Brindle's meriod that he's been on since dating/not dating Victor, and my last client ditched me today for a sick kiddo." She looked at Shaw with a bright smile on her face. "And now I'm having a pretty dang delicious dinner with the world's best boyfriend—yet another highlight of my day."

She offered him a bite of her *Life*, which he happily accepted.

"I was worried about you…" She looked down at her cereal bowl and noticed Shaw set his plate on the coffee table. "I didn't want to interrupt you, Hunt, but I was thinking about you all day. You don't have to tell me anything you had going on today, baby, but please know I'm here if there's anything you do want to talk about." She made sure her eyes met his before she continued. "You can talk to me about Sloane, she's part of you. If you want to keep that part private, that's okay, but please know you don't have to."

He reached for her chin, gazing into her beautiful brown eyes. "Tins, I love you, sugar." He rubbed his thumb along her jaw. "I shouldn't have waited so long to tell you that's how I feel, but it's true. I'll admit that I felt guilty for loving you which I know sounds so ridiculous; but, Tinsley, I'm in love with you."

Tinsley's face flooded with color as she tried to hold back tears. Once one tear finally fell from her eyelid, the rest of them followed like a waterfall. She put down her cereal bowl and immediately reached for Shaw. She crawled onto his lap with her legs on either side of his hips and put her arms around him. He embraced all of her and held tightly as her happy tears flowed freely. Once she felt calm enough, she backed away to touch foreheads with Shaw, locking into his eyes.

"Hunt, I love you too."

"Life's too short to have anything but happy hearts, sweetcheeks." Shaw held her face. "And you make my heart *so damn* happy."

Tinsley chortled through her tears but tried to maintain Shaw's gaze.

"I'd like to revise my answer from earlier." Tinsley said and wiped her eyes with the back of her hand. "This is actually the highlight of my day."

Shaw smiled and reached for her lips. He only pecked her before putting his arms around her again, whispering in her ear, "Mine too, Tins."

They maintained a firm and loving hold on one another. Shaw decided he much preferred this version of such a traumatic anniversary versus the dark routine he'd previously relied upon to get through the day. Now that Tinsley confirmed her mutual feelings for him, he never wanted another dark day in his life. He was ready to fully embrace the feeling of having a happy heart.

Shaw sent a picture Baz took while responding to a call one day. The scene happened to have a litter of cane corso puppies and Shaw couldn't help but say hi to all of them. He had a favorite one all picked out, the white spot on her chest resembled a four point star.

SWEETCHEEKS
🥹🖤 Oh you're going to be in BIG trouble when you get home! Lol He's going to smell those babies all over you. 🐾🐾

He's still my guy. But this little girl…
I can't put her down lol.

Shaw snapped a selfie this time with the black puppy in his arms.

SWEETCHEEKS
I literally didn't know how you could get any hotter and then I end up with these pics. 🖤🐶🖤👍🖤😭🖤🐶

So what are we naming her??

You're going to let me bring her home?!

SWEETCHEEKS
Hunt baby I just want you to be happy. Plus you
know I'm not one to EVER tell you no.

Oh I know

And I'm more than happy sugar.

SWEETCHEEKS
Not as happy as me

You'll have to let me know if you plan on bringing little sis
home for Handsome Harv. He'll need some coping
time before having to share us. And some time to kiss
this relaxing unbothered lifestyle goodbye lol.

Tinsley sent a picture of Harvey laid out on his bed—mostly on his back—he had a hind paw pressed against the wall near Tinsley's station.

Shaw looked at the picture for a long moment while this new, sweet puppy licked his face. His heart melted at the scent of her puppy breath begging for his attention. He smacked his lips at her a few times before texting Tinsley back.

Harv livin the life lol. I love you both so much Tins.

SWEETCHEEKS
We love you too tough guy. Be safe today so
we can see you at home later.

"Tins'll have your damn balls if you show up with a puppy." Baz laughed, watching his partner get wrapped up in this particular puppy despite eight more running around their feet.

Shaw flipped him the bird with his free hand before replying, "Actually, she just asked me what we're naming her. So, she's on board." Shaw picked the puppy up under her front legs now so he could get an unobstructed frontal look at her as she squirmed in an attempt to lick his face again. "She just wanted me to let her know so she can start mentally preparing Harv." He laughed.

"She's really gonna kick your ass now. You didn't tell her these puppies are all spoken for?!" Baz patted him on the shoulder.

"My apartment doesn't allow pets. So, even if they were available, I don't know that I could just take one home."

"Get the *fuck* outta here, fam!" Baz could barely get the words out because he was already laughing. "You don't live there anymore—clearly. I just helped your ass move your fucking Traeger *and* you've set up that damn outdoor living room area. You don't live at the apartment anymore."

Shaw gave the puppy a few more ear rubs before finally putting her down. She scampered off to join her siblings and he headed back to the patrol car with Baz.

"We haven't had an actual conversation about living together," Shaw finally admitted.

Baz laughed at him again. "Is this fear I'm sensing? She really does have your balls already!"

"Fuck off." Shaw gave him a friendly shove. "I'm not scared. I just want the official living together thing to be on her terms. You're right, I've basically moved in already, but under more normal circumstances I'd be asking her to live with me. I'm not about to see if she'd like to sell her house to live in my tiny apartment—she's never even seen it. She's so damn sweet she'd probably insist on me moving in with her on pity alone."

Baz couldn't help but laugh at him again. "Fam, you don't have to be embarrassed of it. I know it's not how you used to live, but there's a reason for it and it wouldn't just be her acting sweet. She loves you, fam. You guys belong together and you need to start acting like the man I know instead of being a little bitch about the topic."

"A little bitch seems fuckin' harsh, bro—it's not like that." Shaw threw his hands up, shaking his head, as he got into the driver's seat of their patrol car.

"Don't lie to yourself too, fam," Baz had no issue in calling him out. "The man I know would've just called it what it is weeks ago and stepped up. You're out here doing all the things but won't say it—won't just fucking tell her you officially wanna live together. You know my ass doesn't need that shit, but you, fam…" Baz shook his head. "That's the Shaw way right there. Always the gentleman and always taking charge. Don't fall short on giving Tins that full experience. She's a goddamn keeper, fam."

Shaw nodded. "I know she is. I don't have any doubt about that at all."

"*AND* you already fucking told her you *love* her! How can talking about moving in together be any harder or scarier than that shit?!" Baz slapped Shaw's leg, continuing to laugh at his partner.

"You wouldn't understand." Shaw shook his head not wanting to explain to Baz that expressing his love was easy because he had a ton to offer behind that. When it came to living together, however, it would be him moving into Tinsley's place. It somehow felt awkward to him that he wasn't the one providing the home.

"Great." Baz swatted his chest this time. "So, you let me know when we're moving your shit."

Shaw finally laughed. "The two fucking things I have?"

"Fam, do you *still* not have a fucking couch?!"

"What the hell would I need one for?" He shrugged. "I don't watch much t.v., I don't entertain, I only went home to sleep and like hell if I'm doing that on a couch when I have a bed."

"Tins got her fucking work cut out for her teaching you how to be human again."

Shaw didn't respond.

"My bad, fam. I didn't mean it like that."

"You're good, bro." Shaw shook him off, pulling out onto the main road heading for another call on their board.

Shaw got home earlier than Tinsley and Harvey that night. Harvey followed Shaw's scent and excitedly ran to him while he grilled dinner on the back deck.

"Hey, bud!" Shaw turned around and grabbed the large jowls that flew around as Harvey jumped.

"Go grab your ball," he instructed him. Harvey scampered back into the house, but soon slammed Tinsley's thigh as he made his way back out with the ball in his mouth.

"Oh, man—sorry, sugar. You alright?" He watched Tinsley's face scrunch.

"Yep." She paused in the doorway.

Shaw tossed Harvey's ball into the yard and then walked to her. He put his hands around her waist and leaned down to kiss her, their tongues dancing around until Harvey dropped his ball at Shaw's feet.

"I'm even better now." Tinsley smiled before looking around. "So, I don't see the little princess anywhere, did you really pass up on that cute little face?"

Shaw's hands drifted down to Tinsley's backside, smiling at her sincerity. She wasn't lying when she asked Shaw what they were naming her, Tinsley was ready to expand the family if that's what her boyfriend wanted.

"All those puppies were spoken for. Plus, I figured we'd want to have a longer chat before adding to the gang." He bent down and tossed Harvey's ball for him before putting his hands around his girlfriend again.

"Is everything okay?" Tinsley looked a little more serious now.

"What?" Shaw picked up on her worry. "Of course, sweetcheeks. No, I just meant that bringing home a puppy would've put a lot more on your plate than mine. I obviously can't take a dog to work and I'm not supposed to have any at my place."

"Well"—Tinsley put her arms up around his neck and looked at his chest—"maybe we do need to have a longer chat then."

"Yeah?" Shaw's strong hands stroked Tinsley's body. "You think Harv's ready for a sibling?"

Tinsley giggled. "I was talking about your place." She finally looked up at him. "It seems to me, this one is our place." She looked around at all the updates Shaw had made, basically transforming the backyard to an outdoor paradise. "So, if you don't want to have a 'your' place anymore, then we should just bring everything to our place." She hadn't looked him in the eyes again.

Shaw gently put his hand under her chin and turned her head until she stared into his eyes. Before he said anything he pressed his lips against hers. Tinsley's lips separated upon impact, turning the peck into a saucy makeout session. The action against one another's lips that left them breathless ended when Harvey barked, demanding Shaw throw his ball.

"I shoulda picked up a puppy today to keep Harv entertained," Shaw joked before tossing the drool covered ball. "But if you're sure you want me intruding on your space all the time, then I'd love to live together, Tins."

"Hunt, baby, you've known I love waking up next to you every morning. I haven't wanted you to leave since the first night you were here."

"Sugar, being with you is exactly what I've wanted. I only go back to my place to make sure my safes are still intact and to shower after the gym." He laughed. "I've had the balls to tell you I love you, but not balls enough to officially talk about living together. I didn't think you'd wanna live at my place and didn't want you to feel pressured about me living here."

Tinsley trapped her bottom lip with her teeth to suppress her grin, placing both palms on his sturdy chest while gazing into her boyfriend's electric eyes. "You shouldn't be afraid to talk to me about anything, tough guy. I love absolutely all of you, Hunt. Something as wonderful as living together shouldn't be a topic we can't talk about." She gestured toward the yard. "And all this? You didn't think I caught on to the fact that you wanted to live together full-time?"

Shaw smiled and lifted her up to hold her. "I would've done all this for you even if you didn't want to live with me. I'm in love not only with you, but with that gorgeous damn smile when you're happy." He puckered his lips for her to peck him before he continued, "but, I'm still a guy. You'll have to accept the fact that it takes me a little longer some-times. I'm workin' on all that, just so you know." He winked.

Tinsley rubbed the back of Shaw's head, her short nails applying the perfect amount of pressure to project her desire. "So, are we going to start grabbing all your stuff tonight?"

Shaw chuckled and set her back down so he could check on the grill.

"Honestly, besides my safes, I could probably move everything over in one trip on my own."

Tinsley thought about how sad that sounded. Shaw had been without Sloane for three years and in that time, everything he had at his house could fit in his truck. She considered the number of trips it would likely take to remove everything from her house and it made her heart hurt. Instead of dwelling on anything that may be hurtful or neg-ative, Tinsley decided to ride the high of their decision to officially live together. She walked up behind Shaw and put her arms around his waist as he rotated a few things on the Traeger.

"It sounds like Baz may need to help you with the safes then, but I'm more than happy to help with everything else. I can't wait for this to be *official* official."

"Well, we've got a few things to discuss before the *official* official happens." Shaw closed the grill and turned around to put Tinsley in his arms.

"Oh?" She cocked her head, smiling.

"You will *not* be maintaining all the bills at this house anymore—that stops tonight." He pecked her forehead. "If I move the safes over here we need to get you to the range so you're comfortable with every-thing I have in there." Shaw rubbed his hands up and down her back before placing his large hands on either side of her face. He encouraged her to look into his eyes, smiling as he delivered his last stipulation, "And, we need to talk about the eighteen extra, unnecessary pillows on the bed."

Tinsley threw her head back laughing. Shaw took the opportunity to sneak a peck on her exposed neck.

"I'm confident and all, but I have to tell you, it's a bit hard to maintain my masculinity when I wake up cuddled next to a pink flower or a plush pair of lips that aren't yours."

"I'm definitely open to a collaborative bedroom update." She elevated onto her tiptoes and softened her voice, "that's my favorite place to spend time with you, it has to be perfect for both of us."

"I've been managing and all." Shaw dramatically rolled his eyes before grinning at his girlfriend. "So, let's plan to address the bed this weekend when we make the move official. Your frilly princess pillow collection days are numbered, sugar."

Tinsley giggled. "A trade I'm more than willing to make."

Shaw walked into the bedroom that night, his face brightened with his smoldering grin when he saw the scene. Tinsley was lying on her side under the covers with her back to the door and all the decorative pillows were situated on Shaw's side of the bed, the lip and flower pillows placed strategically where his head would go.

Tinsley heard Shaw walk into the room and she tried to suppress her giggling. She squealed when he jumped onto the bed and grabbed her from behind.

"You think you're funny, huh?" Shaw teased and nibbled on her neck.

Tinsley flipped around and flashed his favorite smile at him. "I'm just trying to fully indulge in my final frilly princess pillow collection days."

Shaw pushed himself up to his knees, flinging all the pillows off his side of the bed as Tinsley continued to laugh.

"I've been waiting *weeks* to do that." He smiled at her and rolled over to join her under the comforter. His eyes doubled in size when he reached for her. "No jammies tonight?"

She playfully shrugged while reaching down on him. "I figured I'd owe you a little something for the pillows."

"While we're deciding on our new bed situation, I'll go ahead and inform you this is how you'll be getting into bed every damn night from now on."

Tinsley laughed out loud and put her arms around his neck. "No shot, you got in with boxers."

Shaw scrambled to remove them. "Oh, I just didn't know this is the direction we were taking. I'm onboard, sweetcheeks." He pulled their bodies together once his boxers were off.

Tinsley pushed her leg in between his and smirked when she felt his hands as they cupped the bottom of her voluptuous cheeks, giving her a couple of slow, suggestive squeezes.

Tinsley smiled at the gesture and nestled her head further into his neck. "That's my favorite spot for your hands to be." She kissed him just below his jaw.

"Is it now?" Shaw whispered, "I think you may be telling me lies, sugar." His fingertips traced her skin from her backside to the front of her pelvis, giving her a couple of soft passes between her legs.

Tinsley giggled as her leg came higher up to put pressure on his throbbing erection. "That spot's a close second for where I like your hands, tough guy." She looked at him with sultry eyes before continuing. "Because I can think of something else I'd rather have touching me there."

"You'll certainly never have to ask twice around me." Shaw pulled her on top of him by her cheeks. "And my hands will happily continue working this perfect goddamn peach of yours."

Tinsley sat up and started a comfortable pattern with her hips, Shaw's hands assisting with the motion.

"Oh, Officer Shaw, this is *exactly* why that's my favorite place for those hands." Tinsley enjoyed Shaw's touch as he meticulously and firmly helped her rhythm on him.

He held his hands on her cheeks but stopped any movement in them.

"I've warned you to quit the shit with that Officer Shaw routine," he playfully threatened her as his hands made a few passes up and down her thighs.

Tinsley's twisted grin widened as she lowered her chest to his and spoke softly just about his lips.

"What exactly do you plan to do about it?" she flirtatiously asked before biting her lip.

Shaw put his hand on Tinsley's back and flipped them. She now looked up at him with an even brighter smile on her face. She didn't have anything to say at the moment so she simply giggled in anticipation for his next move.

He leaned down and gently sucked on Tinsley's neck. Once he felt her leg rubbing his he grabbed the back of it and placed it over his hip.

Tinsley grabbed his rear end with both of her hands as she enjoyed the feeling of his strong fingers putting more pressure on the back of her thigh.

"You might be providing motivation instead of punishment right now, Hunt."

"I didn't get another 'Officer Shaw', so I guess what I'm doing's working." He winked and continued to love on her.

CHAPTER

Hey Hunt baby—Vance got called into work so he just dropped Laura Loo off at the salon with me. That means we have a little dinner guest joining us tonight. 😊 🥰

Hunt

Two pretty girls to dine with? Harv and I are lucky guys.

Hey I'm gonna stop by the store to grab some graham crapper supplies. I know we wanted to have a little bonfire tonight.

😟 😬 idk if we can do that with Laura Loo… My rents are picking her up and idk about having a fire when they get here.

Hunt

Sugar don't you worry about that. We're having a fire tonight and any other night my girl wants.

😊 🖤 I love you.

Hunt

I love you too. See you soon Tins.

"Shaw's here!" Alaurra squealed, watching Harvey rush the back door when it opened.

"Hey, Laura Loo!" He waved before bending down to give Harvey a good pat down. "Hi, bud."

Tinsley was the last to make her way over because she wanted a longer greeting. Shaw pressed his lips against his girlfriend's puckered ones before slipping his tongue in her mouth which she caught. They didn't indulge long in front of Alaurra.

"Hi, handsome." Tinsley pinched his freshly shaved chin.

"Hi, gorgeous," he adoringly replied.

"Shaw, I'm making bracelets!" Alaurra held one up. "Yours isn't done yet, but I'm making you one too!"

He made his way to the breakfast bar to get a closer look at her crafted masterpieces. "I can't wait to see it, thank you."

"Auntie Tins said your favorite color is blue."

"She's right." He smiled before turning his attention to Tinsley. "Should I go start the grill?"

"Yes, please." Tinsley bit her bottom lip. "I wasn't sure which one you'd be using tonight… and I'm still scared to turn either of them on. I know you showed me like ten times already."

Tinsley felt like an idiot. She'd never had a grill and wasn't the most comfortable taking the lead on either of the devices quite yet. Shaw was quite the grill master with his Traeger and recently added a Black Stone. Tinsley didn't want to break either of his prized possessions due to her lack of knowledge.

Shaw chuckled, rubbing her shoulder. "Sugar, it's okay—I surely don't mind." He kissed the side of her head and then walked out to the back deck.

"Can I help?!" Alaurra stood on the stool.

Shaw stopped in the doorway. "Of course! You can come learn to grill from the master himself."

Tinsley rolled her eyes while smiling at her boyfriend.

"I've got some special treats we can roast over the fire after dinner tonight too," he informed Alaurra now that she stood at the blackstone with him.

"S'mores?!" the little girl excitedly guessed.

"Better than s'mores," Shaw assured her with wide eyes.

Tinsley smiled while listening to them chatting over the grill.

It wasn't long before Alaurra raced back into the kitchen.

"Everything alright, Laura Loo?" Tinsley asked while molding another homemade Parmesan tater tot.

"Yep!" She scrambled for her beads she left on the breakfast bar. "I want to bring this outside with Shaw. I need to finish his bracelet."

"Make sure you measure his wrist," Tinsley encouraged. "He's going to need a few more beads than the one you made for Auntie Tins."

"Yeah because Shaw's big and has all those muscles." She feverishly nodded with a wide eyed smile.

"He sure is." Tinsley left it at that but thought about how perfectly sculpted her boyfriend was.

After everyone had new bracelets—including Harvey—and they'd demolished dinner, they moved down to the newly arranged fire pit area Shaw constructed. He had consistently been building a fire more nights than not since they loved cuddling in front of them so much. With Alaurra joining them tonight, they figured it was a perfect time to put their brand new roasting skewers to use.

"I think I have another amazing idea for these." Tinsley got up from the outdoor sectional to head to the kitchen. Shaw was right, adding a Reese's to the s'more was epic and there was no way she'd be able to just have a normal one again. She returned in no time and Shaw's head fell back when he saw what she carried.

"Oh, sugar!" Shaw's grin showcased his perfect teeth watching Tinsley bring out the tray of brownies she baked the previous night. "You're a genius."

Tinsley cut a piece to put on his graham cracker when Alaurra vocalized her curiosity.

"How come you call Auntie Tins *sugar* so much?"

Shaw smiled, his gaze falling on Tinsley. "Because she's my sugar. I can't think of another name that's sweeter than sugar and that's what Auntie Tins is." He reached out to rub his girlfriend's arm. He stopped when Harvey started barking at the back gate.

"Can we share these graham crappers with Grandma and Grandpa too?!" Alaurra's eyes beamed toward Shaw after she watched her grandparents walk into the backyard.

"Of course," Shaw happily agreed. He watched as Tinsley's dad gave the fire a look and immediately rolled his disapproving glare toward his daughter.

"Hi honey!" Colette's arms flew open to catch her granddaughter who'd raced over to welcome them. "No greeting from my favorite grandson, huh?" Colette watched Harvey who sat up but stayed near Tinsley and the fire pit.

Tinsley softened her eyes, looking down at her beloved cane corso. "He's waiting for you to join him at his new favorite seat in the house."

"My, isn't this the set up?" Colette commented on the new outdoor area under a seemingly brand new gazebo complete with a fire pit. String lights were tastefully placed above the yard and they sat on a brand new outdoor furniture set, complete with a sectional and two additional upholstered chairs.

Tinsley smiled from the comfort of Shaw's arm as she sat next to him on the sectional.

"Hunt's a visionary." She pecked her boyfriend's cheek while the hand placed on his thigh squeezed him.

"Shaw, you did all this?!" Colette continued her initial inspection of the updates.

"I did." He confidently smiled. He was no stranger to working with his hands and had previously taken care of his own house.

"I cheated a bit and got a gazebo that just had to be assembled versus building one, but as long as Tins is happy." He shrugged.

"Grandma, do you want to make a graham crapper with me?"

Colette chuckled. "You'll have to show Grandma because I don't know what that is."

"Shaw taught me. It's a s'more but with Reese's instead of choco-late."

"We sure are lucky to have Shaw around—he does everything!" Colette's eyes smiled at her granddaughter with her hands up.

"Yeah, hopefully keeping an eye on this fire and the things that are going on around it while you girls insist on playing in it." Rick finally chimed in and shot out an irritated exhale as he sat down.

"Grandpa, you shouldn't play with fire. It's dangerous."

"I know. That's why I wanted to give you *all* the reminders." He looked pointedly at Tinsley.

Tinsley stared into the glowing fire to avoid making eye contact with her dad.

Shaw noticed and gave her leg an affectionate squeeze before he slayed a marshmallow onto the roasting skewer.

"Let's try that brownie combo, sugar." He handed the skewer to Tinsley and winked at her.

"Auntie Tins is sugaaaarrrrrrr!" Alaurra sang and popped her hips around while sticking another marshmallow into the fire.

Everyone but Rick chuckled at her and Shaw leaned over to peck Tinsley on the side of her head.

"Shaw, help!" Alaurra giggled.

He sat upright. "Laura Loo, swing that thing over here." He waited for the flaming marshmallow to be close enough for him to blow it out. "I thought you didn't like the burnt ones?" he laughed.

"Yeah, this one's for Grandma."

Colette put her hands on her hips. "Who said I like burnt marsh-mallows?" she sarcastically asked.

"Me and Auntie Tins will take that charred one, Laura Loo." Shaw smiled at Alaurra. "Look how perfect she cooked hers."

"Shaw, what are you doing?! You gotta get the crackers going for us!" Alaurra cracked the whip since he started slipping on his duties.

While Shaw got the graham crapper assembled and ready for a marshmallow he heard Colette commenting on his newest accessory.

"So, you joined the friendship bracelet club, huh?"

Shaw shook his wrist, smiling. "I sure did."

"You're really in now." Colette looked over at her husband who still seemed to be hung up on Tinsley having a fire pit.

"One step closer at the very least." He shrugged.

"Alaurra, are you about ready to go?" Rick asked, furrowing his brows.

"Honey"—Colette turned to her husband—"we're just sitting down for a little dessert, don't rush her."

"Did you have something other than s'mores for dinner tonight?" Rick continued looking for all the ways Tinsley failed to responsibly take care of her niece.

"Grandpa, these aren't s'mores, they're *graham crappers*," she reminded him. "Me and Shaw made smash burgers for dinner."

"I noticed *two* grills up on the porch," Rick made his disapproval known again. "Does your brother know about these new flammable additions you've made while his daughter's here?"

"Vance hasn't been over since we updated the yard," Tinsley admitted.

"We FaceTimed Dad while we were smashing your burger tonight, didn't we?" Shaw pointed out and smiled at his favorite niece.

"Yep! He told me I was doing a really good job!" The little girl beamed brightly, proud of her fun evening thus far. "And he asked Shaw to show him his belly." She gestured to her own stomach, laughing.

"What?" Colette had a curious grin with scrunched brows on her face.

"Oh"—Shaw tried to shake it off—"I had an injury a few weeks back. The doc was just following up to see how it was doing."

"Dangers of the job." She shook her head but smiled. "Good thing you've got so many medical professionals around you."

"Tinsley, pull that from the fire." Rick pointed at the blanket Tinsley had draped over her legs. It wasn't in any danger of catching fire at all, but he wanted to be sure he kept a watchful eye on every movement.

Shaw took, what he hoped, was an unnoticeable breath while listening to Rick.

It didn't take Tinsley long to get up, she folded the blanket and set it next to Shaw.

"I'm going to pick up the kitchen a bit," she decided.

"How 'bout I come help?" Shaw motioned to get up.

"It's okay." She lowered her voice before finishing, "I need a minute."

"Then I'll be in there to help *in a minute*." He reached up and kissed her forehead.

Tinsley didn't get far when Alaurra chased her down.

"Auntie Tins, I need to go get all my bracelet stuff." She scurried to a halt and turned toward Colette. "Grandma, come see what all we made tonight."

Colette was mid-bite on her roasted masterpiece but got up to follow her girls to the house.

Harvey lifted his block head in mild interest but noticed Shaw stayed put so he decided to hold down his warm spot by the fire.

Shaw watched him settle back in so he reached down and gave him a firm side rub before patting his haunches a few times. "Good boy, bud."

Rick wasted almost no time before he started in on Shaw.

"Look, the yard looks great and all, but Tinsley doesn't need something like this back here." He pointed to the fire pit. "I'm not even sure the grill by the house like that is a good idea. Her yard should be simple. She doesn't need all this—it's just a place for Harvey to do his business."

Shaw slightly nodded, he knew this was his opportunity to say what had been on his mind since meeting Rick. It was clear Tinsley's dad wasn't overly impressed with him. He didn't have that opinion very high on his priority list at the moment—he'd work on that later. For now though, he wouldn't allow the disrespectful comments to continue in regards to Tinsley.

"Rick"—Shaw delivered a steady tone—"I'm really not trying to be disrespectful here. I know we haven't known each other long, but I do need to make it known that some of the things you say to Tins aren't sitting right with me."

Rick couldn't believe his ears, he stared at Shaw with a neutral expression under his bushy brows.

Shaw held his hand up, chopping the air in front of him. "Tins is an amazing woman who does quite well for herself and I don't think you give her the credit she deserves. I understand where the fire related comments are coming from, but this is her house and she's more than capable of having these things here."

"You don't know my daughter like I do."

Shaw agreed with the motion of his head. "You're right, we know her and see her in two completely different lights. But I think we can also agree that we both love her. And with that love, we owe her respect. That's all I'm asking for."

"You don't think I respect my own daughter?" Rick's voice got louder.

Shaw was a little shocked that he told Rick he loved his daughter and the only thing he seemed to be concerned with was Shaw's perception of the level of respect Rick was or wasn't giving Tinsley.

"Sir, I didn't say that. What I am saying is the two times I've seen you guys together, there's a certain tone and some insinuations that I'm not a fan of."

Shaw carefully watched Rick for a long moment before continuing, "Your daughter has a brightness about her that you should really see. The doubts you project on her dim that light and it hurts to watch."

"You have no idea what we've been through with her," Rick defended his position.

"I think you may be assuming I don't know about Tinsley's alternative childhood. She fully disclosed that information to me, so I'm aware to that extent and I have to say, her owning a salon and a house and thriving like she is—despite all that? That's a phenomenal woman. It's clear she loves you and wants your approval, but you're a tough audience for her, if you weren't aware."

Rick tried not to project his surprise before he responded.

"I need her to take her future more seriously. She doesn't know how to do that and I'd like for her to be able to take care of herself one day."

"Can I ask what she's not taking care of?" Shaw waited.

"I don't think you'd understand." Rick didn't look at Shaw, he glared into the fire he still didn't like in Tinsley's yard.

"Help me understand then, because what I see is a beautiful, sweet, hard-working woman who loves life."

"You've met Vance, and have spent some time with his daughter, so

I would venture to guess you know the level of expectation I have of my kids and how they conduct themselves. I've known Tinsley would take longer, but she's nearly thirty now and still making poor decisions like these." He gestured toward the fire pit and then to Shaw's surprise, he pointed at Harvey.

"Despite what you think you know about my daughter, it's dangerous for her to be around fire. And she's not capable or mature enough to make adult financial decisions because it's clear a significant chunk of the money she earns goes toward Harvey's care. Which only slows down the growth of her business. She bought an old house—despite me urging her to purchase a new build—and Vance is constantly over here fixing things for her. You have no idea what it's like to take care of an adult child the way I have to watch out for Tinsley."

"Have you ever asked her if she's happy?"

Rick didn't answer him, a scowl took shape on his face.

"I happen to know Tins is very happy right now," Shaw assured him. "I can appreciate you worrying about her having the best life imaginable, but you don't need to worry to the point of putting her down. She's doing amazing." Shaw sat taller, considering his next words but said them anyway.

"Tins won't be doing anything else on her own. I'm here and plan to give her exactly the life she's always dreamed of having. She won't be taking care of this house alone, I'm not about to let her pay for Harvey's care by herself, and as far as the salon goes, I'm ready to help her bring her vision to life. I'm willing to wait for you to offer your approval or blessing about me, but what I won't wait for is you being more respectful of Tins."

They stared each other down when Colette came back out to the fire pit area.

"What are you boys looking so serious about out here?" She stood between the seated men.

"Colette"—Rick didn't look at his wife—"we need a minute."

"Honey—"

Rick held his finger up and finally looked at his wife. "Just a minute, dear."

She watched his eyes and tried to read the situation but finally decided to go back in the house.

"I guess I underestimated you," Rick admitted. "I'll give you that. But, Shaw, I don't think you realize what you're committing to right now. Do you have any idea what kind of money it takes to be successful and have a stable future? I mean, you said yourself, you aren't even sure about climbing from your current position. So, I have to wonder if you're promising all this and yet you're just as immature or incapable of making adult decisions as my daughter is."

"First of all, that's an example of the disrespectful comments that I'd like you to stop with. Tins isn't immature or incapable. Secondly, not only am I fully aware, but I'm more than able to provide a stable future for Tins. And that's in relation to everything she might need—including financial stability."

Rick wiped his face. "Did Tinsley put you up to this?"

Shaw shot out a laugh through his nose. "No." He furrowed his brows. "I'm not doing my job with her if I wait for Tins to ask for things. I never wanted to have to say any of this to you in front of her; as long as you work on showing her more respect, she won't have to."

Rick considered how highly Vance had spoken about Shaw and the clear adoration his wife and granddaughter also had for him. It wasn't just Tinsley who'd fallen for Shaw, *everyone* in his family seemed to love him. He still worried Shaw wasn't what Tinsley needed.

"Look, I get the impression I'm not exactly what you had in mind for your daughter. I respect that we don't know each other all that well and like I said earlier, I don't have a problem earning your approval over time. But what I will tell you is I've been nothing but respectful to Tins and I'd do anything to keep her happy. I may just be a city cop, and not that it's really *anyone's* business, but I have absolutely no debt and I'm damn smart with money. I cleared two-hundred thousand last year alone being on patrol. It's not the bottom of the barrel career you may think it is."

For the first time since they'd met, Rick finally looked relieved. Shaw was a little surprised it wasn't a more impressed look or feeling of shame for Rick being so judgemental, but he'd take it.

"I'd really like to simply move forward just getting to know Tins's family without the suggestive tones and judgements if we can. Tins and I both deserve that chance at the very least. I don't plan on disappointing her or you."

Rick considered the entire conversation, at no point was Shaw smug or condescending toward him. He'd directly, and privately, informed him what was on his mind. His thoughts were interrupted when his granddaughter came skipping out to the gazebo.

"Shaw, Auntie Tins said maybe you can help me with this for school." She held out the paper for him to read.

Shaw smiled at the brightly colored flyer. "You want me to come to your school?"

"Yeah, because it's for our job days and they want those jobs to come to school." She pointed at the list of careers the school specifically requested, which included law enforcement and other first responders. "Daddy will be there too! You guys can both see all my friends."

"I'd love to." He gave her a quick squeeze around her shoulders when she sat down next to him. "Can I take a picture of this so I know what I need to do?" He reached for his phone.

She quickly nodded in excitement.

"Uh oh, did Shaw get roped into going to school?" Colette smiled upon her approach. She looked at her husband for any indication that things had gotten more uncomfortable after she left the private conversation he wanted with Shaw. Rick didn't look upset, if anything, he looked like he was more relaxed than he'd been since they walked in and saw the fire pit.

Shaw smiled at Colette. "Actually, my partner and I have done a few career days. I can contact the school tomorrow. We like to bring the cruiser out and can sometimes wrangle in a canine team to join us." He looked at Alaurra. "I'll be sure to wear my cool new bracelet that day too." He held his wrist up.

Alaurra gushed and hid her face behind his shoulder.

He didn't want to embarrass her anymore than she seemingly was so he changed the topic.

"Auntie Tins isn't in there cleaning the whole kitchen, is she?"

"She's putting dinner stuff away," Alaurra confirmed.

"I'm gonna go help her." He got up. "Can I get you guys anything? Does anyone want a drink?"

Colette and Rick both shook their heads to politely decline.

Tinsley was surprised her parents had stayed so long. She really started to wonder what happened when Shaw was outside with her dad alone. She looked his way several times and it seemed like her dad's mood shifted to a much lighter one than he originally had that night. The four adults enjoyed drinks and conversation now.

Alaurra tried her best to stay awake but eventually fell asleep sharing a blanket with Tinsley. Shaw didn't mind at all when the sleeping six year-old sprawled out and her legs kicked themselves over his lap. He didn't skip a beat in responding to Rick and simply covered her feet with another blanket before resting a hand on her calf. Tinsley stroked Alaurra's hair since her head landed on Tinsley's lap.

"Shaw, honey, you sure are quite handy." Colette was still hung up on how different Tinsley's yard looked. "How'd you pick up all these talents?"

"Thank you." Shaw smirked. "My dad taught me a bit here and there, but I've done plenty of trial and error on my own. I'm not one to sit still very often." He shrugged.

"So, house projects? Or do you have other specialties?" Colette took a sip of the wine she had in her hand.

Shaw rubbed Tinsley's shoulder, he'd never disclosed his previous love of motorcycles to her. "I'd say I'm a bit mechanically inclined as well. I used to have an itch for building motorcycles."

Tinsley whipped her head toward him and smirked.

"Just a hobby really." He fondly shook his head. "I'd get completely thrashed bikes and restore them. It was turning into more of a collection because after all that work I had trouble letting go of any of them." He laughed at himself. Remembering several times Sloane scolded him for bringing home yet another bike when he had a handful to choose from already.

"Do you still have all those bikes?" Colette asked while Rick waited in anxious anticipation. He wasn't wild about the idea of his daughter riding on a motorcycle. Just as he'd gotten more comfortable with Shaw, he had to drop this news on them.

Shaw shook his head and took a swig of his beer before answering her.

"I actually sold the entire collection a couple years ago." He shrugged, not wanting to deep dive into the why of that decision. "It just wasn't a hobby that suited me anymore."

"I have to say," Rick's voice started sternly. "I'm relieved to hear that was an itch you scratched *before* meeting my daughter."

His gaze held Shaw's for a split second before his lip curled and he chuckled.

Shaw returned his smile and joined in the laughter around him.

"Yeah, my parents hated them too," he admitted.

Colette made sure her granddaughter was sleeping in the backseat before she spoke to her husband.

"Are you going to tell me what happened with you and Shaw tonight?"

Rick didn't respond right away.

"Dear, I've known you long enough to read you," she pointed out. "I know you've had your doubts about him and I know I walked out to a serious conversation tonight. We may have left on good terms, but don't try to hide the fact that something else was going on tonight."

Rick took a healthy breath and checked his rearview mirror before answering.

"He's not the useless tool I originally took him for," Rick finally admitted.

"Useless tool? Rick, that's hardly fair that you *ever* made that determination of Shaw." Colette shook her head.

"I said I was wrong."

Colette laughed. "That's *not* what you just said," she called him out. "I happen to love him, he's perfect for Tins. Have you ever seen your daughter that happy? Genuinely happy?"

Rick knew she'd never been so happy.

"I don't love that he's a cop," Colette decided. "I'd prefer a less dangerous profession, but otherwise he seems to be quite the match for Tins."

Rick wasn't interested in sharing the entire conversation with his wife, but seeing the look of hope and happiness on her face, he decided to share some of it.

"He told me he loves Tinsley."

Colette reached over and held her husband's hand with one of hers and the other just above her heart. Her face swelled over with joy.

"You better start liking the kid, Dr. Adams. Shaw's here to stay."

Rick picked his wife's hand up and kissed the back of it.

"I hope so."

It made Colette happy to hear Rick was coming around. She understood why her husband was so tense now and accepted the mood she had interrupted earlier.

CHAPTER
Forty Five

Shaw invited Tinsley to a barbecue with Baz and the Haywood crew one Sunday afternoon. His second set of parents, Mama T and Pops, hosted the entire family pretty regularly. Shaw hadn't introduced his girlfriend to everyone quite yet; he thought this would be the perfect opportunity for her to meet his second family.

"Tins." Baz wiped his meticulously manicured beard while stretched out on an outdoor chaise lounge. "Now that we're better friends—I gotta ask—still no awkward or hard feelings about the whole ghosting thing, right?"

"Bro!" Shaw shook his head, chuckling. "You don't need to be all sad that you took her out on a date only for her to pump the brakes when she found out you have a much hotter friend." He propped his feet up on the coffee table in front of them and put his arm around Tinsley.

"Fuck you, fam." Baz laughed and stuck his finger up at his buddy.

"I mean, technically speaking"—Tinsley smirked at Shaw—"Baz never took me out." She shrugged and looked over at Baz again. "I drove myself *and* we basically went Dutch."

Baz fought a smile. Tinsley had, in fact, put plenty of money down to cover more than half their bill before rushing away to be with Harvey.

"Not only that," she continued, perking her brows at Baz, "a Tinsley date always ends in a nice little tickling and you never got that."

Both Shaw and Baz burst into laughter.

"You fucking admitted *that* shit to her!" Baz rolled on his side across the chaise he was sitting on. "I can't fucking believe she's still around." He slapped the cushions a few times trying to contain his laughter.

Tinsley and Shaw intertwined their fingers and chuckled along with their friend.

"You boys are straight rookies and need to attend the school of Brindle to up your little name calling game. That's what you two should be ashamed of." Tinsley noticed Tilly still across the yard. "I'm assuming Tilly was an app find. Was she blessed with a nickname that she knows about too?"

Both Baz and Shaw looked at one another, they definitely didn't want to disclose Tilly's name.

"Nah"—Baz adamantly shook his head—"Tilly's just Tilly."

Tinsley noticed Shaw's eyes quickly shoot to the ground. She knew then it wasn't true, but she wasn't going to dwell on it at all. She could ask him later if it mattered that much to her.

"Oh, so that's how you knew she was special to you? I get it." Tinsley grinned.

Shaw rubbed her hand and took a visible sigh of relief.

"To answer your original question"—her gaze fell upon Baz—"Hunt managed to get you out of me having any hard feelings about your rudeness." She looked at her boyfriend with stars in her eyes, rubbing his hand with her thumb. "Things worked out how they were supposed to."

Shaw pulled her in to place a long kiss on her forehead.

Baz nodded. "I agree. But, we had to meet otherwise this woulda never happened." He gestured between his friends. "So, in a way, you both owe me."

"Get the fuck outta here!" Shaw laughed. "You must not have made Tilly pay for that first date, otherwise her ass would've run off just like Tins did."

Baz flipped his best friend off. "Goddamn, do I need to take Tins out on a real date to make up for my misstep?" He choked out a laugh.

"You fucking wish," Shaw shot back with a smile on his face.

Tinsley smirked and put her hand up. "You had your chance, Baz. Hunt's the only one I'll be tickling from now on."

They were all laughing again when a new guest joined them.

"This fuckin' guy!" Baz shouted and stood to greet the man. "It's been a minute, Cuz."

Shaw assumed they'd see Craig, but he wasn't ready for the interaction. Craig was Baz's cousin, Chief Haywood's son, and the man Shaw saw at the chop shop during his off-the-books car jacking investigation. Craig had given his parents trouble while in school; mostly moronic teenager moves like cutting *and* failing classes, petty theft, pot, and the occasional graffiti. His dad had always figured out a way to get him out of any real trouble so Craig never did anything about improving his ways.

"Sup, fam?" Craig slapped hands with Baz and then looked at Shaw, his fist extended. "What's good, brother?"

Shaw stayed seated and only knocked knuckles with the criminal.

"We've forgotten our manners, I see." Craig reached toward Tinsley, offering his hand. "I'm Craig."

Tinsley smiled and gently accepted the gesture. "Tinsley," she kindly replied.

She noticed all the gold this guy wore. He had a pinky ring and two thick, gold bracelets on the hand she shook, his diamond earrings were almost just as big as the ones Shaw got her for her birthday, and she counted at least four chains around his neck, one of which had a nearly five inch solid gold Jesus hanging on a cross. He didn't resemble Baz, his frame was much smaller, although he did have a muscular physique that he showed off in a white wife beater tank top and a simple pair of black jeans. He kept his hair in braids that didn't quite hit his shoulders and he didn't need to keep barbered facial hair like Baz since the thin line of hair on Craig's lip barely qualified as a mustache.

An uneasiness consumed Shaw watching Craig around Tinsley.

"These two fools can't do anything alone, I see." Craig laughed, shaking his head before taking a seat on a piece of the outdoor sectional.

"Both gettin boo'd up together, isn't that sweet?" He smacked his thick lips at his cousin.

"Fuck off." Baz laughed as Shaw offered Craig a hand gesture for his comments.

"Auntie over there giving Tilly the business, I see." Craig's head motioned toward the women.

Baz smiled. "They've been getting along quite well actually—Mama T likes this one."

"Shit, where you boys finding these dimes?" Craig stared at Tinsley, taking her in from head to toe. "Do you work with Tilly?"

Tinsley shook her head, having no idea where Tilly worked. "No, I met Tilly through Baz."

Craig's eyebrows went up and Shaw watched him give Tinsley another admiring glance.

Shaw was already on edge around Craig because of what he saw at the chop shop a couple weeks ago; it didn't help that he looked at Tinsley in an appreciative manner now.

"Hey, Tins." Shaw clutched her thigh before he stood and held his hand out. "I wanted to show you something."

Baz looked at his partner, fully aware that his demeanor changed since Craig came over to sit with them. He understood Shaw may be protective of Tinsley since his former fiancée was taken from him so suddenly, but he never knew his best friend to be possessive—especially not around family. That was the anxious energy he felt off Shaw.

Tinsley smiled at her boyfriend, completely oblivious to who she just met, and accepted Shaw's strong, outstretched hand.

Shaw noticed it was perfect timing for getting Tinsley up when he saw two more men walk into the backyard. He immediately recognized them from the chop shop, anger now battling the wrath he'd felt watching Craig eyeing Tinsley. He walked Tinsley toward the house as the men made their way directly to Craig; it made him wonder if anyone else from that night would be joining them. The last thing he needed was the woman who stabbed him showing up and having to deal with that exchange. He needed to take his girlfriend home, or at least out of the Haywood house.

"Tins, sugar, let's get out of here."

"Hunt, are you okay?" Tinsley picked up on the change in his demeanor.

"Let's talk about it once we're outta here." He checked on the new guests through the slider to see Craig introducing his friends to Baz.

Tinsley watched Shaw's inspection of the newcomers and felt his typically calm presence become dangerously protective; she trusted her boyfriend and knew he'd be true to his word and address it later. "Can we at least say bye?" she asked when his focus returned to her.

"Yeah," Shaw agreed and they did a quick sweep to offer their farewells.

As they walked out to Shaw's truck, another car pulled up to the house. Luckily, the sports car parked on the street and Shaw had Tinsley under his arm on the opposite side. He immediately recognized the woman who stabbed him sitting in the passenger's seat. She got out of the car and looked in their direction. Shaw instinctively hid as much of Tinsley as he could manage while not alarming her to any possible danger near them. He made eye contact with the woman and her eyes widened—he knew the recognition was mutual. Shaw noticed the driver was another woman, not one he could recall from that night, but it was clear they were making their way to the Haywood house.

Shaw hastily walked Tinsley to the passenger side of the Raptor, making sure his body blocked the woman's view of her the entire time.

"Tins, I need you to put your sunglasses on and when you get in the truck I want you to scoot down in the seat."

Worry consumed her face. "Hunt"—she rubbed his forearm—"are you sure you're okay?"

"Please, sugar." He reached for the sunglasses on top of her head and put them on her face. "I promise, I'll tell you what's going on, but for now I need you to listen to me."

Tinsley slowly nodded, clutching his forearm even tighter.

Shaw kissed her forehead and then made sure to shut her door once she settled into her seat. He walked around the truck, watching the woman make her way to the Haywood house. Her shocked eyes looked over her shoulder again at Shaw just before they passed through the front door.

"Fuck." Shaw exhaled. He started his truck and pulled his cell phone out.

He hoped Baz would see his text in time to not innocently share anything. He didn't have to hope for long because his phone started ringing almost immediately after he sent his message.

"Hey," Shaw answered in as even of a tone as he could manage.

"Fam, you good?"

Shaw let out a larger than average exhale. "We gotta talk, but not right now. I need to tell you some shit."

"Kinda scaring me, fam. Are you out front still? I'll come out there."

"No." Shaw shook his head and pulled away from the house. "Let's link up when you're done there. But like I said, don't say anything about me to Craig or any of his friends. Don't tell them where Tins works, pictures—absolutely *nothing* about her either."

Tinsley looked over at Shaw, he had never seemed so anxious, she felt his concern in her own chest.

"Hunt, fam—" Baz tried.

"Bro, I'll spill later. I need you to finish the day with fam as if nothing's going on. I know Mama T looked suspicious enough when we left. Just spin some kinda shit, but don't give any indication that there's anything wrong."

"You know I've always got your back, fam. But shit, you sure you're good?"

"Yes. Call me when you've got a minute later."

"Will do, take care."

"Thanks, bro." Shaw hung up and set down his phone in the cup-holder. He checked his mirrors again before looking over at Tinsley.

"It's Craig, isn't it? You have to tell Baz what happened that night… huh?" Tinsley's soft voice hesitantly asked.

"I'm sorry, Tins. I didn't think it would get like that so quickly. It's not unusual for Craig to be there, I just haven't seen him since the night at that chop shop." Shaw reached for Tinsley's hand, interlacing their fingers. "When we got up I saw two more guys who were there that night. They've never been to a Haywood function. I don't know why Craig brought them along, so that's why I suggested we leave. I just didn't want you there if any of them knew I'd been around."

Tinsley's hold on Shaw's hand tightened.

"I didn't mean to scare you, I just needed to get you out of there." He contemplated not even saying anything else to her but wanted to fully disclose the situation. "That car that pulled up as we were leaving"— he took a breath to consider how he'd deliver the message to his already upset girlfriend—"that passenger was the one who stabbed me. I have no idea who she is, but she was headed into that house."

"Hunt…" A single tear rolled down Tinsley's cheek, she reached over and kissed the side of Shaw's face, practically cutting off the circulation in his hand with the tense hold she had on him.

"I've gotta tell Baz everything."

Tinsley watched her boyfriend's agitated face as he drove them away from Craig and his crew. She'd been worried since Shaw's change in behavior, but having these facts now, terror consumed her mind when she realized the likely result once Baz found out. Shaw promised her he wouldn't do any more vigilante bullshit, but she couldn't deny this situation would likely warrant some kind of reaction she wouldn't feel comfortable with. She agreed something had to be done about Craig. She didn't, however, want that solution to result in anything harmful happening to her tough guy.

CHAPTER
Forty Six

Shaw had waited for a text or call from Baz since they left the Haywoods, so he immediately responded.

"Fam." Baz approached the booth Shaw sat at in the corner of the bar. "You good? This ain't like you."

"Bro, there's a lot of shit I need to tell you." Shaw put his elbows on the table and looked over as Baz made himself comfortable across from him. "I'm gonna need you to let me tell you *all* of it—and please try to keep your shit together. You're my brother. I fucking know what you've done for me in the past." Shaw's gaze held Baz's, projecting the memory of Baz finding out about what Shaw did to Sloane's murderers. "Don't think I've ever taken that for granted, or not loved you for it."

"What happened?" Baz assumed Shaw had done something that would require him to pull some strings with the family again.

"You know me, you know I spiraled after Sloane. No one's more familiar with that than you." He checked Baz's expression. "I haven't quite gone to *that* length ever again, but basically every night since then I've been going out doing some similar dumb shit." Shaw's forearms rested on one another, he quickly scanned the immediate area to be sure no one was within ear shot. He paused his admission when the waitress appeared at the end of their table.

"Can I get you something to drink?" the server asked Baz while she set a coaster on the table in front of him.

"Uh, sure, how 'bout a Modelo, please," he ordered, reaching for a chip. Once the server left the table Baz dipped his chip in salsa and reminded Shaw, "I told you we never needed to bring that shit up again."

Shaw nodded. "I know. I just wanted to make sure you knew this isn't exactly like that." He pulled himself closer by his forearms and lowered his voice, "Remember that fucking degenerate wife beater from a few weeks ago?"

Baz stopped chewing, eyes widening at the realization it'd been his partner who went back to visit that loser.

"Shaw, fam—"

Shaw put his hand up. "I know, bro—I know. That's the shit I'm talking about. It's been a fucking lifestyle for nearly three years."

"I thought it was just good fucking karma that he ended up in the hospital."

The server came back to drop off Baz's drink.

"It was forced Karma," Shaw admitted after the server was out of range. "Bro, that's just one of the infinite number of vigilante things I've fucking done. I'm not proud of it, but I'm not exactly regretting all of it either."

"Fam, you know I've got your back. What happened?" Baz asked without judgment. He'd always be in Shaw's corner, no matter what he did. He couldn't imagine anything that would change his mind about that. Helping him cover up murder of all things solidified the fact that there wasn't a crime he could think of that he wouldn't have his buddy's back.

Shaw sipped his beer, swallowing hard. "I stumbled on something a few weeks ago and I should've fucking told you then, but I didn't." He set the bottle down. "You know all the carjacking shit that's been going on?"

"Of course."

"Well"—Shaw rolled his eyes at having to make this delayed admission—"I've been doing a little investigating of my own and I know who's behind it."

"Shaw, fam, what the fuck? We have to tell—"

"Bro, wait." Shaw put up his hand. "Let me explain." He looked up from the Modelo bottle into Baz's eyes. "Remember when I called out of work a few weeks ago?"

Baz nodded, apprehensive about what Shaw would disclose.

"It was because I got hurt pretty bad." Shaw lifted his shirt to show his best friend the scarring on his torso. "Took a fucking knife to the abdomen and have another one on my damn back."

"Fam." Baz, with wide and disbelieving eyes, scooted closer to examine the barely healed wound. "What the hell happened? That's a serious fucking scar, Shaw."

"I know."

"You've gone dark on me before, but why would you shut me out of that? I've never judged you. Why didn't you tell me you wanted to look into the carjacking shit? I would've had your back, you know that."

Shaw shook his head, picking at the Modelo label on his beer. "I can't explain it. It was some shit to do because I've been fucking lost for a while, bro. I'm not exactly proud of how I've been coping, alright."

Baz took a healthy breath, watching Shaw he knew there was a lot more he still hadn't shared. He tried to calm himself by grabbing a chip.

"Bro"—Shaw looked up at Baz, his face and voice projected the severity of what he was about to disclose—"Craig and his crew are responsible for those carjackings."

Baz's face looked like he hadn't heard a word that just came out of Shaw's mouth.

"The two guys he brought to the house today, and at least one of those women, have *all* been involved. That fucking bitch is the one who stabbed me and I know for a fact she recognized me when we left."

Baz sat in disbelief, he was completely lost for words, and his face expressionless.

Shaw started from the beginning, telling Baz about all of the investigations he'd done, how he came across the chop shop, the night of the incident, Tinsley's involvement—all of it. Even after his detailed accounting of everything, Baz still hadn't spoken a word.

"Do you guys need another round?" The server stopped by to check in, noticing both men found the bottom of their beers.

Shaw ordered him and his partner another round, waiting for her to leave before he coaxed Baz to say something.

"Bro, what's on your mind?" Shaw asked.

Baz nodded a few times but his eyes were elsewhere. He waited for the server to drop their drinks and fresh chips and salsa at the table.

"I know Unc loves us. We're his boys"—Baz looked up at Shaw—"but I dunno if we can go to him with this."

"I know," Shaw gravely confirmed.

Baz took another drink. "You sure you're good, fam?" He gestured toward Shaw's injury.

"I'm straight." He nodded. "Got really goddamn lucky in more ways than one."

The men sat across from one another, sipping beer and picking at chips in silence.

"No more of that fucking solo bullshit," Baz firmly stated when he finally looked up at Shaw. "No matter what, we go at this together."

Shaw reached his fist out to his best friend to confirm.

When Baz got up to use the restroom Shaw checked in with Tinsley, he knew full well she'd been worrying since the second he left that night. He and Baz hadn't exactly planned out the evening yet, but he assumed they'd make a move sooner than later.

> Tins sugar, I'm still gonna be with Baz for a while. I didn't want you to worry. I love you.

Tinsley had been nervously waiting for anything from him. She knew Baz wouldn't turn his back on Shaw, but their plan moving forward was the thing that scared her most. When she saw his text she immediately replied.

SWEETCHEEKS
I love you too Hunt. Is everything going alright??

> Baz and I are straight. Idk what we're doing about all this though.

SWEETCHEEKS
Hunt please just BE SAFE and come home to us tonight.

> We're still at the bar but I promise I'm coming home to you sugar.

SWEETCHEEKS
♥♥♥♥

"Fam." Baz sat down at the table. "What if we take Unc up on that offer to join the task force?"

Shaw shot a quick laugh through his nostrils. "And have the *entire* department find out it's Craig? Trust, I thought about that tactic too just to fucking make that shit stop, but you think that's the right move?"

Baz solemnly shook his head. "I honestly don't fucking know. I'm so pissed at Craig right now. I know he's done dumb shit his entire life, but this? And then bringing that shit to mama's house? I'm gonna fucking kick his ass just for that alone."

Shaw motioned to the server that they'd take another round of Modelos.

"Maybe we do that?" Shaw shrugged.

"What? Kick his ass?" Baz chuckled.

"Yeah. I mean, it may take a bit to find their new place—I can't imagine they stayed at that shop when they realized I stumbled on it. Not to mention, I guarantee you whoever that bitch is, she probably told Craig she saw me at the house today."

Baz looked at Shaw for a long minute, the wheels in his head spinning. He reached for his phone, his fingers flew across the screen before putting it to his ear.

"Hey baby girl," he greeted Tilly. "No, I'm still with Shaw."

There was a short pause.

"Hey, real quick. Those girls talking to you today at mama's, did you get their names?"

He nodded while slowly spinning his Modelo bottle.

"Uh huh. Which one was which?"

Shaw leaned over the table and whispered, "The Latina one with the big gold hoops and slicked back ponytail."

"Yeah, Mia—she say anything about Shaw?"

Baz looked down at the table while Tilly talked.

"Baby, no." His oversized fist covered his mouth in an attempt to stifle his laughter. "Even if Shaw was asking because he was somehow interested, I wouldn't let him do that shit to Tins." He rolled his eyes at Shaw. "We're not asking because anyone's interested. I just need to know what you guys talked about."

Shaw threw his hands up and rolled his eyes. He always had his doubts about Tilly, apparently she had her own doubts about Shaw.

"Did you tell her?"

There was another pause.

"Let's just not talk to Mia anymore… No." Baz let out an irritated exhale. "I'm not," he argued. "We can talk about it later but for now I just need you to pull back from talking to her anymore."

Baz lowered his voice and turned his head from the table.

"Are you really gonna be like that right now?" His hand slapped against the table. "Then go out with the girls. Alright then." He hung up and looked annoyed.

"You good?"

Baz flicked through his phone but answered him in an agitated tone. "She gets this fucking attitude about other women sometimes. It's dumb shit. You know as well as anyone I haven't been fuckin' around on her." Baz looked up, holding out his phone to Shaw. "This is her, right?"

Shaw would've remembered her face anywhere. "Yes, that's the bitch who stabbed me. She's in on that shit."

"Tilly said she did ask about you. Wanted to know your name and how you knew us." Baz shook his head. "My B, fam. I didn't say anything to Tilly, she didn't know."

"It wasn't gonna stay secret for long." Shaw shrugged.

"She did ask about Tins—"

"Please tell me Tilly didn't say where she works or anything." Shaw's face practically begged.

"She knows her first name and that she does hair, that's all. But Tilly and Mia are on the socials together now. I think her and Tins connected on there not too long ago too. Tilly also told her that you guys are dating and living together. But Tilly didn't tell her where or anything."

"Fuck."

"Fam, it's gonna be alright. We're gonna figure this shit out."

"We have to do it soon, I don't want all that shit lurking around— *especially* not around Tins."

"I know."

Shaw felt a cold sweat go down his back realizing Tinsley was basically at the salon right now. He'd dropped her off to hang with Brindle because he didn't want her to be alone while he met with Baz.

"Bro, you got Tins on Instagram?"

Baz nodded.

"Pull her up, does she have her salon on there?"

Baz flicked the screen of his cell. "Yeah, the addy and pictures of it—"

Shaw grabbed his phone. "Shit." He scrolled, anyone with half a brain could figure out exactly where her salon was. "Can anyone see Tins's profile?" Shaw had to ask because he didn't have any kind of social media and Tinsley's profile would have shown Mia exactly where to find her. Not only that, but Harvey was all over the page, he'd never be mistaken for anyone else because of his features.

"Yeah, I'm pretty sure she's got a public profile," Baz confirmed.

"We have to go." Shaw gave Baz's phone back and then reached for his wallet to leave cash on the table. "We have to go get Tins, she's at the goddamn salon right now."

Baz was immediately as unsettled as Shaw now that he realized exactly what was going through his partner's head.

"Tins"—Shaw had her on the phone within seconds—"you still with Brindle? Are you at the salon?"

"We are. Are you okay, Hunt? Baby, you sound upset." Worry tainted her voice.

Shaw's chest released a large sigh of relief.

"Sugar, stay in the apartment. Don't answer the doors for anyone until I can get there."

"You're scaring me." Tinsley's throat tightened, she could feel heat crawling up her neck and she tried not to cry. "What happened?"

"You're gonna be alright Tins. I just want you to stay put though, okay?"

"Hunt—"

"Tins, we're fine, okay? I'm on my way to you. I'll see you in like fifteen minutes, just stay in the apartment with Brindle and I'll call when I'm there, okay?"

"Okay," Tinsley finally agreed and tried to wipe the single tear that had escaped.

"I love you."

"I love you too, Hunt."

Shaw hung up the phone and walked out of Poquitos with Baz right next to him.

"Bro, that bitch has full access to Tins if she saw her Instagram already."

"Fam." Baz tried to calm his partner down. "Keep a level head. I know what's going through it right now. She's gonna be fine."

"I need to check," Shaw insisted and hurried to his truck. "I can't even think about going anywhere else right now."

"I'll meet you at the salon," Baz confirmed before splitting ways. He fired up his Hellcat and made it a point to keep pace with Shaw's Raptor. His partner would definitely end up in jail if Craig or any of his crew found themselves within a ten mile radius of Tinsley. Baz felt the pain and grief that had lived within his best friend after Sloane's death. He knew, without a doubt in his mind, Shaw had flashbacks of Sloane's tragedy consuming his mind while he raced to Tinsley. Despite Craig being a blood relative, if push came to shove, Baz would, without hesitation, ride or die with his brother, Shaw, over everything.

Tinsley only loved the text and headed toward the apartment door.

"Is Shawberry here?" Brindle asked, sprawled out on his couch. He noticed Tinsley's demeanor become increasingly anxious after talking to Shaw on the phone but respected her when she said she'd fill him in later.

"Yeah, he and Baz are here. I'm gonna go talk to them for a minute. I'll be back up."

"Do you, Boo. I'll even be kind if Black Casper finds his way up here too." He winked at his best friend who still looked worried.

Tinsley offered him a quick smile before she put slippers on and headed down the stairs.

Harvey jumped excitedly when he saw Shaw through the glass door Tinsley tried to unlock.

Shaw fully engulfed his girlfriend the second she cracked the door.

"Hunt, are you okay?" Tinsley mumbled, her head buried in Shaw's strong chest.

Shaw rubbed the back of Tinsley's head before kissing the top of her hair. His breathing returned to a normal rate, he never wanted to let her go.

"We're fine, sugar." He massaged her scalp and rocked them.

Harvey got a little more demanding so Shaw gave Tinsley a final squeeze before reaching down to give the not so patient dog his greeting as well.

"Tins." Baz nodded at her before giving her a quick hug.

Tinsley looked at the duo with worried eyes. "Are you two all good?"

"Yes," they both immediately confirmed in unison.

"That's my boy"—Baz gave Shaw a healthy jab—"I'd have his back no matter what kinda shit he stepped in."

Tinsley shot a flat, grateful smile at Baz before she turned to Shaw. She didn't say anything, she hugged her torso and waited for him to start talking.

"Tins, we've gotta chase Craig and his crew down tonight." He looked at her. "I know that's not what you want to hear. I know I promised no more vigilante bullshit, but this isn't that—this is bigger."

Tinsley didn't move or respond.

Shaw picked up on the disappointment in her eyes.

"Tins"—he cupped his hands around her soft face—"sugar, we *have* to. His crew knows who I am now—which I'd deal with—but that shanking bitch looked you up on Tilly's Instagram. I'm sure of it."

"Hunt, you *promised* me." Tears threatened on both of her eyelids as she maintained his gaze.

"I can't just wait for something to happen to you, Tins. You have to know that." His thumbs stroked her face. "This is different. Baz and I are both going to deal with this, this isn't some solo vigilante bullshit."

"It *is* the same." She cut in through her tears and put her hands on his chest. "Hunter, I know why you started that vigilante bullshit. You're not in the right mindset to be out there tonight."

"I'll be with Baz, I'm going to share my location with you—Tins, it's different. I promise"

"Hunt, I can't let you do this," Tinsley cried. "I understand it's different because it's Craig, but you'll be going in with way too much on your mind." She shook her head. "I love how protective you are—I do—but knowing she looked at my social media isn't going to help you with all of this tonight. It's going to make you irrational and you *know* that."

Shaw gazed deep into her brown eyes. He knew she was right about him having an edge given what they'd found out about Mia, but he wasn't willing to admit that to her at that moment.

Tinsley knew her boyfriend already had his mind set, no matter what she said. She terrorized herself with the thought of him never coming back, she'd seen firsthand how close Shaw had been to losing his life. She thought, of all people, he'd be able to understand where she was coming from. The tears were uncontrollable at this point and she wiped her face before continuing.

"I don't want you going backwards… I thought we already talked about all this?"

"We did," Shaw finally agreed and pulled Tinsley into his chest. "I'm sorry."

"I don't want you to be sorry, I want you to be with me." She couldn't stop sobbing at this point.

"Tins"—he stroked her hair—"I want that too."

She thought about her next words carefully, but looked up at him with terrorized eyes and asked anyway, "do you?"

Shaw looked puzzled, as if he didn't hear what she asked. "What? Tins, what do you mean?"

Tinsley's fingers swiped from the bridge of her nose to her cheeks taking a stream of tears along with them. She stuttered upon her inhale, taking a deep breath hoping to gain as much of her voice as possible.

"I watched you knock on death's door, Hunt. I feel like you're just going up to ring the doorbell this time." Her palms consumed her crying face. "Hunt, I can't compete with Sloane and your baby. I *know* that. I know you're always going to love them and I understand and accept that." She wiped a steady stream of tears away, uncovering her face but refusing to look at her boyfriend. "I just feel like you're actively going out and trying to find a way to be with them. You *know* what happened last time you went out there—" she was balling now.

"Sugar, no. That's not it, I want to be here with you." He pulled her back into his chest with a firm and comforting hold consuming her. "And, Tins, I'm not going alone."

Her body didn't respond to him, she held her face.

"I don't care. I don't like *either* one of you going. This is a really bad idea."

"Tins." Baz took a cautious step in their direction. "We've been partners for eight years and we're both still here. We got this."

Shaw backed up enough to put his hands on either side of her shoulders, staring at her face.

She continued to sob, turning away from him to walk back toward Brindle's apartment. She barely got two steps when they all watched Brindle marching through the doorway.

"What the *hell* is going on?!" Brindle rushed to his best friend. "Boo, what happened? Are you okay?" He held her tightly, glaring at Baz and Shaw.

Tinsley continued crying under the comfort of Brindle's embrace.

"Someone better start fuckin' talking. What did you two do to her?"

"Brin—" Shaw held up his hands.

"Don't Brin, me, Officer Shaw. My girl doesn't cry like this for nothing. What the fuck happened?"

"It's complica—" Shaw started.

"My ass!" He gave Baz a once over. "And it's no surprise *you're* in on whatever this is."

"Brin…" Tinsley finally mumbled through her tears.

Brindle moved Tinsley back just enough to take a quick peek at her face.

"Boo, let's go upstairs." He rubbed her shoulders.

Tinsley nodded and let Brindle usher her toward his apartment above the salon.

Harvey trotted after Tinsley a couple steps before turning around, cocking his large head at Shaw. The cane corso, confused and conflicted, finally darted toward the apartment after Tinsley.

"Bro"—Shaw looked at Baz—"I can't leave things hanging like that with Tins. I gotta go talk to her."

"I know." Baz nodded his head toward the apartment. "Take care of baby girl and then let's roll."

Shaw reached up, gripping his best friend's shoulder, taking a deep breath before following his girlfriend. When he rounded the corner to head up the stairs he heard Brindle's apartment door slam. He knew Brindle would require an unreal level of coercion to be able to talk to Tinsley. There was no way he could simply leave without talking to her though. He calmly made his way up the steps and gently knocked the back of his hand against the door which elicited barking from Harvey. He could hear Brindle throwing a fit on the other side of the door but couldn't decipher what he was saying. He waited another moment of Harvey still fussing at the door and Brindle going on a million miles an hour before he knocked again. He wasn't surprised at all when Brindle ripped the door open with a look that could kill on his face.

"What?!" Brindle didn't let Harvey out and only cracked the door enough for him to be partially visible.

"Will you please come out here and talk to me for a minute? I can't leave without talking to Tins, but I want to talk to you first." Shaw held a confident tone in his voice.

Brindle crossed his arms, taking a long, icy moment glaring at Shaw before he responded to him.

"Hold on," he finally spat but shut the door without coming out.

Shaw took a step back from the door and waited. He inhaled a deep breath hoping Brindle would actually come back out there and he wouldn't have to knock again. He listened to Harvey groaning from inside and could hear him sniffing under the door.

It didn't take as long as Shaw anticipated for Brindle to fling the door open again. This time he quickly shut it behind him and then leaned against it with his arms crossed. He stood up straight and flung his arms around his sides. "Well?!"

"Brindle"—Shaw held up both of his hands and shook his head—"I know how this looks. And please believe me, it fucking tears my heart to see Tins that upset. There's a lot going on that I don't think you know about."

"Obviously." Brindle's quick, terse voice sliced through the air.

"I *love* Tinsley. That hasn't and won't be changing at all," he assured him. "To make a very long story short, I inadvertently put Tins in a dangerous spot and I need to go out and do something that she's not happy about. I told her I wouldn't be going out to do dumb stuff anymore, but I can see how this looks like me going back on that word now." He took a large breath but kept his focus on Brindle. "Tins is still my world and I don't blame her for being mad at me; but I think you and I can at least agree that her safety is pretty damn important. I don't feel good about just waiting to react to something that might happen. Baz and I need to go out tonight and make sure shit *doesn't* happen." Shaw closed his eyes for the slightest second while shaking his head. "I'm sure this doesn't completely make sense right now, but please just trust me. I love your best friend more than you'll ever know. All I want is to be with her, but I *have* to do this tonight."

A staring showdown took place, Shaw felt like Brindle's hackles were finally relaxing and he was less likely to reach over and slap Shaw compared to what his demeanor would've suggested about five minutes ago.

"I know I'm not in a really great position to be asking for favors, but I need a couple from you, Brindle."

Brindle's entire chest puffed out from the breath he took and he rolled his eyes before responding, "I'm listening."

"I need you to let me talk to Tins. I know she's upset, but I can't just leave without talking to her."

"She looked like she was done talking *and* listening to you," he sassed back.

"I know." Shaw nodded.

Brindle gave him another harsh once over. "Is this Black Casper's doing? Pulling you into whatever shit you two've got goin' on?"

"No." Shaw shook his head to take ownership. "No, this is on me. Baz is actually helping me and the shit I stepped in."

"If I let you in this house and she wants you gone, you need to leave *immediately*."

Shaw looked at Brindle for a long moment—he wasn't sure he could promise that. He considered vocalizing that concern, but instead nodded to confirm.

"Okay," Shaw agreed. "I have one more request from you too."

"Let's hear it." Brindle's hand spun in a circular motion as he rolled his eyes.

"I'm gonna talk to her about me taking her home while I'm out. Do you think you can come with us and stay with her until I'm back home?"

"I don't like this cryptic shit," Brindle snapped.

"I don't like the idea of her being so upset and then being left alone while I'm out. Not to mention I don't want her at the salon right now. In fact, I don't want either of you here right now."

"Well, shit, now you've got me worried. What the hell is going on?"

"Brindle, it's a long story, but someone who may want to get to me knows where Tins works. I just want her to be at home when I go out and try to fix this."

Brindle's eyes widened, beginning to understand why everyone was so upset.

"Victor's on his way here."

"Can you text him and have him come to our house instead? We've got a guest room set up now too. If you guys end up staying, that's more than fine. We all just need to get out of here soon though."

Brindle took a large breath. "You're going to apologize to her, if those aren't the first fucking words I hear from your mouth when I open this door you'll be sorry." He stared at Shaw.

"I will *absolutely* apologize to her. Brindle, you know how I feel about Tins. I don't want to hurt her, but I also need to protect her."

"Don't make me regret opening this door for you," Brindle warned before cracking the door.

Harvey quickly ran to Shaw, hopping around in front of him. Shaw slowed down to give Harvey a proper greeting while Brindle walked to Tinsley who was curled up on the couch.

Brindle put his arms around his best friend and whispered to her for a bit. He finally looked back at Shaw before making his way to his bedroom to give them some privacy.

Shaw felt a stab in his heart seeing the pain he'd caused Tinsley consuming her typically glowing face. He cautiously made his way to her, squatting near the couch right in front of her.

"Tins, sugar…" Shaw caressed the side of her face, carefully wiping tears with his thumb before leaning in to put his arms around his distressed girlfriend.

Despite her disappointment she threw her arms around Shaw's shoulders and held him as tightly as she could.

"I love you and I'm sorry I upset you. I'm so sorry, Tinsley. I *promise* I'm coming back to you." Shaw held firmly to her back and head, squeezing her even tighter. "The Undertaker himself couldn't keep me from you—you know this. I love you, Tins. Trust me, I'm coming home to you," he reinforced.

Tinsley's eyes were swollen, bloodshot, and filled with tears as she listened to him basically begging her to simply accept this is what had to be done.

"I can't lose you, Tins." Shaw finally backed up and put her face in his strong hands. "You and Harv are my whole damn world and I can't let anything happen to you."

Tinsley wiped her eyes but still hadn't looked at him.

"Tins… I don't know what else to do. The only way I know how to keep you safe is to go out to try to fix this. Do you have a different solution? Sweetcheeks, I'm all ears." He briefly paused, watching his girlfriend do her best to accept these terms. "I hate that I hurt you like this, but I think this is the only way."

"Hunt," her broken voice started softly, "I love you so much—" a jagged breath interrupted her. "I can't lose you." Her watering gaze finally looked up at him. "I'm scared."

"I know, sugar." He pulled her in, placing her head against his sturdy chest. "I'm scared too. That's why Baz and I need to go out and try to make it safe for *all* of us again."

"Swear on everything that you and Baz are coming back tonight."

"Tins, that's the only way Baz and I roll. I swear on everything we're both coming back tonight."

Tinsley just needed to hear the words. She wasn't naive enough to think it would be as simple as Craig sitting at home crocheting with tea, being interrupted by her boyfriend and Baz who would politely request he stop the whole carjacking thing. She knew it would take them time to find Craig—since his friend likely informed him who she saw that afternoon—and on top of that, she didn't know what the guys were planning when they did find Craig and his crew.

She acknowledged both Shaw and Baz were more than capable and tough as nails men, but Craig had more bodies and less morals on his side—that's what worried her most. Playing dirty would likely be how the winner was crowned in this situation. Shaw wasn't a stranger to darkness and had done some highly questionable things in his time. Those were the thoughts Tinsley would rely on to ease her mind throughout the night. The vigilante bullshit he'd become so good at would play in his favor with the Craig situation. That experience and the thought of keeping Tinsley safe wouldn't allow Shaw to lose.

CHAPTER
Forty Eight

Tinsley couldn't hold Shaw tight enough when he came home. It wasn't late, it was the early hours of the morning, the sun already slicing the sky with a sliver of gold.

"Thank you for keeping your promise, tough guy."

"I love you, Tins."

"I love you too." She felt a tear drop down her cheek. "Where's Baz?" her muffled voice spoke from his chest.

"He's headed home." Shaw rubbed his hands up and down Tinsley's back, placing multiple pecks to her hairline.

She popped her head up from his strong chest. "Is that a good idea? Does he want to stay here?"

"I asked him." Shaw shrugged. "I think he may go to Tilly's."

"Can I talk to him?"

"You want me to call him?"

Tinsley shrugged. "It's not that I don't believe you, I just want to talk to him."

Shaw dialed Baz and handed his phone to his girlfriend.

"Sup, fam? You good?" Baz sounded concerned.

"Hey, Baz… It's Tinsley."

"Tins? You guys alright?"

"Yeah, sorry." Tinsley grabbed her forehead. "Baz, do you want to stay with us tonight? I—I just want to be sure you're okay and that you're safe."

Baz took a deep breath, Tinsley was a good one. "Tins, thank you, but I'm straight. You and Shaw just enjoy what's left of the night. We're gonna get this thing handled. Don't worry about me."

Tinsley looked up at Shaw. "Baz, I'm gonna worry about you—about *both* of you."

"Tins, your boys have each other's back—always, okay?"

She stayed quiet for a long moment before she accepted what he said. "Thank you, Baz."

"Always, Tins. I love you guys, you're fam."

"We love you too, Baz."

There was an extended pause on the line.

"Hey… Any chance I can talk to Shaw?"

"Of course," Tinsley quickly agreed. "If you change your mind, you're *always* welcome here."

"Thank you, Tins."

Tinsley handed the phone to her boyfriend and slid her arms around his waist.

"Hey, bro." Shaw held Tinsley with his free arm.

"Fam, you guys good?"

Shaw squeezed his girlfriend. "Yeah." He took a deep breath. "I don't love that we didn't get what we wanted tonight. Thank you though, bro."

"Always, fam." Baz nodded. "Take care of baby girl tonight, she sounds stressed."

"I know," Shaw grimly confirmed.

"I'll catch you sometime tomorrow."

"Yep, call if anything comes up."

"Same, fam."

"Night."

"Later."

Shaw put his phone in his back pocket. He gently rocked his girlfriend as his lips moved down to rest firmly on the top of her head.

He knew she was crying so he rubbed his hands up and down her back. Harvey started to get restless so Shaw decided it was time for all of them to go to bed. He reached down and lifted Tinsley off the ground to carry her to their bedroom. He kicked his shoes off and shut the door before walking them to the bed. Shaw situated Tinsley in front of him and then consumed her from behind. His head nestled behind hers before whispering in her ear.

"Tins, sugar, I love you." He brushed her hair back from her face. "We didn't find Craig or his crew tonight. We're gonna have to keep trying though." His hold on her tightened when she wiped tears from her eyes. "I'm gonna end this. Just remember, every damn night I'll come back to you, Tins—I promise."

Tinsley took a minute but she rolled over to face him.

She reached up and gently held his chin. "I love you, Hunter Evan Shaw. Please don't ever break that promise to me."

Shaw felt gutted just staring into her broken eyes but he held her gaze. "Tinsley Emma Adams, my love for you will bring me home every single night. *Nothing* is going to stop that."

Tinsley slid her arms around Shaw's neck to hold him close. They eventually fell asleep firmly clutching one another.

CHAPTER
Forty Nine

S HAW CALLED OUT FROM WORK THE NEXT DAY. THERE WAS NO PART of him that would allow Tinsley to simply be back at the salon before he made a few security modifications there. He planned to install multiple cameras, a new lock system, a small safe, and prepare her with the idea of carrying a firearm. She initially pushed back since her mom had an appointment that day. That was an argument she lost before she started; Shaw didn't even let her drive herself to the salon.

Shaw walked to her station with his phone out after he'd installed a new keypad on the front salon door. "Sugar, what's a number you girls will all remember for the door so I can get this programmed?"

Brindle was uncharacteristically quiet all morning watching Shaw very meticulously installing an entire security system; but he offered his suggestion anyway.

"Boo, use the Pac Ave apartment number. You know that's a number we'll never forget and it's not easy for anyone to just guess."

Tinsley nodded, taking Shaw's phone to enter it just before they watched her mom walk into the salon.

"Good morning!" Colette greeted with a bright smile on her face. "Oh, Shaw, what a pleasant surprise, honey."

"Hi, Colette." Shaw opened one of his arms as she made her approach.

"What are you doing here?" she asked while taking a few steps over to hug her daughter.

"Just getting some cameras and a few other security items taken care of."

"Honey"—she looked at Tinsley—"what happened?"

"Side effects of having a cop for a boyfriend," Shaw quickly answered with a grin on his face as he tried to ease everyone's concerns, including his own.

Colette chuckled. "Well, I won't be objecting to this increased level of security. Your father's going to be happy about that too." She settled into her daughter's chair to start her service.

A quiet rumbling soon consumed the salon while everyone did their best to hide the genuine stress from Colette.

Tinsley squeezed her mom's freshly washed hair in a towel when Shaw approached for the umpteenth time that day already.

"Hey, sugar, are you allowed to have cameras outside the building as well? I want a couple angles of the exterior too and I'll need to drill into the walls."

"Anything I do like that just has to be put back to the original condition whenever my lease is over."

"Perfect." He leaned over and pecked the side of Tinsley's head before stalking to the front window where he'd left his tape measure.

Harvey decided he could help out so he got off the comfort of his bed to follow Shaw. Tinsley didn't respond verbally, instead she worked on combing her mom's wet hair out.

"He looks like he's on a mission today," Colette commented.

Tinsley tried to mask her worry. "He's just in work mode." Her face lightened and a small smile escaped.

They all turned their heads when the front door opened.

"Hey, Baz," Tinsley offered a soft spoken greeting with a smile. Relief set in when she saw him. She knew he was a capable man but the thought of his own cousin being a criminal and Baz having likely stayed home alone last night had Tinsley's mind worrying.

"Hi Tins, how's it goin'?" He leaned in and gave her a one-armed hug.

She shrugged with a flat smile, not wanting to disclose anything in front of her mom.

"I saw the truck out back, Shaw around?" Baz had his hands on his duty belt.

"Yeah, he just went back there. He actually may be outside, you're welcome to go look for him." She gestured toward their breakroom.

Colette's eyes followed Baz and then pumped her brows at her daughter.

"You just attract all the best looking officers, huh?"

Tinsley playfully rolled her eyes.

"Oh, Baz *wishes*." Brindle flicked his wrist around.

Tinsley didn't scold him this time, she laughed along.

"That's Hunt's partner and his best friend," she clarified.

"Jesus." Colette put her hand on her chest. "I already thought Shaw was a looker, it doesn't seem fair the two of them get partnered up. Probably breaking hearts all over Tacoma."

"I've been checking their fine asses out since they responded…" Brindle's voice trailed off when he realized he was oversharing.

"Responded?" Colette looked at Brindle.

Brindle rattled his head around. "Not responded," he tried again, "when they first came to just do like their neighborhood checks." He tried to shrug it off.

"I see," Colette accepted his answer even though the salon seemed a little off that day.

"If not for Victor, I'd be cursing Tins for catching Shawberry's eye." Brindle tried to lighten the mood.

"Oh, yes! Brindle, honey, tell me about the new beau. Tinsley tells me things are pretty serious with you two," she gushed. "How exciting?!"

Brindle never had an issue bragging when something good was going on—he made no exception on the topic of Victor. Tinsley had always admired Brindle's ability to lean so heavily on the good in his life, despite a rough upbringing. She listened as Brindle caught Colette up on his love life and his official *boyfriend*, Victor.

"Hey, fam." Baz ruffled Harvey's head before opening the back screen door to join Shaw.

"Hey, bro, how's work? Crusty Karl isn't inside making my girl's salon a mess, is he?" Shaw stood on a ladder situating a camera to have a full view of the doorway.

"I left his ass in the car. He's nosey as fuck, I didn't want him all up in the business."

Shaw continued working without a verbal response.

"Was gonna see if you wanted to go over to Unc's tonight." Baz shrugged. "Was thinking we can take his temp on how Craig's been—you know, see if he's been weird about us. Or we can try rollin by Craig's again?"

Shaw drilled the camera in place and then stepped down the ladder. He took a large breath before responding, "what time? I wanna finish everything here and I'll need to talk to Tins. She's trying, but I know she's gonna be upset."

"Any time, fam." Baz shrugged and held his hands up.

"Tilly working?"

Baz shook his head with a sour look on his face. Aside from his facial expression, there was an obvious tone in his body language.

"You good, bro?" Shaw took a better look at his partner, knowing something else besides Craig was eating at him.

"Yeah." Baz waited a minute before confessing, "Tilly and I haven't talked since Poquitos."

"Bro, what?" Shaw gave his partner room to share more if he wanted.

"She went out with the girls—after being all pissed I asked about those chicks—and hasn't answered calls or texts since." He rolled his eyes. "Dumb shit."

"You need to go take care of that, bro?"

Baz shook his head. "Fam, you know me. Shit is what it fuckin' is."

Shaw looked down for a minute before he responded to Baz. "I'm sorry shit's so fucked right now. I shoulda told you about all of this when it first happened."

"Don't start apologizing and feeling bad about Tilly since you had to listen to Tins tell me she loves me last night." Baz wiped his goatee to hide his smirk.

"Fuck off." Shaw laughed but delivered a quick jab to his best friend's bicep.

"I tried to warn you she'd always have a lingering desire for Big Daddy," Baz continued to tease.

It felt good to laugh. Shaw realized how stressed he'd been for a straight twenty-four hours now that his body allowed a positive reaction to something.

"I'm gonna kick your ass," Shaw warned, shaking his head with a smile. His smile faded and he took a more serious tone, "I *am* sorry for not telling you sooner, bro."

"I'm not mad at you. This one's on fuckin' cuz. I think we should look for him again tonight—not go to Unc. I'm more inclined to kick his ass than anything else right now. Little fuck has been in need of a good fucking beating for quite some time to straighten his ass out."

Shaw threw his hands up in a motion to agree with his partner. "You know I'm fuckin' down."

"Talk to Tins and then let me know. I'm off at the regular time tonight."

Shaw held his fist out to dab Baz.

"Will do."

Baz reached down to give Harvey a farewell scratch before heading back into the salon.

"Bye, Tins." Baz waved as he made his way by her station.

Tinsley looked at Baz in her mirror but turned around to talk to him. "Did you find Hunt?"

"Yeah, he and Harv are out back getting the place up to the Shaw security standard." He winked.

Tinsley smiled. "Be safe out there, Baz."

"Always am," he assured her before walking through the door. He gave her another friendly wave as he passed the salon window.

"I guess Black Casper's growing on me," Brindle admitted but still rolled his eyes.

"Black Casper?" Colette's face scrunched.

Tinsley chuckled. "You don't want to know." She made sure to shoot Brindle a warning through her eyes.

Besides Shaw checking in almost every five minutes, the day at the salon carried along like any other; Brindle gossiping in the most animated fashion with anyone who would listen, Tinsley happily creating beautiful masterpieces on the heads of each of her clients, and good old Handsome Harv being the goofy guy he always was. Tinsley was taken by surprise when she noticed the time and the fact that she'd just finished up her last scheduled appointment for the day. She knew Shaw had planted himself in the breakroom to quadruple check that all the new cameras were operating, recording, and streaming at optimum levels.

"Hey, tough guy." She grinned at her boyfriend, leaning against the doorway watching him concentrate on his phone.

The second he heard her voice his face lightened and he looked up at her from across the room.

"Hey, sugar, you all done for the day?" Shaw made his way to Tinsley.

"I am," she confirmed with a smile and looked up at him once he was close enough for her to put her hands around his waist.

Shaw leaned down to meet her lips as his hands squeezed themselves into the back pockets of her skin-tight jeans. They fully indulged in the pleasure of the rhythm their mouths always found with one another. Shaw slowed them down and whispered to Tinsley, "is Brindle around?"

"Officer Shaw, are you thinking about Brindle right now?" She smirked.

Shaw pulled one of his hands out of her pocket and gave her a quick swat before squeezing her cheek. "I wanted to know how long my leash was for this little session *you* started."

Tinsley's head fell back and she giggled. "The session *I* started, huh?"

"Yeah," Shaw confirmed, "you start 'em, I finish 'em." He pressed his lips against her neck.

"I hate to inform you, not only is Brindle still here"—Tinsley's head came back up so she could look her boyfriend in his eyes—"but you're on a choke chain with all this until you come back home later."

Shaw realized Tinsley already knew there would be a repeat of the previous evening's activities.

"Sugar, I—"

Tinsley shook her head and interrupted him when she softly placed one of her fingers on his lips. "Hunt, baby, I really don't want you trying to explain anything to me. I love you, and I appreciate everything you've done today to make me safe here. I still don't like you and Baz out there"—she looked down—"but I understand," she admitted.

Shaw hooked his finger under her chin and gently encouraged her to look at him.

"Tins, I love you too and I won't break my promise to you."

She didn't know how he could guarantee something like that, but she'd trust him to keep his word. That's all she could do as she stared up at his mesmerizing green eyes.

Shaw lovingly held her gaze and her waist, slowly swaying them. "Can we grab a quick dinner before I drop you off with the girls?" Shaw asked.

Tinsley took a deep breath and put her hands on her boyfriend's sturdy chest. "Should we see if Baz wants to join us for a little Frisko Freeze date?"

"Only if you back up that whole date comment since he's being included now." Shaw smirked.

She giggled and rolled her eyes playfully. "You and I can still be on a date, tough guy. We'll just have a chaperone this way." She shrugged and cocked her head to the side. "Because I wasn't bluffing about your choke chain—no boyfriend gifts until you're safely back at home tonight."

"That's fair, sugar." He pecked the top of her head and they gathered their things to head out for the night.

CHAPTER
Fifty

A FEW NIGHTS WENT BY WITH THE SAME ROUTINE; SHAW AND BAZ rolling around town looking for any sign of Craig and his crew while Tinsley anxiously waited for any kind of update and ultimately for them to come home safe. Shaw had been pretty good about checking in via text throughout each night, but one night in particular their location was stagnant and he hadn't sent anything for almost an hour. That night resulted in barely two hours of sleep for her and the next day turned into a struggle at work.

"Boo." Brindle snapped his fingers. "Are you even listening to me?!"

"Sorry." Tinsley's eyes fluttered and she looked at him. "I didn't catch that last part, what did you ask me?"

"Bitch! You weren't damn listening to anything I just said." His head whipped around before he took a longer look at his best friend. "Are you alright?" he finally asked.

"I'm just really tired," she tried to assure him. "This whole thing…" Tinsley decided not to elaborate too much in front of Brindle's client while she waited for her next appointment. "I just need to work on falling asleep earlier."

They all turned their heads when the salon door opened—it wasn't

Tinsley's next appointment and only she and Brindle were at the salon for the day. Neither of them recognized the woman who walked in with a baseball hat on her head.

"Hi," Tinsley's friendly tone greeted the woman.

"Hi," the woman returned and looked around the salon.

Tinsley's stomach turned at the thought of who this woman looked like. She'd never got a really good look at the woman who stabbed Shaw when they saw her at the Haywood's, but this woman *could* be her. All she remembered was dark hair, a similar build, and had heard Baz refer to her as Mia in one of their planning sessions before the stalking in the night routine they'd been doing. Her breathing quickened as she approached the woman. Since everything came to a head and the guys hadn't been able to resolve anything, Tinsley had been on high alert.

"Can I help you?" Tinsley smiled despite the worry.

"I was just walking by and I love the look of your salon."

When the woman turned at the sound of Harvey getting out of his bed Tinsley took the opportunity to quickly dial Shaw and hang up. She hoped he may be in a position to call her right back.

The woman stretched her hand out for Harvey to sniff, the good-natured cane corso excitedly ran to his toy bin before the woman was able to pet him.

"Thank you. Was there a particular service you were interested in?" Tinsley tried to get more information out of her and a wave of relief hit her when her phone rang. "I'm so sorry, one second, please."

"Hey, sugar," Shaw greeted. "Did you just call? Are you alright?"

"Uh." Her voice cracked, now very nervous about what she said in front of this potentially dangerous woman. "Uhm, hey Shaw, I think maybe I butt dialed—sorry."

Shaw's brows immediately furrowed and he quickly shook his head, Tinsley *never* called him Shaw—Officer Shaw playfully on occasion, but never just Shaw.

"Tins, baby," Shaw tried to mask the worry in his voice. "Are you alright?"

"I don't know, it was in my pocket so I think that's what happened."

Shaw barely moved the phone from his mouth. "Hit the sirens and get to the salon," he instructed Baz, who didn't question it at all. "Is Craig there?"

"Nope. Shaw, I gotta go, a new client just walked in and I think she's got some questions about the salon."

Fuck. Shaw thought, *it had to be Mia.*

"Tins, listen to me. Get behind that counter right now, the glock is right there, you just have to put your thumb on that lock box. Keep your phone on, do *not* hang up, baby."

"Okay, sorry about that. I love you."

"Sugar, I love you too, we're on our way."

Tinsley pretended to hang up but instead put her phone on speaker and set it on the counter so Shaw could still hear them.

"Oh, I have a regular stylist, like I said, I was just walking by and I loved the decor—I just wanted a closer look." The woman turned and appeared to be checking out the back wall above the sinks that was covered in wallpaper. "Who did you use to design the salon?"

"I selected everything." Tinsley tried to smile and noticed her hand shaking while she reached her thumb to the lockbox that opened immediately.

They were only a couple blocks away but it may as well be ten miles for as anxious as Shaw felt. He couldn't even check the cameras while his phone held the call, he wanted to get a visual confirmation on Mia and the exterior of the salon in case Craig and his crew planned to ambush the place.

"Drop me in front and I need you to run around back in case there's some shit going on back there."

"Shaw," Baz's firm voice commanded his full attention, "keep your head, bro, we're almost there."

He didn't acknowledge him, he continued listening to Tinsley's call and held the door handle, ready to jump out the second they were close enough to the salon.

Shaw unclipped his glock but kept it on his hip, he didn't want to completely burst through the door not having confirmed Mia was in the salon, but he still moved with haste. Tinsley stood behind the counter like he'd instructed her and he blew out a wave of relief to see her unharmed.

"Hey, sugar." He made his way toward her but had eyes on the woman whose back was to him while she took photos of the salon.

"Hi, tough guy."

Shaw watched his girlfriend's entire demeanor relax seeing him; he walked straight for her and put his hand on her shaking one that rested just inside the small gun safe.

"I want something similar to the shelving you have back here, it's still functional but that style is so unique and blends perfectly with the aesthetic in here." The woman went on and on before turning around, jumping a bit to see a large police officer in the salon now when she hadn't even heard anyone come in.

Shaw's shoulders relaxed—it wasn't Mia. He rubbed Tinsley's shoulder and slyly closed the lock box to let her know they weren't in danger.

Once Tinsley realized she'd set off a false alarm she gave Shaw an apologetic look and then turned to answer the woman. "I actually got those from Ikea," she admitted. "I stained them though because they looked really cheap when I got them."

"Good to know." The woman nodded and snapped another photo of Tinsley's station this time. "I really appreciate you letting me take a few photos, this place is just gorgeous. I'd love to do something similar."

"I didn't know you were in the middle of something, sugar." Shaw pecked the top of Tinsley's head. "I was just stopping by to see if you wanted lunch, I'll head in the back until you're done." He smiled at her and squeezed her hand. He offered Brindle a quick nod and flat smile when he walked by his station.

"Bro, they're good," Shaw confirmed when he reached Baz who'd made his way through the back of the salon. "It's not Mia."

Baz holstered his glock. "Thank God."

"Tins wasn't too far off though, the girl's in a hat and has some similarities. I probably should've trolled Mia's socials so she knew exactly who to watch for, that's my B."

"It's always better to be safe than sorry," Baz pointed out and they turned when Harvey came charging toward them with a completely shredded and previously stuffed mailman in his mouth.

"Hey, Handsome Harv." Shaw ruffled the dog's sides.

"Hunt, I'm so sorry." Tinsley came around the corner next. "Hey, Baz—sorry, guys."

Shaw gave Harvey one more firm rub and then put his arms around Tinsley. "No, sugar, I'm glad you called."

"Yeah, don't be sorry about that, Tins," Baz confirmed.

"That was a slick little 'Shaw' routine too." He pecked her forehead.

She looked up at her brave boyfriend. "I was hoping you'd pick up on that."

"I'm glad you're safe, Tins." Shaw's arms tightened around her.

"Are you guys ready for lunch at all? I can call over to the Kims' if you're feeling Korean barbecue? It's the least I can do for interrupting your day for a false alarm."

"Tins, you don't owe us anything." Baz yawned while stretching his arms over his head. "I'm down for some short ribs though."

"Yeah, we'll stay close for lunch," Shaw confirmed. "What do you and Brin want?"

Everyone took a quick lunch together, easing into the afternoon now that the threat of Mia slumming around was laid to rest. They all knew the feeling would be temporary with Craig still in the wind, but they'd take the outcome of the day now that everyone was safe.

CHAPTER
Fifty One

"**G**ODDAMN, BRO." SHAW SHOOK HIS HEAD, LAUGHING AFTER Baz had handed him his phone. "What the hell have you been doin' on here?" Shaw scrolled through Baz's dating app. He noticed eight different chats Baz had going on.

"Fuckin' Big-Titties is getting to be too much work with that jealous fit she's been throwing over nothing. She ain't even talked to me for over a week now—since we were at Poquitos. She was good, but not that goddamn good in bed to be dealing with that shit."

"She's around though, right?" Shaw didn't want to think anything sinister had happened since she made friends with Mia. Their after work searches for Craig and his crew hadn't been successful.

"Been posting on the socials just fine, so yeah—I'd say she's around."

"Sorry, bro."

"That's not on you, fam," Baz disagreed, continuing to drive along their normal route. "Scroll through to that chat I've got with Trina."

"Damn!" Shaw laughed. "Going from Big-Titties to version 2.0 or what?!" Shaw looked at the profile first rather than going to the chat. "Baz, I'm telling you, it's time to find yourself a good girl. This shit's gonna land you in the exact same spot as Big-Titties. Look at this thirst trap!" He held the phone out for Baz.

Baz grabbed Shaw's wrist to pull the phone closer. "That's a new pic. I haven't seen that one yet," he commented on the large chested woman lying on a bed in lingerie.

"So, she's updating her profile with something like *this* while you guys are chatting? 2.0 is still fishing, bro," Shaw warned.

"Well, drop that convo with her then and see what else I've got going on in there," Baz instructed him.

Shaw deleted the chat thread and selected the next girl. "I thought you had a rule about these girls?" Shaw gave his partner a side eye. "I'm not trying to be rude at all, it's your big ass that established these rules; but judging by her pictures, I'd say she doesn't meet your weight requirement."

"She got a cute face." Baz shrugged. "I wasn't planning on taking that one out on a date."

"You can be such an asshole." Shaw shook his head, laughing. "Actually"—Shaw lifted his focus off Baz's phone—"Tins's girl Farrah is single now, what about chatting with her?"

"You know I don't like that short hair shit."

"Bro!" Shaw spat out a laugh. "She can grow her hair out if it's that big of a deal."

Shaw wiped his face from the uphill battle he had figuring out what Baz really wanted when their radio interrupted them.

"Shaw, Baz, there are multiple reports of suspicious activity at an abandoned house, possible battery of some kind in progress and getting louder. They're describing two men's voices violently arguing."

Shaw reached for the radio. "Any shots fired or eyes on weapons of any kind?"

"Not that they've observed."

"Alright"—Shaw refreshed the board on the laptop—"I see it on here now, we're headed that way."

Baz blew out an exasperated breath and cracked his neck. "Another damn day in paradise."

"Wanna take bets on this one?" Shaw smirked.

"Next bar tab says it's a crack deal gone bad." Baz smiled.

"You've got *no* imagination." Shaw shook his head, grinning. "I'll see your bar tab and raise you a bottle of whiskey that says we have to go break up a homeless fighting ring run by Big-Titties 2.0. You know, since we like running into your deleted app dates and all."

Baz laughed out loud and slapped his leg before flipping his partner off.

"I never took 2.0 out on a date," Baz clarified.

Shaw shrugged and offered his hand to his best friend to shake on their bet.

Before Shaw would seal the bet he added a bit more. "*And* if one of these guys doesn't have pants on you're getting that one this time. I had to grab the last goddamn naked perp."

"Shit, I dunno, fam." Baz pulled his hand back.

They still chuckled about Baz's indecisive dating life when they got to the scene of the call.

"Let's hope we don't run into 2.0." Shaw smirked before stepping out of the car.

Before either of them even had time to shut their doors, gunshots rained upon them. Both officers took cover but Shaw's side of the car took heavier fire than Baz's. He swiftly made his way behind the vehicle where they both waited, trying to figure out what was happening. There was a small break in the firing so both men ran for cover near the abandoned house they got called to.

"Fuck!" Baz scrambled behind an air conditioning unit. "Shaw, you good?!" he shouted once there was another break in the gunfire.

"I got fucking hit." Shaw watched blood soaking his right bicep as he posted up against a house. He also knew something hit him in the back on his way from the car. He completely lost his breath when he felt the impact of that bullet but knew it hadn't punctured his vest. "I'm good."

"You sure?!"

"Yeah—I'm calling for backup," Shaw confirmed. "You got eyes on anyone?!"

"No, you?!"

"No!"

"Where you hit, fam?"

"My vest and my arm."

Shit, Baz thought. "Fam, I'm coming your way."

"You're good, I'm good. Let's make sure we know where they're coming from before anyone moves."

"Fuck," Shaw groaned after calling in for backup. He put his hand on his bicep and realized it had grazed him rather than being buried in his arm but still bled pretty steadily.

A few more gunshots made their way toward him so he strategically worked his way around the corner of the house where he was able to see Baz.

"Bro, what the fuck?!" Shaw looked at his partner.

"You sure you're good, fam?"

"Yeah, just my goddamn arm. It feels like shit, but I'm fine." Shaw finally made his way to Baz so they could both take cover behind the aged air conditioning unit. He turned slightly to show Baz his back. "You see anything back there."

"Fuck." Baz reached over and plucked the bullet from Shaw's vest. "Got goddamn lucky. We need to either hunker down until backup gets here or we need to get moving before the shooters find us. There's at least two."

"My guess is more. I didn't see shit when we pulled up, did you?"

"No." Baz tucked himself toward the unit when they heard a peppering of gunfire. This time the bullets hit the side of the house just feet from them.

"Looks like we're not hunkering down for backup. We need to move," Shaw suggested.

"May as well go into the house—better than being out in the open."

"You wanna cover first, or me?"

"You go, fam, I got you."

Shaw gave a stern nod and looked around to be sure he wouldn't walk straight into any obvious firing. Soon after he made his way around the next corner of the house he let out a quick, sharp whistle for Baz to make his move while he covered them. Once Baz was around the corner he kicked in a rickety door with his glock up to take cover from inside the house and wait for backup.

CHAPTER
Fifty Two

"Hey, Vance," Tinsley answered her phone as she was between appointments with her last one only about ten minutes away.

"Tins"—her brother's voice was firm and hurried—"get down to the hospital *now*. I'm going into surgery, you need to be here *right now*." He hung up the phone without another word.

Tinsley felt her entire stomach turn in agony, trying to choke down the bile that surged as her head spun. Her fingers trembled across the screen of her phone to dial Shaw. Tears steadily poured from her eyes and she couldn't catch a breath.

"Boo, what happened?" Brindle worked on the final touches of his client's cut, worried as he watched his best friend.

Tinsley got Shaw's voicemail so she dialed him again while struggling with her coat.

"Brin, he's not answering!" her voice was hysterical.

"Vance?"

"No, Hunt!" she sobbed.

"Boo, he's at work. What happened? Weren't you just talking to Vance?" he tried to calm her down.

"Vance said go to the hospital right now and then he hung up on me." Tinsley tripped over the mat at her station. "Something's wrong," she cried out and tried to dial Shaw again. "He never misses my calls!"

Brindle couldn't swallow as he choked on what felt like an entire lemon making its way down his throat while his heart constricted. He felt every single emotion that came out of his best friend—he never had to be the level-headed one.

"Tinsley"—he held her shoulders—"give me your keys, I'm driving. We'll take Harv and figure out what's going on, okay?" Brindle told his client he'd square up payment later and then put Harvey's leash on. It didn't take him long to barge into Lacey's appointment in the back room to let her know they had an emergency and she had the shop. As they ran to Tinsley's car he quickly texted Victor asking him to come to the hospital as soon as he could.

Tinsley dialed Shaw over and over with nothing but his generic voicemail picking up each time. She took a break from his number and dialed Baz—same result, nothing but endless ringing until his voicemail.

"I don't know who else to call!" she sobbed and dialed Shaw again.

Brindle reached over the console and held his friend's leg as he tried to get to the hospital as quickly as possible.

"Boo," he tried to calm his voice. "Just keep dialing, they can't always answer and maybe they just have their phones on silent." All he could do was hope that was the case, he really didn't know what they'd be walking into once they got to the hospital. His best friend didn't even acknowledge Harvey when he put his head over the passenger seat as she frantically called Shaw again. Brindle watched her entire arm shake as she put the phone up to her ear. He'd watched her with a drunken crying episode once but this wasn't that. This was absolute heartbreaking terror she projected; from her helpless, sobbing cries to the endless tears and the shattered movements in her shaking body. Brindle had never wanted to take pain away from anyone as much as he did watching his best friend while she battled the feeling of her entire world collapsing.

CHAPTER
Fifty Three

"I'M SORRY, MA'AM, FAMILY AND LAW ENFORCEMENT ONLY IN this area right now." A nurse held her hands up, not allowing Tinsley or Brindle any closer to the emergency room.

"She's fucking family! Let her through!" Brindle argued. "Get Dr. Adams out here."

"Sir—" the nurse held her hands up again as an officer walked toward them after picking up on the commotion.

"What seems to be the problem?"

"Is Hunter Shaw in there?!" Tinsley nearly shouted. It was a pain-filled guttural sob that escaped as she begged for any information.

"Ma'am—" the officer held his hands up.

"Hunter Shaw!" she wailed. "What about Baz? Is Bastian Haywood here?! Please!" she cried. "Please, tell me Hunt's okay—tell me they're okay!" She gripped Brindle as her knees gave out on her from the frenzied panic that she was in.

"Ma'am, I understand you're upset, but—" the officer tried before Brindle was cutting in.

"You don't understand *shit*! It's a simple question. You can't tell us the names of the officers back there?!"

"Please." Tinsley reached for the officer but a woman crying her name interrupted them.

"Tinsley!"

They all whipped their heads around and watched as Baz's mom and dad both ran toward the nurse's station.

"Honey, did you see them? What's the status?!" Mama T cried.

Tinsley completely folded. Baz's mom at the hospital confirmed her worst nightmare—both Baz and Shaw were in fact the officers who had been brought in.

Brindle dropped down to help pick his best friend up off the floor. "Tins." he fought his own tears and held her as tight as he could. "Boo…"

Mama T leaned down to place her hand on Tinsley's shoulder and she looked at the officer.

"What do you know?" Mama T asked the patrolman.

"Mama T"—He was familiar with her and tried to be gentle in his response—"we were told no information at all can be relayed to anyone for any reason until the Chief is here."

"*Fuck that!* You know me, and I'm going back there!" Mama T insisted.

"He's on the phone with us right now." Baz's dad held it up and put it on speaker. "Rog, tell 'em. I need to see my kids. Don't you fucking deny us of that."

There was a large, forced exhale on the other end of the line but Chief Haywood gave the approval.

Mama T grabbed Tinsley's arm as Brindle lifted her off the ground to bring her along with them.

"Just family," the officer reiterated and put his hand up.

"This is Shaw's wife—she's family."

The officer looked at her, glanced at Tinsley's hand, and then back at Mama T. She dared him with her eyes to question her any further.

Brindle squeezed her shoulder. "Tins, I'm gonna go check on Harv and get him set up with Victor. I'll be right back up—you call or text if you need me before that. I love you, Boo."

Tinsley hugged her best friend and quickly followed Baz's parents through a set of doors to be in the waiting area of the emergency room.

Victor watched Brindle's tear-filled approach. He'd arrived at the hospital just minutes earlier and waited anxiously near Tinsley's 4Runner. Victor put his arms around his boyfriend, squeezing tightly.

"Brin, what happened?" He rubbed his hands up and down his back.

Brindle shook his head. "I don't know yet, but Shawberry and Black Casper are definitely in the ER and no one's talking."

The air in Victor's lungs escaped all at once as his chest deflated. "Oh Brin, I'm sorry. How's our girl, Tins?"

"Understandably hysterical."

"So we just have to wait here?! Marcus, where are the boys?" Mama T cried as her husband held her with tears in his bloodshot eyes. They were allowed just outside the operating rooms, but no one told them anything else.

The waiting area quickly became chaotic with all the police officers as hospital staff raced around responding to the three critically injured men who'd been brought in.

Tinsley checked her phone for the millionth time as if this was all a big mistake and Shaw was going to return one of her eighty-four missed calls. Her head turned when she heard her name. One of the nurses who had worked with Vance for years approached. She'd attended plenty of family events to where she and Tinsley were quite friendly with one another.

"Tins, what are you doing here? Are you okay?" Kaitlyn came up beside her, rubbing her shoulder.

"Kaitlyn"—Tinsley shook—"can you tell us anything about the

cops who were just brought in? Kaitlyn, please—p-please tell us they're gonna be okay."

The nurse remembered Vance telling her not too long ago Tinsley was dating a police officer. She knew she shouldn't say anything at all but Tinsley's demeanor made her want to vomit from the pain projecting in her tone and through her terrorized expression.

Kaitlyn reached out and put her arms around Tinsley to whisper, "Tins, try to keep it together right now because I shouldn't be sharing information, okay?" She waited until Tinsley nodded while still sobbing.

"I'll go talk to the EMTs who are still here to get specifics, but two officers were brought in with multiple gunshot wounds." She paused and held tighter when Tinsley's legs gave out. "Shhhhh, Tins." Kaitlyn's hold intensified to help hold her up. "I don't know which one's which, but they're both in bad shape. Vance is in there with one of them and Dr. Massy has the other—they were both taken into surgery immediately upon arrival."

Tinsley absolutely couldn't hold it together, she sobbed into Kaitlyn's scrubs.

"Tins," Kaitlyn tried. "Girl, I know. You gotta be strong right now," she reminded her. "Take one big breath for me and then let me go talk to the EMTs before they leave." Kaitlyn could feel Tinsley shaking, she could hardly stand so Kaitlyn tugged her toward a chair. Once Tinsley sat in the chair, Kaitlyn reached down for her shoulder, giving it a quick, comforting squeeze before heading down the hall.

"Tins, did she have any answers?" Mama T's desperation consumed her tone.

Tinsley wiped her eyes, jagged breaths interrupting her attempts at communication.

"They're both in surgery," she managed before choking on another inhale. "She said they came in with multiple gunshot wounds." Her body shook and she was soon engulfed by both Mama T and Marcus. "Kaitlyn said she's going to talk to the EMTs to find out more," Tinsley mumbled through their embrace.

No one spoke, they continued to hold each other. Tinsley and

Mama T felt Marcus pull away after a few moments of collective crying that didn't seem to have an end. When Mama T looked up to see why her husband had left them, she noticed her brother-in-law, Chief Haywood, walk into the waiting area with a puffy face himself.

"Rog." Marcus swiftly made his way to his brother. "What happened?"

Chief Haywood put his hand over his mouth just before a fountain of tears came flooding down from his face.

There was no time for him to answer as a set of doors flung open and everyone turned their attention to the bloody doctor making his way to the waiting area. For the first time in over an hour Tinsley felt slight relief; it wasn't Vance and it was a man so, it couldn't be Dr. Massy. Kaitlyn told her those were the doctors working on the two officers who'd been brought in.

Chief Haywood made a beeline toward the doctor as he removed his surgical mask. All the officers watched in agitated anticipation for any news on their brothers in blue.

"My boys?" Chief Haywood begged in a tone no one had ever heard from the typically brave and stoic man.

The doctor took a sigh of relief delivering this news, he put his hands up, palm facing the chief. "Your boys are still in surgery, Chief. We just lost the perp," he disclosed with little empathy.

Everyone watched in wonder as Chief Haywood's sturdy frame dropped to his knees. He was like an unruly child begging his mom for another sweet treat before bed as he held on to the front of the doctor's scrubs, wailing.

Marcus put his hand on his brother's shoulder and squeezed.

"Rog, the boys are still in surgery—bro, they're strong. We're *not* giving up on them." He bent over, giving his brother a firm, headlock-style hug around his neck.

Chief Haywood dropped further to the ground and slammed his fists on the tile floors.

"Not *my* boy!"

The officers looked around at each other wondering why the Chief was so upset.

"I want to see him!" he managed a distressed shout. "I want to see my boy!" Chief Haywood stared at the ground on all fours while crying out.

Tinsley thoughtfully put all the pieces together, Chief Haywood *was* talking about his boy. He was talking about Craig. He knew before he got there that his son was the third individual brought in that afternoon. By the looks of Baz's parents—and everyone else in the room—none of them knew.

The doctor knelt down to Chief Haywood and spoke at a volume that no one else, not even Marcus, was able to hear. Inaudible mumbling continued between the men. Without even a glance toward anyone, the doctor helped Chief Haywood up and they walked back through the double doors.

"Rog? Roger!" Marcus called out but neither one of the men turned around.

CHAPTER
Fifty Four

"**V**ANCE!" TINSLEY SHOT UP ALMOST AN HOUR AFTER CHIEF Haywood made his scene. Her disheveled brother emerged from the double doors, covered in blood, a surgical mask hanging around his long neck. She couldn't see his expression because her eyes were completely filled with tears as she stumbled toward him.

Vance quickened his pace toward his sister, he put her in his arms the second she was close enough. He'd never held anyone as tightly as he held onto Tinsley at that moment.

Tinsley wailed into her brother's chest, struggling to vocalize any words as she tugged on his scrubs.

"Please," Tinsley's terrorized voice managed, piercing her brother's heart with the force of a thousand swords.

Vance spoke in a low, cracking tone close to her ear, "Shaw's stable right now."

Her entire body melted into him, crying even harder but this time it was relief settling into the heavy sobs.

"He's not out of the woods," Vance cautioned. "But Tins, he's still with us."

"Thank you," she croaked.

Tinsley shook, losing her balance so Vance pulled her in even tighter and swallowed the lump that grew inside his throat.

It didn't take long for Marcus and Mama T to make their way toward the sibling duo.

Mama T put her hand on Tinsley's shoulder. "What's going on with the boys?"

Vance lifted his head from his sister's, his exhausted eyes peering at the couple.

"Are you Mr. and Mrs. Haywood?"

"We are," Marcus confirmed.

"I was in Shaw's room, but I just checked in with Officer Haywood—we're still working on him."

Tinsley stayed in the comfort of the familial embrace but reached to the side of them to hold on to Mama T's hand.

"Officer Haywood has a punctured lung and a lot of internal bleeding," he spoke gently. "They're still trying to stabilize him."

Tinsley felt Mama T squeeze her hand, crying out from the uncertainty.

"And Shaw?" Marcus hesitantly asked.

"He's stable right now."

"Can we see him?" Tinsley whipped her head up from her brother's chest, starting to find her voice again.

Vance took a deep breath and stared at his sister, he had never seen her so upset. Not even the night of the fire when they were kids.

"Tins, I don't think that's a good idea." Vance was used to the visual horrors of the emergency room and even he struggled with the state Shaw was in. He couldn't imagine his sister would respond well to seeing him, despite his stable state. Her eyes, broken and full of tears, begged him. He took another harsh breath and despite his better judgement, he agreed. "If I do, you guys all have to promise me you'll leave the second we ask you to." His concerned eyes fell upon his sister. "It's not common practice to have anyone in the operating rooms." He looked at Baz's parents. "And I'm sorry but it's not possible at all to see your son until he's out of surgery—we can't contaminate that room."

They both gravely nodded, it was Marcus who answered for him and his wife. "Understood."

"Tins?"

"Vance, I just need to see him… please."

There were two nurses in the room with Shaw when the small group arrived. Tinsley couldn't keep herself together when she saw the love of her life lying on the operating table. He had an oxygen mask covering a large portion of his face and from there it was absolute chaos on his entire body. His uniform was in pieces, the emergency room had shredded it to get to each of the gunshot wounds. Every bandage on his body was already stained in blood—she counted at least four massive injuries that she could see while swiftly making her way to her boyfriend. She didn't ask permission when she held his hand, reaching down to softly peck his forehead as a resurgence of tears consumed her face. Her nostrils filled with the distinct scent of a hospital, laced with a hint of copper while her lips lingered on his skin.

"Tins," Vance came up behind her. "Aiden and Lucy will stay in here with you guys for as long as it's safe. I'm gonna get scrubbed up to see if I can help with Baz." He gave the two nurses a flat smile and squeezed his sister's shoulder one last time before he turned around.

"I love you, Vance—thank you."

"I love you too, Tins." Vance let himself out of the room.

Tinsley couldn't help herself, she kissed Shaw's forehead again before another round of sobbing started. Every emotion she'd felt the first time she watched Shaw fighting for his life came back ten-fold based on the grave scene in front of her. Shaw was the strongest person she'd ever known and her heart ached at the possibility of losing him. She pecked him once more, whispering to him, "I love you, Hunt." She rubbed his hand with her thumb as she clung to him. "Stay with me, tough guy."

Marcus and Mama T slowly flanked her sides.

Baz's mom reached out and gave Shaw a very maternal-like caress from the crown of his head to the side of his face. "Shaw, I'll kick your ass if you even think about leaving us."

Her friendly threat triggered a small smirk on Tinsley's face.

"Has he been awake at all?" Tinsley asked the male nurse who stood closest to them.

Aiden, Vance had called him, shook his head. "He passed out in the ambulance and at this point, while he's stable, he likely won't wake up for a while. We put him under anesthesia to work on him."

Tinsley gently ran her fingers on his chest where she noticed a particularly disturbing bruise near his heart.

"He's lucky to have been wearing that vest." Aiden gestured toward Tinsley's gaze. "He has an equally gnarly bruise on his back—four shots hit his vest. That one"—he pointed toward his heart—"there was a bullet stuck partially in his badge, that metal plate in the vest saved him from losing his life to that bullet."

Tinsley's stomach turned again but her heart soared with gratitude that he escaped death.

"He was shot eight times?" Tinsley asked in disbelief.

"Yes," Aiden confirmed as he watched Lucy, the other nurse, walk out of the room. "Four to the vest, one that grazed his bicep, one in the shoulder"—he pointed each of them out even though it was very obvious where he had been hit—"caught him just below the vest here, and then the big one, here, just missed grazing his femoral artery." He tapped his finger in the air at the only bandage below Shaw's waist.

Tinsley's face was covered in tears thinking about how even a millimeter difference on any of the shots could have ended Shaw's life. She leaned over again and a couple of tears dropped onto Shaw's face just before she placed a prolonged kiss on his brow line.

CHAPTER
Fifty Five

A CONSISTENT, SHORT BEEPING NOISE WELCOMED HIM BACK TO CONsciousness. His entire body was in pain, despite the hurt throughout his chest, he tried to take a deep breath and realized something was over his face. He fought his heavy eyelids to see what was around him. His blurred vision took a minute to adjust before he was able to identify he was in a dimly lit hospital room with the lights of the city glowing through a large, round window. The thing that obstructed his view—and most of his face—was an oxygen mask.

Shaw's head rolled to the side and quickly noticed his girlfriend curled up next to him. Her head that donned a loose bun rested near his pillow so he couldn't see her face, but she clung to his fingers with one of her hands and the other gently held the top of his hip. He wanted the mask off to talk to her. He finally managed to get his hand up to his face, pulling on the mask to get it up over his head felt like lifting an entire squad car because of the bullet that had grazed him and the one that went through his shoulder.

The machine monitoring him immediately tattled with hurried and high-pitched alarms. He fully expected to not only wake Tinsley up, but that a nurse would rush in. He watched Tinsley's head pop up over his pillow, her swollen eyes locked into his while her lips curled down and quivered. She looked to be in an, understandably, distressed and exhausted state of mind so Shaw tried to lighten the mood.

"Did you take my pants off while I was sleeping again, ma'am?" Shaw asked with a strained voice that felt like sandpaper passing his lips.

Tinsley burst into tears the second she heard him. She tried to restrain herself from consuming his body completely and instead reached up and crushed her lips against his. She gently but assuringly held his face and head, not ever wanting to remove her lips. Tinsley finally backed up, slightly breathless, just enough to speak softly to him.

"Oh, Hunt"—she let out a sigh of relief with even more tears in her eyes before pecking him once more—"I love you."

"I love you too, Tins." Shaw gently squeezed her hand in his reply. "Thank you for being here."

Her brows furrowed, but slowly developed an assuring smile. "Of course I'm here. Baby, I'm so glad you're awake," she cried while scooting on his pillow.

The door of Shaw's room opened, interrupting them just before a nurse appeared from behind a privacy curtain. "Officer Shaw," she greeted. "I see you're done with your oxygen mask, huh?" She offered a smirk and made her way to his bedside, stopping at his monitor to halt the continuously bothersome alerts since they weren't needed.

"Yeah," he quickly confirmed and tried to lift his head when she reached for the mask he had discarded but ended up lying on the cord of.

Tinsley sat up but never let go of her boyfriend's hand. She watched the nurse fussing with the IV on Shaw's other hand and she slid herself off the bed so she could have full access to ensure everything was in place.

Shaw turned his head toward Tinsley when he felt her get up. His hand tightened around hers and she squeezed it to assure her tough guy she wasn't going anywhere else.

"Your vitals are actually looking pretty good, Officer Shaw," the nurse confirmed. "I'm going to send a doctor in here shortly, but for now, can you tell me your level of pain on a scale of one to ten—ten being unbearable?"

"Uh, like a five?"

"Hunter." Tinsley looked at him with accusing eyes. "I know you don't like pain killers, tough guy"—she smiled down at him, one palm caressing the side of his head—"but please be real about how you feel right now." Her smile transformed into a more concerning look through her eyes.

The nurse chuckled watching their interaction.

Shaw tried to take a deep breath despite the sharp pains that shot throughout his chest. He was definitely much closer to that ten than he was willing to disclose initially.

"Okay," he reluctantly agreed. "Probably a solid eight."

Tinsley's eyes widened at him as her brows rose, halting the loving pattern she'd been drawing on his hand with her thumb.

"Nine and a half," he conceded.

The nurse continued to laugh and offered him a bit of relief. "Well, I'll note that but keep you where you're at for now on the pain medicine. If you hit that ten, or just feel like you need a little extra, just press this button here and we'll get a bit more going for you."

"Thank you." Shaw took another controlled breath and lifted Tinsley's hand to his mouth for a quick peck.

The nurse plugged in a few more notes on the computer. "Do you need anything else to make you comfortable right now? Pillows? Blankets? I'll bring you a water here shortly as well."

Shaw shook his head. "No, I'm fine." He peered up at his girlfriend. "Do you need a blanket, sugar?"

"I have a couple over on that pull out." She gestured toward the bed she was supposed to be sleeping on instead of Shaw's.

More of his voice came back to him and he started to finally look more alert when he turned his attention back to the nurse.

"Do you know how my partner's doing?"

The nurse initially looked across the bed at Tinsley before she addressed Shaw.

"I'm not assigned to your partner—"

"You can't tell me how he's doing?" He scrunched his forehead before he turned his focus to look at Tinsley for more information.

"Baby"—she rubbed his leg as her eyes welled up—"Baz is still sleeping."

"I'll give you guys some privacy." The nurse patted Shaw and then offered Tinsley a flat smile before leaving the room.

"Tins, please tell me Baz is gonna be okay?" Shaw swallowed hard, his grip on her hand tightening.

Tears cascaded down her face, tilting her chin down as she tried to steady her voice. "I won't lie to you, Hunt, Baz was in worse shape than you were when they got you guys here… And I know you don't feel great right now."

Shaw reached his free hand up and held his forehead.

"Vance came to talk to me when they finally got Baz out of surgery. He was in surgery for almost two hours longer than you were. He had a lot of internal bleeding and one of his lungs collapsed," she cried with more than a steady stream of tears now. "I haven't seen him, but Mama T and Marcus haven't left his side. He's not alone, baby."

Shaw's hand tugged on Tinsley to come closer to him. She didn't hesitate and soon snuggled next to his head, noticing her boyfriend struggling to fight off crying.

"I know"—she softly rubbed the side of his head with her fingertips to try to console him—"Baz is a tough guy too, he's stable right now, Hunt. Vance and the rest of the doctors are doing everything they can."

"That's my brother," he choked out and felt a few tears drop down his cheeks.

"I know." Tinsley squeezed her boyfriend even tighter.

"He saved us… That mother fucker Craig. I'm going to kill him. All of them."

"Hunt." Tinsley lifted her head so she could look into Shaw's eyes. "Craig didn't make it. He came in here with you guys, but they lost him shortly after I got here."

Shaw watched her face because she looked like she planned to share more.

"I don't know if everyone else knows, based on the texts from Mama T I think they figured it out. Chief Haywood was here, he made a bit of a scene when he got the news, but everyone just looked confused."

"What kind of scene?"

Tinsley shook her head. "He was completely shattered and on the ground, crying. He left with the doctor and I haven't seen him since. Mama T didn't say anything else about seeing him either. I don't think they're allowing anyone in that room with Baz—his uncle included."

"Did they get the other shooters?"

"Baby, they only found three bodies on the scene. No one else came here with you guys besides Craig."

"Shit." Shaw held his head. "I don't even know how many were there; bullets were just flying every-fucking-where. I knew Craig was there. That fucker was waiting for us in that damn house, we—"

The nurse walked back in the room. "Officer Shaw, I've got some water for you." She set it on a side table which she slid close enough for him to grab when he was ready. "I've also been asked if you're seeing any other visitors right now? There are two detectives outside who'd like a word as soon as you're able. They know you're awake."

"No," Tinsley firmly answered for him. "They can wait until my br—Dr. Adams comes and checks on him."

Shaw looked at Tinsley when her hand gripped his even tighter.

"Hunt's safety and well-being is much more important than whatever they want right now. I want him to be fully checked before anyone, besides family, is allowed in." Tinsley spoke with finality but had a kind undertone given the nurse was simply the messenger.

"I understand," the nurse agreed. "Don't worry, they may be the law, but in our house we do what's best for the patients first. I don't see any reason for them to come in here before the doctor."

"Thank you." Tinsley was overly grateful she wouldn't have to put up any kind of fight, the evening had been stressful enough.

The nurse made herself scarce and Tinsley waited for the door to be shut before she looked at Shaw again.

"I'm not leaving you in this room alone with any of them." She shed a few tears as her voice broke, "I don't trust anyone right now and I'm scared if I leave—" crying consumed her voice.

"Sugar"—Shaw pulled on her again—"The worst part's over," he tried to assure her.

She blew out a large breath. "You know I can't lose you, Hunt."

"I love you, Tins."

"I love you too," Tinsley cried before lying next to her boyfriend on the hospital bed.

They heard the door opening again and Tinsley popped her head up, hoping she wasn't about to see the detectives that she just told the nurse to leave outside.

"Nine damn lives." Vance shook his head but looked relieved. "I've seen you spend two of those now. What are we gonna do with you?"

Tinsley choked out a laugh and wiped her tears with the back of her hand.

"Doc." Shaw smiled and did a quick nod. "I sure appreciate you bringing me back to life again."

"Well, Tins was being such a baby about it." He rolled his eyes while giving his sister a hug. "You don't listen too well when it comes to keeping yourself outta trouble." Vance shot his accusing eyes at Shaw. "Lucky for you, you're one tough son of a bitch." He took his hands out of his pockets and walked to the computer near Shaw's bed. "I'll admit, I was genuinely worried there for a bit."

"I owe you, man. I could probably never repay you or thank you enough for everything. But truly, thank you, Vance."

"Last time I said you could thank me by not sustaining these types of injuries anymore. I guess I had to specify gunshot wounds in addition to stab wounds." He leveled his gaze at Shaw. "But how 'bout this time I just say you can thank me by not upsetting my sister like that ever again. I think that would cover basically anything you'd need my assistance for."

Shaw chuckled through his nostrils. "I promise to try my best." His eyes adoringly lifted to meet his girlfriend's gaze. "I don't like seeing her beautiful face so upset. Plus, I'd like to stick around and enjoy life with her."

Tinsley leaned down and gently connected with his lips.

"I'll let that one slide, but let me get out of the room before it gets all hot and heavy."

"Vance." Tinsley rolled her eyes but smiled.

"Back up, perv—I need to check my patient." Vance lightly elbowed his sister and tugged the stethoscope off his neck.

It was refreshing for both Tinsley and Shaw to have Vance's awkward personality in the room at that moment, it made the severity of his injuries slightly less worrisome to hear the teasing. Tinsley peered down at Shaw and they shared a quick, loving smile with one another before Tinsley snuck into the restroom while Vance continued his examination.

"Great, now that she's gone"—Vance started, moving the chestpiece along Shaw's pec—"what level of detail would you like about what happened while you were on the table? I only gave Tins the high-level because I didn't think she could handle anything else while you were still out."

"I can hear whatever it is you need to share with me." Shaw nodded. "Thank you for shielding her from anything else."

"Well, we did lose you for a hot second shortly after you got here— had to give you a bit of a shock to get the ticker pumping again. Honestly, I wasn't sure if you'd come back from that. I nearly had to call it after that *and* all the damn blood you lost. That abdominal wound didn't do you any favors at all—your vest should've covered that one. I guess you ran out of all that luck after the four that hit your vest didn't penetrate all the way through." He shrugged and swung the stethoscope around his neck, reaching for a small flashlight this time. "Whoever assembles the damn vests these days needs a medal, this bruise here"—Vance pointed to Shaw's muscular chest, just over his heart—"I don't think I need to say it out loud what would've happened without the vest."

Shaw's gaze ventured off into space, the day had been a whirlwind and he tried to place what all had happened during that call. He remembered the first couple of hits, but half of them were complete news to him; he had no recollection of the abdomen shot actually piercing his skin. He did, however, remember he and Baz injured and sitting together on the floor in that house. At least two shots that Craig received also lived fairly vividly in his mind as they came from Shaw's gun.

"Did I lose you?" Vance asked again when he didn't get a response the first time.

"Sorry." Shaw looked up at him. "I missed that."

"Your head feeling alright?" Vance asked and shined the small flashlight into Shaw's eye again with a concerned look on his face.

Shaw nodded and then looked over when Tinsley appeared in the doorway of the bathroom. "My head's good, a little groggy, but no, I just was thinking."

"Baby, are you okay?" Tinsley gently caressed the side of his face with one soft hand and carefully set the other on his torso.

"Yeah." He tried a more assuring nod and tone this time. "I actually… Hey, Doc"—he looked up at Vance—"I'm not trying to sound like a little pansy ass, but any chance you can hold off those detectives for a bit? I need my head straight before they get any kind of statement." He watched a wave of worry consume Tinsley's sweet face, he picked up her hand and immediately assured her, "I promise, I'm good. I just mean I need to really be sure I give a clear and concise statement. I can't be hesitant about anything during that interview. So I want a bit of time to collect all that before having to talk to anyone."

"Absolutely," Vance agreed. "You give me the word when you're ready, until then I won't sign off on anyone but family in here." Vance smirked, shoving his hands in his pocket. "And for the record, you may be many things, but a pansy ass *definitely* isn't one of them."

"Tough Guy Club President," Tinsley confirmed with a prideful smile.

Shaw rubbed her hand in return but looked up at Vance again. "Can you tell me about Baz? Tins said he hasn't been up yet. Is my guy gonna make it?"

Vance took a deep breath and didn't look at either of them, he found a tile on the floor to start talking to. "The short answer is it's really hard to make any predictions right now." He shook his head and in that motion found it in him to meet Shaw's gaze. "The next couple of hours are going to be *very* critical for him. He wasn't breathing on his own when he came out of surgery and he was in there for quite a while, but he's giving himself a fighting chance. He's basically your only competition when it comes to being the Champion of tough SOBs, I'll say that much." Vance sat on the end of the bed, bending his leg, propping an ankle on his left knee. "Dr. Massy is going to be handing everything off with Dr. Leigh here pretty soon, we have to do a shift change so you'll likely have Dr. Leigh too. But I'll tell you she's phenomenal, she's going to take good care of Baz and they already know I'll be flying my helicopter over every single move with the two of you. Not to mention"—he looked at Tinsley—"Dad's on his way."

Tinsley's face tried to hide her surprise. She felt there'd always been something slightly off between her dad and Shaw. He left the ivory tower up at Harborview hospital to oversee their care, even if it had to be through Vance and not his controlling-ass calling the shots directly. For that alone Tinsley was eternally grateful. Her brother was obviously a stand-out doctor, but he developed into that because he learned from the very best.

"Mom's been in the waiting room for a couple hours. I've been updating her, but I also told her she can stay there until she gets the Tinsley green light."

Tinsley got up so she could walk over to hug her brother.

"Don't get all sappy on me now," his sarcastic tone rang throughout the room as he pretended to push her away. He wasn't one to offer sincere affection, he preferred a bully-style love for his sister whenever he had the opportunity. "This counts as your Christmas gift for the next couple of years."

Tinsley laughed. "I'm okay if you count this as my Christmas gift for forever, Vance. I love you. Thank you for everything."

"Don't tell anyone, but I guess I love you too. Even though you're annoying as hell most of the time."

Tinsley rolled her eyes just before she poked him in the side with her fingers.

Vance's body jerked at the sensation, he returned the gesture by yanking her arm to scratch his knuckles against the top of her head. "See, *annoying*," Vance reiterated.

Tinsley readjusted the bun Vance ruined when she replied, "And while I love mom dearly, Hunt hasn't been up all that long. Can we just have a bit before anyone else comes in?"

"Of course." Vance stood and puffed his chest out. "Let me just go inform everyone who the law is around here."

Tinsley and Shaw smiled at him. Vance winked and left the room.

"Do you need anything?" Tinsley asked as she gently stroked Shaw's head, running her fingers through his disheveled hair.

"Just you"—he smiled—"And maybe some water."

Tinsley beat Shaw to the water jug the nurse had brought in and held it for him. Her phone buzzed in her pocket while he drank.

"Has your phone been blowing up?" Shaw asked before putting his lips around the straw again.

"Just Brindle and Mama T mostly." She looked at the text, it was Brindle checking in. He sent a picture of Harvey who laid in a ball on the foot of the bed with him and Victor in the guest room at their house. Tinsley smiled and held out the phone to Shaw. "Well, you scared Brindle enough to allow Harv in the bed with them, he's never even allowed Harvey to sit on the couch with him."

"Good ol Handsome Harv." Shaw smiled and then noticed the time on Tinsley's phone. "Shit, is it really past two?"

"Yeah," Tinsley confirmed and quickly texted Brindle back.

"Will you come lay with me, sugar?"

"Of course." Tinsley found her comfortable spot next to Shaw and covered them with a blanket. "I don't think the last nurse was too pleased to see me up here when they came in for their first check, this gal seems like she's gonna be okay with it though."

"Oh, I'll tell them where they can go if anyone has a problem with you up here." Shaw smirked. "Don't let this damn hospital gown fool you, I can get up if I need to."

Tinsley giggled. "Just take it easy there, tough guy." She delicately rubbed his chest with the tips of her fingers for a bit before looking at him. "Thank you for staying with me, Hunt. I don't know what I'd do without you."

"I told you, sugar—the Undertaker himself couldn't keep me from you." He leaned down to place a gentle peck on her forehead. "I know you like seeing me at home every night and while I won't be able to do that tonight, I sure tried."

Tinsley exhaled into a small grin. "Being right here with me is more than enough." She squeezed his hand. She meant every word. She'd gratefully be anywhere with him—alive and well—versus the alternative. "Do you want to talk about what happened?"

"Tins, I just want to soak in the feeling of being able to hold you right now."

Tinsley sat up so Shaw could slide his uninjured arm behind her. They had always been like puzzle pieces, fitting perfectly together, no matter what snuggling position they chose. She nestled her head into his neck and her hand reached to lace fingers with his.

"I do want to tell you, sugar, but later, okay?"

"Anything you want. I love you, Hunt."

"I love you too, Tins."

CHAPTER
Fifty Six

IT HAD BEEN A COUPLE LONG, EMOTIONALLY EXHAUSTING, AND PHYS-ically painful days in the hospital, but they were finally going to visit Baz. They stabilized him several hours after Shaw, but the partners weren't permitted to have an opportunity to exchange stories before the investigators took separate statements from each of them. The second those investigators left Baz's room Mama T gave Shaw and Tinsley the green light to come visit.

"Sugar, I don't know about you pushing me around in a damn wheelchair." Shaw looked at his girlfriend with suspicious eyes when she parked the wheelchair next to his bed.

Tinsley shook her head. "I love that tough guy in you—you know that—but we're not arguing about this one, Hunter."

"You just don't want anyone else checking out my ass in this back-less gown they've got me in." He rolled his eyes but swung his legs over the hospital bed to prepare for the grueling two step journey to the wheelchair.

Tinsley stood between Shaw's legs and reached for either side of his scruffy face. "Yeah, let's go with that." She stared deep into his eyes before pressing her lips against his. Shaw took the opportunity to grab her rear with his arm that wasn't in a sling. She happily indulged in a longer exchange when his tongue pushed through her lips.

"Maybe we can take a few minutes before visiting Baz," Shaw suggested, smiling against Tinsley's lips.

She giggled in response. "Yeah, I don't think your leash is gonna be all that long while you're healing, tough guy." She gave him one final, juicy kiss before backing up to grab a duffle bag.

"Brindle brought you some clothes. If you want I can help you change, unless of course you want to go visit Baz in your assless dress?"

"It's a *gown*, sweetcheeks," Shaw corrected her.

She rolled her eyes playfully at him. "Here sir"—she smirked—"why don't you just hold my shoulder while I help you out, huh?" She knelt down to get his shorts on each of his legs to make it easier on him.

Shaw couldn't help but roll his head back with an enamored smile plastered on his face. The first time they met, Shaw had offered his shoulder while he freed her heels from the treacherous grate in her salon.

"Thanks, ma'am." Shaw grinned, holding her shoulder to help himself to a standing position.

"Oh, your big ass is too good to get up and say hi, huh?" Shaw greeted his best friend.

"Fuck. You. Fam." Baz flipped him off. "Goddamn Princess coming through on wheels."

Tinsley pushed Shaw right next to Baz's bed, the partners slapped hands and Shaw reached over to pat Baz's shoulder.

"Bro." Shaw gave him a few firm squeezes to his shoulder.

Tinsley approached the other side of Baz's bed as he laid on his back. She leaned down and hugged him as best she could without him having to move at all. She quietly spoke into his ear, "thank you for keeping your word, Baz—and for pulling through. I love you guys and can't lose either of you." She kissed his cheek before she stood back up. "So, don't ever scare me like that again," she added.

"Hey now"—Shaw sarcastically narrowed his eyes at his girlfriend and his best friend—"don't get any ideas about running off on a date without me now."

"Baby, we'd invite you too," Tinsley teased him with a wink before she pecked her boyfriend and rubbed his shoulders. "Baz, are they treating you right, or do I need to go chat with the doc?"

Baz grinned. "They're doing alright, considering."

"This one"—Shaw gestured toward his girlfriend—"has been giving the entire place, our guys included, a run for their money." He held her hand, smiling at her. "So, if you need anything, you just let us know."

Baz nodded with a grateful smirk.

There was a short moment of silence in the room and Tinsley felt like she should give them some privacy. She pulled her phone from her pocket.

"I think I should try to coordinate with a few of my clients before Brindle runs everyone off with his sass." She put her hand on Shaw's uninjured leg and gave him a few loving squeezes. "Are you two going to be alright in here if I just step outside?"

"We're good, sugar."

"Can I get anything for you guys? Pillows, adjustments, food, water?" she rattled along.

Shaw chuckled. "You've done a ton, Tins, we'll manage—and if not we've got that button for the nurse."

"I'll just be right outside the door," she assured him, she couldn't help but give him a parting kiss on his lips, she'd never waste an opportunity for that. She rubbed Baz's shoulder and made her way to the door.

The best friends waited until Tinsley shut the door completely before they looked at each other again.

"How're you actually feeling, bro?" Shaw looked at his partner, giving him the 'don't lie to me' look.

Baz managed to get his hands up to cover his face as he slowly and carefully let out an exasperated breath.

"Shit's so fucked, fam." He paused, still covering his eyes. "I don't even know where to fucking start."

Shaw shook his head. "Bro, you don't have to worry about any of that right now. Get your big ass healthy so you can get outta here, that's it. Everything else is gonna be alright—we did what we had to do."

"You goin home?"

Shaw shook his head. "They said maybe a day or two. Tins is already workin' the staff though, she's not really happy we're still separated and doesn't love the idea of us going home and you being here alone."

"Mama T said Unc hasn't been around." Baz checked his best friend's expression. "I guess the boys've been in and out with all the fuckin' gossip too." Baz took as deep of a breath as his lungs would allow. "Sounds like we're getting the hero titles… I know we did what we had to…"

There was a long pause in the room as both men stared off into space with their own thoughts.

"It doesn't feel like real life," Baz finally said in a tone that was full of grief and disbelief.

"I know what you mean." Shaw agreed with his head. "Bro, that entire thing was a fucking set up for us. We have to remember that—it was us or them."

"I told Internal Affairs it was me."

"Bro." Shaw rested his hand on Baz's broad shoulder.

Baz stared blankly into the wall across from the bed. It took him a long minute before continuing, "I told them the truth."

Shaw stayed quiet, he wasn't entirely sure what the whole truth was. He'd been in and out of it while they waited in the house for back up. The last thing he clearly remembered was forcing himself to sit up against a wall near Baz. He'd watched his partner gripping the outside of his pectoral just under his vest as blood spewed. He knew both of them had been hit several times. He also knew they'd hit at least two of Craig's guys—and Craig himself.

"I killed Craig, I killed my cousin." Baz claimed with no inflection in his voice.

Shaw gripped his shoulder a little tighter.

Baz rolled his head to look at Shaw. The events flashed clearly in his mind, Shaw had passed out and slumped against the wall as Craig held his gun directly over his best friend's head. Baz didn't want to tell Shaw how close the Grim Reaper had been. "He would've taken your life, fam. I couldn't lose my brother."

"I don't have any fucking regrets for putting any of them down." Shaw held his partner's gaze. "I wasn't about to lose you either, bro. Thank you."

Baz used the strength he had to lift his fist for his buddy to knock.

"You see Unc yet?" Shaw assumed that family reunion would be unpleasant.

"Nope." Baz stared at the ceiling tiles above his bed, letting the air sit. "Pops won't even discuss it, I gotta believe they've talked to him."

"I'll ask Vance if he's seen him around."

"Yo, you got your phone?"

A short chortle shot out of Shaw's nose. "My phone's fucked, bro. I need to get a new one."

"I've been asking for my shit, no one knows where my phone's at."

"I'll have Tins ask around, we'll find it, bro."

The guys soon made small talk while watching a random college basketball game on the wall-mounted television in Baz's room.

Tinsley ordered the guys lunch to keep them from having to eat hospital food for their entire stay. Their lunch delivery man sauntered through the door shortly after noon.

"Does someone need mouth to mouth in here? Your nurse has arrived!" Brindle popped his head around the door and smiled at his friends. "I brought special treats too, besides myself that is."

Shaw and Baz looked at each other, rolling their eyes, smiling. Brindle was someone they were learning to love versus simply tolerating him on Tinsley's behalf.

"Actually, Brindle"—Shaw smirked—"Baz here was just talking about a nice little sponge bath."

"From the goddamn nurse in the pink scrubs you asshat!" Baz quickly clarified and swung a pillow at his buddy.

Tinsley shook her head giggling at them.

"Oh, Black Casper, I think I'd be better at it." He pumped his eyebrows at Baz and gave him a friendly pat on his leg that was slightly exposed.

Baz scurried to cover his thigh and shot Shaw the finger when he caught his partner laughing.

"And why the hell do I still have to be Black Casper?! I deserve a better nickname."

Brindle pulled out the MSM Deli requested lunch he picked up for everyone when he replied, "Oh, honey, that's *always* gonna be your damn nickname." He waved a small white bag at Tinsley. "Boo, I did get some magical cookies, but *Farrah* baked as well and asked me to bring them here for our fave boys in blue." He winked.

"That's *super* sweet of her." Tinsley smiled and pumped her eyebrows at Baz.

"Yeah." Shaw looked at Baz with a devilish smirk. "Super duper sweet."

"Goddamn, you all are too fucking much." Baz unwrapped the Mike's Deluxe he ordered but continued shaking his head. He didn't want to admit it out loud, but finding Tinsley and Brindle had been exactly what he and Shaw needed in their lives. His parents walked in shortly after and Tinsley handed them a couple sandwiches as well. Baz looked around the room, despite not having Tilly there, and nearly losing his life, his heart was full.

Shaw noticed his friend lost in the conversation around them, he watched Baz for a long minute. His buddy's hair was unusually long and slightly out of place. He couldn't remember a time Baz let his facial hair be anything less than perfect, it reminded him of a much younger Baz. He'd been, undoubtedly, the best friend a guy could ask for and Shaw was damn grateful for him in an infinite number of ways.

"Shawberry"—Brindle subtly bumped into his favorite beefcake—"you sure are staring awfully hard. Does Tins need to worry?" he teased.

Shaw rolled his eyes but smiled. "I'm just lookin' around, grateful for all the reasons I have to keep death from catching up to me."

Brindle rubbed Shaw's shoulders and everyone continued to enjoy their lunch together.

CHAPTER
Fifty Seven

SHAW WAS FINALLY RELEASED FROM THE HOSPITAL. HE AND TINSLEY had gotten themselves into three separate arguments since his discharge papers. Round one went to Shaw when he insisted on walking himself out of the hospital, compromising with a crutch instead of being pushed in a wheelchair. Rounds two and three were Tinsley's when she not only carried multiple bags out of the hospital room, but she also managed to get herself behind the wheel despite the valiant effort Shaw gave to take that responsibility.

Shaw's parents flew in the day after he and Baz were rushed to the hospital and since then had not only caught up with their son they'd been missing for over a year, but they fell predictably in love with Tinsley.

"Are you sure you're up for the families being over tonight?" Tinsley put the 4Runner in park and reached for her boyfriend's uninjured leg. "I know your parents are staying with us, but I can talk to my fa—"

"Sugar," Shaw smiled, interrupting her, "*our* family is more than welcome to hang out tonight. I'm totally fine." He picked up her hand and interlaced their fingers together before lifting it to press his lips against her soft skin. "Plus, everyone's already here and I smell food."

"Yeah, tough guy, they all made dinner for your homecoming." She leaned in closer to her boyfriend, soaking in the color of his sexy green eyes, every random freckle on his face, the tint of his lips—every single detail that she was so grateful to still have gazing back at her. "I sure love you, Hunt," she finally broke their silence with an ear to ear grin on her face.

"I love you t—"

Alaurra yanked on the passenger door, opening it to greet Shaw, "Uncle Shaw! I made you something because you're out of the hospital now." The little girl showed him a handmade card.

"Hey, Laura Loo!" Shaw reached his arm out to put it around his favorite niece before he accepted her thoughtful art project.

Harvey soon joined them, excitedly slamming into Alaurra before Tinsley grabbed his collar to ensure he didn't end up on Shaw's injured leg. The handsome, yet clumsy, dog belted out a high-pitch sound none of them had ever heard out of the goober.

"Harv," Tinsley encouraged him to calm down so Shaw could get out of the truck. "Sit, buddy." She held his collar to keep him from jumping when Shaw stepped out of the 4Runner.

"I missed you too, bud," Shaw assured him while playfully ruffling the side of his face as best he could with one arm while trying to protect his leg and not move his torso too quickly.

"Laura Loo"—Tinsley struggled with an excited Harvey—"will you please go open the gate for us?"

She feverishly nodded and ran for the wooden gate to the backyard that had shut when Harvey bolted out of it.

"Go get your ball, bud," Shaw instructed Harvey, hoping it would give Tinsley a break from restraining him.

The dog was ecstatic to have his favorite ball thrower back at home. Brindle refused to touch any of his drool covered toys and Victor didn't have the arm or the stamina needed for an acceptable game of fetch like Shaw did.

"You do remember he's gonna charge you like a bull when he finds that ball, right?" Tinsley chuckled watching their dog run into the yard.

"He'll be alright. I missed that goofball," Shaw admitted.

"He obviously missed you too." She reached for his hand to lock their fingers, her need for simply touching him intensified since almost losing him. "Not as much as I missed having you home though."

"Helen, you little shit!"

Tinsley smirked up at Shaw when they heard Vance scolding Harvey as they made their way through the back gate. They couldn't wait to see what the mischievous dog did to earn that reaction.

Vance picked up a plate from the ground and Harvey finished licking his chops.

"Sorry, Vance. What did he eat?" Tinsley asked and held her hand out to slow Harvey down in his hurried approach to Shaw.

"Alaurra's entire plate," he informed her.

"Harv!" The little girl chuckled before chasing him which helped keep him from jumping on Shaw.

"Hey, son." Shaw's dad, Gary, walked toward them to help Tinsley with her purse and a bag she managed to grab from the car.

A collection of greetings made their way around the yard as everyone acknowledged their arrival.

"Here, Shaw"—Rick stood from his chair—"why don't you take a seat here and we can grab you a plate. Your dad made the most delicious ribs."

Tinsley didn't say anything but she appreciated how quickly her dad decided Shaw wasn't the worst. He projected more concern over Shaw's recovery than she could've ever imagined and had made genuine conversation with him since his stay in the hospital.

"Shaw, son, do you want me to make you a plate?" his mom, Denise, asked. She stood behind him and attempted to shove a pillow behind his back when she saw him readjusting his position in the chair.

Tinsley silently chuckled listening to both of Shaw's parents refer to him as Shaw. It seemed everyone, aside from her, called him Shaw. They'd even talked to Tinsley about Shaw's brother, Jason, who they referred to on a first name basis. She didn't love that their first meeting happened because of her boyfriend's life threatening emergency, but she thoroughly enjoyed both Denise and Gary. Shaw looked more like a nephew than a son, especially when she saw Jason's picture, which was a spitting image of what she assumed Gary looked like twenty-five years ago. Gary's hair was completely white, he wore glasses that dated him even more, and he was about three inches shorter than Shaw. His mom stood at about 5 '5", didn't appear to be as health conscious as Shaw, and her hair that touched just below her ears had already grayed. Shaw had previously told Tinsley his dad was several years older than his mom, but she would have guessed that by looking at the couple anyway.

Tinsley noticed how Denise fussed over Shaw, he tolerated it, but she could tell he didn't want all the attention—it didn't help once her mom joined by asking him if she could get him something to drink or a sweatshirt.

"I brought dessert, Shawberry." Brindle made his way to the group surrounding Shaw and pumped his brows. Shaw had enough chatter around him so he only nodded at Brindle.

Tinsley predictably scolded Brindle with her eyes before standing behind her boyfriend and wrapping her arms around him. Her lips found the top of his head and gave him a firm peck before she leaned down to whisper in his ear.

"Baby, I'm gonna go put something together to keep Harv occupied, if you need an out from all the attention and excitement you just ask me for some chocolate milk and I'll subtly bail you outta here."

Shaw reached up with his good hand and gave her a quick, loving squeeze to acknowledge her offer. "Thanks, sugar."

Tinsley placed a firm kiss to his cheek before she encouraged their conflicted cane corso to follow her instead of romping around his dad's feet.

"Auntie Sugaarrrr," Alaurra sang and did her newly developed age-appropriate hip-popping dance.

"Alaurra." Rick looked at her with a light warning casting on his face.

"Rick, leave her alone." Colette rolled her eyes at her husband but chuckled along with their granddaughter. She thought it was adorable that Alaurra took so much interest in Tinsley's little nickname.

Shaw felt exhaustion not only throughout his body, but his mind was tired too. His heart filled with gratitude to be surrounded by family, and he was indeed happy to have found Tinsley.

Brindle and Victor were the last to leave that night, they'd both been a phenomenal support system while Shaw was hospitalized. Harvey developed a new love for Victor but quickly ditched him when Shaw came home. Denise and Gary went to bed hours before they left so once Brindle and Victor said their goodbyes it was finally time for Shaw to sleep in his own bed with the love of his life.

"I'm not sure you want to start all that, tough guy," Tinsley flirtatiously warned Shaw, whispering as his hand at the end of his uninjured arm wandered between her legs. "I'm thinking some boyfriend gifts are in order versus anything else while we're sharing a wall with your parents."

"Boyfriend gifts, huh?" He smirked. "What happens if I'm in a giving mood?"

"Baby, you're always in a giving mood," she reminded him, giggling.

"That's your fault." He kissed Tinsley's favorite neck spot, knowing full well what it did to her every time. "If you weren't so damn sweet and sexy…" He tried shrugging but had to stop and attempted to mask the pain in his shoulder. The doctor-ordered sling hindered all his current plans but assisted healing after a bullet went through his shoulder and another grazed his bicep.

Tinsley noticed a quick jerk of his body when he tried to roll on his side. She realized he put way more pressure than he needed to on his injured leg. She made her best effort to get him in a more comfortable sleeping position and even more than that, she wanted to win the final round of arguments for the day.

"Hunter"—her soft and gentle hand caressed his handsome face— "it's bedtime, tough guy." She bit her bottom lip, carefully crawling over him with her knees on either side of his hips. "So, I'm gonna need you to lie on your back." Tinsley gently encouraged her boyfriend to roll off his side, which he did *immediately*, likely thinking she'd let them go full speed right out of the hospital.

"Sugar, you're gonna tease me like that when I'm already down?!" He choked out a short laugh after Tinsley straddled him for all of two seconds before sliding off of him.

"Not teasing"—she crawled in between his legs and started to move down toward the foot of their bed—"just planning to offer a boyfriend gift." She winked at him as he tossed his head back, smiling. "And let's just agree that this is your fault that you won't be *giving* any gifts this evening."

"Come back up here," Shaw managed to hook her chin, encouraging her to meet his lips.

She wholeheartedly fulfilled his request before giving him his boyfriend gift. Tinsley's knees were on either side of his waist but she made sure to be on all fours to avoid any pressure on his healing body. She had to agree it was a perfect compromise given Shaw was somewhat limited in what he could do with his limbs since they were about fifty percent functional—really sixty since he always liked to push his own limits.

"I knew you'd give in," Shaw suggestively pointed out as their lips grazed one another.

Tinsley giggled. "All you're getting up here is a smooch, tough guy. So, I'm *not* giving in, you're taking the L this round."

"Tins"—he reached his good arm up to caress the side of her soft face—"I wouldn't dream of calling this an L, but if this is losing with you, I'll happily take the L for the rest of our lives."

She carefully set her pelvis on top of him and hovered above his lips. "Hunter, I love you."

Shaw reached up to completely entangle his fingers in her soft hair before he replied, "I love you too, sugar."

Their lips tenderly met to exchange a couple soft pecks before the intensity rose. Their mouths danced to the comfortable rhythm and familiarity of the love surging between them, both knowing they had a long future ahead of them full of love and all the things their hearts had ever wanted.

I LASTED AN ENTIRE WEEK STAYING WITH MAMA T AND POPS BEFORE I was begging to take Shaw up on he and Tins' offer to come stay with them. When leaving the hospital I knew the chances of anyone around me letting me go home alone was zero at best. Mama T was pissed to have me head out, but to soften the blow I reminded her how often Tins' brother, the Doc, had been visiting since Shaw was released from the hospital. She, fortunately, believed that was my main motivation for requesting a change in venue.

Staying with Mama T and Pops was fine until it wasn't. Mama T couldn't leave me alone for five whole seconds, the entire family was divided once the details of what happened started to spread, and my final fucking straw was Mama T nearly demanding to help me in the shower because she was afraid of me passing out or some shit.

After spending four days with my best friend, I already felt a shit ton better about everything. I did go through a twenty-four hour period of self-loathing watching how much the tables had turned when I first got here. The last few years I was the one who always had a few girls around. And now, when I was at my lowest, I watched my best friend with *the* girl. I shook that off pretty quickly because that's my brother and I'd been praying to see him come out of the shadows for years. Their love was effortless and being around them gave me hope that I'd one day find whatever it was I've been looking for.

The last couple weeks let me know whatever I was searching for, it wasn't Big-Tittie Tilly. She apparently tried to resurface a couple days after I got released from the hospital but according to Shaw, Tins shut that shit down. Tins had us both fooled into thinking she only had a sweet side. Whether this feisty nature was always there, or she quickly picked it up when we got injured, I'll never know. But Tins is a ride or die. Dating her didn't work out for me, but having her turn into one of my closest friends has been a pleasant damn surprise.

Shaw and I did our best to listen to the doc and simply relax and recover, but of course the two of us always managed some dumbass fuckery to get into. Tins had been a damn angel with all the shit she did for us, it made me almost sad to think I'd be going back home at some point. I'd never really been much of a gamer as an adult—neither had Shaw—but recently that's how we spent some of our days.

"Fuck you, fam," I tell the fucker as I spent yet another life failing to correctly time the mine cart jump on Donkey Kong Country. "It's my turn to be Kong, you've had him for like the last hour." We played as a team and Shaw claimed to have accidentally given me the wrong controller but did nothing about just trading me since we started.

Shaw laughed. "Just because you're the taller one in real life doesn't mean you get to be Kong. I'd still be better than you if I had to be Diddy." He skillfully hopped across the broken tracks before hitting a barrel to drop me in the cart behind him. "I'm also the more muscular one—this makes sense."

"In your *goddamn* dreams," I chuckle.

"Sit your ass in the back and take notes."

"Oh because I'm black I gotta sit in the back, huh?" I shot back with a friendly shove.

"Shut the fuck up!" he choked out a laugh but kept his focus on the game. "Your ass is back there because you already wasted one of our lives and you need the master to show you how it's done. I'll put us on my back, as per ushe."

While Shaw spewed his nonsense, Harvey charged into the living room and cost us another one of our lives when he stepped on the cord to the controller trying to greet Shaw.

"Party foul, Harv!" Shaw lightly scolded the dog before grabbing his jowls and letting his goofy-ass hop his top half on Shaw's lap for a proper greeting.

Harvey was beginning to grow on me. I really did think he was about the ugliest dog I'd ever seen the first time I met him. But after learning more about him and spending time with him, he was actually a really good dog. Not to mention I loved watching his attitude as he walked all over my best friend and Tins—the dog knew how to work *both* of them. I was getting a preview of how their life would be when they started poppin' out babies. The 'funcle' in me couldn't be more excited.

"Come here, Harv." I coaxed the dog over with a piece of my Rainbow Berry Airhead Extreme. He climbed on the couch between me and the arm of the sofa where he propped one of his front legs against to sit like a gentleman. The cane corso took another bite of candy and then gave Shaw a bit of a side eye.

"Tins is gonna kick your ass if she catches you feeding him any more candy." Shaw warned me and I slid Harvey another piece just before we heard Tins making her way to the living room.

"How're my favorite guys doing?"

She walked behind the couch to smack a quick peck on my cheek— as she had been each day she got home from work that week—and then she turned to my best friend and laid a longer kiss on his lips.

"Hi, sugar," Shaw greeted her. "How was work?"

"Long." She took a noticeable breath as she stood upright. She put a hand on each of our shoulders and then looked at the TV.

"I hope you guys just started. How embarrassing if you've been playing all day and you're only at the Monkey Mines. I'm going to have to tell Vance he should just come back and get his Super Nintendo because it's being disgraced."

"Damn, fam." I shook my head. "How long's the abuse been goin' on?"

Shaw flipped me off, a gesture that would never get old between the two of us.

I wasn't even thinking about it when I offered Harvey another chunk of my candy.

"Baz!" Tinsley immediately jumped all over my ass.

"My B, Tins." I tried to hide my snickering.

"He's sleeping with you tonight. You can deal with the gas you're giving him right now," she threatened. "And where's your phone?"

I quickly grabbed it from my pocket.

"Mama T called me because she couldn't get a hold of you." Tins looked at me with accusing eyes.

I rolled my head back against the couch to catch her accusing gaze. I knew Mama T had called and texted a few times, I just wasn't in the mood to talk to her today.

"Judging by your face, I'd say you're aware she was looking for you." Tins was sweet, but she had no issue in calling me on my shit.

"Tins, you're supposed to be helping me with all that; and she's supposed to be letting me rest and recoup over here."

"I do have your back," she confirms but I knew there'd be more coming. "So, I won't hound you to return her call."

She smirks at Shaw, I knew she was gonna have some other smart-ass remark to follow it up. Tins put both of her hands on my shoulders and stood behind me, lowering herself to my ear before delivering the rest of the news. "Because she's coming over in about a half hour with dinner."

"Tins!" I complained. "Shaw, a little help, fam?"

He was little to no help as he threw his hands up, more or less laughing at me.

"She's making her famous cajun hot chicken if that makes you feel any better."

Her disclosure about the menu did help.

"Sugar, do we have stuff to make your mac salad?" Shaw's face waited in anxious anticipation—it must be legendary mac salad for him to be so excited for food that wasn't some form of red meat.

"We do"—she smiled and leaned down to peck him again—"I'm gonna go put on some comfy clothes and get started on it."

Shaw motioned to get off the couch and called out to her, "I'll help, Tins."

Tins giggled as she turned around. "You guys are supposed to be resting and recovering. You just worry about making it through the Monkey Mines before I have to sit down and show you how it's done."

Shaw and I both lifted our fingers, grinning once her back was turned.

"Fam, I can't tell you how much I appreciate you guys letting me stay like this."

Shaw laughed. "Are you fucking kidding me? Bro, you know you're *always* welcome here."

We watched Harv hop off the couch and follow Tins into the bedroom before Shaw continued, "You don't have to thank us, we're family."

I'd do the same thing for Shaw, but they'd both gone above and beyond to make me feel at home. I'd never had a girl with wifey vibes and Shaw letting me see that life by sharing Tins let me know I needed that kind of girl—not the little fuckboy feasts I'd been treating myself to.

I looked toward their bedroom to make sure Tins wasn't headed back to us before I lowered my voice, "I'm gonna kick your fucking ass if you don't lock that down soon."

Shaw threw his head back laughing and switched the tv over to the Celtics game we wanted to watch.

"I'm not playin', that's wifey. What the fuck are you doing?"

"You don't have to tell me"—he quickly glanced at the bedroom door—"I've *known* this."

"You got a ring then?"

He shook his head and I was ready to jump all over his ass until he responded.

"I've been shopping, I just haven't found the right one yet. Plus"— he gestured to his leg—"I need to be able to get down on one knee and that's gonna be a little difficult right now. You can get your big-ass panties out of a bunch though, I'll find the right ring and I plan to talk to her dad soon."

"Atta boy!" I reach my fist over and pat the side of his shoulder a couple times. "Just don't get mad when she walks down the aisle right toward my handsome ass. You know how much she likes Big Daddy in a suit." I barely got that last sentence out before having to brace myself for Shaw's heavy fist.

"You'll be lucky if you live to see that wedding, fucker."

We settle down—barely—when Tins walks back into the living room. Her house fits crack me up, I have no idea how she can still look so hot but wear such baggy-ass clothes. It's gonna be damn hard to leave this house when I'm feeling better, these two have given me hope for a brand new future I didn't know I wanted. Well, the three of them I decide when I see that goofy-ass dog, who I love too, come barreling into the room again with a damn ball in his mouth.

Brindle

"Hey, Boo!" I greet Tins when I hear Harv thrashing his uncoordinated body through the backroom. I'm hoping to see less bags under her eyes today. She understandably looked like hell for a while there, but it was high-time she started looking like the damn ten she was.

"Hi, Brin."

She'd always been terrible at hiding her emotions and I tried not to be as sassy when I heard her tired voice.

This was the third day that week she came to work in a basic, high pony—not like my boo at all. More than one day was her tell of not getting enough sleep, waking up late, and then having to make a mad dash out of the house. Not to mention, it was the third day in a row she showed up without a coffee in her hand.

"Come here, Boo." I go over and put my arms around her and set my head on top of hers, wishing I could knock that pony right off it. "Victor's ass has me tracking my steps these days so I walked down and got your coffee this morning."

"I thought you guys made a health pact?"

I could hear the smile in her voice and it lifted *some* of the worry I had. She still had it in her to call me on my shit, bitch wasn't completely lost yet and that made me smile.

I roll my eyes and grab her shoulders to push her away from me a bit to look at her. "Okay, so I *agreed* to be more active so Victor doesn't have to hear me complain while he's dragging me all over Cabo."

I felt bad leaving Tins when it seemed like she could still use some support, but the boys had been getting better, *finally*—even doing light duty at work, and every ounce of me was ready to be in tropical weather with my boyfriend. Tins would never let me hear the end of it if I cancelled on her behalf.

"Thank you, I didn't have time to stop by the stand this morning. I appreciate it, Brin. No matter what the motive was." She graciously accepted the coffee and then looked up with a tired smile to greet her client who was right on time.

As if he had a damn tracker on her, Shawberry texted me just as he had everyday since she'd come back to work.

SHAWBERRY
Good morning Brindle. Did Tins make it in yet?

I took a deep breath watching my boo go through the motions to try to be okay and mask her actual exhaustion before I replied.

Yes beefcake.

Your girl is here.

Wearing the THIRD high pony I've seen her in this week though.

You gotta start pulling your end of this deal and get that woman to bed on time!!

I assumed she wouldn't have time for her iced mocha so I did get her one .

🍓SHAWBERRY😣

Thank you for that. I swear, she's been getting
to bed on time. Trust. I've been trying to get
her to ease up around here. I'm not completely
incapable. Working on getting her to trust that.

Well, I'm gonna start telling her I can see
the bags because this isn't my boo. 😵

Perhaps I wasn't clear on bedtime though.

INTO bed is one thing

Sleep is another.

My boo can lose some sleep if you're doin something
to ease her into that slumber each night. 👅👅👅

Your body may still be recovering but if I'm
not mistaken those fingers and that mouth
of yours are working just fine. 👋

I hope you've been putting BOTH to good use 👁️👅

🍓SHAWBERRY😣

Brindle we don't do girl talk lol. That still
applies even in this situation.

I'm just sayin, Shawberry.

I wanna see a tired ✨ glow ✨

Not just tired 😴 😴 😴 😴 next time she comes in here.

My boo needs caffeine and some ding-a-ling!! 👅

Idgaf if Black Casper is in the house. Take care of
my boo because I can bring her coffee but I'm sure
as shit not trying to give her any kind of glow.

🍓Shawberry😫

I'd kick anyone's ass who tried that with her,
including yours.

Ooooooo Shawberry!!

Don't tempt me with a good time 😏

🍓Shawberry😫

I'm gonna bring her lunch today, can I get you anything?

Ooooo and lunch?! Shawberry I'm gonna
have to tell Tins you're coming on to me.

🍓Shawberry😫

I take back my offer lol

No take-backsies beefcake.

I already have it in writing.

I do have to rain check your offer tho.

My ass has to fit in this new suit I just got so I'm
on the whole meal prep thing until Cabo.

🍓Shawberry😫

On the countdown already, huh? When
do you guys leave again?

Four days. 🍃😋😎❄️🌮🌯🔥🏝️

Unless of course you don't get your ass in line
and take better care of my boo that is!!!! 😤

🍓Shawberry😫

You just worry about fitting into your mankini or
whatever the hell. I've got Tins. I appreciate you looking
out, but she'll kill you if you skip out on that trip.

Shawberry if I didn't know any better I'd
think that line was a subtle request for a
pic of me in my new mankini.

SHAWBERRY
I'll talk to you later Brindle, thank you for
getting Tins coffee this morning.

Shawberry will forever be one of my favorites to tease, it's even better than getting under Tins' beautiful damn complexion. In fact, the only problem I have with that man these days is why the hell it's taking him so damn long to propose to my boo. I'll give it to him, he had a life-threatening injury and all, but if he doesn't already have a ring for that damn woman, I'll really have to scold his ass. Sure, I've noticed Team Hetero usually takes a little longer than the U-Haul-style race to the alter my community thrives in, but if he doesn't already know Tins is wifey then he doesn't even deserve her.

"What are you looking for, Boo?" I ask, noticing Tins digging around in her cupboard looking extra anxious.

"I can't find my round brush, I know I just cleaned it last night before I left." She moved a few baskets around in her station cupboard that was disgustingly immaculate and organized.

I look at the small pink cart she always has pushed against the wall near her station where all four of her round brushes were neatly laid out. I calmly walked over and put a hand on her shoulder while she crouched down, still looking on the shelves.

"Boo, have a sip of that coffee you desperately need and I'll find it for you."

She takes my offer and I pluck her favorite round brush from her cart. I let her take a healthy sip before I close the gap between us and put my arm around her and hold her brush out.

"Thanks, Brin." She blows out a breath and leans her head on me.

"I think *you* need to go to Cabo, Boo."

Tins giggles and rolls her eyes. "I can't be gone from work again like that right now, I'll happily live vicariously through all the photos I know you'll be sending me."

"And you're *sure* you're gonna be okay here without me for an entire week?"

"Brin, this is huge—your first vacation with your boyfriend?" Tins shook her head and took another drink of her coffee. "Not to mention, you really deserve some time away in general. You have no idea how much I appreciate you for all your help with Harv and the salon the last few weeks."

"Anything for you and my favorite beefcake," I remind her as I squeeze her again. I felt her mindset was good enough I could pitch her a bit of shit she definitely needed to hear. "If I see this damn high pony one more time this week though, you're getting shoved in my suitcase or I'm cancelling the trip."

She let her head fall back with her glowing smile. "Deal," she finally agreed.

I love that bitch, but she's lucky she's got me to keep her in line from time to time. Her ability to be a flawless fucking dime one second and a hot damn mess the next is something that needs to be studied. She's right though, I do deserve this vacation, it can't come soon enough. Since meeting Victor I'm more excited for the future than I've ever been. No more slummin' it on the apps, I've got a man who worships me on the daily.

I'm pissed having to go back to reality in less than forty-eight hours. Cabo's been fucking paradise and just when I didn't think it could get any better, Victor gave me the greatest non-sexual gift I've ever received. I couldn't wait to tell my boo.

VICTOR PROPOSED 👬👩‍👦!!!!!!!!!!!!!!!!

OMFG 🐼

I'm not doing any of that proposal shit
with the whole MOH thing.

Just know I'm expecting your juicy ass to be
standing next to me when I say I do.

BOO CAN YOU BELIEVE THIS?!?!?!!?!?!?!?!

I'M GETTING MARRIED 💍 💍 💍!!!!!!!!!!!!!!!!!!!

I gave zero fucks that it was almost two o'clock in the morning—this announcement wasn't gonna wait. I planned to post to the socials immediately, but not before my boo got the news. She had all of ten seconds to respond to me before I posted without her congratulatory text though. Fortunately for her, she responds timely.

🐨Boo🐨
OMG!! I'm SO HAPPY for you Brindle Boo!!!!
I love you guys!! 💍🍌💍🍌💍🍌💍🍌

GAAHHHH!!!! This is soooo exciting, and
OBVI I'll be your MOH!!!! 🐼🙌

Duh bitch—I was telling you you're my MOH, not asking.

So get ready!!!!!!!!!!

🐨Boo🐨
You two better NOT get married down
there while on vacay!! 😒 😒

I WISH.

Except you know me.

I need a full on production to walk down the aisle. 💃🤵

I don't think we'd be able to put that together
in the next three days while we're here.

Plus I'll need even more time to get this body right.

Those pictures last for fucking ever.

Boo
Brin you're going to be the MOST beautiful
broom. I can't wait!!!!

I know bitch!

Victor's so lucky.

Boo
Hunt says to tell you guys congratulations
and also he's happy to see Victor swooning
your ass since you're stubborn.

You can tell Shawberry I'll be texting
his ass separately.

I still owe him a pic of me anyway.

Boo
He said his phone broke, send it to
Baz instead.

Group text it is.

I've gotta run Boo.

I wanted to tell you before the socials though.

My FIANCEE would like to start the celebration in the
sheets and I'm not about to say no.

I already have my social media pic and caption cued up and hit post the second I read Tins' text. She might think I'm joking about texting Shawberry, but I'm not in the least bit. That text is waiting for the morning though because I've got a *fiancée* to take care of.

HUNT PUCKERS HIS DELICIOUS LIPS AT ME JUST BEFORE I HEADED out that morning. I, like always, completely melted into him and enjoyed every second and every inch of his tongue playing with mine. The only thing I don't like about kissing him is when it ends.

"You gonna be alright on your own, sugar?"

I *love* it when that man calls me sugar. Hunt's always treated me differently than any other guy has, but always in a better way. I'd been called babe and honey multiple times by different guys. Hunt made it a point to call me something that really meant more to him and was unique to me—that made my heart swoon over the word off his mouth every single time.

"Unless you want to join me, I think I'll be alright on my own for this one. Thank you for letting me do this, baby."

Hunt's thick fingers pluck the loose strand of hair setting on my cheek to gently place it behind my ear.

"Of course, Tins. I actually think it's sweet of you to want to go— it's about time you two meet." His confident smile eases my nerves, letting me know he's sincere about this decision. I wasn't sure when I asked him about this initially, but that man has a knack for always giving me everything. We'd only just come back from Brindle's extra-ass destination wedding two days earlier and when Hunt made me the happiest woman in the world on that final day of the trip, I knew this was something that wasn't just a thought—it was a necessity.

When he presses an extended kiss to the top of my head, I take full advantage of putting my arms around his perfect body to feel secure and loved within his embrace. Connecting with Hunt, on every level from emotional to physical, will always feel like home and I will *always* crave more—he's the epitome of soulmate in every sense of the word.

"I'll be back later, tough guy. I love you."

"I love you too, sweetcheeks. Take your time today. Harv and I will be here when you get home."

I can't help but reach up for one more kiss before I head out.

I actually had two stops to make, the first being Met Market to pick up a special bouquet. After I let the florist know I simply wanted an arrangement of nothing but the most beautiful red flowers they had available in the shop, I snuck inside the market to grab a quick snack. *The Cookie* crossed my mind for all of two seconds before I decided I didn't want to leave Hunt out of that experience, I'd stop by and pick up fresh ones before coming back home—it was only fair. The bouquet didn't exactly flow, but it was a burst of red perfection to include roses, dahlias, peonies, lilies, alstroemerias, daisies, and two other flowers the florist named but I couldn't identify or remember the names despite her attempt to educate me.

Somehow I managed to drive all the way to my destination without playing any music—my mind was elsewhere.

"Hi Sloane…" I suddenly felt very unsure of myself as I walked to her gravestone. Thoughts raced through my mind, practically too fast for me to register—*Was this truly okay? Was it disrespectful to show up at her gravesite? Should I have done this much earlier? Have I gone completely crazy for wanting to do this? What if her family shows up? Oh gosh, should I have taken my engagement ring off?!* I couldn't keep up with everything, so I tried some box breathing before anything else.

When I felt my heart rate settle down I looked at the dedicated vase attached to Sloane's grave. I wasn't sure why someone would have left stems with no flowers—maybe it had a sentimental meaning or something? I noticed how dried out the stems were and there wasn't any water left in the vase, so I did take the dead pieces out before placing my bouquet in there.

After properly fluffing the flowers I brought, I looked up at the headstone. Tears immediately flooded my eyes when I read the inscription.

Fondly loved and deeply mourned
Sloane Elizabeth Walsh & Little Man

♥

There are no goodbyes for us.
Wherever you are, you will
always be in my heart.

My heart broke thinking about what had happened to them. Sloane was only twenty-five years old, a week away from her third trimester, and barely a month away from marrying the love of her life before she was senselessly and violently taken from this world. There wasn't a single thing about that scenario that seemed fair. I thought about the devastation of the uncertainty I experienced when Hunt was shot and how much the thought of losing him still haunted me. I had no idea how Hunt ever managed to get out of bed, or go on in general, when Sloane died. *None* of them deserved what happened.

When Hunt officially moved in he shared a few photos with me and I understood why Sloane caught his eye. She was gorgeous. I did find it funny she and I looked nothing alike; apparently Hunt didn't have a type. Sloane was tiny, she had shoulder length, strawberry blonde hair, green eyes, an almost unnoticeable sprinkle of miniature freckles, and sharp features.

"Sloane, I'm…uhm, my name's Tinsley." I use the back of my thumb to try and gently wipe a couple of tears. My voice is already shaking and I've barely just introduced myself.

"I know you don't know me…"

I can't help but look down at the flawless and stunning round cut rock Hunt put on my finger not even a week ago. I'd never been so sure of anything in my entire life. As I stare at the diamond ring I can't help but think about how none of this would be mine if not for Sloane. A wave of guilt consumes me.

"You're an enormous reason for my fortune in landing Hunt—" I can't even finish my thoughts when I start sobbing. It takes me a minute to gather myself—also thinking about how ridiculous it is that I am even saying all this out loud—she could likely hear me if I sat here in silent thought.

"He wouldn't be who he is without you, Sloane. I know you're his guardian angel and I hope you know how grateful I am to have been chosen for his heart. He's my entire world and I promise you, I will *always* take care of him. I don't take the privilege of his love lightly."

I have to pause to wipe my eyes and collect my voice that can't go two sentences without another round of sobbing. This turned into a much more difficult visit than I could have ever imagined. It was a visit I definitely wanted to make. I wasn't sure if it was some kind of approval from the universe I was looking for, or just the want and need for expressing the gratitude I felt for the life I now had, or if it was also the fact that I wanted to get an apology off my chest—either way, I needed to be here talking to Sloane. It didn't seem right for me to accept a life with Hunt and not pay my respects to the woman who had a heavy hand in giving me the life I always wanted with the man of my dreams.

"Sloane, I'm *so* sorry." I finally fall to my knees and end up settling my backside on my calves, holding my face to try to stop the tears.

"You had *everything* and you deserved that life. Hunt didn't just love you, that man *still* loves you. You're forever in his heart and I'm happy to share that space." I can't catch my dang breath, even if I had prepared a speech for this, it wouldn't have stood a chance against these emotions.

"He's the most amazing man I've ever met and I know there isn't a scenario where I end up with this version of him if not for you, Sloane. I have you to thank for my happiness." I barely get my last thought out because of the tears I'm choking on.

"I'll *never* take the gift of Hunt for granted. I plan to give him every-thing he wants out of life—there's nothing I wouldn't do for him." Since

Hunt showed up at the salon, injured from being stabbed, I knew I'd do absolutely anything for that man. I needed to be sure Sloane knew that, I needed her to know Hunt's heart and happiness would be more than safe with me.

I looked around at the beautiful day developing around me. The sky shined the perfect blue, a light breeze blew through just when the sun started shining a little too warm, and the birds were singing. I sat in silence, knowing I could've blubbered along, but it was Sloane's turn to assess me. I reached for the headstone and brushed away a few stray blades of grass. My fingers swept over the words that gutted me, 'Little Man.'

I'd only ever seen Hunt around Alaurra and his nephews, never any babies, but I knew he'd be an amazing father—assuming he still wanted that title anyway. Hunt gave me a CliffsNotes version of the multiple arguments he and Sloane had entertained relating to naming 'Little Man.' Based on the names he was willing to share, I had to agree, Hunt was right for standing up against names like Silas and Otto. I took that as an indication that he and I may not have those types of arguments. I know it's Hunt's to keep in his heart, but I always appreciate when he shares a sliver of that life. At first, I thought it may be uncomfortable, but it actually makes me fall harder for him—if that's even possible. I've fallen head over heels at least a trillion times over for my tough guy already.

I didn't realize I'd been sitting there for over an hour when I looked down at my incessantly buzzing phone—I knew it'd be Brindle. He was on his damn honeymoon but found time to send an infinite number of suggestions for the Man of Honor outfit he'd like to wear on me and Hunt's big day.

Hunt proposed while we were in Cabo for Brindle and Victor's wedding; but he had, appropriately, waited until the happy couple took off for their honeymoon. When Hunt originally suggested we extend our trip, I assumed it was because he knew I'd need an actual vacation after BRINDLE: BRIDEZILLA EDITION finally said I do. While I'd been hoping to spend the rest of my life with Hunt for a long time now, I truly was taken by surprise when he asked. It still felt surreal.

I shoved my phone in my pocket and readjusted how I sat in the grass near Sloane's grave. A light breeze pushed its way through as I watched the arrangement I brought gently blowing along with it. It wasn't a strong wind, but enough for two small ladybugs to land safely on one of the peonies, hanging on for safety between the petals of the sturdy flower. I felt it was fitting to see a pair of red bugs that day, part of me felt like it was the universe telling me it was okay to be there and I could embrace my future with Hunt. I put my hand behind the peony to steady the little creatures who flew to one of the daisies, immediately picking at the pollen.

Sitting in the serene silence with Sloane was exactly what I needed; it somehow felt like I knew her. I'd honor her and allow her to rest peacefully by loving Hunt with my entire heart for the rest of my life.

I snuck into the front door early that same evening after hearing Hunt and Harv out in the backyard. I wanted a moment of watching my favorite guys before making my presence known. Hunt had just thrown a rubber tennis ball for Harv off the back deck and then turned to the grill. He plucked a pair of tongs from the side of the Traeger, and in his other hand he held a beer bottle—a view that would *never* get old.

Harv was back in no time, flinging the ball from his drool-filled mouth to watch it roll the rest of the way to Hunt's foot. He'd mastered his technique to place the ball perfectly every time. I watched him tap his feet just before barking because Hunt didn't immediately acknowledge him.

"You can chill, bud," Hunt lightly warned him, "I'll burn your steak if you wanna keep yelling at me like that."

I couldn't help but join them at that point, Harv alerted Hunt of my presence when he stopped barking and instead made a charge toward the slider. For the umpteenth time, Harv ran right into the screen and popped it out of the frame.

Hunt and I share a predictable sigh, but I greet Harv while Hunt fixes the screen that he leaves open to avoid another accident. I meet the love of my life on the threshold of the slider and throw my arms around him, feeling his beer bottle against my back as both of his strong arms hold me tightly. Nestling my head into his neck while he securely holds my entire body up is one of my favorite feelings. Hunt feels like home and I don't ever want to leave the house.

SHAW

Tins and I just passed our twenty eight month mark—not that I'm counting—and I couldn't be more grateful to have that woman in my life. For such a degenerate like myself to have wound up with the genuinely sweetest damn angel didn't seem fair; so, I worked tirelessly everyday to prove that I was worthy of her. Tins had saved my life multiple times and in more ways than one—I'd never be able to pay her back for the way she loved me. She fully embraced my demons and never shied away from the darkness that had consumed me before I met her.

I couldn't stop watching her as she slept-in on an unusually gloomy August day. We had developed a habit of staying in bed for the better part of the morning on our mutual days off. I'd woken up almost an hour ago and had spent each passing second fighting every last urge to wake her up.

We were forced to, once again, keep the physically intimate part of our relationship at bay for several weeks because of my dumb ass and the stitches that my body couldn't seem to live without. Not to mention, Baz shared a wall with us for a few weeks and we weren't always the most quiet. Actually, Tins was always the loud one, I blame myself for her volume but I'll never regret it and I'll always crave more. It'd been practically a year, but we were still playing some serious catch up for lost time since our house guest went back home. That catching up had been nothing short of heaven.

I couldn't keep my hands to myself any longer after a visual of the previous night flashed in my mind so I finally made my move. Tins was a side sleeper and she faced me so I crawled over her to hold her from behind. I barely nuzzled my head into her neck when I felt her pushing her hips back toward me.

Her sleepy voice melted my heart.

"Mmmm, good morning, tough guy."

She reached around to confirm it wasn't my knee or elbow poking her when I got behind her. Each time that hand came back and caught me with her ring, I felt more validation in the round cut being perfect for Tins—no corners poking into my bare skin.

"Good morning, sugar," I reply as she gives me a gentle tug. Her hands are just goddamn perfect… And that ass that she loves backing into me—it unravels me every damn time and I'm addicted.

"Did I miss the alarm again?" she asks as she continues to work the sexiest rhythm against me.

I reach around to put my hands between her legs and she whimpers.

"I couldn't wait for the alarm anymore," I fully admit with zero shame behind it.

"You know this is how I prefer to be woken up anyway." She rolls over and I waste no time positioning myself between her flawless fucking thighs.

"I'm happy to oblige, every morning for the rest of our lives," I promise while gently thrusting toward her.

Tins bites down on her bottom lip and all I want is to give her every pleasurable feeling all at once.

"Are you putting that in your vows?" she manages despite the squirming in her hips.

"I'm not telling you anything I have in there yet. I want to see your gorgeous face on our wedding day when you hear them for the first time." I nibble on her neck and can tell she's slipping her thong off.

"Hunter, you better take those boxers down because now that you woke me up, I'm ready for you to take care of me like you want to be my husband."

Her calling me by my first name is like taking a hit off your favorite drug; the high I get everytime is inexplicable. I immediately follow her directions with a grin on my face, this week can't go by quick enough. Not only have I been ready for Tins to be my wife, but the Honeymoon we have planned out is going to be—hands down—the best experience of my life…so far.

"You're not wearing that tank top while I take care of you, sweetcheeks," I inform her before removing the sheer garment.

Her arms land around my shoulders as she smiles up at me. "Show me what you got, tough guy."

"Oh, you already know what I've got."

"I love being reminded," she tells me and hooks her leg around mine to pull me in—as if I wasn't already headed for her.

Every time with Tins feels like the first time—forever won't even come close to being long enough with her.

I stood just outside the slider, watching good old Harv sniffing around the backyard when the side door opened. With my cereal bowl in hand I take a few steps towards the mudroom to see who it is.

"Don't you two fucking knock?" I shake my head at Baz and Brindle who walk in like they own the place—an hour earlier than scheduled.

"Hey fam, we thought keys meant we didn't need to knock." Baz smiled at my attire, I knew what flew through his irritating-ass mind in that smug stare.

I'm still in a damn pair of boxers with no shirt, just having loved all over my fiancée, and now likely subject to Brindle's damn ogling. That thought alone should have me calm enough to hide my lingering feelings for Tins. I'm only thankful that I threw on actual boxers versus my normal boxer briefs. I thought I was fairly comfortable with Brindle's humor, but somehow—especially lately—he manages to outdo himself.

Without his husband here right now he's sure to say some shit that'll have me taking ten steps back in my comfort journey. I really thought he'd tone down his obnoxious advances once he got married, unfortunately for me, getting a husband significantly increased his suggestive damn behavior.

"Oohh, Shawberry! Is that your glock or are you just happy to see me?"

"Shiiiit," Baz drew out, "that little pocket pistol?"

I throw a finger up at Baz before grabbing a cereal box to hide behind and make my way to the bedroom for a pair of sweats—*and* a shirt.

"I enjoy that view too, beefcake!"

Unfortunately, I hear Brindle's parting comment echoing down the hall. I do feel a little better when I hear him squealing as Harv greets him with what I know is a face full of drool.

"Hey tough guy," the sweetest voice I'll never get tired of listening to calls out from the bed. "Is Brindle out there harassing you again?"

"Yes," I tattle, setting the cereal box on the nightstand.

Tins sits up and crawls across the bed until she's able to put her arms around me as I take a seat on the mattress.

"Hunt, baby." She pecks just behind my ear and I feel instant goosebumps. "He turns that up because he knows how much it makes you squirm."

She does me no favors in hiding the front of my boxers when she reaches down for me while nibbling on my ear.

"You've gotta know my love is more than real to be putting up with Brindle's ass for the rest of our lives," I tell her and I get not only a seductive rub down the front of my boxers, but her addictive goddamn giggle right in my ear.

"Those two made the mistake of showing up way too early this morning. They're not supposed to be here for another hour." She continues her massaging pattern that has me feeling like another round is in order.

"We need to take *both* of their keys back," I decide after their unannounced and certainly unwelcome premature arrival.

"Boo! We don't have time for all that, you better be ready to leave soon!"

Tins smirks and I roll my eyes when we hear Brindle hollering from the living room, no doubt calling on every ounce of his self-restraint to not make himself comfortable in the bedroom with us.

"You're early," my goddamn perfect fiancée responds. "I'm gonna pretend I don't hear you right now!"

"Bitch, I'll come back there," he threatens.

"Only if you want to see my lady parts!"

Baz repeatedly slaps his big ass hands on the hallway wall. "I guess I'm comin' back there instead," he jokes.

"Ew!" Brindle scoffs. "I'd say it'd be worth also catching a glimpse of my favorite beefcake, but he already gave me a show, I'll settle with *that* mental polaroid that'll be dancing around in my head allllll day."

I grab my temples and Tins immediately swings around to straddle me on the bed, instantly changing my mood. I accept her plump lips on mine and squeeze the peach that's had me obsessed since the first time I laid eyes on it.

"I still need to shower, tough guy," she reminds me but grinds down on my lap and gently scratches her perfectly manicured nails through the back of my hair. "Any chance you want a little show while you're getting dressed this morning? Or perhaps we should be conservationists and share the shower?"

"Hell yes!" I emphatically reply while standing us both up. I'll happily put up with Brindle's ass if this is my reward. I grab Tins' robe but only to throw over her shoulders as she clings to me, we have to make it across the hall and I'm sure the two little dumbasses are still standing at the end of it.

My peripheral catches them on my first step out of the bedroom, I keep my pace and get us on the other side of the bathroom door.

"We have almost an hour of pretending you fuckers aren't here yet. So, grab food and go make yourselves at home *outside*," I suggest before shutting and locking the bathroom door.

"An hour?!" Baz laughs. "Please, you and pocket pistol are a thirty second show, at best."

"That's all?" Brindle chimes in.

I can still hear their dumbass commentary until Tins turns the shower on. I almost liked it better when Brindle maintained a healthy level of hatred for Black Casper. The two of them are insufferable some days, I shake my head, chuckling while dropping my boxers. Looking over at my gorgeous future wife immediately clears my mind of our two best friends obnoxiously interrupting our morning.

"Are you ready for some full service treatment, tough guy?" Her bright and picture-perfect smile stings my heart in the best kind of way.

Everything about Tins makes me so damn excited for every second with her. Sure, I'm looking forward to our future, but bathing in every ounce of all she has to offer makes my life worth living. We have so many plans for our future together, the only thing holding me back from breaking my finger on the damn fast forward button is how satis-fying the journey has already been.

ACKNOWLEDGMENTS

WILL FOREVER BE A TACOMPTON KIDDO. I WAS BORN AND RAISED here in Tacoma (aka Grit City) and have only lived elsewhere when I attended WSU (Go Cougs!). This gritty little city will forever have my heart, I don't give one single EFFFF how many times it's featured on *Cops* or how gross it can be from time to time. It's super gorgeous out here and it'll always be home. If you're familiar with the area I hope you enjoyed some of the little shoutouts of REAL LIVE PLACES in our little slice of heaven in the PNW.

I had the privilege of going on an official ride-along with the Tacoma Police Department for some book research. I learned a lot and have to admit some of their protocols didn't quite fit my storyline, lol. I *did* listen and take notes, Officer Knutsen, but the people like drama!! Lol I *super* appreciate the opportunity to take a ride in the passenger seat to see behind the scenes a bit. Also, a HUGE shoutout to Detective Faivre and Ms. Nicole for getting me connected with the ride-along. I sure appreciate it and despite me deviating from some of the terms, procedures, etc. I got a ton of inspo and really enjoyed the experience. It's not an easy job trying to keep the city safe—people are straight FERAL these days, so I applaud the boys and girls in blue for putting up with the nonsense around here.

[Side Note: I hope I've redeemed myself with anyone who was under the impression I don't like law enforcement after reading about freggin' Mike in Starstruck. They're like every other profession—you've got some rockstars but also some corn-filled turds in the mix.]

These books don't come together overnight or simply by my hand/brain—it takes a dang village!! In addition to the amazing individuals mentioned above, I have to always shout out the one and only woman behind ElfElm Publishing LLC—Thank you SO VERY MUCH, Niss!! Making my literal novel dreams come to life isn't an easy job (I'm a difficult crowd, lol), but you do it well and nail it every single dang time!! Sure, I write the content. But the job of then reading my mind based on chicken scratch notes, poor attempts at digital mock-ups, and ten trillion convos in-between other convos because I need to be sure to let you know about one last detail that I rely on you remembering because my final brain cell is hanging on by less than a thread—THAT'S actually the heavy lift as far as getting these books out there. Thank you for being patient with me, thank you for supporting my visions (even when I don't even know what they look like), thank you for always telling me my content is good (even if you've had to lie a time or two, lol), and above all—thank you for being a friend!! 🙋🏻‍♀️👋🏻

Finally, I have to, of course, thank all my family and friends who continue to offer their support!! ☺️💕 You guys have no idea what it means to have that. I get giddy/nervous/excited when people ask me what I'm working on because I just want to vomit all the ideas right out of my head to share with you all. I'm in struggle city with the socials, but the in-person connections have been amazing!! Thank you so much if you've ever reached out or spent time chatting at a market—I do truly enjoy meeting new friends. The love that y'all have shown gives me the confidence to go forth and keep putting out content. Grit City has actually been a quick little project so I didn't have the chance to spread the news of it too widely, but the ones in the know were defs here for it—so thank you for that!! I hope you loved Grit City as much as I do and that you'll stick around for what's to come!! 🖤💕🤍🥰

STAY CONNECTED

I would love for you to stay connected!!
Here are a few ways:

Baley Noal Official Website

As of November 2024 I officially have my own website!! You can find links for purchasing all of my books, news, and EXCLUSIVE MERCH. Not to mention, this is the site where I'll drop BONUS CONTENT related to my books!!

@baley.noal

Get real time updates and see what else I create by following me on Insta. I would LOVE to hear from you!! (Seriously, I super love connecting with all of you.) I'm also a huge fan of giveaways, so if nothing else, follow along for a chance at some exclusive freebies. ☺ 💕

Spotify

I've created a playlist that is FULL of *Grit City* vibes. If you'd like to know what I was listening to, or felt inspired by for a few scenes, check out the playlist.

Amazon Author Page

It's free to follow and you'll be updated when I have new content available.